BLACK FLAGGED REDUX

a novel by

Steven Konkoly

Book Two in the Black Flagged Series

First edition

ISBN: 9781477401392

Dedication

For Kosia, Matthew and Sophia. My favorite people in the whole world.

Acknowledgments

I have more people to thank for a variety of critical roles, which underscores the fantastic response I have experienced from my previous novels, *Black Flagged* and *The Jakarta Pandemic*. I'm going to switch up the order here, so be patient.

Drum roll please...

To my wife, the very first pre-reader. She has developed an insightful, critical eye for my writing and knows when I wander too far astray. I know a number of writers who don't let their partners read their *magnum opus* until it's a finished and polished product. I say pass it along in the early stages.

To Jeroen ten Berge for a stunning cover design. Words can barely describe his ability to simultaneously capture both the core of a book's theme and the essence of a writer's vision.

To my pre-readers...the list grew significantly since *Black Flagged*. Bill, who listened to my original concept for this book and told me "you can't do that." This is the best kind of advice a writer can receive, and he was dead right; Joe H., for colluding with my wife and pushing me to tighten up the main plot. A little "between the eyes" honesty, early in the game, kept me focused on the novel's core; Trent, for finally informing me that I overuse commas. He staged a punctuation intervention that was badly needed. He also gave me some deep insight regarding my writing style, which will pay dividends in the future...and on the final version of this book; Bruce, for providing excellent feedback and another comprehensive redline; Glen, for finally identifying the right genre for the *Black Flagged* series. Technothriller. Dead on. Welcome to the team and thank you for your insight about character development; Nancy, for providing an additional female perspective. G36C assault rifle or M4A1? Who cares, right? She looked past all of this and focused on the characters and the story. I need this, since I often get a little too preoccupied with the technical details; Finally, to Jon, a long-time reader and the most recent addition to the pre-reader crew. He was one of the earliest reviewers of *The Jakarta Pandemic.*

To my writing group for their fantastic initial reaction and advice. I learn something new every time we meet, and you guys really squared me away with the start of *Black Flagged Redux.* I will forever tread lightly with back story. I would apologize for the violence you had to endure reading my selections, but Joe S. topped it with his amazing undead novel. Joe, I owe you a debt of gratitude for your encouragement of my writing career and your input regarding my latest book. Congratulations on finishing *The Reawakening.* Coming soon?

To Felicia A. Sullivan, still my editor extraordinaire. I'm one book closer to writing another post-apocalyptic thriller. You can see some of the potential in *Black Flagged Redux*...who says I can't write a zombie novel?

To the finishing crew, who took the final product and ensured readers were getting the best experience for their money. Pauline, Stef and Joe Bunich. I still owe Joe B the rest of a certain helicopter scene. One of these days I'll sit down and finish that for you.

Finally, to Russell Blake, a talented author and great friend. Russell has redefined the concept of "dedication to writing" and has an incredible knack for the business side. His blog (russellblake.com) serves as a guiding light for indie authors interested in maximizing their exposure to the reader world. He also writes incredible thrillers. I have included excerpts from two of his most acclaimed novels, *King of Swords* and *The Voynich Cypher*, which are both available for the Kindle at Amazon.

About the author

Steven Konkoly graduated from the United States Naval Academy and served for eight years in various roles within the Navy and Marine Corps. He currently lives with his family in southern Maine, where he works for a major pharmaceutical company.

He published his first novel, *The Jakarta Pandemic*, in 2010. An excerpt from this apocalyptic thriller can be found at the end of this book, along with an excerpt from the next book in his *Black Flagged* series, *Black Flagged Redux*.

Please visit Steven's blog for updates and information regarding all of his works: www.stevenkonkoly.com

About Black Flagged Redux

Black Flagged Redux takes place roughly two years after the events of *Black Flagged.* If you haven't read the first novel, it's not necessary that you go back and read it before starting *Black Flagged Redux. Redux* was designed to stand on its own, however, it will be a much richer read with the first book under your belt.

Unlike the relatively limited geographic scope of the first novel, *Black Flagged Redux* spans four continents and several time zones. In order to make this a little easier on the reader, each scene is stamped with a location and local time. Keep in mind that the scenes occur in chronological order. Here is a short list of the time zone differences between the locations featured in the *Black Flagged Redux* and the U.S. East Coast: All locations in Argentina +2 hours, Kazakhstan +11 hours, Kiev + 7 hours, Moscow/Monchegorsk +9 hours, Stockholm +6 hours.

Character List

In alphabetical order

"Andrei" - Black Flag Operative, Russian Group, assigned to Petrovich's Kazakhstan team

Audra Bauer - Deputy Director of National Clandestine Service

Karl Berg - CIA agent, National Clandestine Service liaison to Weapons of Mass Destruction Center

Dustin "Dusty" Bremer - CIA agent assigned to U.S. Embassy in Astana, Kazakhstan

Goran Brujic - Former paramilitary commander in Srecko Hadzic's White Panther criminal organization

Susan Castaneda - FBI Special Agent, Legal Attaché, U.S. Embassy in Buenos Aires, Argentina

Dr. Valeria Cherkasov - Emergency room doctor, Monchegorsk Central Hospital

Lieutenant Commander Scott Daly - U.S. Navy, SEAL, Assault Force Commander, Operation Bold Scimitar

Rear Admiral Mark DeSantos - U.S. Navy, Head of the Strategic Support Branch under DIA control

Major Stepan Eristov - Zaslon Group Spetznaz leader, Stockholm

Richard Farrington - Black Flag Operative, head of the Russian Group. Wanted by the FBI

Ernesto Galenden - Wealthy Argentinian business tycoon supporting General Sanderson's program

Lieutenant General Frank Gordon - U.S. Army, Head of Joint Special Operations Command

Josif Hadzic - Srecko Hadzic's nephew

Srecko Hadzic - Imprisoned Serbian war criminal, awaiting U.N. trial at the Hague, Netherlands

Eric Hesterman - FBI Special Agent, Domestic Terrorism Branch, Part of Ryan Sharpe's Task Force

Jared Hoffman - Black Flag Operative, sniper, trained by Daniel Petrovich

Konrad Hubner - Black Flagged Operative, European Group, Assigned to Stockholm operation

Darryl Jackson - Brown River Security Corporation executive

Miljan Jendzejec - Former enforcer in Srecko Hadzic's White Panther criminal organization

Alexei Kaparov - Deputy Counterterrorism Director, Federal Security Services, Russian Federation

Major General Bob Kearney - U.S. Army, Head of the Defense Intelligence Agency

Sarah Kestler - White House Counterterrorism Director

"Leo" - Black Flag Operative, Russian Group, assigned to Petrovich's Kazakhstan team

Sergeant Malyshev - Active duty Russian Army, assistant to Captain Sabitov

Thomas Manning - National Clandestine Service Director

Enrique "Rico" Melendez - Black Flag Operative, sniper, trained by Daniel Petrovich

Frank Mendoza - FBI Special Agent, Operations Section One, Al Qaeda Investigative Unit

Jeffrey Munoz - Black Flag Operative. Urban operations instructor, Wanted by the FBI

Brigadier General Lawrence Nichols - U.S. Marine Corps, Head of USMC Special Forces Command

Dana O'Reilly - FBI Special Agent, Domestic Terrorism Branch, Lead Analyst for Ryan Sharpe

Daniel Petrovich - Black Flag operative, aka Dario Russo, Marko Resja, Wanted by the FBI

Jessica Petrovich - Black Flag operative, aka Natalia Russo, Zorana Zekulic, Wanted by the FBI

Yuri Prerovsky - Federal Security Services (FSB), Russian Federation. Assistant to Alexei Kaparov

Anatoly Reznikov - Rogue Russian Scientist

Captain Maxim Sabitov - Russian Army reservist, leader of Monchegorsk uprising

Brigadier General Terrence Sanderson - U.S. Army retired, Black Flag program founder, Wanted by the FBI

Hans Schafer - Black Flagged Operative, European Group, Assigned to Monchegorsk and Stockholm operation

"Sergei" - Black Flag Operative, Russian Group, assigned to Petrovich's Kazakhstan team

Ryan Sharpe - FBI Special Agent, Domestic Terrorism Branch, Task Force Commander

Frederick Shelby - Director of the FBI

Gerald Simmons - Assistant Secretary for Special Operations and Low Intensity Conflict

Dmitry Solomin - Russian Foreign Intelligence Service (SVR), Stockholm

Captain Vasily Tischenko - Russian Air Force Special Operations helicopter pilot

Lieutenant Colonel Grigory Zadornov - Russian Federation Army, Battalion Commander

REDUX:

"Latin, derived from reducere:

Returning from war or exile."

IN THE BLACK

2:30 AM
"Dock Sud" (South Dock)
Buenos Aires, Argentina

Daniel Petrovich shifted his elbows slightly and stared through a small handheld spotting scope at the building one hundred and sixty meters away. Situated strategically among several dozen stacks of partially rusted, multi-colored maritime shipping containers, the modest, unattractive two-story structure didn't garner much attention on any given day. This particular Wednesday proved to be an exception, though to the casual observer, it looked like any other late night in the sleepy, working class barrio, on the southern outskirts of Dock Sud.

The areas immediately beyond the container yard's high walls were quiet, except for the cars that passed in the distance on Avenida Juan Diaz de Solis. Since he had arrived two hours earlier, only three cars had turned off Juan Diaz and penetrated the sizable slum squeezed between the container yard and a vast sea of fuel storage tanks that extended all the way to the Rio Plata waterfront.

He reconfirmed the presence of two sentries stationed outside of the building: one on the roof of the two-story building and one pacing a small wooden deck located on the second floor. The sentry on the deck guarded a door at the top of an adjoining, external metal staircase. Lights blazed behind the curtains inside the windows on the second floor, leading him to assume that the ground floor was deserted and possibly not connected to the upper level. The outer staircase further supported this theory.

The rest of Petrovich's team waited in the shadows of three separate container stacks surrounding the structure. The building and all adjacent stretches of flat gravel were bathed in the orangish-yellow glow cast by several strategically placed sodium vapor lights, which prevented the rest of the team from approaching any closer. Only the two sentries stood in the team's way at this point and removing them was his job.

Lying prone for two hours on the hard metal container was starting to take its toll on his concentration, and he found himself shifting every couple of minutes. He employed active breathing techniques to take his mind off the fact that his hip and elbows were beyond the point of finding comfort on their new metal home. He gently placed the spotting scope next to his elbow and pulled the dark gray thermal shielding blanket over his head, nestling in behind his rifle. The rooftop sentry scanned the dark areas of the container yard with a portable hand scope that may have thermal detection capability. The blanket was designed to conceal Petrovich's thermal signature and worked well against low-power handheld scopes, but would do him little good against the kind of sophisticated thermal imaging equipment found mounted on aircraft or vehicles.

He sighted in on the rooftop sentry through the ATN MARS6x-3 night vision scope attached to a silenced Heckler and Koch MSG-90 rifle, placing the sight's center red dot on the man's upper chest. At this distance, with the ambient glow of the surrounding sodium vapor lights, the bright green image was crisp. He could have used a conventional scope for these shots, but as soon as the sentries went down, electricity to the yard would be cut to maximize confusion in the building.

Based on intelligence provided by Ernesto Galenden's contact in the Buenos Aires Police Department, a high level meeting of Chechen street bosses was scheduled for tonight, which always preceded the arrival of a large, "tri-border" area, Andean cocaine shipment destined for Europe. He might need the night vision scope to deal with any men left outside to guard the VIP vehicles, which still hadn't arrived. They anticipated a possible total of twenty targets at the building. Their mission was simple. They were to kill everyone on-site. *Señor* Galenden wanted to both send the Chechen mafia an unforgettable message and put an end to their increasingly violent encroachment on his legitimate dock interests.

Four minutes later, his patience was rewarded by the staggered arrival of three expensive, oversized SUVs. The drivers maneuvered the SUVs to face away from the building and parked them side by side, away from the four assorted cars and trucks already parked at the base of the building. All of the truck doors opened at once, and several men exited and walked toward the metal staircase. He didn't count them. One of the breach teams would take care of that. Instead, he noted that two heavily armed men stayed with the vehicles. They positioned themselves on the exposed side of the nearest vehicle, a silver Mercedes SUV, and lit cigarettes.

"All teams, this is control. Proceed."

"Over watch, out," Petrovich whispered.

Through his earpiece, he heard the rest of the teams confirm the order. At this point, everything hinged on Petrovich's shooting. The three breach teams would move once the roof sentry dropped to the ground, which might require a little more patience. He wanted to hit the man while he stood on the edge of the far roof, so he would tumble to the ground. He couldn't be sure of the roof's thickness, and an unusual overhead thud during a tense meeting would not be a good start to their operation.

Petrovich steadied the crosshairs, which had already been adjusted for the distance and a steady six knot breeze. The roof sentry touched his right hand to his ear for a few seconds, which was a tell that he had just received orders through an earpiece. It was a hard habit to break, even for a seasoned professional. The guard moved toward the far edge, and Petrovich was willing to bet he had just been ordered to keep a close eye on the areas behind the building. They already had three men watching the front.

He kept the red dot centered on the man's upper back and started his breathing drill. Slow, predictable breaths, allowing him to gauge the rifle scope's natural drift. He gently added pressure to the sensitive trigger, and the rifle bucked into his shoulder, the large silencer barking a sharp hiss that was unlikely to attract any attention. The sentry lurched forward from the impact of the 175 grain hollow point projectile and disappeared over the edge.

He zeroed in on the second sentry and fired a hasty shot, knowing that the first round had passed over the remaining sentries, travelling at over 2100 feet per second, and the sound would be unmistakable. The second projectile struck the man center mass, and the wall behind the guard turned dark green in his scope. By the time he had quickly centered the crosshairs on one of the two guards near the SUVs, all three of the breach teams had reached the building undetected. Two of the teams ascended the stairs, and one climbed an affixed ladder on the far side and headed for the roof.

He fired two shots, quickly alternating between the guards on the ground, dropping each of them unceremoniously to the hard gravel. One of the SUV windows shattered, reminding Petrovich that the high velocity rounds seated in his rifle's magazine tended to exit humans at these ranges, unlike the smaller caliber hollow point projectiles fired from pistols. He checked the bodies for signs of movement. If one of them managed to operate their handheld radio, the breach team would have a big problem. He saw an arm move for one of the compact assault rifles lying in the gravel. Petrovich's rifle bucked, and the movement stopped. He quickly changed rifle magazines and aimed at one of the second-story windows, waiting for the lights to go out.

He didn't envy the teams tasked with entering the building. Everyone inside was heavily armed and anything could go wrong. He felt lucky to be lying on top of a quadruple stacked shipping container, nearly three stories up, well removed from the danger below. Things had worked out decently enough for Jess and him in Argentina, and he had no intention of taking a bullet to help Sanderson pay off a debt to one of his crony supporters.

❧

Five minutes later, over six hundred miles away near the Chilean border, General Sanderson's satellite phone rang. He answered the call and listened for a few seconds.

"That's great news, Rich. See you back at the ranch." He leaned back in one of the leather chairs situated around the lodge's stone fireplace and relished in the team's success, the program's success...*his* success. He had sent twelve operatives into Buenos Aires to execute a high risk raid on behalf of Ernesto Galenden, their "unofficial" sponsor in Argentina, and it had gone off without a hitch. This was fantastic news, given that Sanderson had decided against fully stacking the team with their most experienced operators. With a number of them just over a year into their formal training, the newer recruits needed opportunities like these to hone their skills and instincts.

The final body count at the container yard had been eighteen. He suspected that the message would be received clearly by the remaining

Chechen mafia heads, and if not, Sanderson would gladly send them another. He wanted to keep Galenden happy. The headquarters compound and surrounding training areas turned out to be ideal, and he needed at least another eighteen months in Argentina before he could start pushing the newest batch of operatives into their assigned areas of operation (AO). Presently, he could deploy most of the operatives into their AO's for short assignments, but they lacked the fine tuning necessary to ensure their longer term survival. Fine tuning that came with consistent practice and patience.

So far, the program's progress had exceeded most expectations, despite the challenges involved in getting the Middle East program off the ground. Viable recruits for this group had proven difficult to find and screen, especially candidates with prior military or law enforcement experience and most importantly, fluency in either Farsi or Arabic. Sanderson had overstated the program's Middle East capabilities when he struck a sudden truce with Karl Berg and the CIA two years ago. He knew that Berg had seen a healthy portion of the original Black Flag files and would believe that Sanderson had re-engineered a new program to face America's biggest perceived threat: radical Islam.

The fact that Berg had gone "off the books" to hire a covert assassination team had led Sanderson to believe that Berg was a player. He was an expert at reading people, and Berg struck him as the kind of career CIA officer who normally worked within the system, but who had enough salt to cross the line if the potential payoff was big enough. Sanderson had been correct in all of his assumptions, and once Berg accepted the deal over the phone, there was no turning back.

In less than two years, Sanderson planned to have the entire program fully capable of conducting sustained operations throughout the world, right on the doorstep of every pressing threat to U.S. national security. At that point, it would only be a matter of time before they stumbled onto something big enough to give him the leverage needed to pull his program back into the fold as a legitimate and necessary extension of the United States.

For now, he had the generosity of several wealthy and extremely influential powerbrokers who professed the same commitment to worldwide stability as Sanderson, but their support came with a price. The occasional "favor" had turned into a monthly distraction, which provided his operatives with real world experience, but also underscored the fact that he was no longer ultimately calling the shots. Sanderson's practical side had long ago come to terms with this arrangement, but for a man who had "run the show" for decades, it gnawed at him. The sooner he could break free from these shackles the better.

General Sanderson stood up and pushed the remaining glowing ashes around in the fireplace. The fire had long ago died, but the embers had kept him warm enough while he waited for word from the team. He turned off the light, relying on instinct to get him to the front door of the headquarters lodge, and opened the wooden door to step outside into the frigid winter night. A thin layer of snow covered the ground, illuminated by the first quarter moon that beamed through the valley at a low angle above the Andean foothills. The valley was deathly silent, except for the sound of water trickling past larger rocks in the exposed riverbed ahead of the lodge.

He stepped onto a worn path to his right and cleared the lodge, crunching the freshly fallen snow under his boots. He glanced around, confirming that all of the compound's lights were out, except for the one he had expected to see shining through the thick trees of the forest. His last duty of the night would be to let Jessica Petrovich know that Daniel was fine.

The Petroviches remained somewhat of an enigma to Sanderson. He had never met two people more tightly connected than Daniel and Jessica. He had limited information regarding their relationship in Serbia, but he was convinced that something had happened in Belgrade to seal these two together forever, aside from their audacious plan to steal over a hundred million dollars from Srecko Hadzic. He wasn't overly concerned about their secret, but it kept him from fully trusting them.

He could already sense that Jessica was losing her interest in the program. Much to his surprise and pleasure, she had embraced her duties as an instructor with a raw eagerness that painfully contrasted Daniel's less than enthusiastic arrival at the compound. Gradually, they had reversed roles, and now he found Daniel deeply immersed in the program while Jessica was drifting, which wasn't the only thing that worried Sanderson. Lately, she struck him as less emotionally stable than when she first arrived. If he couldn't control—or at least predict—her behavior, she could quickly become a major liability. It was something for him to consider, and watch with a keen eye.

He softened his footsteps as he turned down the path that would lead him up to her door. Terrence Sanderson didn't have many fears. An active thirty year career in Army Special Forces had cured him of that useless emotion. Still, as he slowly approached the Petrovichs' timber A-Frame, he kept imagining Jessica inviting him inside and cutting his throat. Most men might have a different fantasy about Jessica Petrovich, but for Sanderson, his thoughts about her always involved a quick, razor-sharp knife. She was starting to get under his skin, and he didn't like it.

BLACK TIDE

Early April 2007

Chapter One

8:05 PM
Foothills of Kurchatov
Republic of Kazakhstan

Anatoly Reznikov stared at the fading ribbon of cerulean blue sky over the darkened steppe. He sat in the back of a cheap Russian four-door sedan, likely rented at the airport in Semipalatinsk (Semey), where he would soon board a privately chartered aircraft. From there he would fly unescorted to an airport in western Russia. Generous prepayments ensured that he could walk straight from the plane to a four-wheel drive vehicle, with no questions or hassle. Of course, this had all supposedly been arranged for him by his new partners, while he worked on their product at the laboratory. Reznikov didn't expect them to honor the final terms of the contract, so he had made his own arrangements.

The driver was still headed vaguely in the right direction, but Anatoly knew the man had taken a subtle turn down a dead end spur, which might have gone unnoticed in the dark, especially if he hadn't been paying close attention to every single action, facial expression…even word, uttered by his partners, as the project neared completion. It also helped that he could understand what they were saying, a fact he had kept secret from everyone, especially his new "partners."

Over the past few weeks, he had overheard some interesting conversations about "covering their tracks" and "getting rid of any links." The phrases had churned his stomach and made it nearly impossible for him to focus on the transfer of his product to the delivery devices. He had expected to be killed at any moment, either in the lab or his room, and the suspense had nearly crippled him as he played scenario after scenario in his head, trying to determine if they had realized that either of his assistants could complete the final steps of the project without his help.

He had become a nervous wreck during those weeks, plagued by stomach problems, unexplained sweating episodes, and numerous other symptoms of severe paranoia. All of that suddenly vanished when they announced that he would be transported to the airport as agreed. His "friend" Ahmad spoke right in front of him to a rough-looking man Reznikov had never seen at the lab complex: "Get rid of him."

As soon as the words were spoken, Anatoly felt calm, almost relieved. He found himself looking forward to the ride. Finally, he could get on with the plan he had set in motion nearly three years earlier, when he first tried to contact these traitorous jackals.

He wished there had been some way to keep the final product out of their hands, but this crew didn't mess around and there had been no opportunity to sabotage the project while keeping what he needed. He wouldn't get the second part of his payment, but it didn't matter. He had exactly what he had set out to obtain sitting in two innocuous, specially designed, thermos-sized coolers, snuggled into the backpack sitting next to him.

The car continued for another minute and then slowed to a stop.

"I think we took a wrong turn. I need to look at the map to try and make sense of these dirt roads. This is the middle of nowhere," the driver said in broken Russian.

The driver opened the door and walked forward, unfolding a map. The front passenger joined him, and they flattened the map on the hood, examining it with a flashlight for a few seconds. Suddenly, the interior roof lamp bathed the car in a dingy orange light and the man in the rear passenger seat next to Anatoly started to exit the vehicle. He exchanged a few words in Arabic with the men huddled around the map and stuck his head back in the car.

"It's an old Russian map. They need your help reading it," Ahmad said.

"No problem," he said.

Reznikov opened the door to join the three Al Qaeda operatives, who were staring quizzically at a map that had given them no problems on previous occasions. As he approached, the new passenger pointed to an odd cluster of hills to the southwest.

"We're trying to figure out where we are. Can you see if those hills break apart in the middle? If they do, I know exactly where we are. You might have to walk down the road a bit," he said and went back to the map.

"Sure," Anatoly said and continued walking.

As he reached a point alongside the three men, he drew a compact GSh-18 pistol from a large flapped pocket on his dark brown overcoat and fired two 9mm hollow point bullets into each of their heads. He started with Ahmad, who faced him on the other side of the hood, and rapidly dispatched the remaining two extremists, before they had even straightened their bodies in response to the deafening noise.

In the reflected light of the car's high beams, he watched the mystery passenger's body slide down the side of the car, taking the blood and brain matter-stained map with him. Ahmad and the driver lay on the road next to the car. In the dusty illumination of the dropped flashlight, he watched Ahmad's left foot twitch erratically, until it slowed and stopped.

Satisfied that the men were dead, he returned to the car and opened the trunk. Inside, he found exactly what he had expected. A cardboard box filled with spray bottles of cleaning solvent and assorted rags. Like Reznikov, his "partners" had no intention of returning a blood-stained car to the rental agency at the Semey Airport. He took the cleaning supplies and grabbed the flashlight from the side of the road. He'd start with the larger brain pieces.

Chapter Two

1:24 AM
Caucasus Mountains
Southern Dagestan

Captain Vasily Tischenko fought with the controls as he tracked the infrared navigation lights of the lead helicopter through the incredibly tight, tree-lined canyon. His grainy perception of the scene through night vision goggles (NVGs) told him that he had plenty of room, and his limited experience flying similar missions validated the deceptive green image that flickered and changed without warning. He had supervised the detailed route planning with the other pilots and knew logically that the Mi-8MS "Hip's" rotors had ample clearance from the rocky, pine-covered sides of the small river valley, but he had long ago learned never to trust anything but his instruments while flying at night.

Unfortunately, the only useful information he received from his cockpit controls told him that he had one hundred feet between the helicopter and the ground, and the altimeter hadn't been installed with night-vision flying in mind. Normally, he could check the altimeter and trim gauges with a flicker of his eyes, but the night vision goggles severely limited his field of vision, requiring him to move his head and take his eyes off the helicopter ahead of them.

He despised flying with NVGs and relied on his co-pilot to check several instruments for him, most importantly, their route. His co-pilot monitored a recently installed low light GPS screen and called out their position relative to the calculated track, which gave him some reassurance that they wouldn't slam into the side of the valley. Tischenko figured that if the lead helicopter didn't crash and burst into flames, they would probably be fine on the approach. He had enough distance between them to avoid a deadly pileup.

As with all Alpha Group Spetsnaz operations, the pilots had been given scant details regarding the nature of the target, only the ingress and egress routes, timeline, and expected support tactics. Tischenko had only flown two other missions for Alpha Group, and one had been aborted thirty minutes into the flight. The other had been a fairly straightforward insertion, in an uncontested landing zone near Grozny.

Overall, Tischenko's year in Chechnya had been quiet, as most of insurgency had been quelled by the time his helicopter squadron had started its year-long rotation. This had suited him well. A ready supply of SA-7 "Grail" surface–to-air missile launchers had been distributed to the rebels by mutinous Chechen regiments, and dozens of helicopters had been lost in similar operations during the early years of the insurgency. Helicopter losses were a rarity these days, which gave Tischenko all the more hope that he would make it back to attend his daughter Elena's third birthday party.

The captain's stomach pitched as the helicopter unexpectedly dropped fifteen feet, and he nudged the collective to raise the 22,000 pound chunk of metal back to a steady altitude. He was careful not to overreact, since the close walls of the canyon would not be very forgiving of an overcorrection. The helicopter bucked again, and he repeated the process, fighting a sudden torque problem, as wind shears from his own rotor wash came back from the valley walls directly across his tail. He delicately applied pressure to pedals that controlled the tail rotor blade pitch, and kept the fully-laden assault helicopter pointed at the center of the Alpha One. He had fought thousands of these small aerodynamic battles since entering the river valley fifteen minutes ago, and could barely wait to get out of these narrow confines. He sensed no change to the vibrations of his helicopter, which settled his stomach…slightly. He could detect the slightest changes to his helicopter and could often detect a problem before the helicopter's own fault sensors.

He wished there was an easier route to their target, but he understood the need for their clandestine approach. Three helicopters were about to drop sixty Alpha Group "special operators" onto a single site, which meant their target was important and probably heavily defended. He figured they had another minute before banking hard left and dropping directly into the middle of the insurgent base.

Once he made the turn, his helicopter would be less than one minute from dropping twenty of Russia's most highly trained Spetsnaz into the darkness. There would be no room overhead to hover and provide cover fire for the commandos. They had been instructed to climb out of the valley and use the nearby hills for cover until the operation had concluded. If requested, one helicopter would return for close air support. Luckily for Tischenko, that task fell to Alpha One.

"One minute to Final Waypoint," the copilot said over the internal communications circuit.

Following standard procedure, the copilot flashed the muted dark red lights in the troop compartment, which would let the commandos know that their insertion was imminent. They knew the drill better than Tischenko's crew and would be moving around the compartment making last second preparations. His two gunners would start to spin the barrels of their GshG-7.62mm miniguns, in preparation for the short period of time they would be allowed to engage targets of opportunity on the ground. It would be the only support Alpha Group would receive from the air, and his gunners wanted to make it count.

Roughly one minute later, Tischenko watched Alpha One's shadowy green profile start to change as the massive helicopter banked left and disappeared behind the adjacent valley's rocky spur. He would execute the same turn and line up on Alpha One as soon as he was clear of the same tree-covered outcropping. He expected all hell to break loose when they accelerated into the hidden valley.

A few more seconds passed, and he could tell that his own helicopter had crossed into the secondary valley opening. He caught sight of Alpha One's infrared taillights through his night vision and adjusted the cyclic to put the helicopter into a sharp left turn. He steadied on Alpha One with a clever manipulation of his pedals and watched as the lead helicopter picked up speed, seconds away from inserting its team.

His copilot flashed the troop compartment lights twice in rapid succession, and Tischenko felt the helicopter jolt as the doors on both sides of the modified special operations helicopter slammed open, ready to disgorge their human cargo. He felt the crisp mountain air rush into the cockpit and fill his helmet. Adrenaline coursed through his veins, as Alpha One flared, and two thick ropes dropped from each side of the hovering black beast. Once the helicopter settled a few seconds later, figures started to rapidly slide down the ropes, and Tischenko tried not to count them. He needed to focus on the narrowing gap between his rotor blades and the trees, since reconnaissance photos and survey maps indicated a tight squeeze before the valley opened up into the perfect hiding place for a high value insurgent base.

He found his helicopter approaching Alpha One too quickly and reduced the forward cyclic, waiting for the lead helicopter to dip forward and speed away. Once Alpha One started moving forward, he would move Alpha Two into position for his turn. Given the tight fit within the valley and the limited flat ground near the insurgent base, mission planners had decided against trying to fit two helicopters into the LZ at one time, especially at night. One miscalculation could be catastrophic. Alpha One's miniguns started firing, sending continuous streams of green tracers into the darkness on both sides of the helicopter.

"There he goes," the copilot said eagerly, before Tischenko could process the fact that Alpha One was speeding away.

He generously pushed the cyclic, and the helicopter lurched forward. His copilot continuously called out the distance to the final Assault Point using the GPS system, which was accurate to one meter. Tischenko was a skilled pilot and brought the Mi-8MS "Hip" right into position, flaring at the last second to completely stop the helicopter's forward motion. As the helicopter settled, the first thing he noticed was the unmistakable sound of small arms bullets clanking into his helicopter. He couldn't hear the source of the gunfire, but one of the lower cockpit windows spider-cracked, followed by the window immediately to his left.

"Stable at Assault Point. Deploy Alpha Team!" he yelled into his helmet microphone.

"Alpha Team deploying," he heard.

His own helicopter's miniguns barked like buzz saws, spitting hundreds of 7.62mm bullets per second back into the insurgent positions. Through his peripheral vision on both sides, he saw thick streams of green tracers float away from his helicopter. They had a full-scale battle on their hands in this shitty little valley. Alpha One had warmed them up and escaped untouched. *Lucky motherfuckers*, he thought momentarily, before he immediately regretted the thought.

Alpha One had cleared the LZ and just started its ascent from the valley, when at least two flashes caught Tischenko's attention. The flashes came from the left side of the valley, and his mind didn't have enough time to process more of the scene before his night vision flared bright green, blinding him. He held the controls steady, as every natural instinct programmed into his body fought against him. The Spetsnaz team had already commenced fast-roping to the ground, and he could not break his hover. Any sudden changes to the aircraft's stability could hurtle one or more commandos fifty feet to their death. He had to settle himself and wait for the "all clear" from his crew chief, who was directing the fast rope operation. He pivoted the night vision goggles out of his face and took in the scene. What he saw gave him little hope of ever seeing his wife and daughter again.

Alpha One had activated its decoy flare system, which fired eight blinding magnesium flares into the air behind it, rendering his night vision equipment useless. The flares landed on the ground and completely illuminated the entire valley, including his own helicopter. He couldn't see Alpha One beyond the burning flares, but a crunching explosion and a billowing orange pillar of fire didn't leave much to Tischenko's imagination. He needed to get out of here before the insurgents could reload their rockets.

"Chief, how much longer?" he yelled into the helmet microphone.

"Half of the team is out. We're doubling up on the ropes. Five more seconds," came the abrupt reply.

One of the cockpit window panels above his copilot's head shattered, and a bullet ricocheted through the cockpit. Several more bullets struck the reinforced glass around them, which miraculously held. The miniguns belched sustained bursts of withering fire back at their targets as Tischenko counted the seconds aloud. Seven seconds later, his crew chief screamed through the headset that they were "all clear."

He decided to skip the low level egress route chosen by Alpha One and pushed the cyclic and collective together, favoring the collective. Alpha Two rushed forward, ascending rapidly. His IR missile sensors started to flash and a harsh tone blared in his headset, but he resisted the impulse to launch his own flares, knowing they would likely rain down on Alpha Three. The missile threat never materialized, and Tischenko's helicopter rose above the valley, racing for an adjacent range of hills. He could see enough without the night vision goggles to keep them safe for now, until they were inevitably called back into the valley to pick up the Spetsnaz.

"You need to redesignate helicopters, Captain," the copilot said.

"Standby," he said and opened a channel to the ground force

commander and the other helicopter.

"Redesignate call signs. Flight Hotel Victor Four Three Two is now Alpha One. Flight Hotel Victor Four Three Three is now Alpha Two, over," he said.

"This is Alpha Command. Out."

"This is Alpha Two. Out."

Tischenko enjoyed a few more seconds of peace, hovering in what he hoped was safe airspace.

"Alpha One, this is Alpha Command...request close air support in vicinity of Assault Point. Alpha Strike units will designate targets for your gunners using IR pointers, over."

Shit, this was going to be the longest—or possibly the shortest—night of his life. At least he wouldn't need his night vision goggles. The flares and burning wreckage had transformed the valley into an inferno.

"This is Alpha One, thirty seconds from commencing gun run. Mark targets in two-zero seconds," he said.

"This raid better be worth it," he muttered, as the orange glowing valley reappeared ahead of them.

Chapter Three

6:45 AM
Strigino Airport
Nizhny Novgorod, Russian Federation

Anatoly Reznikov squeezed the armrest tightly as the Hawker 800 business jet floated above the runway for two seconds, then abruptly dropped onto its landing gear. He felt the airbrakes decelerate the sixteen-thousand-pound aircraft from one hundred and sixty miles per hour to less than twenty in fewer than five seconds, pressing his abdomen uncomfortably against the lap belt. It wasn't the smoothest landing he'd ever experienced, but he understood why the pilots had chosen to sacrifice comfort on this particular approach.

Cross winds from a massive storm system north of Nizhny Novgorod had plagued the small aircraft since the pilots started their decent, and had intensified as they lined up with the runway. Reznikov had considered requesting that the pilots divert the flight to a different airport, but his arrangements for a hassle-free transfer had been made for Strigino Airport and couldn't be guaranteed anywhere else. He was carrying a suppressed pistol and two stainless steel cooling cylinders, a combination of items unlikely to pass through even the most cursory security checks typically associated with private business travelers, especially if special monetary arrangements were not already in place.

The aircraft slowed further, and Anatoly loosened his safety belt. The first person he expected to see upon exiting was Gennady. The man had already been paid half of a very generous fee to personally ensure Anatoly's uncomplicated transfer to a rental car. He had met Gennady once before, immediately prior to arriving in Kazakhstan to begin work for his former "friends." Knowing that he would not be theoretically allowed to leave the laboratory site again until the work was completed, he had made all of these arrangements in advance. All Gennady needed was a phone call, and he could have a business jet flown from Novosibirsk to Semey within four hours, all at considerable cost, of course, which was why Anatoly expected to see Gennady himself personally standing at the bottom of the Hawker's cabin door stairs. Gennady's absence would signify a considerable problem, one that could only be solved with the pistol readily accessible in his black backpack.

He glanced through the rain-splashed cabin window at the scene unfolding on the edge of the runway. The private terminal area loomed ahead, and shadows of the runway crew hurried through sheets of rain to prepare for the jet's arrival. The shiny concrete was illuminated by massive terminal lights, which dimmed with each passing rain squall. The sun had risen a half hour earlier, but the heavy rain clouds shielded the airport from any signs of dawn. Now that the aircraft was still, he could hear the rain pummeling the aircraft's thin metal shell and feel the wind buffeting the aircraft's frame.

After a few minutes, the jet moved forward into its final position in front of the terminal and stopped. Waiting at a safe distance, several airport personnel converged on the aircraft, disappearing underneath the cabin. He heard the usual assortment of sounds associated with post-flight maintenance and spotted a fuel truck speeding toward the aircraft. The jet would undoubtedly be back in the sky within the hour, headed toward its next thirty-thousand-dollar passenger. It was money well spent on his account. The flight had put him within a reasonable three-day driving range of his target. Unfortunately, his budget didn't allow for another flight like this one, or he would have flown all the way to St. Petersburg. From St. Petersburg, he'd face an easy, one-day drive to the Kola Peninsula.

One of the pilots stepped back into the cabin. "Sorry about the landing. I wanted to get this thing down as quickly as possible in those winds. We'll have you on your way in a few minutes. Feel free to empty the minibar. The company stocks premium liquor, and it's a little known secret that everything is included in the price of the flight," he said, tipping his pilot cap.

"Thank you. I think I might take a few bottles for the road."

Reznikov unbuckled his seatbelt and made his way over to the minibar near the front of the cabin. Upon opening the small refrigerator, he smiled. Indeed, they'd spared no expense with the liquor selection. He placed several miniature bottles of vodka in the side pockets of his backpack and secured the straps. A hand touched his shoulder, startling him.

"Don't forget to take this. Glen Ord, thirty year, single malt. $300 a bottle," the pilot said, pulling a bottle out of the cabinet above the minibar.

"Now I understand the cost of the flight," he said, accepting the bottle and then handing it back. "I never developed a taste for Scotch. Vodka is my poison."

"A true Russian. Not many of us left these days. In that case, try this instead. I like to make these bottles disappear from time to time."

He reached into the cabinet and removed a bottle of Rodnik Vodka, which Anatoly knew for a fact would cost nearly $500.

"If I flew this jet, they would all go missing. Many thanks, comrade. I have the perfect occasion in mind for this bottle."

"Ground is ready for you to disembark, Mr. Pavlenko," the co-pilot said, sticking his head into the doorway.

The pilot turned to the door and pulled a small handle to the left, breaking the door's airtight seal. Reznikov watched him lower the door, which served as the staircase, slowly to the tarmac. A gust of wind whipped rain inside the cabin, and Reznikov hiked the backpack over his shoulders. He stepped forward and saw Gennady standing at the bottom of the stairs struggling to hold an umbrella, a useless gesture given the sideways rain. It was a good sign, nonetheless. The money paid to Gennady had left an impression. Wasting no time, he walked down the stairs.

"Put that ridiculous thing away, and help me with my bag."

"Your bag is already taken care of," he said.

"Then, let's get the fuck out of this rain," Reznikov said, still holding the vodka bottle as Gennady led him to a door reserved for "special" customers.

Once inside the door, Gennady turned to Reznikov with a worried look. They stood in an abandoned, poorly lit reception area outfitted with a couch and table set. The room opened into a hallway that led further into the terminal and likely emptied into a discreet area where certain customers could disappear without any official fanfare.

"We have a problem. Two gentlemen arrived about an hour ago asking questions about you. They had basic flight information and used the name Reznikov."

"Russian?"

"Barely. I'd guess Chechen by the looks of them. Filthy, dark-skinned Muslim mongrels. Out of Moscow probably. They had rough details and a picture of you. Unfortunately, they were spreading money around, and people here were talking."

"So much for a private terminal," Reznikov said.

"The money was just a formality. Everyone here knows what they are, and nobody wants to be dragged out behind the terminal for a private conversation," he said.

"Where are they now?"

"Waiting inside the terminal for you," Gennady said.

"Where is my car?"

"Already checked out and waiting for you in the private parking lot."

"I need you to do something for me. I want you to tell them where my car is and suggest that they wait for me in the parking lot."

"Are you crazy?"

"Just do what I say, then get back to Novosibirsk."

"I don't like the sound of this. I don't need the Chechens on my ass. And what about the rest of my payment?" he said.

"I can transfer the rest to you in Novosibirsk, or you can collect it here…but only after you convince the men to wait for me in the parking lot," Anatoly said.

"I don't like this."

"Then don't get paid. It's your choice."

"I need a kicker for doing this. Fucking with these people is serious business," Gennady said, "and you never mentioned they were involved."

"They weren't. This is a simple job for them, nothing more. You'll be fine."

"I'm not fucking with them unless you double the remaining fee," Gennady said.

"Double? I'll give you one and a half times the remaining fee," Reznikov said.

"You have it here?"

"Yes. You'll get it after I deal with these guys. I have your cell phone number. I'll call you when it's done and I'll drive around to the terminal to meet you," Reznikov said.

"You better not fuck me over on this," he said.

"Gennady, this has all gone very smoothly so far. I've paid you as agreed, and you've delivered the goods. I just need you to help me get out of here. You'll get your money, and then you can disappear to Novosibirsk. It's a win-win situation. No blood on your hands."

"We'll see about that. I'll call you when they're on their way to the parking lot. Until then, stay right here," he said and walked briskly down the hallway.

When Gennady closed the door, Reznikov took the suppressed GSh-18 pistol out of his backpack and thumbed the safety off, sliding it back into the cushioned compartment normally reserved for a laptop. He would need to access the pistol quickly. He removed a second eighteen-round magazine from a smaller compartment on the backpack, and stuffed this into one of his coat pockets. He left the top of the backpack open and stood up, straightening his coat. He walked down the hallway to the same door used by Gennady a few minutes earlier and opened it.

He found himself in a sparsely furnished, windowless office with an access door to the outside. The room's only source of light came from a small, translucent window on the door, which barely cast enough light to see into the furthest reaches of the room. Fresh rain pooled on the floor just inside the door, and he could hear the rain drive against the outside walls. If Gennady betrayed him, they would come for him through this doorway. There would be too many witnesses on the tarmac for the men to enter through the runway door.

He closed the door leading back into the hallway and positioned himself behind the desk, which sat in the darkest corner of the room to the right of the hallway door. He kneeled down below the top of the desk and took out his cell phone, switching it to vibrate. After returning the phone to an inside pocket, he reached into the backpack and withdrew the semi-automatic pistol, holding it steady in his right hand.

Five minutes later, his phone buzzed. After the third extended vibration from his coat pocket, he heard a crash beyond the hallway door and was glad he had trusted his instinct regarding Gennady. He knew the man wouldn't have the balls to go through with his plan. He wondered if

Gennady had intentionally turned on him, or if the Chechens had simply given him no choice. Either way, it didn't matter. If the men sent to the airport were indeed Chechen mafia, then Gennady couldn't return to Novosibirsk.

The sudden appearance of the Chechens meant one thing to Reznikov: Al Qaeda had quickly discovered that he'd escaped from Kazakhstan, and they desperately wanted him dead. He could understand why. He had left their makeshift laboratory eight hours ago, with two self-cooled cylinders that they had fully intended to recover upon his execution. Now, he was on the run with enough virus capsules to poison two cities, and Al Qaeda had no idea what he planned to do next.

He'd overheard enough to know that Al Qaeda planned to strike several European cities with the virus, and he'd been fortunate to memorize several addresses where containers would be received and held for a coordinated attack. He wasn't sure how he could use this information, but was certain that it would hold some value if he was ever captured. He'd also heard plans for shipping the virus overseas to the United States, through a medical supply distribution company in Germany.

It all added up to a major attack on the West by Al Qaeda, which is why they wanted him dead. The last thing they needed was for Reznikov to release the virus first, putting the World Health Organization and every other major international health ministry on high alert for further attacks. The capsules were specifically designed to poison municipal water supplies, and an isolated attack would lock down every water facility throughout the world, leaving Al Qaeda with few viable deployment options for their virus.

He didn't care one way or the other whether Al Qaeda succeeded with their plans. He had a specific target for his own virus capsules and that was all that mattered. If he could escape from the airport, he'd be at his target city within three days. Less than a week after that, the Russian government would watch helplessly as the city of Monchegorsk was put out of its misery.

He heard voices muttering from the hallway, and bright beams of light penetrated the privacy glass on the hallway door. The lights suddenly disappeared and everything became still again. He watched the doorknob closely, barely poking his head over the desk. The doorknob reflected some of the light from the outside door, and after a few seconds he was certain that it had turned. He ducked his head quickly, a fraction of a second before the door crashed open, slamming against the wall and cracking the inset glass window.

Footsteps filled the room and bright lights swept the walls and corners. He prayed that his head was far enough below the lip of the desk to remain unseen by the light focused on his corner. He tensed and prepared to make the first move, expecting bullets to rip through the desk at any moment. He started to lift the pistol upward when the light above his desk vanished and a grim voice sounded out in the darkness.

"He's not here either. What the fuck are you trying to pull on us?"

Gennady answered them timidly. "I told him to wait back there. Don't worry. He can't go far. He doesn't have the keys to the rental or his luggage. We'll find him," he said, and Anatoly heard a key chain jingling.

"You're not finding anyone," one of the men said.

The comment was followed by a deafening gunshot, which spurred Reznikov into action. He rose swiftly, extending the suppressed pistol forward with two hands, and repeatedly squeezed the trigger. Each flash from the suppressor showed a progressively macabre scene, as he fired into the center of each briefly illuminated figure, alternating back and forth between the two men until the slide of his pistol locked back. By the time he realized that the pistol's magazine was empty, the two men started sliding down the opposite wall, leaving dark, glistening trails of gore. He didn't hear a grunt or groan from either of the two men, as their bodies slumped to the floor.

He changed pistol magazines and walked over to Gennady's body, using one of the dropped flashlights to illuminate the man's face. His eyes stared up at the ceiling, and a single red dot on his forehead trickled blood down the side of his temple. Reznikov turned the flashlight on his body and located the keys to his rental car. Now, he just needed to figure out where to find his baggage, and he could be on his way.

With Gennady dead, the rental car would be untraceable. Gennady had rented the car in Moscow, using false paperwork, and driven it to Nizhny Novgorod himself earlier today. He looked down at the man again and shook his head. He'd hoped to kill the traitor himself, but maybe this would work out for the better. By the time the police straightened out this mess, if they ever did, the world would be different place.

Chapter Four

8:22 AM
FSB (Federal Security Services of the Russian Federation) Headquarters
Lubyanka Square, Moscow

Alexei Kaparov slammed his right fist down onto a stack of papers that littered his desk and extinguished his cigarette into a crowded ashtray with his other hand. He lifted the report, which had been unceremoniously tossed into his daily slush pile, and squinted at its contents. Not even a simple folder, or anything. The single most important piece of information he'd seen in months had been unceremoniously added to the never-ending shit pile of papers on his desk. It might as well have been thrown in the trash. What about a priority flagged email? How long have they had email? Important shit like this still ended up travelling ungodly distances, only to be buried under a rubble pile. It really wasn't his team's fault, but he was pissed at the entire system.

If any of Kaparov's subordinates could have heard his frustrated internal dialogue, they would have agreed with him on several of his points, especially the part about the rubble. The deputy counter-terrorism director's office was a disaster, with loose stacks of paperwork scattered everywhere, sitting on top of boxes of paperwork that needed to be filed. Despite the appearance of chaos, Kaparov could find anything he needed and reviewed every single document that found its way into the room…as long as the paperwork was placed on top of his desk. He made a point of clearing through the desk every day, and then refilling it with new documents, or old ones he had decided to resurrect.

Daily, he scoured field reports from hundreds of FSB and Foreign Intelligence Service (SVR) agents, looking for any clues, signs or trigger words that might indicate a potential chemical or biological act of terrorism on Russian soil. When he came across the four-page Southern District FSB intelligence summary of a recent counter-insurgency raid in Dagestan, he settled in for some interesting reading. Raids into Dagestan were rare, and the report piqued his interest. He could have just as easily dismissed the report. Threats limited to the volatile Caucasus Region were analyzed by another deputy director, leaving Kaparov's crew of analysts with the rest of Russia.

On page three of the report, he nearly had a heart attack. He felt a tightening in his chest and glanced down at the top drawer of his desk, which ironically held both a package of Troika cigarettes and a small plastic bottle of nitroglycerine pills. Right there, buried nonchalantly in the report, was a dangerous name. The fact that the name had been discovered among documents recovered from an Al Qaeda stronghold in Dagestan was even more disturbing. He chuckled at the thought of dying from a heart attack in his office. Maybe someone had slipped the name in the report just to trigger his death. They would probably take a look around at the mess, eyeball the ashtray, and shrug their shoulders.

At 57, Alexei Kamarov wasn't exactly a picture of good health. Slightly rotund and stuffed into a dark brown suit, his skin was devoid of color and almost matched his similarly dull gray, yellow-tinged hair. Only a hawkish, blood-vessel-riddled nose gave his face any contrast and also served as a beacon for his unhealthy habits, cigarettes being only one of many bad choices Kamarov made on a daily basis. Seeing the contents of the report not only turned his nose a few shades darker, but also ignited a craving for one of his other bad choices. Fortunately, he no longer kept a bottle of cheap vodka in his lower desk drawer. Those days in the Lubyanka were long gone for all of them. He was lucky to still have his cigarettes.

He stormed to the door of his office and opened it abruptly, which turned several heads in his direction.

"Someone find Prerovsky immediately! Goddamn it, I want this shit filed electronically," he said, waving the report at nobody in particular. "We're living in the fucking dark ages here, and we're missing shit left and right!"

Now everyone was looking in his direction, at a very atypical burst of emotion from their director. Several analysts broke from their seats, to either look for Agent Prerovsky or just get out of the way.

"He's over in another section. Caucasus Division," a female agent replied, who didn't appear to be moving from her computer workstation.

"Well? What exactly are you waiting for? A personal invitation to get off your ass and find him? For a bunch of analysts, you seem to have trouble connecting the dots. I need Prerovsky here immediately! I don't pay him to work in the Caucasus Division! He works here, and if you value your job in my division you'll fucking find him immediately!" he said, and retreated into his office, leaving everyone to scramble.

The door slammed shut, and he listened to the beehive of activity on the other side of the flimsy gray door. *That went well.* A little fire under their asses worked miracles from time to time. Kaparov was careful not to verbally explode on them too regularly, like many of the other directors and mid-level managers within Headquarters. It served no purpose other than to alienate, though every once in a while, he felt the need to show them that they weren't working on easy street. Granted, his division wasn't the busiest, but it was no less important than any other division, and on a day like today, it might be more important than anyone would care to admit. Just as he sat down to look at the report again, he heard a knock at the door.

"Come in," he barked, and Yuri Prerovsky opened the door, stepping in tentatively.

"Shut the door. We have a problem," he said.

Agent Yuri Prerovsky, second in command of the Bioweapons/Chemical Threat Assessment Division, shut the door and walked over to a crude folding chair opened next to his boss's desk. "What's all the commotion?"

He threw the report down on the end of the desk closest to Yuri. "Have you seen this report?"

Yuri studied the first page and thumbed through it. "I haven't read it. I catalogued it and placed it on your desk two days ago. I think we received it by mistake. It should have been routed to the Caucasus Threat Division if anything…hold on," he said, studying the document, "actually, it was routed to them as well."

"Read page three and you'll see why it was routed to us," he said and waited for Yuri's response.

"Fuck…how did Central Processing miss this?"

"They didn't. They got it to the right desk, but didn't bother to highlight Reznikov's name or put an alert in the computer! Anything to bring this to our attention. He's at the top of our list for fuck's sake!" he yelled, instantly calming back down and holding his hand out for the report.

"Two days you say? Shit." Kaparov lit a cigarette from the pack of Troikas in his desk. "The raid occurred five days ago, and this is the speed at which we receive crucial information?" he said, deeply inhaling tobacco smoke.

"There isn't much here, and we're not likely to dig the rest out of Alpha Branch. I'll try though," Yuri said.

Kaparov exhaled the smoke toward the ceiling and regarded Yuri. He was young and smart, part of the new generation of law enforcement agents that hadn't been trained under the KGB. He wasn't part of the paranoid, compartmentalized thinking that had served mother Russia so miserably for nearly fifty years. The fact that he had no hesitation to walk upstairs to the infamous branch that handled FSB Spetsnaz Operations was a testament to the new days.

Agents like Prerovksy gave him hope that the change was real. Two decades ago, walking up to the KGB Special Operations Branch without an invitation could easily end your career, and if you were on your way up there to ask the wrong kinds of questions, you could wake up the next morning in a Siberian detention camp. Times had fortunately changed, but old fears were hard to shake.

"It's worth a try, but the report entry doesn't indicate much more than a few scattered ledger entries regarding Reznikov's visit to the camp and a reference to recent activity in Kazakhstan. That's Reznikov's old stomping grounds. He was fired from the VECTOR bio-research facility in Novosibirsk, just a few hundred miles away from the Kazakhstan border. He supposedly disappeared en route to an interview at its sister institute, barely three hundred miles away in Stepnagorsk, Kazakhstan.

"Yuri, I have a bad feeling about this. Reznikov's been nosing around Al Qaeda for three years, with what I can only assume is one purpose: to strike some kind of funding deal to complete his research into weaponized encephalitis. Even during the heyday of the Soviet bioweapons program, that research was banned."

"But they still did it," Yuri said.

"Unfortunately, considerable research continued, and VECTOR was one of the primary sites that violated the Kremlin's decree. Of course, it stopped for good in 1978."

Yuri cocked his head and cast a curious look.

"Ah, the benefits of being a remnant of the old guard. Lots of loose lips back then, without any glue to keep them shut. Rumor has it that the entire scientific team associated with the project was executed by firing squad on the front lawn of the facility. Reznikov's father was supposedly among the group executed. Nobody really knows. There was no official record of the executions, as you can imagine. What we do know is that Reznikov's mother fatally shot herself on the same day, and Anatoly Reznikov went to live with the mother's sister somewhere south of Murmansk. The father just disappeared from record."

"No wonder Reznikov is a little off."

"A little? He was a vocal proponent of continuing his father's research. Can you imagine how well that was received at VECTOR? Within a month of being hired there in 2003, he suddenly started talking nonsense about how modifying encephalitis genomes could save the world. That fucker went under surveillance within the hour, and emails from certain research staff hit my desk quicker than you can imagine. Whether the rumors about 1978 were true or not, nobody wanted to be summoned to attend an impromptu picnic on the front lawn. Know what I mean?"

"So, where do we go with this?" Yuri said.

"I'll walk this up to the Investigative Division. They'll need to start sending agents out to Kazakhstan and all potential laboratory sites in the area. Only God knows what's in this for Reznikov, but if he's aligned with Muslim extremists, we have a big problem. Al Qaeda won't be funding his research to improve their image on the scientific scene. This can only lead to one thing. Bioterrorism attacks on European and U.S. soil. Hell, if Chechen separatists are involved, which is a fair assumption given the Dagestan connection, then we're looking at possible attacks right here in Russia. We need to assume the worst. Let's get our team looking in the right places for any more information. I'll stop by Alpha Group on my way back from Investigative, unless you have a contact there."

"Well, I do have special access to a lady friend up there," he said, grinning.

"I don't even want to think about your concept of 'special access,' Yuri. If I don't have any luck with them this morning, I'll pay for you to take her out on the town tonight. And they said we were out of the spy business," Kaparov said, shaking his head.

Chapter Five

9:35 AM
United Nations Detention Unit
The Hague, Netherlands

Srecko Hadzic sat impassively at a thick stone table, contemplating the warm, salty air that wafted through the enclosed courtyard. The "Hague Hilton," as some critics liked to call it, was located in the Dutch seaside town of Scheveningen, less than a mile from the North Sea, but Hadzic had never seen any of it. His room didn't come with a view. None of the cells did. To Srecko, this was far from any Hilton Hotel he had visited and an ungodly affront to his nature.

His tenth cigarette of the morning smoldering between his stubby, yellow-stained fingers, he glanced up at the clear Dutch sky and swallowed his pride for the hundredth time since he was rudely awoken by the guards this morning. A surge of rage always followed, but by midday, he would start to feel slightly level as the strong emotions abated. This would last until something seemingly innocuous would vomit all of the rage and indignity right back up in his lap, and he'd have to start over trying to come to terms with his situation.

He'd been slowly rotting in the United Nations Detention Center for seven years, watching one former Serbian colleague after another leave for various reasons. Some were indicted and sentenced to lengthy prison sentences. He didn't envy their fate. They were rumored to have been transferred to Germany for imprisonment. Others had been released pending further trial proceedings, a feat not even Srecko's lawyers could accomplish, which only served to fuel his daily rage.

Above all, nothing stoked his anger like the luckiest of his former Serbian "friends," who were suddenly freed from custody when the chief prosecutor for the war crimes tribunal, Carla Del Ponte, simply excluded them from the draft indictments of "criminal enterprise" leveled against Milosevic's regime. Her indictment focused on Slobodan Milosevic, essentially ignoring several other key members of the regime, who Srecko knew had ordered many of the crimes that held him firmly entrenched in his own cell.

Not one of them looked back or offered their support to him as they scurried to freedom like cowardly pigs. Now, the number of true Serbs in the detention unit was dwindling, and his trial had been postponed for another year, forcing him to mingle with the disgustingly impure Croatian and Kosovar dogs roaming the floors here. There was no shortage of war criminals in the detention center, from all sides of the war, and he had to sit around on a daily basis and make small talk with the very people he had tried to ruthlessly stomp out, on behalf of the traitors who had turned their backs on him. He had little to look forward to, but the visit today from one of his most trusted and cherished allies might give him a renewed sense of purpose. The chance to taste the sweetest nectar of life. Revenge.

The nondescript, gray metal door leading out of the courtyard opened, and Josif Hadzic stepped through the solitary breach in the courtyard's walls. Josif had changed significantly since Srecko's imprisonment, transformed from the young, scrawny, awkward nephew into a muscularly lean, handsome, young Serbian man. His thick black hair, prominent brow, and deep-set brown eyes proclaimed to the world that he was of pure Serbian stock. A true testament to the cause Srecko had spent his entire life fighting for…and for which he had been summarily discarded by the so called "patriots" that now lived in luxury.

Despite Josif's soft, almost serene composure upon entering the courtyard, Srecko harbored Josif's secret. He was a dedicated ultra-nationalist, like his uncle, after having seen the direct impact of the NATO-imposed restrictions on their just campaign to carve out a little space for the true Serbia. His family had lost everything due to their allegiance with Milosevic's army, but fortunately, none of them had been imprisoned. Josif's father, Andrija, Srecko's younger brother by three years, had wisely kept his nose out of the seductively lucrative spoils of Srecko's enterprises.

He had taken care of his brother, but always from a distance. He respected Andrija's choice, and his brother had served loyally in the regular Yugoslavian Army for several years, fighting for the cause during the Bosnian war. Now, Josif's family was in shambles. His father an absent, raging alcoholic and his mother a catatonic drone working several shift jobs in the outskirts of Belgrade. She refused to accept the modest amount of money Srecko had offered to keep them afloat. "Poisoned money," she would say.

Josif started visiting Srecko during the early days of his incarceration at The Hague. Srecko immediately recognized the hunger and intelligence in his eyes. He soon arranged for Josif to stay close by in Amsterdam. Srecko had unfinished business and plenty of hidden money to keep an underground organization alive. More than anything, he needed loyalty that would not abandon him in his time of need.

Josif walked briskly to the stone table. "Uncle," he said, and Srecko rose from the table to hug him with the cigarette still burning in his right hand.

"My Josif. Have you brought me some good news?" he said, glancing at the hardcover book in Josif's hands and signaling for the young man to have a seat at the table.

"Always good news, Uncle. And a gift. I know how fond you are of the Fruska Gora National Forest," Josif said and slid the book toward his uncle.

"One of the thickest, most mysterious forests in the world. We used to take a lot of trips there, your father and I. Lots of good memories…and a few bad," he said and raised a knowing eyebrow at Josif.

"I think you'll find page twenty-three to be your favorite," he said and looked away at the sky.

Srecko opened the book and casually thumbed through the pictures, stopping once or twice to admire the picturesque scene of a forest engulfed village, or a hidden waterfall. He stopped on page twenty-three and his eyes narrowed to a reptilian quality. Page twenty-three was not part of the original picture book's publication, but rather a cleverly-designed and professionally-inserted counterfeit addition. Designed to look the same in structure and layout, the half-page-sized picture had nothing to do with the Fruska Gora National Forest from an outsider's perspective. To Srecko, the photograph had everything to do with the forest.

"This was taken recently?" he said, still staring intensely at the picture.

"A few days ago in Buenos Aires. Our guy emailed the pictures while they finished lunch."

"Do we still know where they are?" Srecko said and looked up from the photo.

Josif lowered his head slightly in a subconscious deference to his uncle.

"No. Once they started walking, our guy found it impossible to follow them without tipping them off. I'm sorry about that, but..."

"No need to apologize, Josif. Never apologize. Not even to me. This is great work. It shows great patience and intellect, my nephew. Very important traits to have," he said, glaring at the picture.

"They'll show up again. That bitch is predictable and has a taste for expensive things. She won't be hard to find. As for him, tell our people to be extremely cautious. This one is capable of just about anything."

"What would you like to do about them, Uncle?"

"I want them dead, but first, I want to know what they did with my money. I don't care what needs to be done to get this information out of them. They're trying to indict me on charges that I ordered the systematic rape of over two hundred Kosovar whores...why not add another rape to the list? Or two."

"We'll try for both, but what if we can only grab one?"

"Grab the woman first. I can't stress to you how badly I want her to suffer...and I want to see it on video. I have a DVD player, and I'm getting tired of the usual movies."

Josif grinned and stood up. "Understood, Uncle. I'll keep you informed. See you next week," he said and his grin faded into a deadly serious gaze.

"You know, the security here is pretty terrible. I'm worried about your safety," Josif said.

Srecko stifled a laugh at the audacity of what Josif had just implied.

"Perhaps one day it will come to that, my nephew. For now, I'll let the lawyers work their magic. One of my dearest friends was granted a provisional release a few weeks ago. Haven't heard a word from him since, of course," Srecko said.

"Mr. Stanisic hasn't disappeared, as some expected, which is a good thing. Maybe the lawyers can get you the same deal," Josif said.

"Maybe," he said and hugged his nephew.

He watched Josif stride toward the door, which buzzed and opened from the inside. He waved one more time at his nephew before the door closed, sealing him off from his only contact with the outside world besides his lawyers. He sat down slowly and removed a crumpled pack of generic cigarettes from the front breast pocket of his wrinkled gray collared shirt. He tapped a cigarette and lit it with a disposable butane lighter retrieved from the back pocket of his threadbare pants. He took a long drag on the cheap tobacco, then exhaled the thick smoke through his nose several seconds later, tapping his free hand on the picture in front of him.

Staring at the picture of Marko Resja, or whoever he claimed to be now, sitting alongside that supposedly beheaded whore, stoked the deepest embers of his seething rage. He started to feel sick and immediately took another nicotine-filled drag on his cigarette, igniting the tobacco embers in a fierce orange glow that lasted for three seconds. The wave of nicotine filtered through his bloodstream and entered his brain, triggering pleasure receptors, which barely cut into the anger. It gave him a moment of clarity to process a few level thoughts.

Two years ago, by sheer luck he had stumbled across Resja again. He had been sitting around a large fold-out table on a different floor in the detention center, attending the "release" party of Idriz Dzaferi, one of the Albanian terrorist leaders his paramilitary unit had scoured Kosovo trying to kill. Apparently, the testimony against Dzaferi hadn't been compelling enough for the tribunal to move forward, and once again, Srecko found himself eating cake and "celebrating" someone else's release. As he pushed the tasteless cake around his mouth, his eyes were drawn to the common area's television screen. Two images, side by side, appeared on the CNN feed, and Srecko froze, unable to chew.

The screen showed a man named Daniel Petrovich, wanted in connection with a string of high profile killings throughout the Washington, D.C., area that included the brutal slaying of a police officer and several military contractors. He disappeared after a spectacular neighborhood shootout with FBI and local police that landed several more law enforcement agents in the hospital. Daniel Petrovich? Srecko knew this man by another name. Marko Resja.

Srecko still hadn't made the connection between the stolen money and Daniel Petrovich, until he studied the fleeting image of the woman on the screen. Jessica Petrovich. That's when he almost choked on the mouthful of cake still mulling between his clenched jaws. She looked different now, but he knew he was staring at that deceptive snake, Zorana Zekulic. The woman responsible for the theft of his money, or so he had been told…by the man apparently married to her in the United States! The man who had thrown her supposed head down on the ground before him.

It all made sense to Srecko in those few seconds. Marko Resja's sudden disappearance had been no coincidence. He had engineered the entire thing with the help of that cunt. The theft of over 130 million dollars, leaving him high and dry in Belgrade with a bloodbath on his hands. On May 27, 2005, over cake and fruit punch at the United Nations Detention Unit, he swore to God and the Serbian people that he would see these traitors' heads roll. It gave him a renewed sense of purpose and temporarily lifted him above the fact that he was sitting at a hastily assembled card table amidst two dozen other chubby fifty-year-olds; most of whom had run successful criminal enterprises on the Balkan Peninsula, but now were reduced to eating yellow cake and drinking Kool-Aid like toddlers.

The memory faded, and Srecko Hadzic snapped the picture book shut. He smothered the cigarette against the side of the stone table and got up to leave the courtyard. The fresh air was killing him.

Chapter Six

10:35 AM
FBI Headquarters Building
Washington, D.C.

Special Agent Ryan Sharpe adjusted the files on his desk and checked his watch for the fifth time in the last minute. He was nervous about this meeting. His career hadn't exactly flourished since General Sanderson and his crew popped up and decapitated HYDRA. The Black Flag group vanished into thin air and proved near impossible to track. The quick revenge demanded by the FBI's director, Frederick Shelby, never materialized, and his significantly smaller task force began to shrink with every uneventful month, until he was finally absorbed by the Domestic Terrorism Branch.

The time they had spent scouring the earth for traces of Sanderson's organization hadn't been completely fruitless. His task force stumbled upon some unsavory funding links between foreign organized crime syndicates and a rising domestic ultra-nationalist terrorist organization, True America. Soon after establishing these links, he had been given command of a specialized task force dedicated to investigating foreign funding sources linked to homegrown domestic terrorist groups. Thanks to Director Shelby, Sanderson's crew had been designated a Tier One domestic terrorist organization, which re-landed Sanderson high on Sharpe's list of priority investigative targets.

He had the best of many worlds working for the DTB, a renewed sense of purpose, job security and the ear of Director Shelby, who had vowed to bring the wrath of God down upon Sanderson if Sharpe ever located his new stronghold. After reading the preliminary report forwarded by Special

Agent Mendoza, he felt goosebumps. Something about the ATF summary gave him the first real glimmer of hope he had experienced in nearly two years.

Sharpe heard a familiar knock at the door and stood up to walk around the desk. "Get in here, Frank," he boomed.

Special Agent Frank Mendoza entered, followed by Special Agent Dana O'Reilly and a short, angular-faced female wearing a navy blue suit jacket over a sharp-collared white blouse and matching dark blue trousers. She looked extremely serious, and her dark blue eyes pierced the room with a hint of disapproval. She wore an ATF badge clipped to her suit lapel.

"There he is. Special Agent Mendoza. Recently promoted to Ops Section One. You better not give up my favorite chair," he said, vigorously shaking Frank's hand.

"Well, it needs to find a new home. My so-called 'promotion' landed me in a cubicle. It's a whole different world down there. Small fish in a big pond. Ryan, this is Special Agent Marianne Warner. She leads the task force that nabbed Javier Navarre."

"Special Agent Warner, I can't thank you enough for taking the time to meet with me. Please have a seat," he said and nodded at Dana O'Reilly, who closed the door behind them.

Once they were situated in his cramped office, he opened the file sitting at the top of the smallest pile on his desk.

"Special Agent Warner, tell me a little more about Javier Navarre?"

"My task force had been watching him for quite some time. He specialized in what we consider to be exotic, special order weaponry. Not the usual crates of former Eastern Bloc discounted Kalashnikov rifles or RPG-7's. High end stuff. Modern assault rifles, large caliber sniper rifles, armor piercing ammunition. Scary shi…stuff, from our perspective."

"Please speak freely here, Marianne. Special Agent O'Reilly curses like a trucker, and Mendoza here, well…he taught me a few words I didn't learn in college," Sharpe said.

"I might reinstate that HR complaint," O'Reilly said.

"Don't listen to her. She's still pissed I dragged her along into Domestic."

"Shit, we all wanted to get away from you," Mendoza said, and they all laughed.

"Anyway. Please continue, and remember, these people are about as real as it gets in these organizations," Sharpe said, and Warner's face relaxed slightly.

"So, as much as we'd like to keep crates of assault rifles off U.S. soil, the special orders concern us the most. The crates go to groups that are easy to track, and the big orders or shipments are relatively easy to discover. We're all over those, so to say. It's the smaller, specialized orders that slip through the cracks and end up in very dangerous hands. High level drug cartel groups…not the street enforcers, but cartel execution teams or high value target protective details that operate on U.S. soil. They don't attract much public attention, but they're very real and pose a significant danger to law enforcement personnel that stumble on the wrong house, at the wrong time."

"Like last year in Dallas?"

"Exactly. Latest generation G-36C assault rifles equipped with enhanced optics and armor-piercing bullets. The Dallas PD SWAT team lost eleven men on final approach to the target building. All but one from headshots, most of which punctured their Kevlar helmets. These are the kinds of weapons we try desperately to keep off U.S. soil. Mr. Navarre was a key player in this realm, which is a small, exclusive group. With most arms dealers we track, quantity is usually the key to profit. Not with this group. It's highly competitive, cutthroat to be precise, and the clientele is brutal. Russian mob, South American drug cartels, and most recently, U.S. ultra-nationalists. Navarre had been around for nearly two decades, which is an eternity to survive dealing with these groups."

"You're speaking of him like he's dead," Sharpe said and leaned back in his chair.

Warner raised one eyebrow and looked across the office at Mendoza and O'Reilly.

"This hasn't been released for intra-agency consumption yet, for obvious reasons…but Mr. Navarre was shot in the face during a transfer from the Federal Courthouse to the Metropolitan Detention Center in Los Angeles. A Mexican gentleman with terminal pancreatic cancer and a very well forged California driver's license fired three "frangible" 10mm bullets from a pistol at a range of five feet and tried to turn the gun on a U.S. Marshal, who had already drawn his service pistol. We didn't get a chance to question the suspect."

"How many days had he been in custody?" Mendoza said.

"Five. We discreetly snatched him out of a Beverly Hills home after DEA received a tip from an actress turned recently busted coke distributor, who wanted desperately to stay out of jail. The homeowner, a surprisingly well known director and kingpin for the coke distribution, apparently loved guns so much that he'd been paying Navarre exorbitant amounts of money to personally deliver the latest weapons. Bad timing for Navarre. The DEA's snitch thought Navarre was the drug connection.

"We get called in when DEA finds the director's vault. This guy had a weapons stockpile that would put all of our agencies' combined SWAT arsenals to shame. Anyway, you can imagine Navarre wasn't very happy being snatched off the street like that. He didn't know who to blame, but kept a level head. I think he sensed that we had a spotty case at best against him because he lawyered up and shut up really quick. He did, however, have a few tender moments before his lawyer arrived."

"Which is why we're here," Mendoza added.

"Navarre knew better than to start talking about the cartels, not that it made any difference in the end. Still, drug cartel activity remains one of the highest priorities for the ATF and DEA, so we started there. Javier was a shrewd businessman…his long tenure a testament to that fact, so before his team of lawyers could shut him up, he got a little cocky. He told us that we were being played by our own agents, and that he could prove it.

"He wanted immunity for this information, which at that point wasn't even a suggestion we were willing to entertain. Not until he expanded his theory a bit. Of course, we kept the talk alive and spoke about the amazing immunity deals granted to big time catches. His eyes widened a little and he told us more. According to Navarre, he'd been supplying some top shelf equipment to Argentinian contacts in Bolivia. Enough to equip a SEAL team. His exact words. He had also arranged smaller weapons cache deliveries for what he believed to be the same group in several locations around the world: the Middle East, northern Europe and western Russia."

"Why did he think this was an inside play?" Sharpe said.

"He suggested these were rogue DEA assets. Undercover assets. Said they spoke flawless Spanish, every nuance and inflection, but he just knew they weren't Argentinian. He couldn't place it at first, but then he said it hit him. It was the way they carried themselves. He knew they were American. He got panicky and started to investigate the contacts. Navarre's assets traced one of the men back to Buenos Aires, where he vanished. He did the same with the rest and couldn't find a trace of them. He stopped dealing with them."

At the mention of Buenos Aires, Sharpe glanced at O'Reilly, and Agent Warner continued. "I figured he was grasping at thin air, trying to come up with some conspiracy theory nonsense to get us thinking about a deal. Either way, he was killed before any further discussions could progress. His lawyers kept him buttoned up good. Nothing really came of this information, until my team entered it into the intra-agency database, with the search tags 'rogue U.S. assets' and 'Argentina,' among many others. That's when I got a call from Special Agent O'Reilly."

O'Reilly broke into the conversation.

"Right. The tagged information came to me through a routine system alert, since we're subscribed to get any information tagged close to this title. I get over two hundred alerts per day, but 'Argentina' caught my eye. This information got tagged again with 'domestic terrorist group' less four hours later."

"My techs added this tag because one of the agents recalled being told by Mr. Navarre that these guys were collecting weapons right here in the U.S. When pressed further, Navarre verified that one of the meetings took place on U.S. soil," Agent Warner said.

"As soon as I saw this, I called Frank and Marianne to compile any information regarding Navarre's business contacts. I know Navarre supposedly dealt with Al Qaeda at some point, so I figured Terrorist Operations would have a file on him. Photos, aliases, travel records...anything. That's when I stumbled upon an incredible coincidence in the ATF files. I found a picture of Navarre with a suspected buyer in Amsterdam. ATF didn't have any follow up information on the buyer, but I recognized the photo immediately. Robert Klinkman...or in this case Reinhard Klinkman."

At this point in the conversation, Sharpe stood up and picked up a different file on his desk.

"Sorry to hit you with this, Agent Warner, but I wanted to do this in person and not over the phone. I need to permanently requisition all files associated with Javier Navarre, as directed by this executive Justice Department order."

"What? This is highly—"

"Unusual? Yes, it is, but I'm not prepared to completely yank this out from under your feet. I understand this may feel like a rude slap to the face after all of the work your team has put into tracking and assembling evidence in Navarre's case, but the link between Mr. Klinkman and Mr. Navarre now falls under Compartmentalized Information Security Category One classification."

"Jesus Christ," Warner muttered.

"Not even J.C. has access to this information," Mendoza quipped, failing to amuse Warner.

"I want you to work with Special Agent O'Reilly to sort through all of Navarre's files, and see if we can find any more links like these. I'm specifically interested in Navarre's travels to South America. This has all been cleared by the assistant director in charge of your investigative division, and I have CIS Category One paperwork here for you to sign…whether you accept the assignment or not."

"Do I really have a choice?" she said.

"Probably not, but we really need your help with this. You know Navarre's case inside and out, and with Navarre shot dead by the Sinaloa Cartel, your investigation is running on fumes. Trust me, I know the feeling. This is a great opportunity to work on a project that has the direct attention of my director and a few extremely high-placed officials in the Justice Department."

"How did you know the Sinaloa Cartel killed Navarre?"

"Sign those papers, and Dana will explain it to you. Navarre's murder was big news in certain circles. Is there anything else that will help make this temporary transition any less painful?"

"We should bring over my lead data analyst. He can work directly with Dana to speed up and optimize the process of merging and analyzing the files," she said.

"Dana, please make this happen and ensure that the CIS agreements are fully explained, signed and filed. Welcome aboard, Special Agent Warner," he said and extended his hand for a formal handshake.

Agent Warner accepted the file in one hand and shook Sharpe's hand briefly without saying a word. Once O'Reilly and Warner stepped out of the room and the door was shut, Mendoza sat back down.

"Good to see you again, Frank. Looks like we might be back in business."

"We? I'm working on Muslim extremists, not Black Flag. I have to admit, you might be on to something finally," Frank said.

"I have a gut feeling about Argentina. This is the second link in three months. We busted Victor Almadez flying back into the country using false papers."

"Part of the reconstituted list?"

Since the Black Flag file had been stolen in its entirety by Colonel Farrington, and the late Harris McKie had been parsimonious in the dissemination of its contents to the FBI during his short stint as gatekeeper in the Sanctum, Sharpe had less than half of the list of living Black Flag operatives. His reassigned and significantly reduced task force spent the first six months creating the missing list. They started with missing persons reports filed within a block of time extending two months before and after May 26, 2005. Specifically, they categorized male adults, aged thirty years or older, and started to compile a surprisingly large list of missing males. They eliminated any reports filed by direct family members, since the families of known east coast and Midwest operatives had either disappeared with the operative, or had gone to live with relatives in protest.

The only home they found occupied had contained Jessica Petrovich, and there had apparently been a good reason for that. The FBI's database had been hacked shortly after Edwards temporarily vanished from the grid. The cyber-attack appeared to be a simple probe, using Edward's computer and intranet password. Probably designed to confirm the information released by McKie to the FBI and view any key FBI assumptions that might hinder their vanishing act.

Once O'Reilly's team of data analysts compiled a list of missing males that fit the general demographic pattern, they further narrowed the field by discarding any profiles without prior military service. Known operatives to that point had been one hundred percent connected by military service, and this assumption whittled the list down to a manageable number. Examination of known operative military and personal backgrounds yielded no discernible pattern for further breakdown of their list. Black Flag operatives came from every branch of service, often from specialties not directly tied to combat, and examining personal history data offered a vastly diverse picture with no connections. At that point they started the real work, creating a database alert system linked to friends, relatives, work contacts...hundreds of variables that might trigger a possible contact event with one of the ninety-eight contacts on their list.

Their hard work produced tangible results on February 8th of this year, when the system alerted Special Agent O'Reilly to the fact that Victor Almadez's grandfather, living in Santa Fe, New Mexico, had passed away unexpectedly from a heart attack. Based on the alert, Sharpe issued the highest level priority terrorist alert for Victor Almadez, providing enough imaging data for both TSA and Customs to effectively utilize their new facial recognition software systems.

Three days later, customs agents at the Dallas/Fort Worth International Airport seized Manuel Delreyo after debarking an American Airlines flight that originated in Buenos Aires and made a stop in Santiago, Chile. Almadez/Delreyo proved to be as difficult to read as the escape artist Jeffrey Munoz, and Sharpe couldn't shake the feeling that they were being played again.

He had been so badly burned by Sanderson's Munoz play that he felt tinges of paranoia as soon as he received the phone call from Customs. Two months later, they still had Almadez in custody, held under some very tenuous Homeland Security Act provisions that wouldn't hold up if put under any public scrutiny. Unfortunately for Almadez, he was a nameless prisoner stuffed away in an obscure detention facility designed and administered by the Hallister Corporation. Sharpe wasn't worried about Almadez.

"The capture kept me from being fired and resulted in my transfer to Domestic. The last nod from Director Shelby I can expect. Unfortunately, Almadez hasn't said anything substantive, other than a promise to 'take this personally' if he doesn't see a lawyer by the end of June."

"He's willing to wait four months?"

"He said, 'I'm a patient man, and I understand your predicament...I'm willing to wait four months,' and that was it," Sharpe said.

"You're going to let him go, right?"

"Not with the Navarre link. I'm going to start poking around down south. Argentina and Bolivia."

"You gonna bring the CIA in on this?"

"No. I don't trust the CIA after the Black Flag debacle. Too many aspects of that day didn't add up in the end. Jeremy Cummings is paid nearly two hundred thousand dollars to assemble an off the books team to kill Petrovich. All we get from the CIA is the suggestion that this might be a revenge play by Serbian nationalists. A little too convenient that they stumbled upon the same connection regarding Petrovich and Resja so quickly. The CIA liaison, Randy Keller, vanishes from the face of the planet after walking into a Georgetown residence that literally explodes minutes later. And the payment to Cummings came from an extremely sanitized money trail leading nowhere, deposited into his account after he was killed. The director himself told me to keep the CIA out of it. I'm going directly to our counterparts in Argentina and Bolivia. We have a good working relationship with Argentine Federal Police."

"Argentina's a big country…let me know how I can help. We're still shaking down the Navarre/Al Qaeda connection, but it doesn't appear to have any meat. Even a scumbag like Navarre kept his distance from that group."

"Thanks, Frank. Always a pleasure. We should grab a drink soon. My treat," Sharpe said.

"Damn straight. Good luck with this. It would be nice to nail Sanderson to the wall. He set the domestic Al Qaeda investigation back two years with his stunt," Mendoza said.

"I'm keeping my fingers crossed on this one. Catch you later, Frank."

"You too," he said and closed the door as he left.

Sharpe had enough confirmation to contact the FBI legal attaché at the U.S. Embassy in Buenos Aires, but he'd have to be careful. The embassy crawled with spooks, and the wrong conversation, at the wrong time, could bring the CIA into the fold. He desperately wanted to avoid this and needed to do a little more research into Dan Bailey and Susan Castaneda, resident legal attachés in Argentina.

Chapter Seven

2:24 PM
Monchegorsk Water Treatment Plant (A District)
Monchegorsk, Murmansk Oblast, Russia

Anatoly Reznikov was both surprised and relieved to find the water treatment plant nearly deserted. Construction on the modern, mostly automated facility had been completed two years ago, ushering in a new era of clean drinking water for the residents of Monchegorsk. Three decades too late in his view. The previous plant, which had stood guard over the city water supply for as long as anyone could remember, relied upon a disinfection process to purify the water, but did little to prevent the flow of heavy metals into the citizens' blood streams, including his own.

The Norval Nickel plant had been the main source of industry in Monchegorsk since the early 1930s, resulting in an ever-growing population boom that served the needs of Norval Nickel, further expanding the company's lucrative nickel and copper mining enterprise. For all that the residents of Monchegorsk did for Norval Nickel, the multinational corporation gave little in return, aside from poor wages and a harsh work environment that would have made Joseph Stalin cringe. More than seventy percent of Monchegorsk's population worked in some capacity for Norval, with the vast majority performing hazardous mining jobs or unregulated, unskilled jobs in the processing plants. Reznikov's uncle worked the mines, and when Anatoly joined the family in late 1978, not much had changed in terms of work conditions from the early days of Norval Nickel.

The corporation had invested little money in the city's infrastructure, despite the efforts of environmental activists and the few citizens that dared to defy Norval's stranglehold on both the city and the local communist party. The effects of the smelting plant's pollution on the population's health was no secret, but asking the wrong questions in the wrong place came with serious risks.

The best case scenario involved employment termination and immediate eviction from company subsidized housing, which could put a family on the streets in the middle of the night in harsh winter conditions. The worst case scenario varied by level of activism. A one-way train ride to Siberia was reserved for persistent, unorganized agitators. Sometimes these were family trips, which added to the deterrence factor. Organizers or nosy environmentalists either disappeared suddenly or slowly bobbed to the surface in the polluted Moncha Lake, which fed into the ineffective water treatment plant. Despite the growing voice of concern about the effects of heavy metal poisoning, the Norval Corporation continued to deny the mounting body of evidence, and instead produced more dead bodies. Norval was finally called to task by the Russian government in 2001, on behalf of Norway, Sweden and Finland, who had been the unwilling recipients of several million tons of sulfur dioxide (acid rain) over the past several decades. Permission was "granted" for NEFCO (Nordic Environmental Finance Corporation) to provide regional loans that would be used to improve several offending industrial plants near the Kola Peninsula and provide funding for localized environmental improvement projects.

The Monchegorsk water treatment plant made the top of the list, which was probably influenced by the fact that senior Norval officials held influential positions on the Murmansk Oblast's Natural Resources Agency executive board. The Natural Resources Agency had replaced the State Committee for Environment Protection in 2000, when President Vladimir Putin abolished the organization, which resembled the U.S. Environmental Protection Agency.

The Natural Resources Agency was the organization responsible for managing the commercialization of Russia's natural resources, and the move was seen as a direct measure to ensure that most environmental decisions favored the major corporations. Due to the overwhelming international pressure of the Kola Peninsula's pollution problem, Putin's government decided on a work-around. They leaned on Norval Nickel to accept NEFCO's low interest loans to clean up Monchegorsk.

By that time, the Monchegorsk plant had launched nearly one million tons of heavy metals into the air each year, including nickel, copper, cobalt, lead, selenium, platinum and palladium. The ground concentrations of platinum and palladium in the soil near the plant were so severe that mining of surface soil for these metals had become economically feasible in the past five years. Add decades of concentrated acid rain to the mix, and the health effects on the Monchegorsk population were devastating.

Anatoly grew up in a poverty level neighborhood wracked with stunted growth, pediatric and early adult cancers, severe mental disabilities among adults and children, neurological disorders resembling early onset of Alzheimer's, and frequent unexplained seizures. The local hospital was owned and administered by Norval Nickel, which only served to compartmentalize and minimize the problem.

Reznikov had been lucky to join his aunt and uncle well past his early developmental years. He had been spared eight years of toxic exposure, and the results were dramatic. In the ten years he spent with his new family, he watched everyone in the filthy, cramped apartment suffer from Norval Nickel's irresponsibility. His aunt died of pancreatic cancer five years after he arrived, and he experienced the daily sadness and brutality of his uncle slowly losing all semblance of mental function. Less than one year after his aunt's death, his uncle had been banished to a local mental hospital.

His three cousins, two boys and one girl, all younger than him by a few years, never grew at the same rate as Anatoly and barely progressed in school past a fifth grade level. They had all been remanded to state care when his uncle had been institutionalized. When Anatoly graduated from secondary school and left for Moscow University, his cousins resembled drones: void of personality, intelligence and drive. Ten years earlier, they had been drastically different, similar to him in so many ways. He had painfully watched them suffer under Norval Nickel's reign of terror in Monchegorsk, transformed into empty shells, unfit for employment outside of Norval Nickel's mines.

That was the cruel irony of life in Monchegorsk. They had been placed into the custody of mother Russia to live in a state sponsored orphanage, but the orphanage was funded by Norval Nickel, and the children were funneled back into the very jobs that put them there in the first place. Anatoly's case had been different. He showed strong academic promise in science and math, so he was awarded a place at Moscow University to study biological engineering and chemistry, compliments of Norval Nickel, with the understanding that he would return to the corporation to work as an engineer. Reznikov never fulfilled his obligation, though he was seconds away from observing a promise he had silently made to his cousins and his own parents.

By honoring his father's legacy, Anatoly Reznikov had discovered the perfect way to exact revenge upon a corporation that had slowly destroyed his adopted family and a government that had brutally murdered his parents. He would also make a fortune. If everything went according to plan, his payment from Al Qaeda would look insignificant compared to the series of increasingly larger payments he could demand for his services or his product.

He walked briskly across the long, grated catwalk toward a sizable brick building on the other side of a vast sea of light green, flattened metal domes. The domes capped immense underground tanks, which housed the disinfectant side of the Monchegorsk plant's treatment process. The other side, located uphill, utilized a rapid sand filtration system, combined with a state of the art membrane filter. The combination of the two ensured the removal of any suspended particulate matter, including heavy metals, before the water was finally transferred to the field of tanks he now crossed, for the final step of the treatment process.

From these tanks, the clean water was pumped to the city's reservoirs through a massive pump station, which could be accessed from the building he rapidly approached. He glanced around furtively as the building loomed closer, painfully aware that there was no way to soften the loud clanging of his boots on the metal grating. Maybe the sound didn't matter. He had breached the treatment plant's fence line where it ambled too close to the edge of one of the city's forest preserves. Wearing a suit and a long winter jacket that showcased fake city credentials, he had approached the complex's buildings from an angle that would conceal his approach until he could find a way to access the pump station building.

He had watched the station for a full day, noting the number of personnel and their patterns. For the most part, there hadn't been any. The automated facility was monitored by a control station toward the front of the complex, which he would avoid altogether, though he didn't think he could completely dodge all of the cameras. He just needed to get into the pump station, where he could effectively and quietly deal with anyone that came to investigate his presence. He assumed that an alarm would sound when he broke into the pump station and had prepared accordingly.

He walked up to the door at the end of the catwalk and stared at the covered button pad to the right of the door. Not a problem. He had anticipated the possibility that every door at the new facility would utilize new technology and had researched methods to breach similar systems. Several black market electronic devices had been available, but each device was specific to certain systems, and he didn't have room in his backpack to bring along one of each device. Even if he had, there was no guarantee that any of them would work on this door. A better solution had been offered by his black market contact. A compact circular saw, specially designed to cut through door locks. The saw featured a five inch metal cutting saw blade, which would give the blade enough depth to cut through dead bolts or locking mechanisms when placed flush against the crack between the door and frame.

He slipped the nylon backpack off his shoulders and kneeled in front of the door to open it. A few seconds later, he wrestled the gray saw out of the backpack and attached the power cord to a customized battery that had been guaranteed to provide fifteen minutes of continuous operation. He examined the door again and decided to start with the most logical point near the door handle. He inserted the thin blade into the door crack a few inches above the handle, and felt no resistance as he placed the saw flush against the door and frame. He depressed the black trigger and the saw roared to life, emitting a high pitched squeal that made him nervous. *No way to turn back now*, he thought and moved the saw slowly down the crack.

The blade met with brief resistance at handle level, but continued to move effortlessly with Anatoly's hand. He felt no resistance a few inches past the handle and stopped the blade. Could it have been that easy? He pulled the saw blade out of the crack and placed it on the grate before standing up. He grasped the handle and pulled, surprised when the door gave no resistance and swung open. He examined the door for a few seconds and determined that the blade had done no obvious damage to the door, besides cutting the locking bolt. When closed, he doubted anyone would be able to tell it had been cut. Anyone approaching the door would punch in their code and open the door, unaware that it would have opened regardless of the numbers punched into the keypad. Not wanting to waste another moment, he dragged everything through the doorway and closed the door, noting the time on his watch.

The first thing he noticed was the industrial grade humming sound of the pump. He had expected the noise inside to be louder. The pump station descended one additional story below the entrance level and housed two massive centrifugal pumps, one of which pumped water to the city's storage sites at any given moment. The other served as a backup, in case of a maintenance issue. The active pump was rotated weekly, to increase the longevity of the incredibly expensive system. He would need to identify the active pump and then locate the water sample collection/testing node, located somewhere forward of the pump.

The only consistent activity he had noted at the plant yesterday had been an hourly visit to the pump station. A technician dressed in gray overalls, carrying a black plastic case by its handle, had ambled down from the control station and entered the station through the door on the other side, reemerging a few minutes later. He used the same door, which was closest to the control station, each time. He presumed the man had taken a required hourly sample of the water for analysis. The sample collection node would take water directly from the system and would represent his best opportunity to introduce his product into Monchegorsk's water supply.

He descended the metal grate staircase, able to see both pumps through the porous metal flooring. They were aligned in parallel, separated by a raised grated catwalk, but joined by various metal pipes and mechanical structures. The staircase emptied onto the end of the catwalk nearest to the intake from the disinfectant tank field. The station's humming grew louder as he approached the catwalk, but remained within tolerable limits. He saw a pair of blue noise protection headphones on a hook at the bottom of the stairs and noted how times had certainly changed in Monchegorsk. It didn't take him long to figure out which pump was active. He only had to lay his hands on one side, and then the other, to determine that the right side pump was active.

The catwalk was installed halfway up the side of the pump, which put him in a position to examine the top of the pump and all of the attachments leading into it. The pump itself was taller than Reznikov and extended the length of two SUV's. The catwalk design made it easy for him to examine all of the components, and within seconds he had located the sample collection node. Located to the rear of the pump, near the stairs, he had momentarily overlooked it. Like everything in the plant, it was labeled, making this easy beyond his wildest dreams. The node had four latches, which ensured a tight seal. Reznikov had some trouble opening the latches and looked around for a tool that might be designed for the purpose. He didn't see anything useful and cursed as it took him nearly a minute to get two of the latches open.

The latches were designed to seal tightly, but this wasn't the problem and Reznikov knew it. As he struggled with the third latch, he started to tremble in anger. He hadn't escaped completely unscathed from Norval Nickel's legacy. He had suffered neuromuscular damage that mainly affected his hands and feet, resembling peripheral neuropathy at its worst and slight tingling at best. It had plagued him as a biochemist and rendered certain routine tasks unpredictable. He had developed an angry patience for his condition, but this was not the time for him to have a problem with his hands. The third latch opened, and he stopped. His hands felt like they had been squeezing a metal bar for hours, cramped and shaky. Ignoring the pain, he wrenched at the fourth latch, opening it in a fit of rage. Now sweating in the forty degree room, Reznikov better resembled a depraved madman with the intention of poisoning an entire city's water supply.

He placed the backpack next to him and removed a thermos-sized metallic container, setting it down on the grating. He paused and looked at the pump again, his composure returning. The pump was bigger than he'd expected, which meant that his original calculations for water supply contamination might be inaccurate. He examined the pump from front to back, taking it all in. This was definitely a higher capacity pump. He didn't want to use all of the product in his possession, but this was not the time to make a mistake. He decided to pour both containers into the water system.

He had hidden enough core samples of the virus to create other batches and knew exactly where he could find a few more containers. The Arab traitors had spoken of several specific locations and timelines, so he could always "meet" them for a surprise visit. He'd finish up here and hide out in St. Petersburg until he was sure that the virus had done its job. Once he was satisfied that Monchegorsk was ruined, he'd head to Sweden. His eavesdropping had provided him with an address in Stockholm. After that, a quick trip to Copenhagen could bring him to another address, if he felt ambitious.

Once he possessed more virus, he might provide an anonymous tip to Interpol regarding the other addresses and planned attack locations, or maybe not. He truly couldn't decide, and it never occurred to him that this ambiguity indicated a dangerous deterioration of his mental state. Though he wasn't aware of it, Anatoly had suffered more than neuromuscular damage during the ten years spent in Monchegorsk. The long term mental impact of accumulating lead, cadmium, nickel and copper in his brain had been significant, gradually leaving him obsessed and unable to sustain empathy. He only vaguely processed the cruelty of his actions and how it would affect thousands of innocent people. These blurry thoughts were swept aside by his obsession with both delivering a damaging blow to Norval Nickel and teaching the Russian government a lesson. He had convinced himself that this was the right thing to do, so with no hesitation, he released the pressure fitting on the cylinder sitting on the catwalk.

There was a brief hiss, and he was able to twist the top free, exposing thousands of transparent tablets. He poured the contents of the cylinder into the six-inch diameter opening and repeated the process with the second cylinder. Thousands of tablets sat in the one foot deep miniature dry well, waiting to be introduced into the water system. Anatoly shut the sample node's lid and refastened the four latches, which turned out to be infinitely easier than opening them. Once closed, he activated the dry well and heard the mechanism working. A red light turned to green and the mechanism stopped. He activated the mechanism one more time just to be sure and waited twenty seconds for the cycle to complete. Once the light turned green again, he endured the pain of opening the latches to inspect the chamber. The chamber was dry, and the tablets were gone, on their way to infect the city's water supply. He quickly resealed it.

Each tablet contained concentrated, weaponized encephalitis virus, surrounded by a thin gel coating. The virus within the clear gel coat had been given a dark red color in the lab, so each tablet looked like a menacing eye, which underscored the virus's potential. The gel coating was designed to last roughly thirty minutes before releasing the virus into the water. He knew that water leaving the plant would end up in a massive storage tank that constantly filled and emptied into the city. The concentration of virus would be more than adequate to infect the entire supply and continue to infect it for several hours. The charcoal filters installed between the disinfectant tanks and the pump station would ensure that any remaining chlorination would not be enough to kill the hardened virus Reznikov had developed. Only a strong anti-viral water treatment course could accomplish this, and these were nearly nonexistent in public water treatment plants.

The virus tablets would reach the main storage tanks partially dissolved and remain at the top of the tank for a few minutes, until they released their payload, which would sink and spread throughout the tank. Later that day, pipes in every household and business within Monchegorsk would contain contaminated water. Within three to five days, the city's hospital and medical clinics would be overwhelmed by patients complaining of severe headaches and rapidly progressing flu-like symptoms. A few days after that, the city of Monchegorsk would descend into chaos, taking Norval Nickel along with it.

The Russian government would face one of its biggest challenges in recent history. How does mother Russia contain the news that a city of 54,327 people had imploded, with no plausible explanation? He couldn't wait to see how they'd try to contain the news. Based on Russia's notoriously poor human rights track record, he felt confident that it would be a disaster for the Putin government.

The virus combined several of the nastiest viral encephalitis traits he could genetically manipulate. He had started with a particularly virulent and highly infectious strain of Venezuelan Equine Encephalitis (VEE) and had gone to work modifying its structure. He enhanced the virus's focus on the limbic system, specifically targeting the temporal lobes, which caused victims to exhibit rabies-like behavior. The recurrent hallmark behaviors he had observed through human experimentation included: severe aggression, marked destructiveness, primitive impulses, and transient disorientation or catatonia, often followed by hyperactive episodes. Brain damage had been severe in most of the cases they examined, and nearly seventy percent died within a week of showing symptoms.

The remaining thirty percent deteriorated at different rates, with varying degrees of brain damage. Like every disease, some got lucky, though they were usually the first to fall victim to the madness that descended on the others. Once the virus had been tweaked to his own desired specifications, they had conducted a practical test. Twenty "volunteers" each drank a glass of water spiked with the same concentration of virus that he calculated would be present in every sip of water throughout the city. Roughly eighty percent contracted the virus, though he took steps to ensure all of his test subjects were infected. The eighty percent statistic had made him smile. He relished the complications this would present to the Russians.

Now that the virus was in the water, his next task was to get out of here undetected. He jammed the cylinders back into the backpack, along with the mechanical saw, and withdrew a silenced semi-automatic pistol from one of the other pouches. He debated whether to head up the stairs, or hide in the station and wait. He couldn't imagine that the station didn't have an alarm rigged to the doors. Yesterday, he had timed the technician's journey from the central station to the pump station and averaged it to six minutes, if he didn't stop for a cigarette. His watch showed six minutes and thirty seconds, which he blamed on his damn fumbling hands. Glancing around the station, he chose to stay and hide.

The pump itself was massive, providing numerous hiding places, and he saw another staircase at the end of the catwalk. He might be able to squeeze underneath the end of the pump or the wide outflow pipes on either side. If the technician decided to walk down to the catwalk and poke around, he would be forced to use the pistol. It would be his last resort and buy him enough time to get out of town, but depending on the city's response, it could jeopardize the entire plan. He would walk the technician out of the building at gunpoint and push him over the catwalk onto the domed tanks. He hoped it didn't come to that because his hands were trembling from the latches, and he could barely hold the gun straight. He might need every round in the pistol's magazine.

Just as he tucked himself under one of the huge outflow pipes on the right side of the station, he heard the door above him open. The technician entered through the front door and shut it behind him, pausing on the grating above. The man walked around for a minute, presumably checking some of the diagnostic gauges above, and started to descend the stairs. Anatoly's pistol hand was shaking, and he was afraid that he might fire the pistol accidentally. He depressed the safety lever to prevent an unintended discharge. He further squeezed himself under the pipe and along the outside of the pump. He would be undetectable if the man stayed on the catwalk.

He had a hard time hearing the man's footsteps over the vibration and hum of the pump, but knew he was drawing closer along the catwalk. The sound of the metal grating increased and suddenly stopped, indicating that the man was at the top of the second set of stairs. He could picture the man leaning over and determining if it was worth his effort to take a further look. He jammed himself further back, willing himself to be invisible to the man. A few moments later, he heard footsteps heading back down the catwalk, followed by the stairs. Less than a minute later, Anatoly was alone in the pump station.

He decided not to press his luck. He replaced the pistol, keeping the pouch unzipped, and left the station through the back door. He knew it would trigger another alarm, but figured the duty crew would consider it to be a glitch. They'd watch the sensor from their comfortable seats all day, and when it didn't happen again, it would be forgotten. He wondered if anyone would have the presence of mind one week later to make the connection. Based on the human testing results in Kazakhstan, he sort of doubted it.

Chapter Eight

2:10 PM
Legal Attaché Section, U.S. Embassy
Buenos Aires, Argentina

Special Agent Susan Castaneda took another look at the manila folder on her desk and picked up the phone to dial Ryan Sharpe. He had contacted her a few days earlier with an odd request, which had been easy enough for her to research without attracting any attention. Sharpe wanted to know if the Argentine Federal Police (AFP) had started any investigations within the past three years into any fledgling terrorist or paramilitary organizations, with a focus on regional arms smuggling or cross-border operations. He was also interested in any unusual paramilitary style operations or violence over the past few years. Sharpe had been detailed enough with the focus, but nebulous beyond that.

He stressed the importance of keeping this quiet, and she understood why. Word had a way of getting around in the embassy, which made it difficult to get any real work done, even in a stable country like Argentina. So she had scheduled a leisurely lunch with one of her AFP counterparts, in a location of the city not known for embassy traffic. She trusted this law enforcement agent as much as she could trust anyone in the Argentine government and had given him enough information to dig around for something that might fit the profile Sharpe had provided. He had more or less come up empty handed, though he did provide a few bits of information that might be helpful. She wasn't sure how, but it had been worth a lunch away from the office and her counterpart, Dan Bailey.

Bailey was starting to wear on her nerves and had only been "in-country" for three months. He had chosen an "unaccompanied" tour, leaving his wife and two children behind for the year-long assignment, which was not uncommon for "Legat" (legal attaché) duty. Unfortunately, the reasons for Agent Bailey's choice appeared to go beyond the disruption and inconvenience of moving a family long distance for a short period of time. It apparently had more to do with the likelihood that Dan Bailey's wife might not approve of his weekly visits to local brothels, or that she might take issue with her husband lunching and dining with a different woman nearly every day.

As the senior "Legat," Susan had been approached by one of the more discreet embassy staff personnel, who also happened to work for the CIA, and provided the unsavory details of Agent Bailey's first month in Buenos Aires. His behavior immediately classified him as a security risk, and she was informed that the surveillance would continue. She could barely contain her laughter as the details were exposed, almost wishing that she didn't know about any of it.

None of it was illegal behavior in Argentina, though it strayed pretty far from what was expected from a representative of the FBI. Still, she didn't have any official recourse, beyond some uncomfortable lifestyle counseling and possibly some negative input on his performance evaluation. She was scheduled to leave within the next three months and wouldn't be around for his transfer performance evaluation. For all she knew, her replacement could have chosen the assignment for the same reasons as Agent Bailey. She didn't really care, as long as she managed to get out of here with her career intact.

She eventually managed to make some use of the information provided by the CIA employee. Agent Bailey had logically started with her first when he arrived. She was single, attractive, in her early thirties, and they worked in the same section, though thankfully they had separate offices. The advances had intensified to the point of discomfort and harassment, until she played one of the many Langley trump cards so conveniently delivered to her. One day, she called him into her office and slid a photo across the desk. His face turned ashen when he took a close look at the photo.

"Tranny prostitute #4" had been written across the top of the photo, in black permanent marker, identifying the "woman" at Bailey's door as the fourth transsexual prostitute photographed entering his apartment. Susan was aware that the series ended at #9, but thought #4 was good middle ground. Stunned, he stammered for a few seconds before she laid it on him. She remembered her words clearly.

"I don't want you talking to me again, unless it's official business. The same rule applies to all of the women at the embassy, or any women entering the embassy. Trannies too," she had added, before dismissing him.

Dan Bailey hadn't been a problem for anyone since then, and she smiled at the bizarre train of thoughts that had led her to remember Bailey's predicament. She dialed the number for Sharpe's office, and he answered it after the second ring.

"Special Agent Sharpe," he answered, always sounding crisp to her.

"Agent Sharpe, it's Agent Castaneda from the legal attaché office in Argentina," she said.

"Of course. Please call me Ryan. Thank you so much for taking the time to look into this for me. I'm working on a long shot, but this one is worth the time. I really appreciate it," he said.

"No, it's my pleasure, and it's Susan. Unfortunately, I don't think I found what you're looking for. There's not much in the way of new terrorism or paramilitary organizations. They have some neo-Nazi types that are pretty organized, drug cartels, Russian mob, all the usual suspects, but nothing that really fits what you described. I had one of my counterparts at AFP do some digging, and he came up with a few unusual events, but nothing they are actively investigating."

"I'm looking for anything here, so you have my attention," he said.

"Well, he found a few incidents spread over the course of the past eight months involving Chechen mafia and neo-Nazi gangs in Buenos Aires. Three separate incidents. The biggest incident took place at one of the Chechens' dockyard strongholds, leaving eighteen bodies behind. The police and AFP have no idea what time of day they were hit, but the one thing they all agreed upon was that it was pulled off by professionals using suppressed weapons. Most of the gunshot wounds were precision headshots, and AFP's SWAT officials said that there had been multiple, simultaneous breach points around the building. Ballistics confirmed that the four Chechens stationed outside had been taken down by snipers. AFP thought this was an American or European black op."

"This sounds like more than an incident. No investigation?"

"Not really. Two more hits, smaller in scope, occurred in the following months. A Chechen safe house was hit inside the city, at about two in the morning, and there were witnesses from adjacent buildings and houses. The assailants were in and out within the span of minutes. Witnesses swore it was a government operation. Roughly a dozen attackers in three separate cars hit the building at once.

"Someone managed to fire off an automatic weapon inside, but there were no signs that any of the assailants had been hit. Eight Chechens were found dead and one prostitute broke both of her legs trying to jump from one of the balconies. Witnesses said there were more women in the apartment, but they fled. Nobody has come forward to admit they were in the building, which is no surprise. FPA came to the same conclusion on this one and they're pretty sure one of the Chechens was hit from the outside by a sniper bullet."

"They don't know for sure?" he said.

"I'm not sure they really care. Twenty-six dead Chechen mobsters within the span of a month and only a pair of broken legs as collateral damage. One of the Chechens was identified as senior leadership. My contact didn't seem to indicate that this was a high priority," she said.

"What about the last one?" he said, pretty sure he had stumbled onto something pointing him in the right direction for further investigation.

"Last one happened a few months ago and involved the neo-Nazi group. They've been expanding their influence over the past five years, and it looks like they expanded it a little too far. This one was different. It took place around 1 AM at an underground neo-Nazi slam fest, or whatever the skinheads call them. Heavy metal, lots of 'Heil Hitlers,' hard drinking…usually spills out into the street later and ends up killing or maiming someone without a Swastika tattoo. On this particular night, the reverse occurred. Someone tore through the bouncers with a knife, then lobbed a combination of fragmentation and incendiary grenades into the basement party. Nobody made it out. Estimated thirty-five dead, including the leader of the cell represented at the party. He was shot in the face running down the stairs with his girlfriend from an apartment unit located on the second floor of the house."

"What about the girlfriend?" he said.

"She's the only one that survived the entire attack. Said there were four of them, heavily armed like Komandotruppe."

"I assume that means commandos?"

"Yes, my FPA counterpart has a sense of humor. The woman dragged one of the bouncers out of the blaze, and the forensics team determined that he had been stabbed through the neck, just above the collarbone. Knife plunged through the spinal cord on the same strike," she said.

"Can you get me that forensics report?" he said, feeling his pulse quicken.

"It shouldn't be a problem. Sounds like this might have been helpful?"

"Yes, I think it has. Were there any theories about who was doing this? Other than a foreign black ops team? I'm just having a hard time believing that this isn't being actively investigated," he said.

"Luckily, my counterpart has a little bit of a crush on me and likes to drink Sangria during our lunches. He was hesitant with this information, so I need your discretion," she said.

"Absolutely, Susan. I'll use this to corroborate, but nothing beyond that."

"All right. He said the only serious theory circulating through the ranks was that a man named Ernesto Galenden had hired an outside team to send these groups a message. This might also explain why the investigations have stalled," she said.

"I can't wait to hear this," he said.

"Ernesto Galenden is one of the wealthiest and most influential citizens of Argentina, owning a huge stake in one of the primary oil companies within the country, and of course, dozens of lucrative business ventures. He also owns more real estate than you can imagine. For the most part, Galenden has retained a good reputation in Argentina across the board and has never been implicated in any illegal schemes.

"He owns a vast portion of the shipping waterfront along Argentina's coast, which put him at odds with the Chechens. He hasn't made it easy for them to expand their efforts to ship Andean cocaine to Europe and ports north. Once the strife turned deadly on the docks, Galenden turned to his government cronies to put some pressure on law enforcement, but this tactic didn't prove very effective. FPA thinks Galenden took matters into his own hands."

"It's not a bad theory. You said Galenden owns land all over Argentina?"

"He owns localized assets and buildings in most cities, but the vast majority of his land lies in western Argentina, along the Chilean border. This is where his father discovered oil," she said.

"Interesting. Susan, I trust you to keep this quiet there. I'm working on something very sensitive, and if the wrong person at the embassy found out, I could have a complication that would jeopardize my investigation. I can't thank you enough for the help. I'll be in touch shortly with some more questions, as soon as I figure out which direction to pursue. In the meantime, can you get me the forensics report of the knife attack at the neo-Nazi club?"

"Sure. I'll give my guy at AFP a call. I'm sure he won't mind another lunch," she said.

"Not very sporting of you to lead him on like that, but I'm not going argue against your methods. This was great work, Susan. Talk to you shortly."

She hung up the phone and smiled. She wasn't sure how to classify what she was doing with Federico. Technically, she wasn't leading him on because he had no chance in the first place. Despite his handsome, Italian inspired face, muscular build and pleasant manners, she had never been interested in him romantically. In fact, she'd never been interested in men and was on an "unaccompanied" tour to Argentina. Her partner of eight years, Stephanie, eagerly awaited her return to the States.

Chapter Nine

8:30 AM
FBI Headquarters Building
Washington, D.C.

Special Agent Ryan Sharpe made room for Special Agent Eric Hesterman, which was no small sacrifice given the agent's size. Hesterman, a broad, muscular African-American in his early thirties, stood over six feet tall and took up twice the amount of shoulder room of most agents. He literally dwarfed Dana O'Reilly, who stood on the other side of him, invisible to Sharpe through his large, expensively-tailored suit. At 225 pounds, Hesterman had trimmed down considerably since his linebacker days at the University of Michigan; scaling back in size during law school, and finally settling in at his "target" weight upon graduating from Quantico as a Special Agent. Eric was one of six agents permanently assigned to Ryan's task force within the Domestic Terrorism Branch, and despite the fact that he had no background in finance, he had quickly impressed everyone from Sharpe's veteran finance tracking team. Sharpe could tell by the grins on both Hesterman's and O'Reilly's faces that he had found something.

Hesterman manipulated the screen with a mouse on the computer station in front of them and zoomed the satellite imagery into an area of western Argentina, less than twenty miles from the Chilean border. Suddenly, a yellow line appeared to outline areas throughout the province. Sharpe glanced around at the Joint Operations Center, looking for any faces that were overly interested in his semi-private meeting. Luckily, Hesterman blocked most of the screen from view.

"The yellow line roughly demonstrates Mr. Galenden's land holdings, the best I could calculate using public-sourced documents. Most of it is held within the Nuequen Province, where his father struck oil in the sixties. He holds some vast tracts of land in Mendoza, La Pampa and Rio Negro, but I focused on some of the parameters we discussed and narrowed the possibilities to a few locations. Most of the land is held in national reserve status, though not to be confused with the concept of a nature preserve. A national reserve opens land to the country, but the landowner retains mineral rights and can restrict access to fifteen percent of the reserve. Restricted areas need to be filed with national and provincial government at the beginning of the year, so I started there, looking four years back.

"If we figure that Sanderson started his plans at least a year prior to the events of May 2005, it made sense that he would have already broken ground on his new organization's headquarters, and that the location might not have been on restricted land. Most of the restricted areas retained by Mr. Galenden were located in flatter, arid zones, better suited for oil and mineral exploration. I found three separate filings that immediately attracted my attention and led to the image you're viewing on the screen.

"First, in January of 2003, Mr. Galenden filed for the immediate restriction of a relatively small area here, which encompassed a local airport. Not a big one. Two runways, one capable of landing small jets. The airport was manned by volunteers on weekends and sported a small café, limited fuel and basic air traffic control capabilities. It was used as a weekend leisure stop for pilots interested in some great trout or fly fishing in the nearby foothills. I spoke with one of the volunteers listed on an old website, and he confirmed that it wasn't a busy location. Maybe ten to fifteen planes on a busy weekend. Said the buildings were mostly run down and that pilots couldn't land or take off at night. No lights. He heard rumors that some major improvements would be made to the facility, but hasn't been able to visit. Based on satellite imagery graciously provided by the powers that be, we can now see that this airport has been completely refurbished. The most interesting aspect is this dome right here.

"I had to dig around on this one, but found similar images and determined that this is a remote air traffic control module...RATCOM. The airport now sports a small radar, VFR transmitters, new radio transmitting equipment, new hangars, and of course, lights. This facility can now be used day and night, in any visibility condition, and can remain completely unmanned due to this extremely expensive device. It allows for a real time connection between all of the airport's equipment and a contracted air traffic control site. This site could be located anywhere in the world. There are several companies that specialize in this service, and none of them are located at an airport. It's really quite innovative, if you have the money and don't really want anyone seeing what comes in and out of your airport."

"Could it be a drug operation?" Sharpe asked.

"The thought crossed my mind, but the facility is in the open and the RATCOM system would leave tracks. I asked DEA, and they've seen these used by the big boys for their own personal airports, but never at a distribution point."

"Yeah, it wouldn't make much sense. Can we get the records of traffic into the airport since it became operational?" Sharpe said.

"Eric and I talked about that and decided that it might present a few problems. First, we have no idea which firm handles the site, but this is potentially the least of our issues. Without a subpoena, the firm would have to willingly talk to us, which, given the nature and expense of the service, seems unlikely. I'm afraid that even asking questions might tip off Sanderson," O'Reilly said.

"I think you're both right. What else did you find?"

"A second site was gobbled up by Mr. Galenden at the same time, a hundred square miles surrounding an abandoned town…here," he said, and the screen changed.

"Located about sixty miles south east of the airport, in a mostly flat area. There's not much information available on the site, but I found references to towns rising during the speculative years following the discovery of oil in Nuequen and falling shortly after that. Unless Mr. Galenden suddenly discovered something his father hadn't forty years ago, I'd say this was an odd choice for a land status conversion," Hesterman said.

"It would be a poor choice for a headquarters or training compound. Too exposed," Sharpe said.

"Exactly," O'Reilly added. "There is evidence of significant improvement to the town, but mostly superficial. Cleaned up, a few new structures, but beyond that, not much has been done. One of the ex-military guys said it looked like a combat town."

"Interesting. Close Quarters Battle training site?" Sharpe said.

"Could be anything, but it's fenced up on all sides. Someone wants to keep people from wandering too close. As for a headquarters? Take a look at this," Hesterman said.

The flat-screen monitor changed to a satellite image of trees and a river valley that ran northwest to southeast out of the Andes foothills. Structures were evident along the thick pine tree line, tucked together on the western side of the valley. Several larger buildings appeared in the open, clustered at the northern end of an improved dirt road that ran adjacent to the river. Based on its location in the foothills, and the immediate presence of a decent, shallow river, this would be a fly fisherman's paradise. The area was world renown for trout and fly fishing expeditions.

"Something tells me this isn't a fly fishing lodge," Sharpe said.

"Well, if it is, it's brand new and operates year round. January 2005, Mr. Galenden set aside a massive tract of land in these foothills. Over four hundred square miles of valleys and mountains," Hesterman said.

"How the hell did you find this camp?"

"A ton of patience. I requested comparative pictures, at the highest level of detail available, and spent some time alone with a computer."

"A lot of time. We were pretty sure he had given up and had started surfing internet porn," O'Reilly said.

"If anyone had cared to join me staring at thousands of satellite images, you could have put your dirty minds at rest," he retorted.

"Eric and one other agent volunteered for the job, but after about forty minutes of staring at satellite images, the other agent suddenly found more important work to do," O'Reilly said.

"He nearly slithered on the floor to get out of there. Anyway, after laboriously comparing imagery, I finally discovered a dirt road that did not exist in 2004, leading into this river valley. I subsequently found these structures, which also did not exist in 2004. I verified this by comparing two similar strings of imagery. One taken in October 2004 and the other taken in July 2005. I couldn't find any other changes to the infrastructure of this zone.

"Check this out. Ever hear of Google Earth? It's a civilian application created by Google that overlays publically available satellite imagery onto the entire planet. You can literally scroll around the earth and zoom down to street level. It was launched in 2006. I had heard of it, but I wasn't sure about its accuracy or level of detail. Let me tell you. I'm not sure we need to go crawling to the National Reconnaissance Organization (NRO) anymore. I used it to correlate most of the images, and the level of detail is frightening. I still like the NRO imagery for clarity, but look what we can do with it," he said and started manipulating the screen to follow his words.

"We can start out in Nuequen and travel west along Route 22, heading to Zapala, then turn south on Route 46. Moving along until right here," he said and stopped at what appeared to be a random point on Route 46.

"I don't see anything," Sharpe said.

"That's where Google Earth shudders to a halt for us. The imagery is older than 2005. Hold on...hold on...there!" he said, and the screen split, showing roughly the same image.

"The 2005 NRO image shows an unimproved dirt road. Unfortunately, we can't conveniently follow the NRO imagery like Google. But, if you follow Google Earth for about ten miles or so, you'll come to this point. The NRO imagery shows people around the buildings. Welcome to Sanderson's lair."

"Nice work on this, Hesterman. Almost like finding a needle in a haystack," Sharpe said, pausing for an uncomfortable period of time.

"Worried about taking this to Ward?" O'Reilly said.

As usual, Dana had read his mind. Keith Ward, Domestic Terrorism's director, had initially opposed Sharpe's request to continue pursuing General Sanderson's group, but a few well-placed calls from above had changed his tune on the surface. Ward had expressed enough of his feelings about Sharpe's "pet project" to leave him with no delusions that his direct supervisor felt that it was a waste of time. To be fair, Sharpe and his team had very little to show for their efforts over the past two years, until recently.

During DTB's last weekly department head meeting, he announced the information they had uncovered by ATF agents in Los Angeles, along with their renewed focus on Argentina. The looks from Ward and the other task force leaders painfully reminded him that nobody really cared about his "pet project" anymore. Fortunately, nobody dared to shut it down. A personal inquiry from Director Shelby had a long shelf-life, especially if you had your eyes on moving up in the organization. Since he had never been officially swatted down, Sharpe assumed that Keith Ward had bigger plans at the FBI.

"Actually, I'm worried about not taking it to Ward."

"Bypassing him?" O'Reilly said.

Hesterman backed up from the computer table, so they could all face each other to talk.

"How confident are you in this imagery?" Sharpe said.

"It's all pretty circumstantial, but it's certainly worth a closer look. I'd feel comfortable requesting that NRO give us some face shots," Hesterman said.

"Face shots?" O'Reilly said.

"Close ups from a satellite. It would require the temporary repositioning of a reconnaissance satellite into a stationary orbit above this area. It's not a simple request. So based on what we have here, you'd feel comfortable making the request?" Sharpe said.

"Yes, sir."

Sharpe took his cellphone out of his suit jacket and speed-dialed a number that he rarely used anymore. He stepped into the far corner of the Joint Operations Center and lowered his voice.

"Director Shelby's office. How may I direct your call?"

"Good morning, Margaret. This is Special Agent Ryan Sharpe from DTB. The director personally asked me to keep him apprised of an investigation."

"I remember, Agent Sharpe."

"I have new information pertaining to the case that he needs to see."

"I'll pass this along to him immediately and be back in touch with you to set up a meeting," she said.

"Thank you, Margaret. I appreciate your assistance," he said.

"I'll be in touch," she said, which meant 'don't call back to check on this.'

Sharpe snapped his phone shut and turned to Hesterman.

"Stay close and make sure all of these images are portable and organized. The director's office could call us back in minutes. We don't leave the building until the director does," he said, starting for the door.

"Whoa! What are…wait a minute. I'm not going to see the director," Hesterman said.

Sharpe gave him a strained look and walked back over to him. "Let's keep it down. The walls have ears around here. Of course you're going. I can't make all of this magic happen or explain it nearly as well, though you will have to economize your words and cut out any attempts at humor."

"What? No…sir? I think O'Reilly is the best agent for the job. She's earned it," Hesterman whispered.

"Earned what? I don't want to sing and dance in front of the director. This is all you. The guy sort of gives me the creeps, anyway. Likes to touch my shot-up arm and grimace like he feels my pain. It's a little creepy," she said.

"It's all you, Hesterman. Put on your game face," Sharpe said.

"You'll do great, Eric. Seriously, you know the ins and outs of this imagery, and I liked the way you presented it to me. I can't possibly drag O'Reilly in there again. Admittedly, it's a little creepy when he touches her arm," Sharpe said.

"He better not touch me," Hesterman said.

"No guarantees. Stay close. When the director calls, we jump," he said and left the Joint Operations Center.

Chapter Ten

11:20 AM
FBI Headquarters, Director's Office
Washington, D.C.

Frederick Shelby, director of the FBI, stared intensely at Special Agent Hesterman for several uncomfortable seconds. Sharpe had given Hesterman the full briefing on what to expect from the director and hoped the agent didn't fidget. The director hated fidgeting under pressure, and often did whatever he could to elicit what he considered to be an undesirable trait. Eric held it together, only breaking eye contact a few times, but remaining silent and composed until the director spoke.

"This looks promising, Agent Sharpe. Very promising. Agent Hesterman? Excellent job with this discovery. Solid presentation skills I might add. Sharpe. I would like a moment alone with you," he said and turned to face one of the vast windows in his office.

Sharpe patted Hesterman on the back and winked at him. "Can you find your way back?" he whispered.

"I'll figure it out," he said, suppressing a grin.

Hesterman collected the meticulously prepared folios of support documents and satellite imagery, and removed the portable hard drive connected from the computer connected to the director's wall mounted flat-screen monitor.

"See you in a few," Sharpe said.

Hesterman started to walk to the door.

"Agent Hesterman?" the director said.

"Yes, sir?" he said, turning to face the director, who continued to stare out at the inner courtyard of the J. Edgar Hoover building.

"You had one hell of a senior year playing for Michigan. Starting linebacker for an undefeated season. Rose Bowl win over Washington State," he said.

"Thank you, sir. It sure beat the year before," Hesterman said, not sure if he was pushing his luck.

"Damn straight it did. I lost a considerable amount of money on the '96 season. Made up for it your senior year, plus some, so I won't hold it against you."

"I appreciate that, sir. Wolverine?"

"Lacrosse for four years. Graduated in '62, which was one of the worst football seasons in history up until that point. Keep up the good work, Agent Hesterman," the director said, and Sharpe signaled for him to leave.

"Take a look at this," the director said, still facing the window.

Sharpe walked over to join him and stared out at a busy courtyard, filled with agents and support staff, mostly clustered in small groups.

"Can you imagine? Having the time at two in the afternoon to take a little sun break out in the courtyard?"

"Not really, sir. This is the first glimpse of the outside I've seen today," Sharpe said.

"Well, nobody comes to headquarters to enjoy the sun. Especially not while they're on the clock," he said.

Sharpe made a mental note to avoid the courtyard, even if it represented a shortcut to another section of the building.

"Keith Ward won't be happy to know you've gone over his head with this."

"I felt you needed to see this first, without it being watered down," Sharpe said.

"I can appreciate the fact that you had the guts to do it, despite the consequences."

"Surprisingly, it wasn't a difficult decision, sir."

"That's called personal integrity, and it's by far my favorite trait in a person, especially another agent. I'll need to make a few calls on this. I should be able to convince the right people at the Pentagon that we need a look at Argentina. I presume you'd like to keep the CIA out of this?" Shelby said.

"I assume that was a rhetorical question, sir?"

"Very well, we'll leave our scheming brethren out of this one."

"What will you do if the satellite photos ID our man?" Sharpe said.

"Do my very best to rain fire and brimstone down onto him."

Chapter Eleven

3:45 PM
Nuequen Province
Western Argentina

Jessica's attacker committed nearly everything to the overhand, downward knife strike, leaving her with few options. Her attacker possessed a startling combination of agility and raw strength, which had so far left her with little margin for error. For the past minute, which seemed like an eternity, Jessica poured every ounce of skill, power and most importantly, instinct…into staying alive long enough for him to make a fatal mistake. At one hundred and twenty-four pounds, her five-foot-seven-inch frame was lean and exceptionally muscle toned. She could physically match up against most men in a hand-to-hand combat situation, but her current situation was far from normal. This man was a highly trained killer, with more than an eighty pound advantage, and he'd wanted to taste her blood for as long as either of them could remember.

Instinctively, she blocked the devastating strike with her empty left hand, her brain deciding not to grab the wrist. She didn't know why this decision had been made, but as her own processing ability caught up with her instincts, she consciously flowed with it. She imparted a sharp upward motion against the strike and immediately hinged her elbow, allowing the strike to continue downward with more momentum than the attacker had probably expected. She had feinted a solid block, which if executed would have locked her into a useless strength match. Her attacker had been hungry for this and didn't realize his mistake as she stepped forward and pivoted on her left foot, swinging her blade behind her own back, in an admittedly desperate gamble.

She crouched as her entire body turned along the attacker's right side and her knife hand swung in a blinding arc, burying the blade to the hilt in his lower back. He made a useless attempt to swing his own blade backward to strike her, but missed, as she spun even further behind him. He recognized the severity of his wound and knew it was useless.

The knife hadn't really penetrated his back. The Simknife blade was designed to retract and measure the damage imparted by the knife strike. Based on a number of variables, it pressure released a bright red stain relative to the depth of the wound. Similarly, the flexible "blade" could measure lateral slash intensity. Not surprisingly, the stab wound to Leo's back resulted in the maximum spray radius, leaving a six-inch diameter mark on his blue flannel shirt.

"Shit," he muttered, and Jessica yelled, "Next!"

And so this game would continue until everyone had been given a chance to test their skills against her. For nearly two years, she had trained the new recruits, imparting her knowledge and absorbing skills from the program's "old hands," including General Sanderson. Leo had asked to go first today, since he wanted Jessica fresh. He was hell-bent on taking her down, and when he finally succeeded, he told her that he didn't want anyone claiming she was tired.

She nodded at Leo as the next victim walked toward her.

"First. Last. The result is always the same," she taunted, and he shook his head as a thin grin formed.

"You almost fucked up. It's only a matter of time," he said.

"I wouldn't rely on 'almost' as a key strategy. Now, if you don't mind, I have a few more of your buddies to open up here," she said, just as Sergei, another Russian Section trainee, leapt forward, trying to catch her off guard.

His throat was "slit" within five seconds, and they all braced for the word. "Next!"

She had started this end-of-the-week contest one year earlier and opened it to anyone at the compound. She relished the challenge and remained undefeated. The contest length varied every week, depending on how many willing participants were located at the main compound. Some participants perished quicker than Sergei, and few ever managed to stick around longer than Leo. The whole thing rarely lasted more than thirty minutes, and when it was finished, Jessica found herself physically exhausted, but mentally and sexually charged. She used the contest like a drug, to fuel her weekends with Daniel, not that their relationship needed it.

Although training never really stopped at the compound, Jessica and Daniel had carved out a nice existence, spending as much time together as possible. General Sanderson ran a demanding schedule, but he had been flexible with both of them, given the circumstances that had brought them into the Black Flag fold. Jessica mostly stayed at the compound. Her knife and urban field craft lessons were taught mainly during the week, with at least one weekend practical field exercise conducted per month on the outside, in a major city. For these "practicals," she served mainly as an observer, though she would occasionally test her own deception and disguise skills against the trainees. These were perishable skills that she had no intention of losing to the classroom.

Daniel drifted in and out of the compound, with no discernible schedule. He frequently took trainees to one of several field training areas, some located more than fifty miles away. Unlike Jessica's curriculum, Daniel's training regimen didn't have a set schedule, and the trainees' skill levels varied drastically. One day he would be at the nearby sniper range, the next he would suddenly decide to take them into the field for several days. He followed Sanderson's general sniper curriculum with most students, but for a small core group of promising candidates, he would take them to the far reaches of Ernesto Galenden's massive private reserve to put their skills to the test.

Señor Galenden was one of the Black Flag program's most prominent silent partners and Argentina's wealthiest oil baron, owning a sizable share in the Repsol YPF, a Spanish owned, multinational petroleum company. Most of Galenden's wealth stemmed from his father's aggressive campaign during the late 1950s to buy large tracts of land in the western Nuenquen province. In a gamble based on privately contracted geological surveys, Galenden's father added vast stretches of the barren province to his shaky portfolio. In 1965, when petroleum was "officially" discovered near Rincon de los Sauces, the sleepy cattle town was transformed into the "energy capital of Argentina," and the Galenden family quickly became the wealthiest family in Argentina's history. Nearly 50% of Argentina's proven reserves of oil and natural gas lay under the soil on Galenden family property.

Black Flag's "leased" property extended for hundreds of miles along the western edge of the province, well away from most petroleum industry activity. The area had been designated a "private reserve," which kept most of the public from venturing too far into the territory. For Sanderson, it held everything the program needed. With arid land at the eastern limits of the reserve and the heavily forested Andes Mountains to the west, his operatives could train in nearly any environment. Several abandoned settlements, ranging in size from a small town to rough encampments, sprinkled the property, providing opportunity for urban combat training. The reserve combined unlimited training possibilities with privacy. Privacy provided by remote, geographic difficulty and guaranteed by *señor* Galenden's considerable influence.

Tucked into an obscure Andes river valley forty miles southwest of Zapala, Sanderson's compound took advantage of the natural cover offered by lush, dark green mountain conifers, and the naturally broken and rocky terrain of the Andes foothills. A wide, pristine stream teeming with trout rushed through the open valley a few hundred meters from the nestled encampment, giving the scene a rustic, picturesque feel that could evoke postcard quality images of a nature conservation lodge...if nature conservation activities involved automatic weapons.

Pushed back from the open valley into a gently cleared forest area, the main compound had been constructed with Sanderson's private funds and resembled a small campus of a few dozen log and timber buildings. The compound housed Black Flag's "schoolhouse" activities, along with a general cantina and basic housing accommodations. Operatives lived in private rooms within small dormitories. With the exception of common instruction and messing, operatives separated themselves by assignment to Areas of Operation (AO), for the purpose of language and cultural immersion. As much as practical, instruction, food preparation and recreational activities were designed to be AO-centric and focused on improving their ability to assimilate with indigenous AO populations.

Unlike the first Black Flag program, the new program was not designed to create long-term undercover operatives for strategic placement. The support requirements needed to adequately prepare operatives for deep cover placement proved to be prohibitive and unrealistic given Sanderson's budget and need for operational security. General Sanderson had no shortage of funding for the new program, but the human logistics required to recreate the first program caused Sanderson to rethink the program. The U.S. military had not only provided him with a generous budget, but had also given him a full battery of psychologists and counselors, critical to trainee selection and conditioning. Carefully screened political refugees had been funneled by the State Department to his program and paid generously to live among the trainees to ensure full immersion.

Beyond these limitations, Sanderson had a more practical reason for redesigning the program. Sanderson couldn't afford the time it would take to find candidates suitable for deep cover assignments. Without the screening tools used to find the earliest batches of Black Flag operatives, he now had to rely on a cautious process to recruit new operatives. The process was slow and inherently risky, exposing Sanderson's new program to the outside world more often than he would like. Still, it was the only way to gauge the limited pool of recruits he could access. Mostly hardened combat veterans of Iraq and Afghanistan, the new batch of operatives were different, and he had so far only identified two that would have passed the first program's initial psychological assessment.

The new program created undercover operatives suitable for short term or quick response operations. The first batch of trainees were ready for deployment, though based on Jessica's next three quick kills, the casual observer might consider sending them back through the program for further knife training.

The last body hit the deck with a solid thud, followed by two quick knife stabs to the neck that hissed red paint. Dhiya Castillo lasted longer than any of her previous attempts, having rapidly absorbed Jessica's instruction. For her small size, she fought viciously and relied heavily on her martial arts training to disarm Jessica. Inevitably, all of their matches ended with Dhiya eating dirt, the victim of splitting her attention between edged combat and martial arts acrobatics. With a little patience, Jessica always found an opportunity to knock her off-balance, though she had to admit, as Dhiya shifted more of her attention to the blade, Jessica had experienced some close calls. A few more months of intense knife work would turn the tide for this one, she thought.

With no more takers, she took a deep breath and sheathed her knife. She glanced around for Daniel, who she thought had been present earlier. She shook several hands and accepted a dozen or more slaps on the back as she waded through the group looking for her husband. She saw Richard Farrington breaking free from the group and jogged over to talk to him.

"Rich! I missed you in the circle today," she said.

Farrington turned and regarded her with a grin. "I can only have my ass handed to me so many times in one month before I develop a complex. You start to join us on the range, and I'll jump back into the circle," he said.

"I hate guns, but I might take you up on that. I know Danny likes to see you get your ass kicked. Might bring him around to watch. Have you seen him today?"

"He was there for a few minutes. I saw him head off to the armory."

"Thanks. See you around," she said and took off jogging, energized by the prospect of seeing her husband after his two-week absence in the field.

She still felt a twinge of disappointment that he never stuck around for "the circle." Logically, she knew that their strong attraction and protective instinct for each other would make it almost impossible for him to stay and watch. From an observer's point of view, every attack looked like a close call, and some were closer than she would care to admit. He'd seen the results of the closer calls. A black eye, split lip or bloodied nose wasn't uncommon. Every Friday yielded multiple bruises, and she knew that Leo's desperate attempt to take her down would leave several bruises on her forearms from blocking his devastating strikes. She'd have to wear long sleeves on their trip to Buenos Aires. Luckily, she had been spared any damage to her face.

As she approached the armory door, she heard him talking inside the secure facility. Constructed of log and timber on the outside, the inside of the armory had been considerably upgraded to store the program's weapons and ammunition. Personal weapons were also kept in the armory, though they served no real purpose in the grand scheme of the program, other than an indulgence. Operatives mastered weapons common to their AO and were familiarized with weapons beyond that scope, in case they were needed in a more general role outside of their specialty area.

She entered the armory and heard the distinctive metallic snap of a rifle bolt sliding forward. Daniel looked up as she crossed the threshold, placed his sniper rifle against the bench, and sprang up to greet her. He had nearly two weeks of grit and camouflage grease on his face, compounded by thick, filthy stubble. She knew he would reek of dirt, sweat and possibly urine, but she didn't care. She embraced him, and they held each other for a few seconds, until one of the other operatives grunted.

"I'll be up in about an hour. We need to clean all of the rifles and stow our gear," he said and gave her a quick kiss on the cheek.

"I'd tell the two of you to get a room, but you already have one," said Enrique "Rico" Melendez, ex-marine sniper, and Daniel's most promising trainee.

"Rico, don't upset the lady. I'd hate to see her turn up the heat on you in the 'circle' next week," Daniel said.

"We're not headed back out?" Rico said.

The other trainee started to add to the complaint, but Daniel cut them off. "We're taking a little R&R trip to the city, but we'll be back for next Friday. Jess didn't want to miss out on the fun."

"I need to make sure he's not coddling you guys out there. Put a little balance back into your lives," she said, and her long, black Simknife flashed out of its sheath in a blur.

"Shit. More of that? I thought I wouldn't have to deal with that anymore."

"Nobody has to participate, especially a fragile guy like you, Rico," she taunted, and the other sniper trainee, a harsh-looking Caucasian with a flat nose, blurted out laughing.

"You're fucking pure evil, you know that? You and your husband. And what are you laughing at, Jared? Who the fuck names their kid Jared, anyway?"

"It's a Jewish biblical name. At least my parents didn't idolize Julio Iglesias. Fucking Rico? Living *la vida loca*," he started to sing.

"That's Ricky Martin, you racist Hebrew," Enrique countered.

"I thought they were the same, man. They look the same," he whispered.

"Don't make me come over there and shove this sliding bolt where the sun doesn't shine," Enrique said, and Daniel pulled Jessica out of the armory.

"You might want to get out of here before this escalates. It was a long field exercise. I'm really looking forward to spending some time alone with you. Out of here," he said, and they touched hands briefly.

"They're in separate dorms, right?" she said.

"Thankfully. See you in few," he said.

She kissed him again softly. "The quicker you get me out of here, the better chance you have of getting lucky tonight," she said, turning to walk away.

"I thought my chances started at one hundred percent?"

Jessica stopped and turned around. "That's usually at the beginning of any given day, and goes downhill from there, but when you go into the field and leave me here by myself...you start at zero, and work your way back up. Time's a wasting," she said and twirled around again.

She heard him walk back into the armory, followed by some laughter. She accepted the fact that it might be longer than an hour before Daniel reached their "residence."

As part of their agreement with Sanderson, they occupied a stand-alone residence, unlike the rest of the staff and operatives, which didn't strike anyone as particularly unusual, since they were also the only couple at the compound. Sanderson housed the instructors and other support staff, like Munoz, Parker, Farrington and many others, in separate dormitories from the "trainees," due mostly in part because of the continued immersive environment maintained for each SAO's operative.

On the inside, each of these dormitories was a separate world, where the food, merchandise, furniture, appliances, everything, was imported directly from the assigned SAO. Internet service, satellite TV, magazines, books, even the linen, was all designed to give the trainees lasting, imprinted memories that could spell the difference between success and disaster in an overseas operation. They would be required to blend in with local populations on the surface, and the deeper they could take the deception, the better. Something as innocuous as referencing the wrong magazine or an unavailable satellite channel could draw the wrong kind of attention and bring an operation to a grinding halt.

The post and beam house gave them about 800 square feet of privacy, which included a bedroom loft. Designed in a basic A-frame style, the entire first floor was open, except for the home's only bathroom, which was stashed behind the stairs on the right side of the large room. A large two-story stone hearth, with imbedded wood-burning stove, adorned the left side of the structure and kept them toasty during the frigid, snowy winter months. As Jessica opened the unlocked door, she took in the comfortable, rustic design and felt a slight longing for the home in Maine that she couldn't fully erase from her mind. They had done pretty well given the circumstances, but they both wanted more than this life at Sanderson's commando training sanctuary.

Because it had been in everyone's best interest at the time, they had agreed to stay on for three years to help Sanderson get the program back on its feet. They were growing weary, but continuously assured each other and Sanderson that they would honor the agreement and give it one hundred percent. Jessica had found the work fascinating at first, taking the time to join the trainees in building skills she had never developed with the CIA and had never really needed in Belgrade.

This aspect of "compound" life, combined with frequent trips to Buenos Aires and Patagonia with Daniel kept her focused on what needed to be done, but her interest in compound life waned. Buenos Aires had become an addiction, and even Sanderson had voiced the concern that she might soon spend more time in Buenos Aires hotels than at the compound. Buenos Aires provided a sense of freedom and escape that had at first satisfied her cosmopolitan cravings and need to get away. However, the cravings came stronger and faster, and before she realized it, she could no longer wait for Daniel to return from one of his unpredictably long field exercises. She had previously grown accustomed to a life that couldn't be satisfied in the western hinter-regions of Argentina and needed to get away from here as often as possible.

Nearly fifteen years ago, she had boarded a United Airlines flight at Dulles International Airport as Nicole Erak, a woman who had never been given anything more expensive than a Sony sports Walkman in her life. Several hours later, she had stepped off the same plane at Paris-Charles De Gaulle Airport as Zorana Zekulic, one of several identities that would never be denied any indulgence, no matter how expensive or exotic...until now.

She had been doing better recently. Daniel had committed to giving her solid timelines for his training, so she could plan their trips together, spacing them out more evenly. Tonight, they would fly out of Nuenquen Regional Airport for the short one and a half hour flight to Ministro Pistarini International Airport in Buenos Aires, followed by a thirty-minute taxi ride to their rented flat in the trendy Palermo Soho barrio. They would arrive late, on the last flight out of Nuenquen, but the city would wait. It always waited, and they would spend five days in paradise, to return fully vested once again in each other's bodies and souls. She closed the door behind her and glanced at her watch impatiently. She'd give him forty-five minutes before dragging him out of the armory. She didn't want to miss the last flight.

&

General Sanderson stared at the Jeep Wrangler speeding south along the camp's only road, headed for Route 46, a two-lane provincial road that would carry Daniel and Jessica to Nuenquen Airport. The Jeep's headlights illuminated the deep blue remnants of a shadowy dusk that had crept down the eastern face of the Andes mountain range, bringing darkness to their valley well before flatter lands just ten miles east of the compound.

"We're losing her faster than I had anticipated," Sanderson said.

"She's been through more than either of us can imagine. Frankly, I'm surprised she's lasted this long. I expected her to disappear on one of her solo trips to Buenos Aires," Parker said.

Sanderson was about to respond when Richard Farrington opened the front door and walked inside, followed by Jeffrey Munoz.

"Rich. Jeff. Have a seat," he said, indicating the large wooden table near the open fireplace.

Sanderson tossed another thick, hand-split log into the fireplace, sending a cascade of burning embers up the chimney.

"I'm growing concerned with the Petroviches, Jessica in particular. I'm considering putting them under surveillance in Buenos Aires," Sanderson said, waiting for a response.

"She seems stable enough, for now," Farrington said.

General Sanderson glanced at him with a raised eyebrow, prompting Munoz.

"She's a city girl, General. We can't keep her cooped up here forever. Maybe we could institute a week on, week off training schedule for her. Keep her happy."

"I don't think we're seeing this in the same light," Sanderson said. "Trust me when I tell you that Jessica is highly unstable, emotionally. I spoke at length with our friend at Langley about her…Daniel won't say a word…and from what he shared, they pretty much lost her in Belgrade to severe mental illness, first identified by her handler. We're talking schizophrenia and dissociative identity disorder…multiple personalities. Most likely stress induced, but Berg has gone back through her file and thinks she might have shown some signs of this during training. Either way, she clearly came apart under assignment in Serbia, but somehow kept producing results…right up until the moment she vanished."

"But you knew about her in Serbia, right? That was how you got Petrovich back," Munoz said.

"I didn't make the Jessica-Zorana connection until late in the game. I was aware of Daniel's relationship with Jessica…Zorana, in Serbia, but I never suspected she was CIA. Parker took some background pictures of them in Maine, and I couldn't shake the feeling that something wasn't right about the two of them. Daniel disappeared for three months after sending Hadzic's money into an untraceable zigzag across four continents, and given the pressure on our program back in the states, I had never given his absence much thought. We had the money. He made it out alive. I had other things to worry about.

"I wasn't altogether surprised when he suddenly reemerged and announced that he was done with the program. He was pleasant, which was a change for Daniel, and said he had enrolled in graduate school. I put on the usual dog and pony show to keep him in the program, which was about to fold anyway, but I could tell he had moved on. I should have figured out that something didn't add up. I had always thought the plan to steal the money from Hadzic had been his idea, but now I'm not so sure."

"So, what are we worried about with Jessica? What's her biggest liability?" Farrington said, leaning back at the table.

"I'm worried about losing Daniel. The two of them share an unusually tight bond, and Daniel will do anything to protect her, physically or mentally. If she slips too far into Zorana's personality, we'll lose them both. He'll leave us before his work is done, and I need his skills here to train one more batch."

"Have you talked to Daniel about her?" Munoz said.

"Yes. He admitted similar concerns. He thought the combination of her training duties and frequent trips to the city were dangerous, in that she was being exposed to a set of conditions that evoked strong associations with her last assignment. Look, I can't stop her from going to Buenos Aires any more than I can really keep Daniel at the compound. I've always known that they'd never fully take to the new program. Staying here has been beneficial to both parties. They remain under radar, and we get their expertise. Unfortunately, I think they'll be leaving much too soon, and I'm not exactly sure how long they'll stay hidden in Buenos Aires. The place is crawling with Serbian emigrants. Given their histories, Buenos Aires is not the best city for them, which brings me to the purpose of this meeting."

"Surveillance?" Farrington said.

"Exactly. For two reasons. One, to get a better assessment of Jessica's habits and mental state. Two, because if the wrong people find them, the entire program could be jeopardized. Jeff, I want you to take Mr. Melendez to Buenos Aires for some filthy city air. He could use some time practicing his skills in a more hectic, confined environment. Keep an eye on them. Full surveillance. Pictures of people they interact with, names of places they frequent, schedule, personality observations. Long distance stuff, and for God's sake use disguises. The last thing I need is for either of them to figure this out. Keep an eye out for any competition. If they're being watched, you're authorized to use any and all means to neutralize and interrogate."

"Do you want us out tonight?" Munoz said.

"No. I've made arrangements to have the two of you privately flown out of our local airfield tomorrow morning. You can pick up their trail in Buenos Aires during the day. You'll have plenty of time to observe them. They'll be there for five days. I'll fly you back ahead of them on Wednesday. Bring some goodies to keep Mr. Melendez occupied…you won't have to worry about checking bags."

"Sounds good, General. I'll get the word to Melendez. We'll rent a car at the airport and find accommodations. I assume you know where they'll be staying?"

"Of course," General Sanderson said, and the room fell silent except for the sharp crackling of early season wood burning in the fireplace.

Chapter Twelve

10:07 PM
Monchegorsk City Central First Aid Hospital
Monchegorsk, Russia

Doctor Valeria Cherkasov approached the emergency room's wide automatic doors and paused. In all of her four years at the hospital, the doors had never functioned properly. Several bloody noses had taught her to never assume the doors would open swiftly. This evening was no exception, and her patience was rewarded when the doors hesitated on their tracks and struggled to open. An ambulance pulled into one of three empty parking spaces, which were kept clear of cars by armed police officers. Its emergency strobe lights bathed the concrete walls of the ER parking alcove in icy blue flashes. More cases. Doctor Cherkasov walked through the door into the freezing night and followed a ramp down to the street level, wishing she had grabbed her winter coat. She ducked behind the corner of the hospital and nearly ran into a couple smoking cigarettes. Vasily, an x-ray technician, and Mila, one of the ER's medical assistants, had formed the same idea as Cherkasov—a brief respite from the madness that had descended upon the hospital over the past forty-eight hours.

"I guess the secret is out," Cherkasov said, taking a pack of cigarettes out of the front pocket of her white lab coat.

"That you smoke? Not really. Though you've done a decent job of concealing it. A smoker can always spot another smoker," Vasily said, dragging deeply on his cigarette.

"Ironically, I didn't start smoking until medical school. Some example of health, huh?" she said.

"We won't hold it against you. I might shake you down for a few shots of vodka in town though," Mila said.

"A few shots of vodka sound pretty good right about now," Cherkasov said.

Vasily held an expensive-looking metal lighter out for the doctor, who accepted the offer and inhaled her first lungful of tobacco smoke in several hours. She closed her eyes for a moment as the nicotine did its job, briefly taking her away from the mayhem.

"Everyone will be smoking if this gets any worse. Any ideas, doctor?" he said.

"I've never seen anything like it. I thought it was the flu at first, but some of the patients are starting to show signs of sudden, severe aggression. Others go catatonic, then burst out of it in fits of nonsense. I've seen occasional cases of rabies that caused this kind of behavior, but nothing on this scale," she said.

The words "nothing on this scale" were an understatement given what they were seeing. The hospital had filled to capacity earlier in the day, finally overwhelmed by patients complaining of flu symptoms and severe headaches. City officials had graciously opened an abandoned school building next door to the hospital, to serve as a makeshift site for less severe patients. It took a while for the heating system to be restored, but it now housed at least a hundred patients in cots supplied by the nearby Air Force base. To Cherkasov, this looked like the beginnings of a pandemic and she had sent numerous samples to the main hospital in Murmansk, where they could be properly analyzed. The hospital laboratory here in Monchegorsk was still in the dark ages, and only the most obvious and basic lab confirmations could be made.

She had also insisted on sending several of the early patients, with the hopes of shedding light on the mystery disease's pathology. The signs of aggression in patients disturbed her the most, since it suggested a disease that could affect the brain's temporal lobe, like rabies or encephalitis. The hospital could conduct a spinal tap to collect cerebrospinal fluid, but they had no way to confirm the presence of either disease without a proper laboratory. The hospital in Murmansk was well equipped to do this and even had MRI capabilities, which could detect the temporal lobe damage that might explain the sudden aggressive behavioral swings. They hadn't heard anything definitive from the hospital in Murmansk, other than to stop sending patients.

"I heard that one of the nurses on the third floor was raped right inside a patient room," Mila said.

Dr. Cherkasov didn't want to start down this road, but she saw no real choice.

"It's true. The two men were removed very quickly by police, and the nurse is at a private facility. The hospital administration didn't want a panic among staff. We're taking precautions to prevent future attacks. More orderlies, two person rule..."

"Army soldiers and police," Vasily continued.

"Unfortunately. I heard they activated the military police component of the city's reserve army battalion. I'm not sure if that's a good thing or a bad thing," the doctor said.

"It's better than getting raped in one of the hospital wards," Mila said.

"I agree, but I don't see the situation getting better any time soon," Cherkasov said, nodding at something down the street.

They all turned to look in the direction she indicated and saw several people walking down the street toward the hospital. Nothing to be alarmed about on the surface, but it signified an accelerating trend. The number of people walking in off the streets had increased significantly as the day progressed, and it appeared there was no break in sight. Maybe an armed company of military police wasn't such a bad idea after all. The situation at the hospital could degrade very quickly at this rate. With a population of fifty-two thousand, they had barely scratched the surface with the few hundred patients housed within the hospital and the converted school. They were well above maximum capacity as it stood, and supplies were thinning quicker than anyone had ever imagined. Within twenty-four hours, they would have to turn people away and tell them to drink plenty of fluids.

She stared out over Lake Lumbolka, taking in the fading light of the northwestern skyline. The dark orange sun hovered on the horizon, radiating rich hues that competed with the bleak snow-covered landscape, casting a starkly beautiful reflection over the blackish ice covering the lake. She loved the long days of spring and longed for the endless summer days. Her brief escape was shattered by the sound of gunfire in the distance, from the direction of the city, she thought. The people on the street looked behind them and started to shuffle quickly up the street. Dr. Cherkasov threw her cigarette to the ground and stepped on it.

"You're one of the doctors, right?" said a middle aged man bundled in warm clothing, holding a child in his arms.

"Yes. What's going on?" she said and heard some whimpering from the group behind the man and his child.

"My daughter has the flu and terrible headaches. We all have headaches, and one of the women was attacked. Stabbed in the arm. Things started to go crazy in our building. It's not safe to leave your apartment. We banded together to get some of the sickest people here to the hospital," he said.

"All right, let's get you inside. Come on, help me out with these people," she said to her companions.

Vasily and Mila extinguished their cigarettes and jumped into action, helping to herd the dozen civilians up the ramp toward the entrance. Halfway up the concrete ramp, Dr. Cherkasov was hit by a splitting pain in her head and for a moment thought she had been hit over the skull with a tire iron. She buckled slightly, but held it together, realizing she hadn't been hit with anything.

"You all right?" Vasily whispered.

"Fucking headache hit me like a hammer. I've felt like shit all day, but this was different," she said.

"Welcome to the club. We've all been getting them. Drink plenty of water…it seems to help," he said.

As the doctor approached the door, trailing the group of patients, she heard two more gunshots from the direction of the city.

"Stay alert. Things are getting worse," she said to the police officer directing the ambulance out of the parking lot.

He simply nodded.

Chapter Thirteen

9:02 AM
CIA Headquarters
Langley, Virginia

Karl Berg scanned through the email alerts that had been passed to him by the National Clandestine Branch's Analysis Dissemination group and focused on a new report provided by the Community HUMINT (Human Intelligence) Coordination Center. The brief email didn't surprise him, given the ELINT (Electronic Intelligence) intercept transcripts provided by the NSA two days earlier. It had only been a matter of time.

The veteran agent rubbed his face with both hands and glanced around, giving the entire matter some consideration. He hadn't found the time to unpack several boxes of personal books and curios that he had collected over a thirty-one year career as a CIA agent, ten years of which had been spent behind the Iron Curtain. At 53, he looked a few years younger than his peers, which he attributed to thick brown hair that showed little indication of turning gray. His face showed a different story. The years of stress and long hours had taken a toll, and for the first year ever, he looked as tired as he felt. Beyond the wrinkles and lines, his dark blue eyes held the weariness of making hard decisions and living with the consequences.

He still couldn't shake the regret he felt for leaving Keller in the burning safe house two years ago. He didn't kill the young agent, but he certainly hadn't done anything to save him. It had been a selfish act, fueled by several bad decisions over the course of the day. The attack on the safe house had been his fault for jumping to conclusions about Daniel Petrovich's involvement in the murder of Nicole Erak. There had been no way to know that Nicole was still alive, living under an alias...actually married to the man he suspected of killing her. Her subterfuge had been brilliant and almost made him proud, but it had left him with an awful mess.

He had let his personal feelings explode that day, and two dedicated CIA agents had paid the price. Berg had buried the part where Keller's death ensured that the unholy alliance between General Sanderson and Berg could move forward. Keller's memory had been a potential liability to the proposed alliance, and Berg didn't want to ponder exactly how much this selfish instinct influenced which agent he decided to pull out of the burning safe house first. He knew the answer and it didn't sit well with him, which was why he swore to ensure that it hadn't been a waste. Thinking deeply about the information presented on his screen, he decided to put Sanderson's agreement to the test.

He picked up his desk phone and dialed Audra Bauer, who had been promoted to deputy director of the National Clandestine Service. Despite the fact that he had been Bauer's assistant director in the Counter-Terrorism Center, he wasn't in line to take that job upon her promotion, so he took a lateral transfer into a liaison position with the Intelligence Directorate's Weapons, Intelligence, Non-Proliferation and Arms Control Center. He remained a member of the National Clandestine Service (NCS), where he had served his entire career, but now spent his time coordinating WMD (Weapons of Mass Destruction) intelligence analysis with the hands-on activities of the NCS branch.

It was a newly-created position, thanks to Audra Bauer, who wanted to keep him close, but couldn't bring him along for the ride to the director's office. It was a good move and put several NCS personnel under his charge. There was a persistent rumor that NCS was looking to expand Berg's group into a full Branch within a few years. If he played his cards right, he might be in line for a deputy directorship. Then again, a lot could happen in a few years, and Berg wasn't exactly known for playing it safe. The idea rattling around in his head was a testament to the risks he had no problem taking.

"Deputy Director Bauer."

"Good morning, Audra. It's your favorite Intelligence Directorate liaison," he said, leaning back in his chair.

"I wasn't aware that we had more than one," she teased.

"I guess the distinction is safe for now. Hey, I need to run something by you in person. Have you read the most recent HUMINT summary from our friends in Kazakhstan?"

"Why don't you head over to my office? I have a meeting in about twenty minutes, but we should really talk about this. See you in a few?" she said.

"I'll be right down," he said and hung up the call.

A few minutes later, he navigated the corridors and stairwells needed to arrive at her office on the other side of the building. He greeted a few familiar faces, but pressed forward, not wanting to waste a minute of the rare time he had been given. There were plenty of unfamiliar faces that would have been pissed to learn that Berg had simply picked up the phone and secured time with one of the most sought after people in the National Clandestine Service. Even the office assistants didn't query him as he strode into "off limits" territory near the director's office and conference rooms. He nodded politely and continued, turning into the room labeled Assistant Director on a dark blue placard.

"Mr. Berg, Ms. Bauer is ready for you. No need to knock, sir," her assistant said, attentively observing him from behind a neatly arranged desk.

"Thank you, Liz."

Karl opened the door and was greeted by Audra, who didn't get up from her desk. She was studying one of two flat-screen monitors on her desk, squinting.

"Might help if you turned on some lights in here," he said, making his way over to her desk.

This was the second time he had been to her spacious office. Audra was not a packrat like he was, and there were very few personal effects present. A family photograph; three framed service decorations, which Berg knew were not the most prestigious she had earned, but instead the ones that meant the most to her; a few crisp, colorful authentic prints purchased from a semi-obscure artist in Maine; and neatly organized bookshelves, containing not a single personal book. Audra preferred a modernistic, Spartan environment, and the preference extended to her home, which very closely resembled the minimalist tone captured in her office. All except for her husband's den, which was more Berg's style and must have been a serious compromise in their relationship.

"I like the natural light. I can't stand the institutional lighting of this place...and I'm not about to bring in one of those antique abominations you have around your office. So...as much I'd love to catch up, Karl, I think we'll need every one of the few minutes we have to discuss what I'm reading here. It's not yet actionable in my opinion, but we need to alert some of our good friends in Europe. FBI and Homeland, definitely. I hesitate to put up an Interpol alert, since this is obviously not in the open."

"Then you might want to reconsider the FBI and Homeland. I agree that they need to be notified, but they'll liaison with Interpol as one of their first steps," he said.

"I know," she muttered. "I guess we can work on this behind the scenes, but even bringing some of the friendly intelligence services into the fold poses risks. They'll do what's in their best interest, and if that means a coordinated Interpol effort—or even better, throwing us under the bus and confronting Russia—they won't hesitate."

"We know FSB and SVR agents have been in direct contact with both the VECTOR Institute and Microbiology Institute in Stepnagorsk. The NSA has picked up a ton of chatter centered around Semipalatinsk and Kurchatov, and we're pretty sure they've sent 'unofficial' assets across the border, which would indicate to me that they're searching for something important. It's all rather unsettling. The most disturbing aspect is the Russians' secrecy. They've suddenly rekindled the search for this Reznikov character, who is at the top of everyone's WMD watch list, and they haven't breathed a word of it to anyone outside of Russia. I think we need to activate ground assets and take our own look around Kazakhstan," Berg said.

"Special Activities Division? I don't know. The Russians might be chasing a dead end. I can reassign imagery assets without alerting anyone, but I don't have the authority to activate a Special Operations Group. We can start the ball rolling, but I'm going to need more than a hunch that Reznikov is up to something. Russians snooping around Kazakhstan for a missing scientist isn't going to be enough," she said.

"He's not just any scientist. He's a bio-weapons expert that has been actively courting Muslim extremist groups for at least two years. Maybe longer. We know he's been to Al Qaeda facilities in Africa, and now electronic intercepts suggest he's met with Al Qaeda leadership in Dagestan. The fallout from a partnership between Reznikov and Al Qaeda could be disastrous for the West. The guy was caught trying to steal partially weaponized encephalitis samples from the VECTOR lab, and the Russians tried to kill him for that."

"I'm not going to ask how you know that," she said, shutting down her computer, assembling some files and stuffing them into a nylon executive bag.

"I wouldn't tell if you did ask. I'd like to use 'off the books' assets to do some digging around Kazakhstan. Get me access to imagery associated with the area around Kurchatov and Semipalatinsk, and I'll get you the information you need to get the ball rolling," he added.

She stopped and stared at him, glancing at the door, which Berg had closed behind them.

"Sanderson's group?"

"He has highly trained operatives that wouldn't raise an eyebrow in that region. The team could be on the ground within twenty-four hours. I'd expect actionable intelligence several hours after that."

"Assuming they find anything. No links back to us on this," she stated harshly.

"That's why I want to use them. I'll set up equipment through another source," he said and stood silently, waiting for her final approval.

"All right, make it happen," she said, starting for the door.

"I might need UAV support, in case they find something…or something finds them."

"I'll need to think hard on that request, Karl. I assume you'll want the drone to be armed, too?"

"Well…an unarmed drone is sort of pointless," he said, moving out of her way.

She shook her head and smiled. "Let me see what I can do about the drone. Get me something I can work with here, and let's hope this is all a false alarm on the Russians' end. So far, you've actually been really good for my career. I'd hate to see that change," she said, smiling warmly.

"The day is young. Stick around long enough and you'll find yourself assigned to a liaison position with the Intelligence Directorate," he retorted.

"A fate worse than death. Let's meet up later to finalize things," she said.

"You mean I have to ascend into these hallowed halls twice in one day?"

"You love coming up here and you know it," she said, walking through the door after him.

"I really don't. See you later."

Berg had a few calls to make and could barely keep himself from skipping down the halls. He lived for this kind of action and felt reinvigorated. Time to call in a few favors.

Chapter Fourteen

10:55 AM
FBI Headquarters Building
Washington, D.C.

"Please close the door," Special Agent Sharpe said.

Agent O'Reilly closed the door and joined Agent Hesterman next to Sharpe's desk.

Sharpe turned his flat-screen computer monitor to face them and started to type on his keyboard. "This will be a quick meeting. We have work to do," Sharpe said, edging his office chair toward the end of the desk so he could see if his keyboard commands worked.

A color photograph of two figures filled the screen. The image was crisp, taken from a high angle, and completely captured the faces of both men.

"This satellite image was passed to me by the director himself. Anyone care to guess who's in the picture?"

The man on the left wore dark brown cargo pants and an olive green sweater with a zippered collar. His tightly cut silver hair contrasted the earth tones of his outfit and tanned face. The man had broad shoulders and a clearly athletic, muscular frame. The figure standing to his right was dressed in light blue jeans and a gray collared shirt underneath a worn, dark brown leather bomber jacket. His brown hair was cut short, but didn't resemble a military style haircut. It looked poorly trimmed, with too much of a fade on the side exposed to the camera. To Sharpe, the man looked like he had stepped off the streets of Moscow.

"Are you serious, sir? We hit the mother lode," Hesterman said.

"Classified sources have provided this photo, based on your excellent work. I know this hasn't been the most popular sideshow here in Domestic Terror, but it paid off big time. You're looking at..."

Sharpe switched images to show the gray-haired man.

"Terrence Sanderson and Richard Farrington. Two very big fish in this investigation. We've been tasked to jump start a focused financial investigation of the activities related to the building and funding of the sites you identified," he said, and the screen changed to a wider angle showing the entire river valley.

"I assume you don't want anyone else working on this?" O'Reilly said.

"The director doesn't want anyone else working on this. He wants minimum exposure to this information within our branch. He's specifically worried that our friends in Langley might catch wind of this, and so am I. If a connection exists between the CIA and Sanderson, one wrong word could turn this site into a fly fishing lodge overnight. And you can be guaranteed that Sanderson won't be the activities director."

"What will Director Shelby do with the information?" O'Reilly said.

"That's the big question. Shelby isn't the forgiving type, and Sanderson's stunt was a major setback for the FBI. Not to mention a massive embarrassment. The director wouldn't tell me directly, but I'd be willing to bet that he takes this all the way to the top, where he'll have plenty of support for action against Sanderson."

"A Direct Action mission?" Hesterman said.

Sharpe shrugged his shoulders. In all reality, he had no idea, but it wouldn't surprise him if Shelby and a few of his cronies could convince the right people that Sanderson posed enough of a future threat to America's security to warrant foreign interdiction.

"Even if they did, we might never find out. I asked the director if he could keep us in the loop, and he told me to focus on the financials. He'd like to build a solid case against Ernesto Galenden, which I suspect will serve two purposes. The first being a legitimate way to spur the Argentine government into action against the compound. And the second? Well, if we could prove beyond a shadow of a doubt that Galenden funded and operated a terrorist compound right under the Argentine government's nose, then a direct action mission might be easier for everyone to stomach. Let's start piecing this together like an evidentiary investigation. Understood?"

"Where do we work on this?" Hesterman said.

"That's the good news. We've been upgraded to a recently vacated executive suite upstairs. It'll be tight for the three of us, but I hear it comes with a comfortable leather chair."

"Your old office?" O'Reilly said.

Sharpe nodded.

"I'll head up there and make sure they configure the workstations correctly. Do you need to move anything in here?" she said.

"No. The office upstairs is temporary. The director wanted to get us out of here while we worked on Sanderson. Keith Ward wasn't exactly pleased about this arrangement. He hates being cut out of the loop, and technically we still work for him, so watch what you say. Shelby can exert a lot of influence, but he won't stand a twenty-four hour vigil. Let's get this moving."

Chapter Fifteen

4:30 PM
Brown River Security Corporation
Fredericksburg, Virginia

Darryl Jackson sat hunched forward at his desk, furiously scribbling notes as Karl Berg spoke. He had weathered the investigative storm caused by Berg's last request well enough, though he didn't enjoy the multiple visits from Special Agent Sharpe's crew. All of which paled in comparison to sitting in front of Brown River's board of directors and answering some hard questions about the policies in place for their Brown River Special Operations Group. He had assured them that Jeremy Cummings had sourced the Petrovich operation on his own. As a senior member of the SOG, Cummings had access to the armory and the appropriate personnel. He had also convinced them that Cummings possessed the perceived authority at Brown River to assemble a team without supervision. He assured the board that safeguards had been put in place to ensure that nothing like this would ever happen again on Darryl's watch.

The mysterious six figure payment to Cummings had sealed the deal and kept Darryl from being fired. Everyone except the FBI had bought off on the theory that Cummings had been paid to hunt down and kill Petrovich for overseas clients. He felt guilty about framing Cummings, but the man was dead, and there was no need to complicate matters beyond that for either Brown River or himself. When he finished scribbling, he settled back into his chair.

"Are you sure that's all you need? Last time I did you a favor…well, I almost kissed my retirement goodbye, among other things," he said.

"I appreciate the assist on this one. The embassy there doesn't have the type of gear they've requested. Acquiring this stuff would be a pain in the ass and raise too many eyebrows. Kazakhstan is crawling with Ruskies."

"Five burly men arriving in that shit hole of an airport might attract all the attention they can handle," Jackson said.

"Their arrivals will be staggered, and nobody should be expecting them."

"Famous last words. The gear will be in the back of the rental vehicle. The vehicle will be rented using a bogus business account…just in case it doesn't get returned," Jackson said.

"Always a few steps ahead, eh?"

"When dealing with you, I like to be about a football field ahead at any given moment," Jackson said, and they both laughed.

"Sorry to be a stranger, Darryl."

"Hell, Karl. No need to apologize. I feel the same way. The heat came down pretty fierce on both of us. Scared the shit out of me, to be honest. We're good friends no matter what," Jackson said.

"It's always good to hear that. Thanks again for the help. Anything I can do, just let me know," Berg said.

"Well, since you mentioned it, I do have fond memories of the scotch we used to sip on my patio."

"Green Spot? Single Pot Still…one of the finest and rarest whiskey discoveries from my travels to Ireland?"

"My very favorite and impossible to find here in the states," Jackson said.

"Two bottles are already headed your way, my friend. Save enough for us to toast," Berg said.

"No promises. I'll give you a number for the team to contact when they arrive. Our guy will pick them up at the airport and take them to their rental vehicle. I'll do everything I can to get them a 4X4. They'll need it if they're heading out to the testing sight. I'll be in touch shortly. Catch you later."

"Sounds good. Later, Darryl."

Jackson replaced the receiver and considered his options. Brown River ran a small scale security operation in Kazakhstan, with most of it based out of the capital, Astana. The compound boasted two dozen contractors at any given time. Kazakhstan wasn't considered a high risk location, especially compared to Afghanistan or Iraq. Taking five assault rifles fitted with advanced optics out of their armory would be a big deal. Giving them to another team would be an even bigger problem. Onsite personnel would sense a lost opportunity, and more importantly, lost money. The less he explained to the Brown River group in Astana the better. This would require a little finesse on Jackson's part, or if necessary, some serious ball busting. One way or the other, he fully intended to get the right equipment to Berg's team. He pulled up an intranet computer site on his desktop computer and started looking for the right numbers. He needed to get the ball rolling as soon as possible. He'd like to have this settled before the scotch arrived.

Chapter Sixteen

12:30 PM
Palermo Soho Barrio
Buenos Aires, Argentina

Daniel brushed his bare feet against Jessica's leg and sipped his steaming cappuccino. She wore a bright floral long-sleeved dress, dominated by yellows and mellowed by dark orange and brown tones. Against her dark skin, the dress added to the exotic look she had carefully cultivated since they embarked on their journey south. Every time they "vacationed" to Buenos Aires, she scheduled a visit to her favorite beauty spa and had her hair dyed straight black. This was how he figured out that she had started to sneak away to Buenos Aires on her own, while he was out in the field for extended periods of time, honing the skills of Black Flag's most promising snipers. Of course, even if he hadn't noticed the jet black hair, he had a legion of stool pigeons waiting to inform him that Jessica had run off for the weekend. There was zero privacy out at Sanderson's compound, which was why they relished these trips together.

He stared over his book at her, moving his foot slowly up her calf. She still looked and felt tense, which was unusual for her once they got away from the compound for a few days. He could tell she had something big on her mind and was waiting for the right moment to spring it on him. Everything had been slightly off over the past three days. Their conversation, lovemaking, dancing…all of it felt a little forced, and he could barely stand the suspense. A million possibilities ran though his head, most of them bad, because this was how he naturally approached any problem—from the negative side. Anything positive was a surprise. This pessimism was a natural extension of his practical nature, so he braced for the worst case scenario, which wasn't really well defined in his head. When it came to Jessica, he often had no idea what was coming next, so he usually waited. This time, however, he couldn't stand it anymore. She was ruining a fantastic brunch with her stuffy silence.

"All right, you win, sweetie…I can't take it anymore. What's going on?"

"What do you mean?" she said, placing her mimosa down on the wrought iron table.

"I can go back to reading my book…which I only brought because I can't seem to get a word out of you. It's been a long three days, but at least I've managed to make some progress with my Blake novel."

She quit staring off into nowhere and looked straight into his eyes with a determined look. Her deep brown eyes bored straight through him, and he knew this was the big moment. She was either leaving him or she was pregnant. The latter didn't make sense, considering the amount of alcohol she had consumed over the past few days…another sign that something was out of place.

"I want out. I want *us* out," she said, and he wasn't sure he was relieved.

This was the worst case scenario he had expected, and deep down inside, he really wished he had kept his mouth shut. He released a long, dramatic sigh, which annoyed her based on the frown she flashed.

"We can't leave yet. We've talked about this," he said, which he knew was a weak opening.

"I know we've already talked about it. I want to talk about it again. I can't take it there anymore," she said, giving him a look that silenced a few of the tables adjacent to them at the sidewalk café.

"One more year, and we can go wherever we want. Do whatever we want. I promised him three years…"

"He made you promise three years. It was his idea, not yours. I don't trust him to keep his word. I'm the only knife instructor. You're the only sniper instructor."

"He has others that can teach marksmanship."

"You know the difference."

Daniel shifted uncomfortably in his chair and grimaced. He knew she was right to a degree. Everyone at the compound could shoot extremely well at short and medium distances, under pretty much any conditions, but Sanderson had a noticeable absence of any experienced, skilled snipers. He knew why and didn't want to share the information with Jessica. He was the only trained sniper that had survived his initial assignment with the original Black Flag program. Sanderson didn't have anyone else close to Daniel's experience level and he had been unable to procure a fully trained, experienced sniper in his new batch of trainees. Melendez had recently finished the Marine Corps sniper program, but hadn't deployed to Iraq or Afghanistan to put his skills to the test. Daniel was Sanderson's only qualified instructor for long range, concealed shooting.

"I know. I just don't know what we can do right now. I can't leave him high and dry," he offered weakly.

"Really? He didn't seem to have any hesitation leaving us high and dry a few years ago. We took the easy way out—your words—and it was a big mistake. We should have packed up and vanished. You and I both know we were manipulated. We're still being manipulated."

"We've been over this a million times. There was no way we could have predicted what he was planning, and I didn't exactly hear you argue against killing Ghani," he replied, immediately regretting his comment.

"Ghani was funding Al Qaeda, supposedly."

"That was confirmed."

"Confirmed by whom? Sanderson? A very trustworthy source," she said sarcastically.

"Look, this isn't productive. We've been down this road. What are we supposed to do?"

"I say we walk away. We have more money than either of us could ever spend..."

"I don't know about that," he said.

"Thanks for the dig," she quipped.

"I'm sorry. Seriously. I just don't know," Daniel said.

"I think we need to trust our instincts. If we had walked away from Sanderson in the first place, we wouldn't be international fugitives. We'd have normal lives, somewhere else...but it would be so much better than what we have now."

"We have each other," he said and squeezed her hand.

"I know, but Sanderson used that leverage against you once. What's to say he won't do it again? There's no reasoning with him. I'm telling you that I'm done with his program. I'm pretty sure the only way to leave is to simply vanish. You can mail him a nice card with an explanation if you feel like you owe him anything. As it stands, I don't feel like I owe him a fucking thing. I spent over six years in Serbia, in the company of society's worst, and I never killed anyone. I had ample opportunity, and at times would have liked nothing better, but I didn't. I couldn't. I had a job to do and if I killed every man that took advantage of Zorana, or violated her, there would have been no need for NATO intervention in Belgrade. It was one of the few moral high grounds I could stand on, and Sanderson robbed me of that." Jessica's eyes started to glisten. "I just don't know what I'm doing here..."

"That was my fault. I should never have let you do that," he said.

"You're right, you shouldn't have. But it was my idea. I could have pulled the plug on the whole thing, right up to the point where I jogged up his driveway. I knew better, but I had convinced myself that it was the best thing for both of us. Sanderson had us both under his spell, and here we are on furlough in Buenos Aires. I'm done with him, Danny. You're either with me on this, or we're done," she said and stared up at him fiercely. All the traces of a young woman about to break down crying had been quickly erased.

"I'm with you. Always. Give me a few weeks to make some arrangements."

Daniel's beeper buzzed. He kept his cell phone turned off when he wasn't using it, and so did Jessica. Neither of them needed Sanderson eavesdropping on their conversations through some of the clever technology he kept hidden in his vault at the compound. By the look on Jessica's face, he could tell that she had formed the same thought about the coincidence of the beeper's timing. With Sanderson, they just never knew.

"Your beeper?" she said, shaking her head.

"Makes you wonder," he said and took his cell phone out of the cargo pocket of his khaki shorts.

He dialed the number on the beeper, which he recognized as one of Sanderson's satellite phone connections.

"Daniel. Appreciate the quick response. Sorry to do this to you, but a situation has developed, and a very good friend of ours needs some help.

I'm putting you in charge of the team. I've made arrangements to have you flown directly to an airfield near the compound. I need you at the Aeroparque Jorge Newbery within the hour. It's located on the water, a few miles north of Palermo, so you should have plenty of time to pack up and get over there. Check in at the private terminal. You know the deal. Bring Jess with you, please."

"She's not going to be happy about this," he said.

"I know she won't, but she'll want to be here when you leave. It's an overseas assignment. Something right up your alley."

"Right up my alley, huh? Okay. We'll see you in a few hours." He disconnected the call. "We have to go."

"Are you fucking kidding me? Another critical job neutralizing more of *señor* Galenden's competition?"

"No. This sounds different. Overseas. Let me do this job for Sanderson and I'll work on a plan when I get back. I'm with you, Jessica. I just want to do this smartly."

"Do you ever want to call me Nicole?"

"Every time I look at you," he said with no hesitation.

"I want to be Nicole again." She stood up from the café table.

"I'd really like that. You might have to be Nicola, Nicolette...or maybe Nikita," he said, tucking the bill and some cash under a salt shaker on the table.

"*La Femme* Nikita? I don't think so. Danny, don't look now, but a guy in Mama Gracha's just took a picture of us...I think. He used a small camera or a phone."

"It's on our way back to the apartment, so why don't we casually stroll past and take a closer look," he said.

"Sounds good," she said and leaned over to kiss him and grab his hand.

Daniel and Jessica navigated through crowded tables of the large sidewalk café. It appeared that most of Buenos Aires awoke with the same idea. To take advantage of an unusually warm late April day before the temperatures dropped significantly in May. They hadn't passed a single empty table on their walk to the plaza and had endured a thirty-minute wait to enjoy their favorite brunch spot. Although it was possible to enjoy breakfast outside all year round in Buenos Aires if properly dressed, most locals crowded indoors during the winter months, emerging only on the occasional day when the temperatures rose temptingly into the seventies.

Leaving the restaurant's patio, Daniel felt a little exposed as they crossed the empty street and stepped onto the sidewalk adjacent to the small coffee shop. A few crowded tables lined the café's windows, but most of the business was conducted indoors.

Mama Gracha's was an iconic coffee shop, famous for high end coffee and amazing French pastries. Normally a favorite of Jessica's, they had opted for a heartier brunch across the street, where they could soak in the sun and ingest some solid food to counter the effects of a mild hangover. They had danced at a nearby disco until two in the morning, and neither one of them had tempered their drink consumption. Jessica had been on a tear with sangria all evening, and Daniel had surrendered to the multiple pitchers brought their way. They had slept until eleven and awoken with splitting headaches, which no doubt added to the tension this morning.

As they walked by the window, Daniel spotted the man that had piqued Jessica's interest. He was definitely European, but he dressed like someone who had been here a while: polo shirt and khaki pants. His outfit wouldn't have garnered a second glance on any of these streets. He was likely one of the multitude of permanent immigrants that had recently flocked to Buenos Aires. He looked Balkan…possibly Serbian, but that wasn't unusual in this city. Buenos Aires was home to one of the fastest growing Serbian immigrant populations in the world, which was another reason for them to leave. The Serbian community was tight, and fewer worlds were more closely connected. Add that to the surprisingly small percentage of former Serbian paramilitary members still in custody, and they were always watching their backs in Buenos Aires. Daniel risked another glance.

The man in the coffee shop fiddled with his phone as they passed the window. He never looked up from the device, even while he sipped coffee. For Daniel, the man didn't raise any alarms.

"Maybe just taking a picture of the square. I don't know. Let's take the long way back, just in case."

"A stroll with my husband…punctuated by a random sprint at some point. Fabulous. Glad I didn't wear sandals with heels," she said.

"You know you love me," he said.

"Am I that easy to read?" she replied, squeezing his arm tighter.

"Hardly."

They turned down a side road taking them away from their high-rise three blocks away. Neither of them saw the second man leave an outdoor table on the other side of the plaza and walk in their direction.

ᯅ

Enrique Melendez sighed in the back seat of their rental car. Parked on Nicaragua Street, the off-white, four-door sedan sported a few random dents and scratches, which placed the car right at home on the tight streets, where fitting into a parking space often relied on a driver's willingness to accept collateral damage. Munoz sat in the driver's seat, sipping tepid coffee from a Styrofoam cup. Melendez was sure of this because his own cup had long ago reached room temperature. He had jammed it into one of the cup holders to resist any further temptation to sip the disgusting liquid that their hotel claimed was coffee.

"So, what do you have?" Munoz said.

"They're drinking better coffee than we are…that's for sure," Melendez said, huddled low and staring through a portable hand spotting scope.

"Jesus Christ. We've been off the compound for three days, and you're a food connoisseur," Munoz said.

"I drank good coffee before Argentina. The hotel shit is worse than Sanderson's coffee. You'd think the coffee would be better…at least better than what we have back at camp," he said.

"All the coffee down here is shit," Munoz said.

"No, I'm pretty sure it's just our hotel," Melendez said, snapping a picture through the camera he had been staring through for nearly an hour and a half.

"Actually, it's shit almost everywhere. Right now, it's very likely that Jessica and Daniel are drinking shitty coffee. You see the café across the street? Mama Gracha's? That place has good coffee, because they import the expensive stuff from somewhere else. Argentinian coffee is notoriously bitter and watery because most of their beans are sugar roasted."

"Why would they sugar roast the beans?"

"Most of their beans come from Brazil, which produces nearly two thirds of the world's coffee, but sells the lower quality beans to Argentina and Chile. The rest is consumed by Brazilians or exported to the big operations like Starbucks, Lavazza and Illy. The beans are sugar roasted to conceal the bad quality, and in some cases, to cut the expensive stuff they're forced to buy. Sugar can account for about a quarter of the weight of a batch," Munoz said.

"They cut it like coke?"

"More or less. In this city, if a coffee shop isn't using Lavazza or Illy, it'll taste worse than Sanderson's shit. I make sure he imports the proper coffee for each group. Be glad you're assigned to the South American team…you can imagine the kind of mud the Russian team is pouring down their throats," Munoz said.

"Maybe I shouldn't complain. How do you know so much about coffee?"

"I owned a string of coffee shops in Hartford before all of this started," Munoz said, and Melendez sensed a hesitation.

"Do you miss it?"

"Miss what?" Munoz said, taking another sip of his cold coffee.

"The coffee shops. That kind of life," he said.

"I didn't really have much of a choice in the matter," he said.

Melendez could see that he didn't want to discuss it any further, so he focused on Jessica and Daniel, neither of whom frowned with every sip of the terrible coffee Munoz had convinced him they must be drinking. Three days of stale bagels, takeout sandwiches and bottled water was starting to wear thin on Melendez, though he knew he really had nothing to complain about. He'd allowed himself to get excited about the prospect of hanging out in Buenos Aires. Savory local foods, good coffee, exotic women, nightclubs, swank bistros…he'd let his imagination get the best of him and had instead spent the past few days watching the Petroviches enjoy the fruits of his limitless imagination.

Stakeout work had turned out to be grueling in terms of boredom and vigilance. The biggest rush so far had been carrying a compact concealed handgun at all times and Munoz's insistence that he bring his RPA "Rangemaster Standby" sniper rifle to the car when they were mobile.

The Rangemaster was a British-designed, compact urban system, measuring twenty-eight inches with the stock folded, and easily stowed in a gym bag. The barrel was significantly shorter than a standard sniper rifle, trading longer range accuracy for urban maneuverability, but remaining extremely lethal in the right hands. Melendez possessed a pair of those hands. If their rental car had been equipped with tinted rear windows, he could practice sighting and dry-firing from inside the vehicle. That might make things a little more interesting for him.

"I think we should use a van if we have to do this again. At least a mini-van with tinted windows. I feel pretty conspicuous staring through this camera in front of people walking by."

"Don't worry about it. It's more normal on these streets than you might think. Nobody knows if we're cops, PI's or worse. Even better, nobody cares. Everyone just minds their own business, and as long as the scope isn't on them, they don't care. Even the cops don't give it a second glance," he said, and his cell phone started to vibrate.

"Sanderson," Munoz grunted and answered the call.

"Munoz."

He listened for a few seconds.

"I understand. We'll be at the airport in ten minutes."

"That's it?" Melendez said.

"Correctomundo, amigo. Otra vez...hablamos solamente español," Munoz said in a thick dialect.

"I don't think correctamundo is español," Melendez said.

"I was just testing your skills. Pack up the camera. We need to be at the airport ten minutes ago. Sanderson has a flight waiting for us that leaves ahead of theirs," Munoz said.

"They're heading back, too?"

"Si, señor. Something's up," he said.

The car pulled slowly out of the spot and accelerated down the street, covering the one city block distance in a few seconds. They passed the Petroviches just as they both stood up from the table. Neither of them looked up at the unremarkable car passing by, and even if they had, they would not have recognized Munoz with a mustache and thick, wavy black hair. He normally kept a close-cropped appearance at the compound, and experience had taught him that all he had to do among an ethnically similar group was alter his appearance enough to change the general impression of the observer. As a dark skinned Latino, he could melt into most crowds here in Argentina. Even among the Italians, he would barely raise an eyebrow.

Melendez decided to lay flat on the seat as they passed the plaza. A passenger sitting in the back seat of a crappy car would attract a second glance anywhere, especially since their car was not a taxi. He stayed low for another block, until Munoz told him they were clear. On the way down Nicaragua Street, they passed their hotel without stopping. They had each brought a small duffel bag of clothing and essentials, which they kept in the car. The only things they would leave behind were a few toothbrushes. Melendez relaxed in the back seat and felt some relief that they were leaving. It sounded like this would be a regular gig for the two of them, so he made a mental note to bring a large thermos, his French press, and a one pound bag of Italian roast for the next trip.

Chapter Seventeen

3:00 PM
The Pentagon
Washington, D.C.

Director Frederick Shelby nodded to the marine colonel who held the door open for him and stepped inside the conference room. The stoic marine had met him at the VIP entrance and escorted him through an abbreviated security check. They had spent the next ten minutes navigating the building in silence, which apparently suited both of them. The tight-faced Colonel turned to him once to announce that they were approaching the Plans Section and that everyone had been assembled. Shelby considered breaking his own silence to offer the marine a job with the FBI. He could think of several ineffective jabber-jaws that this man could replace.

The first thing he noticed in the room was a blonde woman in a dark gray suit. She was seated next to a rather fishy-looking man wearing a tan suit jacket over a light blue dress shirt, which was missing a tie. He immediately assessed this man as White House representation.

"Director Shelby, it's an honor and a privilege. I saved you a seat here," Major General Bob Kearney said, who stood up and shook his hand.

Once the director was seated, General Kearney addressed the group.

"We'll make a quick round of introductions. I think we have everyone we might need to proceed with the information presented by Director Shelby." He nodded to the admiral to his right.

The admiral introduced himself. "Rear Admiral Mark DeSantos. I head the DoD's Strategic Support Branch, which is the successor program to the joint DIA and DoD venture created by General Sanderson in the early nineties."

Shelby noted the golden "trident" and naval parachutist wings perched above an impressive row of ribbons on the stocky man's dark blue uniform. His light brown hair was notably longer than any of the other uniformed men in the room, and he appeared relaxed in his seat, wearing a skeptical look on his tanned face.

"Lieutenant General Frank Gordon. Commander, Joint Special Operations Command," said an imposing hulk of a man on the opposite side of the table.

To Shelby, the man looked like a bodybuilder who had accidentally borrowed the wrong outfit. His dark green uniform bristled with insignia that baffled Shelby and stood in contrast to the crisp Navy uniform design. Still, the sheer volume of brushed silver pins and colorful ribbons led Shelby to the same conclusion as the SEAL admiral. They'd seen some serious shit. The next man looked downright frightening.

"Brigadier General Lawrence Nichols, Marine Corps Special Forces Command."

The general's facial skin was so tight and weathered that he oddly resembled a skeleton. His dark blue eyes burned through Shelby who, for the first time in ages, felt uncomfortable. He didn't need to examine the marine's uniform to know that he had seen his share of worldly violence and had stood at the serving end of that table.

The director shifted his gaze to the two civilians at the table. The smarmy civilian dressed in business casual spoke ahead of turn, cutting off the severe-looking woman, who immediately raised an eyebrow and flashed a strained smile.

"Gerald Simmons. Call me Gerry. Assistant secretary for Special Operations and Low Intensity Conflict Capabilities. I'm SECDEF's principal advisor on these matters. If I say it's a go, it's a go," he said.

Shelby glanced back to Generals Gordon and Nichols, detecting no shift in their posture or facial muscles. It appeared that they had a lot of practice dealing with Gerry. He admired their stoicism and restraint because he was pretty certain that he had raised his own eyebrows at the ASEC's statement.

"Sarah Kestler. White House Counter-Terrorism director. It's a pleasure to finally meet you, Director Shelby."

"Likewise, Ms. Kestler."

"And I'm Major General Bob Kearney, Defense Intelligence Agency. I lead the Defense Counterintelligence and Human Intelligence Center, which had a heavy hand in supporting Sanderson's program. The man murdered in the Pentagon two years ago worked in my office. Director Shelby contacted me to set up this meeting to gauge the level of interest in proceeding against Sanderson's new organization. As requested by the director, you have all read the classified summary of events leading to the acquisition of the recent satellite photos and have been given as much information about Sanderson's history as appropriate without considering a serious increase in security clearance protocols. Let me know if you need more information to proceed, and I'll consider issuing LIS Category One approval. I have the paperwork on hand if necessary."

"I do feel like I'm a little in the dark here. How many here have signed LIS Category One paperwork for the rest of Sanderson's file?" Gerald Simmons said.

"Director Shelby, Admiral DeSantos and myself. In all truth, if I approve you, you won't receive any material…it was stolen from the Pentagon's vault two years ago by Richard Farrington, the man standing next to General Sanderson in the satellite photo. He served faithfully in the army for nineteen years, until the day he walked into the vault and stabbed one of my people through the neck with a commando knife. He was part of Sanderson's new program, which poses a clear threat to United States security," General Kearney said.

"Can you break that down better for me? I read the file you provided, and there is no doubt that Sanderson significantly jeopardized U.S. security by destroying the FBI's HYDRA investigation. Our domestic Al Qaeda investigations still haven't recovered. Would that be an accurate statement, Director Shelby?" Sarah Kestler said.

"We're making good progress on new investigations, but yes, it was a significant and costly setback," Shelby said.

"So, now he's in Argentina, raising an army of operatives? People like Farrington? I need a better link to the future security of the United States, before I start suggesting that we either press Argentina to cough him up or take independent action. We all know the stakes involved in either course of action," she said.

"And that's a big part of why we're here. To discuss the viability of options," General Kearney said.

"Let's reach some sort of consensus about the threat before I try to lay anything out in front of the national security advisor," she said.

Although Shelby wanted to fast track an operation against Sanderson and wasn't in the mood to waste time, he appreciated her cautious approach. The director was close personal friends with James Quinn, the president's national security advisor, and his next stop today would be to pay his good friend a visit. With the "War on Terror" fever pitch at its apex in the country, he didn't foresee a problem getting a "green light" from the White House.

"Well, to start, Sanderson is number seven on the FBI's list of wanted terrorists, just under Ahmed Yasin, an emerging young Al Qaeda extremist that we've tried to kill three times already. That alone warrants action, but I understand that we are not talking about a simple Predator drone operation here," Shelby said.

"What are we talking about?" Gerald Simmons said.

"I want Sanderson and his key players in custody."

"Jesus, I was really hoping for something a little easier," Simmons said.

"Now I understand why SOCOM is here," Kestler added.

"The entire operation needs to be shut down before it causes more damage to investigative efforts domestically and internationally. Sanderson is a rogue, and only God knows what he plans next. We have a confirmed link between Sanderson and True America, and his operatives have been accepting arms shipments throughout South America and Europe. He's a deviously intelligent planner and he's had two years to come up with an encore to his last fiasco. Trust me when I say that we can't afford to wait around for his next Broadway production," Shelby said, shuffling through his file for a picture.

"Who knows where his next sleeper agent is hiding? The last one, pictured right here," he said and held up the picture of Farrington, "buried a seven-inch blade to the hilt through an innocent man's heart, severing his spinal cord. Just to steal classified information."

"I'm going to be honest with everyone here and hopefully save some time," Gerald Simmons said. "My boss supports action in this case, and I was mainly sent to assess the viability of suggested options. I notice that we don't have any CIA representation at the table. Does someone have a country assessment from Langley that might shed some light on the possibility of local federal police or military assistance? Obviously, the best case scenario would be to let the Argentine government take care of Sanderson."

"The CIA's absence is no oversight. There were too many irregularities surrounding Sanderson's debacle that couldn't be adequately explained…especially by the CIA," Shelby said.

"Do you suspect they were working together?" Kestler said.

"I couldn't say conclusively, but I've been doing this for a long time, almost 40 years, and let's just say that the numbers didn't add up on the CIA's side of the equation. I don't know if there was any collusion. My gut says no, but I suspect that the CIA tried to specifically eliminate one of Sanderson's operatives. Either way, we need to keep the CIA out of this. General Kearney brought the DIA's assessment of Argentina," Shelby said.

"Overall, the political climate is favorable for Argentinian cooperation; however, we feel that success is highly unlikely. Assuming a successful operation and capture, we have no guarantee of extradition. The extradition treaty is solid, but Sanderson is unlikely to be transferred. Munoz's testimony for an immunity deal was structured to move the day's investigation along so that the FBI could open more layers and figure out if a major terrorist attack was imminent. Munoz can't be touched. He could take a tour of the White House if he wanted. Munoz never directly implicated Sanderson in any of his testimony, and any lawyer worth their salt could argue that Munoz would say anything under duress to get immunity. See where this is going? This may sound outrageous, but the evidence against Sanderson is circumstantial at best. Against most of them, frankly. We have a few solid cases. Richard Farrington's fingerprints were on the knife that killed Harrison McKie. Daniel Petrovich was caught on camera slicing and dicing two Brown River contractors…followed by killing a police detective," General Kearney said.

"And three more Brown River contractors on a suburban street. We've got Petrovich and Farrington nailed. The rest? They're not likely to be held by Argentine authorities," Shelby said.

"Running a paramilitary training center within Argentina's borders? I don't think we have to worry about them being released any time soon," Kestler said.

"I wish it were that simple. Unfortunately, Sanderson's crew is running their operation on Ernesto Galenden's land, and based on recent activity uncovered by my investigative team, we can assume that Ernesto Galenden is fully aware and supportive of Sanderson's activities. Mr. Galenden is one of the wealthiest and politically influential men in Argentina. Sanderson would be tipped off long before an operation could get off the ground in Argentina. Certainly before federal forces arrived at the compound.

"'Even if Argentine forces took Sanderson into custody, Galenden has the clout to set them free. It's too risky in my opinion. If we decide to take Sanderson down, we need to do it ourselves. He's had two years to train and prepare his next batch, plus he has a full complement of fully-trained operatives from the good old days. If he's tipped off and flees, it'll put a damper on his plans, but it won't cut him off at the knees. His threat will linger," Shelby said.

"We need to capture this man and his principal players. At that point, we can work to unravel whatever remains of his network and plans," General Kearney said.

"I assume Sanderson and his crew won't be deposited into the U.S. federal prison system?" Kestler said.

"No, ma'am," Kearney said, "he'll be flown straight to Guantanamo, where he'll remain until he cooperates and dismantles his worldwide operation."

"All right, I'm sold, as long as these gentlemen can convince me that we can pull this off without a major international incident," she said and stared at the two Special Operations Command generals.

General Gordon spread out a few satellite images in front of him and smiled for the first time since Shelby entered the room. It was a meaningless, practiced smile that impressed Shelby. Prior to seeing it, the director thought only he had patented this grin.

"After reviewing the satellite photos and the DIA's best assessment of the situation in that camp, I feel extremely confident that we can pull this off and keep it under the radar, both literally and figuratively. Our Navy's Third Fleet, based out of San Diego, is one month away from sending the Boxer Expeditionary Strike Group to the Persian Gulf. The *USS Boxer* and all of the ships in the Strike Group are at sea conducting a final shakedown prior to deployment, fully loaded with a combat-experienced Marine Expeditionary Unit. This MEU has been reinforced with a Marine Special Operations Company and the uniquely modified helicopters needed to put them into action. The MEU also hosts a SEAL platoon that specializes in direct action missions. I can have another SEAL platoon onboard the *Boxer* within four hours, along with eight of the navy's special operations Rescue Hawk helicopters. HSC-85's "Firehawks" are based right out of North

Island in San Diego. This would give us one hundred special operators, and more than enough helicopters to ferry prisoners.

"Based on DIA and FBI estimates, plus reconnaissance, I estimate the possibility of removing up to forty prisoners."

"Forty? Is that feasible? How many helicopters are we talking about here?" Kestler said.

"Ten. Two marine CH-53ES Super Stallions and eight Rescue Hawks."

"Ten helicopters is an invasion force, General. What are the chances of keeping ten helicopters airborne during a nighttime operation? The targets are as well trained as any of the men that will step off those helicopters. Right?" Kestler said.

"Maybe the use of Tier One operators is something to consider," the assistant secretary of defense added.

"We won't need Delta or Devgru on this one. The operation is too big for either of those units anyway."

"Devgru is SEAL Team Six," Gerald said, directing his comment at Kestler.

"I know what the Naval Special Warfare's Development Group is, Gerald," she replied.

"General Nichols' Marines and the SEAL's can handle this job. General?" he said, nodding to Nichols.

"Given the number of structures and personnel on site, one SEAL platoon would secure the armory and vehicles and set up three or four support positions consisting of snipers and light machine guns. The remaining twenty SEALs and sixty marines would be assigned to secure the structures and prisoners. The helicopters would drop into the valley from an adjoining one, giving them little warning. Within the span of a minute, they'll be facing one hundred fully amped, night vision equipped, locked and loaded special operators...supported by several helicopters capable of spitting several thousand bullets into the compound within the span of seconds. Sanderson is a former special operator himself. He'll recognize the futility of his situation within seconds. So will the rest of his crew. If he decides to go out in a blaze of glory, we'll have a bloodbath on our hands, but it won't last long, and U.S. casualties will be minimal."

"I'm more concerned about the ten helicopters illegally crossing foreign airspace. I'll defer to your expertise regarding the capabilities of the operators," Kestler said.

"Thank you, ma'am," General Nichols said.

"Fortunately, we're looking at a relatively unpopulated stretch from the coast to the border of Argentina, far enough away from the capital or any major airports that radar detection is not a concern. No coastal radar emissions beyond sparse Coast Guard patrols have ever been noted in the most likely area for our helicopters to go 'feet dry.' Once over land, we're looking at a hundred and thirty mile trip to the compound. Forty miles of that is over Argentinian soil. Roughly a forty-five minute ride over land to the compound. The helicopters carry every possible electronic countermeasure available and have been constructed to produce a minimal radar or heat cross section. These birds incorporate stealth technology and are virtually undetectable by commercial radar. Even their rotor systems are dampened to reduce noise. The pilots are highly trained for this type of mission and have extensive real world experience flying missions a lot more complicated. Miss Kestler, if the White House approves the mission, it will succeed."

"I concur with this assessment," Gerald said, and for the first time since the meeting started, a few of the generals subtly shook their heads.

"The navy's Strike Group will be at sea for two more days, conducting operations off Camp Pendleton. If the decision is made before they pull into port, the Strike Group can be in position off the coast of Chile within ten days, assuming the navy doesn't mind burning a little extra fuel."

"I'm sure they'll mind, but given the tasking, they won't have a choice. Gentlemen, thank you for your time. I expect to meet with the national security advisor later this afternoon to get the ball rolling. I think it's clear this operation is worth the risks involved. Sanderson presents a clear and present danger to U.S. security. I'll be in touch," Kestler said, and everyone stood up.

"I think with the Secretary's backing, we'll be in business shortly. I expect to see everyone in the situation room within a few weeks. General, I'll catch up with you later," Gerald Simmons said.

When the assistant defense secretary exited the room, General Gordon shook his head and spoke quietly. "Just my luck to get stuck with that guy. I can barely stand to look at him and I have to deal with him on a daily, if not hourly basis. At least he isn't universally opposed to conducting military operations like the last guy."

"That appears to be his only redeeming trait," the marine general added.

"Frank, Larry...thanks for putting on the 'dog and pony' show. I think the general concept of operations laid out by the two of you will be more than adequate to handle Sanderson. Start working on the details. Director Shelby assures me that all of the right faces are aligned to recommend an operation against Sanderson to the president, and we all know it would be highly out of character for the president to swim against this tide," General Kearney said.

"Sounds good, Rob. We'll get things started behind the scenes. I'll put the helicopter squadron and another SEAL platoon on immediate alert, and we'll start a detailed mission planning session with SEAL Team Three and 1st Marine Special Operations Battalion."

"Thank you, gentlemen. Always a pleasure," Kearney said.

The two generals departed after a brief round of handshakes, leaving Admiral DeSantos, General Kearney and Frederick Shelby at the table.

"Why were you so quiet?" Kearney said.

Admiral DeSantos leaned forward with a slightly anguished look on his face. "I don't know. I didn't have much to add. I inherited the watered down version of Sanderson's program, and to be honest, the more I learn about Sanderson's new program, the more I wish we had something like this...off the books of course. I just wonder if there isn't a way to harness what Sanderson offers," the admiral said.

"In flagrant violation of the Constitution and every known law of the country? Sanderson had his chance and he blew it. Congress shut him down for a reason, and given his complete lack of regard for our nation's laws, or respect for our agencies, I wouldn't expect the relationship to be worth the risk. I like results and I'm willing to bend the rules a little to achieve them, but Sanderson's concept of bending the rules far exceeds anything any of us could live with. The sooner he's out of circulation, the better for all of us. Trust me on that," Director Shelby said.

"I'll be in touch. Thanks for corralling the right people at the right time, Bob. I owe you one," Shelby said.

The director stood up and bid the two DIA flag officers goodbye after extracting a promise that Kearney would keep him in the loop.

Chapter Eighteen

6:35 PM
Nuequen Province
Western Argentina

Daniel stared at the map laid out on the massive oak table in the headquarters lodge and glanced up at the sixty-inch plasma screen TV mounted on the wall just above them. The table had been pushed up against the rustic wall so the team could lay out any paper maps or charts on it and easily cross-reference the material with any of the media that Sanderson had acquired. Currently, it displayed some "borrowed" satellite imagery from the CIA.

"This sounds like a routine site reconnaissance. Why can't the CIA handle this? Or Shitwater? It sounds like Berg is breaking our balls," Daniel said.

His comment was accompanied by a few muted laughs, which were immediately stopped by several serious, condemning stares. Farrington glared the hardest.

"Come on, Sergei. You know you want to laugh," Daniel said and focused on the map again.

"Three bodies on this dead-end road. Russians?" Daniel said.

"Daniel, you're killing me. Unknown on the bodies. Imagery indicates that we might be looking at several more bodies in a mass grave around this cluster of buildings," Sanderson said, flashing his laser pointer at the screen.

Parker sat at one end of the table with a laptop. He moved a mouse connected to the computer, and the image zoomed in on a cluster of buildings far removed from the main concentration of buildings associated with the Semipalatinsk Nuclear Test Site. "The buildings of interest lie about ten miles southwest of the old reactor complex and show signs of recent activity. According to local sources, mining operations in the area had been extensive, but recent imagery doesn't show any mining equipment associated with the activity at this site, and a new, permanent structure appeared about five months ago. The miners typically bring trailers for any onsite needs. CIA thinks we should focus on this site."

"And check out the three bodies?" Farrington said.

"Exactly. The site is to be examined specifically for signs that it may have been used as a laboratory. To answer your question, Daniel, though I don't like to get in the habit of entertaining your endless supply of commentary…the CIA division running this op is chasing a theory, based on some circumstantial intelligence reports. Due diligence. Whatever the case, the Russians are up to something, and the CIA doesn't want to fall too far behind on this one," Sanderson said.

"What are we looking at?" Farrington said.

"The Russians are turning over every conceivable rock to find Dr. Anatoly Reznikov, a disgraced and disavowed bio-researcher. Apparently, a Russian Special Forces raid in Dagestan hit pay dirt. They found evidence that Reznikov travelled to Dagestan to meet with Al Qaeda leaders. Five years ago, Reznikov tried to steal partially weaponized encephalitis samples from Russia's equivalent of the CDC. As you can imagine, this is not a match made in heaven. Only bad voodoo can come of it."

"Why would they keep shit like that around?" Andrei interjected.

"Standard procedure. We do the same thing, even with programs that have been banned for decades. The CDC keeps a sample catalogue of every known disease, natural or manmade. Anyway, they fired him from the lab and blackballed him throughout Russia. He disappeared soon after that. The CIA always speculated that he had been assassinated by the Russians, but apparently that was not the case. Your job is to gather evidence to help the CIA determine if someone, likely Reznikov, had run a lab at this site. It's perfectly isolated, aside from the mining activity, and Reznikov would be familiar with the area."

"What about radioactivity levels? This was the Ruskies' primary nuke testing site for most of the Cold War. I'd like to have kids one day," Daniel said, and this time most of them laughed.

"Now that's a scary thought," Farrington said.

"You'll be equipped with Geiger counters and radiation strips. I can't imagine the need for radiation suits, given the fact that someone clearly used the buildings for an extended period of time. If it's hot, I don't want you sticking around. That'll be your call, Daniel. I wouldn't want to ruin your plans to have beautiful children," Sanderson said.

"I'll be sure to pass that on to Jessica. So, I only have one more question."

"Oh boy," Farrington muttered.

"Although this site certainly fits the bill for a mad scientist's laboratory, I can probably find you a thousand similar locations around the world. How did the CIA narrow this down so quickly?" Petrovich asked.

"I assume they started looking in the areas close to Reznikov's old stomping grounds. The VECTOR research lab is in Novosibirsk, a few hundred miles away, and another major lab is located in Stepnogorsk, roughly a hundred miles to the north in Kazakhstan," Sanderson said.

Daniel glanced at Farrington and raised an eyebrow. Despite their personality differences, he had come to trust Farrington's tactical assessment capabilities, finding them to be remarkably similar to his own. They had worked together to solve *señor* Galenden's problems, and Farrington had been Daniel's first choice for the Kazakhstan mission, although Sanderson had already assigned Farrington to the team. Sanderson had logically placed Farrington on the team because he spoke fluent Russian and was the de facto leader of the Russian AO Group.

The three other men in the room comprised the newest batch of Russian AO operatives. Sergei, Andrei and Leo, all born in the U.S. to Russian emigrants; all former U.S. military special operations soldiers, all currently fluent in several Russian dialects, and trained to blend seamlessly into Russian surroundings. Apparently, the Russian AO training regimen prohibited regular bathing, as all three of them reeked of body odor and sour breath. They looked rough, ungroomed, and slightly aloof. The effect was amazingly effective. They'd fit in on any Russian street, right down to the brands of clothing they wore on a daily basis. If anyone was going to compromise their group, it would be Daniel, who smelled like a blend of citrus and sandalwood soap.

"Looks like it's time to quit showering and shaving," Daniel said.

"You should go for a nice, long run in your clothes," Sergei said in Russian.

Daniel replied in passable Russian, which he had studied in college, and continued at the compound. Still, his Russian skills left a lot to be desired compared to the four men he would accompany to Kazakhstan under the guise of a Russian mineral survey team. He wouldn't be doing most of the talking, which probably gave Farrington a sense of satisfaction and relief.

"Do I have time for a body odor inducing run?"

"*Nyet.* You need to leave within the hour. You'll travel in small groups separately, and I need to route most of you in a fashion that brings you through Moscow. I want you on the ground in Kazakhstan within twenty-four hours. Everyone should head over to the Kremlin and grab all of your clothing and personal travel gear. I need to make a call to finalize your equipment arrangements," Sanderson said.

Daniel glanced at Farrington again.

"Weapons?" Farrington said.

"I'm thinking pistols and a few concealable submachine guns. Nothing that would raise too many eyebrows in Kazakhstan," Sanderson said.

Daniel knew he didn't have to prompt Farrington any further. Pistols and submachine guns were the standard load-out for a low to medium risk operation. Neither of them believed this operation qualified as such. The CIA didn't just stumble across this site without some help. If the CIA found it, they could assume the Russians had found it, too. If the CIA and Russian FSB weren't working together on this one, it would be fair to assume that the Russians had a reason to pursue Reznikov on their own.

"Upgrade the kit to local assault rifles with good optics. It's not uncommon for civilian engineers in these areas to bring heavier firepower. We'll keep most of it concealed in the vehicle," Farrington said.

"I assume you agree with this assessment?" he said, looking at Daniel.

"We're probably not the only ones interested in this site if I'm reading between the lines correctly."

"All right. I'll make this happen. Take a few more minutes to look at the satellite images and make sure everything is marked on your maps in a discreet fashion. I want you driving out of here in an hour. We'll meet one more time in fifty minutes. Daniel, can I talk to you for a minute?" he said and walked toward the empty fireplace.

"I need you back here in forty-five. Your cover will have to be different, and I need to go over it with you. It'll explain why your Russian is rusty, if anyone picks up on that…and the fact that you look like a spoiled, Latin American trust fund kid," he said.

"I wasn't expecting to make any clandestine trips to Kazakhstan. This isn't exactly in my job description," Daniel said.

"I need someone with your instincts and field experience on this one. Farrington is good, but he still needs some fine tuning. This is a great opportunity for you to hand off the baton to him. I know Jessica's heart isn't in the program anymore, though she puts on a good show, and I realize I can't keep the two of you here forever. I've been greedy with your time, and frankly, I didn't think the two of you would last nearly two years. I expected you to have disappeared by now and I'm really appreciative that the two of you have stuck around as long as you have. Give me one more good op with Farrington and then get back here to finish up what you started with your sniper protégés. A few more months tops, and I'll support you and Jessica in doing whatever you choose," he said and stuck his hand out.

Daniel took the general's hand firmly, while eyeing him suspiciously. "Didn't you make this promise to me once before?"

"We never shook on it, if you remember correctly, and a few unavoidable complications arose."

"Well, just to put you on notice, I won't let any complications get in the way this time, and neither will Jessica."

"Fair enough. You better get moving," Sanderson said and slapped him on the shoulder.

Daniel turned to the group still hovered around the table. "Rich, make sure the maps are properly marked and the GPS handhelds are programmed before we leave. I'll meet you at the Kremlin in thirty minutes. Size thirty-two waist. Medium for any shirts—"

"Daniel," Sanderson interrupted, "you'll be joining the team as a travelling executive from an Argentinian mineral exploration company. The company exists, but the reference phone numbers provided to customs in Kazakhstan will forward to a dummy phone center run by an influential Argentinian gentleman who has agreed to help us. You can dress in your usual clothes."

"Well, that sure beats having to stop wiping my ass and taking showers. I'll have to grab some winter gear somewhere along the way. See everyone in a few," he said and walked out of the lodge.

Five minutes later, he finished explaining the situation to Jessica, who had been waiting impatiently for him to return. She wasn't happy with the quick departure, but on the whole seemed all right with the entire package presented by Sanderson. He wasn't surprised by her quick acceptance of Sanderson's proposal. Neither one of them relished the idea of simply vanishing. One more operation and a few more months of training, in which both of them could wrap up their core instruction, was reasonable. Each of them could prepare an interim instructor. Melendez could easily outshoot Daniel, and Jessica wasn't the only qualified knife instructor at the compound. Farrington was more than handy with a combat knife and could take over the training until Abraham Sayar received the final nod from Sanderson.

Sayar had qualified as an edged weapons and hand-to-hand combat instructor with the Israeli Defense Force's Sayeret Matkal (Special Forces), but had been dismissed from service in 2006 for an alleged prisoner mishandling incident during the Second Lebanon War. Born in Israel and transplanted to America by his parents, Sayar returned to his homeland at age eighteen and enlisted in the IDF. Upon his dishonorable discharge, he returned to the States to try and join the U.S. Army Special Forces, but met with no "official" success. Identified by contacts still loyal to Sanderson, Abraham Sayar was recruited for an "off the books" program that suited both of their needs.

Jessica kissed him passionately as soon as he had finished telling her all of the details, and they pulled each other up the thick wooden stairs to the bedroom loft. They made the best out of the remaining thirty minutes, lustily testing the sturdiness of the queen-sized bed that had arrived at the compound nineteen months ago, to the complete chagrin of Sanderson and pretty much every other operative at the compound. They had spent a lot of productive time together in that bed, practicing for the day that they could put all of this behind them and truly start over on their own terms.

They both wanted to start a family at some point, but hadn't seriously considered the idea until recently. The scars of her ordeal in Serbia were still too close to the surface when they had settled in Maine, and he hadn't been in the best mental shape either, still plagued by a sense of transience and paranoia. Only the prospect of making a clean break from Argentina had started them talking about it, and even then they would still wait. He wasn't sure how long, but both of them needed to feel reasonably reassured that the ghosts from their past had finally given up.

Chapter Nineteen

11:35 PM
Monchegorsk City Central First Aid Hospital
Monchegorsk, Russia

Dr. Valeria Cherkasov struggled up the poorly lit staircase to reach the third floor of the hospital. She had spent the last fourteen hours triaging patients in the overwhelmed ER and finally realized the futility of their efforts. Her trek up three flights of stairs, which was a physical feat in itself given her condition, was motivated by self-preservation more than any lofty Hippocratic ideals. The violence spilling off the streets had reached an unmanageable level, even for the heavily armed platoon assigned to the hospital from the reserve Military Police battalion. The ER served as a beacon for the entire city and had effectively become ground zero for the worst cases.

All of the other entrances to the hospital had been heavily barricaded, leaving the ER loading bay as the only point of entrance to the hospital. This had worked well for a while, since the steep ramp leading from the back street gave police officers and soldiers higher ground to control the massive crowd that extended nearly one hundred meters in each direction on the tight road. Once up the ramp, patients were corralled into the concrete walled ambulance parking area for initial inspection.

Triage efforts had devolved into more of an asylum process than a medical one, since the hospital had long ago ceased to exist as an effective medical facility. Patients were screened for severity of disease, with a focus on the far ends of the symptom display spectrum. Patients showing some promise of recovery were provided refuge on the third and fourth floor of the hospital, which were secured and patrolled by military reservists, augmented by the few remaining police officers. These patients were frequently reassessed for possible mental deterioration and removed if they started to exhibit violent or unpredictable behavior.

This represented the other end of the spectrum, and the second floor of the hospital had turned into a makeshift prison for the worst cases they could identify. Dr. Cherkasov and the remaining hospital staff had decided that this service would be just as important to the citizens of Monchegorsk. The second floor had previously contained an inpatient behavioral health ward and had been outfitted with security features not found on the other floors of the hospital. The presence of such a large ward within the small hospital had surprised Cherkasov when she first reported to the hospital, but she soon came to terms with the fact that Monchegorsk had a history of neurological and behavioral disorders, which were most likely related to decades of heavy metal pollution from the Norval Nickel plant.

She reached the second floor landing and nodded at the two soldiers standing guard at the reinforced metal door. Three more guards were posted inside and guarded the controls to the door locking system for the entire floor. Another set of soldiers sat on the other side of the building, in the eastern stairwell, guarding the other exit. Within the ward, all of the patients were restrained to beds, chairs or anything solid and stationary. Occasionally over the past few days, a patient would get loose and try to kill another patient or charge the door. Their rage was usually met by a hail of gunfire, and the body was dumped out of a window.

Cherkasov coughed violently into her thin surgical mask. Since experiencing the first skull splitting headache a few days earlier, her condition had progressively worsened. Flu-like symptoms, just like everyone else. She knew the two soldiers were watching her closely for any signs of sudden unpredictable behavior. Their platoon had suffered its share of casualties from violent behavior directed toward them. They had also seen the illness itself start to claim members of their tightly knit group. For whatever reason, most of the soldiers from the reserve Military Police battalion didn't get sick, and the ones that started showing signs of the mystery illness were significantly delayed from the general population of Monchegorsk.

Her symptoms had also been delayed compared to the majority of the hospital staff and citizens. She started to suspect that maybe the outbreak started while she was visiting friends in St. Petersburg. Two weekends ago she had taken the train to meet up with a group of her medical school friends to celebrate their five year graduation anniversary. They had all completed the final internship requirements for St. Petersburg State I.P. Pavlov Medical University in 2002. She had been fine until the weekend. Now, less than a week after her first headache, she was coming apart mentally and physically. She struggled to hold it together as she approached the soldiers sitting on chairs at the door. She didn't want to end up tied to a water pipe on the second floor.

"Good evening, Dr. Cherkasov," one of the soldiers said, adjusting the assault rifle within easy grasp along the wall.

"I wish it were good, but I don't see an end in sight. Anything new in there?" she said.

"It's getting bad. We had three get loose in the last hour alone. They're chewing through their restraints...and limbs. We can't take any more patients on this floor," the sergeant said.

"I understand. I'm heading up to talk to your platoon commander. I just gave the order to stop taking any additional patients at the hospital," she said, squinting through the pain of a migraine headache.

"You all right, Doctor?" he said, glancing at the younger soldier.

"I'm fine for now. Anyway, I'm going up to discuss an exit strategy with your lieutenant. Once word hits the street that we're not accepting patients, all hell will break loose. Worse than it already is. Hell, we've been pulling the wool over their eyes for a few days now. Bringing people inside for nothing. Maybe we can get some of the people on the upper floors relocated. I don't know," she said.

Cherkasov raised her foot to start the climb toward the third floor when the stairwell went dark. Three seconds later, the emergency lights activated, bathing them in an eerie orange glow. She didn't feel panicked by the darkness, instead all she wanted to do was hug the young private who had advised her to take the stairs. At first she had wanted to punch the soldier, but when he told her that they had no way to get her out in case of a power failure, she had relented and shuffled over to the staircase. *At least something went right today*. She started to laugh at the thought, but quickly changed the laugh into a cough. One inappropriate display of emotion could land her behind that metal door. Laughing in a dark stairwell during the middle of a pandemic easily qualified as improper. The sergeant's radio crackled and he brought it to his ear.

"Understood," he said and knocked on the metal door leading to the second floor.

He turned to Cherkasov.

"I'm pulling my men out of the ward. The locking mechanisms on these doors are dependent upon electricity, but they aren't connected to an emergency backup. Fucking idiots. We'll have to barricade from the outside to keep any of these crazies from escaping."

"Shit. All right. Good luck, sergeant."

Cherkasov continued her journey up the stairs, moving slowly through the severe muscle aches in her legs. She coughed most of the way up to the third floor landing. A bright light hit her face, followed by an authoritative announcement.

"Cherkasov is here," the guard said, lowering his assault rifle.

The light from the rifle's side-mounted flashlight left bright green splotches in her vision.

"Doctor, the lieutenant needs to talk to you immediately.

"Funny coincidence. I was just on my way up to see him."

Cherkasov passed the two grim-faced soldiers and entered the third floor. She was overcome by wailing and whimpering, as hospital staff tried to calm the patients crowded into every conceivable space offered by the modest hospital. Mattresses had been cannibalized from other floors to fill the gaps between beds. The staff and soldiers could barely move through the long hallway, which resembled a refugee camp dormitory. The two emergency lights on the floor, each located above the stairwell doors, barely cast enough light into the room.

To her immediate right, Lieutenant Altukhov and one other soldier sat huddled around a small coffee table that had been pushed into the corner. On the table sat an olive green communications backpack that held a military VHF radio. The lieutenant held the radio receiver to his ear, while furiously scribbling on a partially opened map with his other hand. The enlisted soldier held a flashlight over a map, illuminating the lieutenant's work.

"Hold on, Doc," the lieutenant said, still writing.

Gunfire erupted from below, catapulting the entire floor into hysterics. She could barely hear Lieutenant Altukhov yelling to her over the screams and cries for help.

"Doctor! The ER has been overrun. My men are retreating to the stairwells to cover our escape. It's time to abandon the hospital."

"Escape to where?" she said.

"Anywhere but here. My commander has lost all communications with the squad assigned to guard the power plant. There's no reason for the power to fail. He's pretty sure it was targeted."

"Targeted? By whom? How are we going to get all of these people out of here?"

"We're not. My orders are to leave immediately. Russian Federation forces have blocked all exits from the city and our observation posts report armored vehicles headed in this direction. The major is convinced that the government knocked out the power," the lieutenant said.

"Why would they do that?" she demanded.

The lieutenant folded the map and stood up from the table, issuing orders to the rest of the soldiers in the room. His radioman secured the radio and heaved the backpack onto his shoulders, handing him the receiver, which was attached to the radio by a thick elastic wire. The officer issued orders into the handset.

"What's going on?" she said, grabbing the young radioman.

"Ma'am. We're evacuating the hospital. The lieutenant is ordering the soldiers to hold the stairwells for two minutes. We'll all depart through the east stairwell," he said, pointing to the other side of the room.

"What about the patients?" she said, turning toward the room.

"I'm sorry, ma'am. We need to get out of here before Federation forces arrive," he said.

"Why? Aren't you Russian Federation military?" she said.

The lieutenant gave the handset back to the soldier and started walking toward the far stairwell exit while providing her with the answer to her last question.

"Not any more. Our unit was given orders to strip the armory and vacate the city two days ago. As you can see, we didn't obey that order…we all have families here. They'll shoot us on sight. They've already started to shoot civilians trying to drive north…before they hit the roadblocks."

"No. This can't be happening. I can't just leave these people," she said.

"The choice to stay is yours, but my men are leaving. We'll escort anyone who can move during the next two minutes. After that…they're on their own," he said and continued walking.

Cherkasov looked around for members of the hospital staff. She could see roughly a dozen men and women in green hospital scrubs engaged in calming the patients. She spent the next minute repeating what the lieutenant had told her, careful not to let any of the patients eavesdrop. Some of the staff were as sick as the patients and opted to stay. About half of them started to edge their way toward the eastern stairwell, torn between duty and personal safety. Once the soldiers disappeared, chaos would descend upon the entire hospital, pitting each of them against their own personal hell. Rape, torture, murder, burning…all at the hands of the deranged populace that was sure to swarm the hospital within minutes.

Valeria Cherkasov stood next to the door with the two soldiers left to guard their retreat down the stairwell. One of the men held a two-way radio to his ear, obviously not willing to take the slightest chance that he might miss the final withdrawal order. The radio chirped and he acknowledged the transmission before locking eyes with her.

"It's time," he said.

She glanced into the room one more time and saw one of the older nurses trying to calm a young mother who kept screaming. Her listless child lay with her on the mattress. She froze until the nurse turned her head and nodded, mouthing "go." Cherkasov found herself shuffling through the doorway and down the stairs. As she passed the metal door to the second floor, she heard gunshots inside. She paused on the landing and the sound of dampened gunshots continued. One of the soldiers prodded her with an elbow.

"Keep moving," she heard.

"What's happening in there?" she whispered.

"The right thing to do," one of the soldiers said.

BLACK OPS

Late April 2007

Chapter Twenty

11:40 AM
Astana International Airport
Astana, Kazakhstan

Daniel Petrovich rode an escalator down toward the vast lobby area of Astana International Airport. The modern airport completely upended his expectations for Kazakhstan. He had expected a complete shithole and had instead emerged from his Austrian Airlines flight into a structure that could be used for the next *Star Trek* movie. The newly constructed, glass and steel encased engineering marvel stood in stark contrast to everything he had envisioned about the former Russian satellite country. He glanced up into an immense dome structure that formed the roof of the modernistic lobby. The front of the dome, directly in front of Daniel, held a flat steel girder-supported window that towered several stories high. His first glimpse of the turquoise dome from the window of his sparsely populated flight reminded him that he was indeed landing in a Muslim country.

As he reached the bottom of the escalator, Daniel spotted Andrei sitting on a nearby bench, reading a Russian newspaper. Andrei folded the paper and walked toward him, speaking in Russian. Daniel did the same, hoping his slightly rough Russian wouldn't be a problem. He had sailed through customs as Dario Russo, using Russian only as a convenience for Kazakhstan customs officials. English or Italian would have been a challenge for them and would have attracted more officials to the customs kiosk. His passport had been stamped through Buenos Aires, which didn't raise an eyebrow given his cover as an advanced liaison for a South American industrial company looking to partner with a Russian mining company. Kazakhstan welcomed the industry and the money it brought to their doorstep. Glancing around at the space station known as Astana International Airport, he figured they had plenty of money rolling their way.

Andrei was dressed in a warm gray wool jacket that fell below his waist, which gave Daniel some concern that he might be underdressed. His Iberia Airlines flight had been delayed leaving Argentina, which caused him to miss his connection in Spain. By the time he arrived in Vienna, he had no time to make a purchase at the Vienna airport, where he could find some appropriate winter clothing. He would be the last member of the team to arrive in Astana, and he didn't want to put the operation further behind schedule.

"Good flight, Mr. Russo?"

"Very nice, thank you. Are we ready?"

"The rest of the group is with the SUV outside of Astana. We're loaded up and ready. It's going to be a little crowded. We have a guest," he said.

"I can't wait to meet him," Daniel said.

"He's a little green for this kind of work, but he comes highly recommended from our sponsor."

"Any way we can ditch him?"

"I doubt it. He's not that bad," Andrei said, and Daniel paused before the sliding glass door.

"What's the temperature like?" Daniel said.

"Cold, and the wind makes it worse. This place is flatter than Siberia. Nothing to block the wind. I have an extra jacket for you in the car. Yuri figured you'd need some wardrobe help."

"Yuri is such a mother to me. I can't wait to see him again," Daniel said, before he stepped through the door into a dusty wind.

Chapter Twenty-One

5:59 AM
CIA Headquarters
Langley Virginia

Karl Berg saw Audra Bauer enter the National Clandestine Service Operations Center and check in with the watch officer in the processing area near the entrance. He waited for her at a semi-private computer work station on the opposite side of the room. A dozen additional workstations lined the wall, each situated so that the computer screens faced away from the center of the sizable room. She nodded at him and made her way around the outside of the NSOC. He watched as she passed several floor to ceiling, private cubicles on her left. The room was divided in half by a floor to ceiling, soundproof glass wall, with a translucent glass door in the center.

On the other side of the glass sat a large conference table with black leather chairs, and several workstations organized on the side walls. Three immense flat-screen monitors sat flush against the far wall, surrounding a large wall-mounted projection screen. Nicknamed the "Fish Bowl," larger scale, compartmentalized CIA operations were monitored from this room. When in use, the "Fish Bowl" went "dark," and thick shades would descend the entire length of the glass wall to keep prying eyes off the CIA's most secretive operations.

Berg occupied the only cubicle toward the rear of the room, which wasn't surprising at six in the morning. He could tell that a few of the private cubicles were in use, and judging from his own personal experience using these cubicles, the occupants had probably been sequestered inside for more than twenty-four hours. These cubicles were usually worked in shifts. Luckily, there was an eleven hour time difference between Langley and eastern Kazakhstan, which meant most of the action in Kazakhstan would take place during working hours for Berg. The team would likely arrive at the site within the next four to five hours and be back on the road a few hours after that. If all went well, he could be home in time for dinner.

He ensured that the operations screen on one of the monitors in his cubicle contained all of the active links he had programmed and that the other displayed all of the intelligence feeds he would monitor. The feeds were set to alert him according to the parameters he specified and were further linked to a pager designed to work only in the operations center. He could freely roam the room to grab coffee or use the bathroom.

"Everything good?" she said, standing behind him.

"Yes. They got a late start out of Astana, but they're on the road. They should be out of the area by sunrise. Everything is patched in and ready to go. Our guy is with the team, and SATCOM is clear. I have a direct line to the UAV control room in Kyrgyzstan. Two lines, actually, and a priority line to the Air Force Command Center responsible for the UAV. Thank you. I just hope we don't need it. It's a one-way mission, and I can only imagine that Air Force Special Operations Command wasn't very happy with the setup," he said.

"They weren't, but it helps to be the deputy director of the National Clandestine Service."

"Apparently it does. They assured me that the UAV could be airborne within thirty minutes of my phone call," he said.

"Impressive."

"Unfortunately, it's a minimum three-hour flight to get the UAV in position to help our team. This won't be a quick response close air support mission," he said.

"Like you said, hopefully we won't need it," Bauer said.

"I'll be in here until they're back on the main highway headed to Astana. I've enabled priority search strings on all of our live intercept feeds and I'll be looking for anything that might indicate a problem for them. We're focused on Russian side communications and any satellite transmissions leaving the area in the vicinity of Kurchatov."

"Sounds like you have all the bases covered. Keep me in the loop. I'll have a lot of explaining to do if we are forced to sacrifice one of the Air Force's Predator drones."

"That's why you get paid the big bucks, Deputy Director Bauer."

"Thanks."

"There's something else I'm keeping an eye on," Berg said.

"Related to this?"

"I'm not sure, but I have a hunch it's connected. My analysts came up with a string of Reznikov search parameters, which we inputted into the data analysis system a few days ago. This system looks at everything and puts up flags—"

"I'm aware of how it works, Karl. I haven't been out of the trenches that long," she said, shaking her head jokingly.

"My sincerest apologies for suggesting that you might be more of a bureaucrat than a CIA agent," he said.

"Touché. So what's up?"

"Reznikov grew up in an industrial city south of Murmansk called Monchegorsk. He was sent to live there after his father and mother died when he was eight. The circumstances surrounding his parents' death was suspicious according to one of my Russian sources. Anyway, something really strange is going on in Monchegorsk. ELINT is catching all kinds of military and civilian chatter about quarantines and roadblocks. Communications to Monchegorsk are down, and I'm trying to confirm what's going on, but we don't have any HUMINT assets on the ground there. Assets in Murmansk and St. Petersburg are on the road as we speak. I expect to confirm the presence of roadblocks within the next few hours. The link to Reznikov is too strong to ignore at this point."

"I agree. Do you think he's responsible? Why would he poison the city he knew as a child?"

"Maybe it wasn't a good childhood. I have no idea, and we don't even know if Reznikov is still alive. Muslim extremists have a tendency to clean up after themselves. I'd be surprised if he was still alive, but I'm not taking any chances."

"Good work as usual, Karl. I'll be in the building until this is over. Let's hope we can wrap this up cleanly," she said.

Chapter Twenty-Two

6:40 PM
Highway A345
South of the Karkaralinsk National Forest

Daniel stared out of the front passenger window of their Toyota Land Cruiser at the rolling hills covered with pine trees. They had travelled over two hundred miles south of Astana along the same highway and had seen very little change in topography, though the grass and bushes had started to green slightly over the past hour. Checking the map, he noted that they were passing through the edges of a national forest, which explained the dense pines. Several miles in the distance he saw a few small mountains, similarly covered with deep green trees.

To his left was a different scene altogether. The highway here served as an informal border between roughly carved, pine strewn hills and a vast steppe that extended hundreds of miles to the Russian border. Low, flattened hills kept him from staring at the empty land to the east, which had served as Russia's primary nuclear testing ground for over four decades. They would be driving into the heart of this wasteland, which they had been assured by "Dusty" to be utterly unremarkable.

Dusty had unexpectedly joined their team in Astana and had spent most of the ride silently sulking in the third row, wedged uncomfortably between the team's gear. Assigned to the embassy in Astana as the Economic Development Attaché, he met them upon their arrival in Astana. Karl Berg had insisted that they would need someone familiar with the terrain and local operations, and also presumably to keep them in check. So far he hadn't proved annoying, and according to Farrington, he had proved to be invaluable dealing with Brown River.

The equipment handover didn't go smoothly when the contractors tried to pass off badly damaged, previously confiscated rifles to the team. Farrington took one look inside the oversized duffle bag and zipped it back up, telling them that the weapons were not acceptable. He didn't need to inspect them any further to know that they hadn't been fired or maintained in a long time. One of the folding stocks had been bent, and he saw no optics devices. He did spot one badly twisted front sighting post. A heated argument ensued, and phone calls were exchanged. He never heard what Dusty said, but their tune instantly changed, though the contempt was still palpable in their mannerisms.

They left Brown River's compound with five AKS-74 assault rifles, all equipped with the latest optics. One of them had a 4X ACOG (Advanced Combat Optical Gunsight) scope that was handed to Daniel as soon as he arrived with Andrei at the oversized garage that had been provided by Dusty for their preparations. The ACOG scope gave the rifle a long distance sighting advantage over the red dot sights attached to the rest of the rifles. He was the best suited in the group to make use of the sight.

The weapons were stowed in the back, easily accessible by the three men in the wide back seat, but hidden from view in case they were stopped. Each member of the team, except for Dusty, carried a Russian semiautomatic pistol hidden somewhere. They didn't expect any immediate problems, but didn't want to take any chances. Reznikov had stirred up a hornet's nest of Russian activity, and they had all been assured by Berg and Dusty that the Russians didn't fuck around.

In addition to the weapons, they had various forms of digital recording equipment, night vision gear, biological testing kits and a satellite communications rig. The satellite rig would transmit everything they found from the site, as soon as they had finished their sweep of the structures. Dusty carried their satellite phone, which would be their emergency contact to Langley in case of trouble. They had been assured the support of an armed UAV drone, but were told that it would not be a quick response asset. The drone was located in Kyrgyzstan, with a three-hour flight time to their area. Dusty reinforced the fact that committing the drone to this flight would necessitate a life or death situation, since the drone would have to fly well past its recovery range to reach them. Daniel wasn't exactly sure how they could make use of it, but it made him feel a little better to know that it was an option.

"How much further to the turnoff?" Farrington asked.

"About fifty miles. We'll still have roughly an hour of light when we make the turn. We should be able to make it halfway from the turn to the site before it's pitch black. The last half will take us at least another hour. The roads are pretty shitty out there in the daytime. At night, fucking brutal. I uploaded satellite maps into our GPS. We should have no trouble navigating to the site. Just slow going," Dusty said.

Great, another three hours or so of driving, Daniel thought, watching the deep red sun dip closer to the horizon.

Chapter Twenty-Three

11:38 PM
Foothills of Kurchatov
Republic of Kazakhstan

The site proved to be nearly impossible to find in the dark, and the road conditions turned out to be far worse than Dusty had anticipated. These unexpected factors added two more hours to the trip. Finally, the Land Cruiser slowed in front of a horizontal yellow and black striped pole that served as a makeshift barrier. No sign hung from the pole, but Daniel could see that crudely attached links of thick chain held the pole in place, locked to the side posts with padlocks that shined in the SUV's headlights. He wasn't sure why anyone would have bothered with the gate, since you could drive a dump truck around either side of it. Beyond the hastily constructed obstruction, they could see the scarce outline of several buildings roughly a hundred meters away, superimposed against the faint orange glow of Kurchatov's city lights. He decided to take a closer look at the gate.

"Hold up for a second. I just want to make sure this thing isn't booby-trapped," he said, and Farrington nodded.

Daniel opened his door and stepped out into the frigid air. He was relieved to be out of the SUV. They had driven nonstop for over nine hours, the last four on spine-breaking roads. It didn't help that they drove around lost for nearly two hours before finding the obscured entrance to this road. Whoever left this site last did a professional job concealing the turnoff.

He approached the gate with a small but powerful flashlight and inspected the lock and chain connection on each side, paying close attention to the vertical posts. It all looked pretty straightforward to him and nothing raised his suspicion. He lifted the black and yellow pole a few inches off the posts and didn't see any wires. Nothing attached to the gate, as far as he could tell, but he wasn't one of their explosives experts. He directed the light along the ground to the side of the posts and could immediately tell that the gravel and rock had been recently groomed. He backed up several meters and examined a similar stretch of ground on the same side of the road, noting the difference. A significantly large section of ground immediately adjacent to the post had been raked or brushed. He repeated the observation on the other side and jogged back to the Land Cruiser through a sudden gust of cold air.

"The ground looks groomed on both sides. I don't like it. The gate looks fine. Sergei, you've received some advanced training in improvised explosives. Why don't you grab a set of bolt cutters and take another look at the gate? If it looks safe, cut the locks, and bring the truck up. I'm going to walk up to the site and take a look at the road. Meet you up there," Daniel said.

He reached back into the truck for his backpack and night vision spotting scope as Sergei hopped out of the SUV with a large set of bolt cutters. Daniel walked with him to the right side of the gate and showed him the ground.

"Yep, that looks pretty fucked. Land mines?" he said.

"I hope so. I'd hate to think someone is watching us with their thumb on a detonator. That's why I'm walking ahead of the truck," Daniel said and slapped Sergei on the shoulder.

"And it sounded so selfless and brave a few seconds ago," Sergei said.

"That's part of my unusual charm. It grows on you. Just ask Farrington. See you guys in a few."

Daniel slid over the top of the gate and started his slow, cautious trek up the windswept road, scanning ahead for trip wires and to the sides of the unimproved gravel road for evidence of an IED. He heard Sergei snap the chains, followed by the hollow metallic ring of a hollow pole thrown to the ground. A few minutes into his walk he had the Land Cruiser several feet behind him, illuminating the road far better than his small flashlight. Bathed in light, he felt exposed, but there was no rational reason to be worried. Aside from his team, the nearest human being probably sat huddled up under blankets twenty miles away in Kurchatov.

Ten minutes later, they assembled in front of the first building with all of their gear. They did a sweep of the immediate area with a portable hand Geiger counter, and although the reading was higher than normal, it didn't fall into any hazardous parameter that would preclude them from spending time at the site. Once this sweep was concluded, they shouldered backpacks and split up into two teams of three to examine the buildings. They each carried basic biological/chemical detection lab kits, designed to give an immediate color coded indication of the most common agents: anthrax, nerve, blister, ricin, Ebola, botulinum. Beyond that, they would have to bring samples back in small coolant containers, if they found any.

Three of the larger structures had new stainless steel chimneys, so these were prioritized for first inspection. Daniel had chosen the largest of the buildings, which was a one-story, flat-roofed structure roughly 50x30 feet. They walked the building's perimeter and found a second door at the rear of the building. Continuing along, Daniel located a small vented shed set against the far side of the building. The shed sat on a recently installed concrete slab, and upon opening the unlocked door, he immediately surmised its purpose. Besides the distinct smell of diesel fuel, electrical wiring protruded from the back wall of the shed and rested upon a large metal spring dampener that had been bolted into the concrete. A yellowed, translucent plastic hose protruded from the wall a few feet away from the wires. The shed had obviously been used to house a heavy duty generator, and judging by the small puddle of diesel fuel below the plastic hose, it had been recently used.

Daniel decided to enter through the back door, which was located halfway down the building. The door was locked, but using a small crowbar, they easily forced their way in. A musty, dank smell hit them as soon as they stepped inside the small vestibule, but there were hints of something more familiar.

"What does that smell like to you?" Daniel said.

"Old building, but definitely used recently. I want to say cologne or some kind of chemicals," Andrei said.

They both pulled out larger flashlights and illuminated the hallway. Nothing looked damaged or out of order upon first impression. They cautiously stepped into the main hallway and could easily assess the entire building's layout. One hallway ran from one end of the building to the other, ending at the exterior walls on each side. The front door stood opposite the back door, across the intersection of hallways. Glancing in either direction down the main hallway, they saw several open doors stood on each side.

"Let's split up," Daniel said.

He stepped inside the doorway of the first room and worked the light over the interior. The room was completely bare. Even the light bulb had been removed from the ceiling socket. He examined the walls where they met the floor, looking for anything left behind. He found nothing in the room, which had been apparently swept clean. In one corner he found broom lines in the thin layer of dust. He started to walk out of the room, when he suddenly flashed the light up at the ceiling. Something about the light socket seemed odd.

Examining the socket closely, he started to think that he had been mistaken. It was a standard one bulb fixture, crudely screwed into the ceiling. Nothing unusual, he thought, when he suddenly realized what had caused him to take a second look. The wiring for the socket ran along the ceiling, outside of the drywall. He followed one wire that ran to the light switch and the other that tied into the building's electrical system. Studying the room again, he found the same wiring setup repeated for hastily installed wall sockets throughout the room. The wires were bundled in groups and neatly stapled to the walls and ceiling, and there were enough outlets installed in the room to handle a credit card phone customer service center, or an equipment laden laboratory.

With a small digital camera, he snapped several pictures of the room before walking directly across the hall through another open doorway. He found the same wiring arrangement in this room, but nothing else. He was impressed by how clean the rooms appeared. The building was at least twenty years old, solidly constructed with little flourish. It had probably served as a mineral company's initial headquarters and laboratory years ago, someone having decided that mineral core samples taken nearby looked promising enough to warrant the construction of permanent buildings. Obviously, this hadn't worked out for the company, but someone else had recently found its seclusion and rugged construction suitable for temporary use.

He got down on his hands and knees to inspect the outlet nearest the door and felt his spine tingle. A small wire protruded ever so slightly from the bottom of the half-installed outlet. His mind had been in paranoid overdrive since finding the disturbed gravel near the gate, so the tiny wire had piqued his attention. He slowly pulled the outlet from the wall without a screwdriver, easily separating the heavy duty staples from the drywall. Once removed, he twisted the outlet to examine the back. Nothing unusual.

The outlet was still attached to the wires, and Daniel had to pull the wire bundle free of a few staples to get it far enough away from the wall for an easy inspection. He removed a small screwdriver and opened the outlet box. He didn't like what was inside.

The small, protruding wire turned out to be the antennae for a highly sophisticated listening device. The presence of this device in a random room meant that the entire building was bugged. More likely, the entire complex had been rigged with these tiny UHF passive bugs. The UHF bugs operated on a line-of-sight principle and had limited transmission power. Despite the fact that these were top shelf surveillance bugs, the gentle hills surrounding the complex suggested the presence of a manned hide site, or a remote transmitter hidden somewhere among the buildings. Unfortunately, by handling the outlet, he may have already tipped off his listeners. They would have to compress their timeline.

He gently placed the opened outlet against the wall, hanging from the wires, and walked briskly to Andrei. Upon seeing him, Daniel put his finger to his lips and signaled for him to come closer. In a barely audible whisper, he told Andrei about his discovery and asked him to finish searching the building. He would need to notify the others. After leaving the structure through the back door, he bumped into Dusty, who was staring through night vision goggles at the surrounding hills.

"Looking for trails. The new building is located about fifty meters down that path. Funny they would put it there. I don't get the impression that building codes are big out here," Dusty said.

"Maybe it's a pump station," Petrovich said, trying to keep the conversation natural.

"For what?"

"A well? Geothermal?"

Dusty lowered the night vision goggles, and Daniel could feel the quizzical look on the man's face. Before Dusty could fire back a smart-ass comment, Petrovich quietly filled him in on what he had found and asked him to step inside to help Andrei, while he talked to the others. With two people nosing around in the building, his absence might go unnoticed.

❧

Senior Warrant Officer Grigory Limonov stared through a powerful night vision spotting scope at the compound. Through the green image, he watched as flashlights probed two of the buildings. Dressed in artic level thermal gear, he lay next to Sergeant Mikhail Kilesso inside a small, low profile tent hidden among the larger rocks on the side of a hill eight hundred meters away from the buildings. The tent's opening faced the complex and had been nestled right against two of the larger rocks, allowing the occupants a clear field of vision of the entire site.

Slightly higher in elevation than the building area, they were virtually invisible to the men that had arrived thirty minutes earlier. Even in the daytime, the camouflaged tent had been undetectable, so perfectly placed and concealed, that close-up Russian satellite photos had failed to find them. Constructed of specialized thermal blanketing material, they were also invisible to any infrared or thermal imaging devices deployed from the ground or air, as long as they stayed in the tent.

The two men had been part of the security detachment for the scientific team that had analyzed the site and cleaned up the remaining mess. They had been left behind strictly to conduct surveillance and see if there were any other interested parties. The scientific team hadn't found much in the main buildings, other than a few walls that needed further cleaning, but the building outside of the complex had been a different story altogether. The original six man Spetznaz team had been given few details regarding the site's purpose, but the discovery in the outer building required everyone's involvement. They had spent the better part of a half day digging a hole deep enough to bury what seemed to be an unending quantity of skeletal remains. Not exactly the kind of work any of the Spetznaz soldiers had expected, especially Limonov's team.

They were members of the elite Vympel Group, a Spetznaz unit descended from the darkest shadows of the cold war era, specialized in foreign covert operations. The original Vympel commandos had been trained for deep penetration of enemy territories to conduct sabotage and assassinations in support of conventional Soviet military missions. NATO civilian and military leadership lived in constant fear of these commandos, who were given the task of infiltrating Europe prior to war and unearthing hidden weapons caches. These weapons would be used to kill generals, destroy NATO communications hubs, and cause chaos throughout Europe.

Fluent in multiple languages and masters of deception, they were the most highly trained and lethal arm of the military.

Since then, little had changed about the quality of the men that comprised the Vympel Group, but their mission had undergone a radical shift. Though they still focused on foreign covert operations, they were now one of the Russian Federation's premier counter-terrorism units, focused on weapons of mass destruction. His unit had drawn this assignment due to their familiarity with the Semipalatinsk Nuclear Test Site grounds. Never removing his eye from the scope, he spoke to Sergeant Kilesso.

"Do you think they found the bugs?"

Kilesso shook his head hesitantly, staring through a smaller scope. Both men wore earbuds attached to receiving equipment on the sergeant's side of the tent and had been listening intently to the group's limited conversations. Both of them regretted not placing a bug at the gate. The gate's location was obscured from their view by terrain, and they had no idea if the group had discovered the anti-personnel mines they had buried in the gravel along each side. Clearly, they had not driven the SUV around the gate. The anti-personnel mines were powerful enough to blow out a tire and possibly bend a wheel hub, but unlikely to destroy the vehicle or kill anyone inside. They had placed them as a deterrent, but the crew searching the buildings seemed far from being easily discouraged. They worked quietly and efficiently, methodically working their way through the complex.

"I can't tell. I think one, or possibly two of the outlets have been handled. Not out of the ordinary, in my opinion. I'd want to examine at least one outlet in each building. Especially given the odd wiring setup."

"I agree. We call this one in once they leave. If the motion detectors along the back trail show activity, we call it in immediately," Limonov said.

"Can we leave then?"

"Not likely, my friend. I suspect we'll be here a few more days, especially if this site has become popular," Limonov said.

Petrovich reached Farrington's building and softly opened the door. He stepped inside and was immediately met by Sergei, who held a finger to his lips and shook his head. Daniel was relieved that they had made the same discovery.

He walked up to Sergei and whispered, "Found the same thing in our building."

They both joined Farrington, who was in one of the rooms at the end of the hallway studying the furnace, which looked relatively new. Scanning the room with his flashlight, he didn't see an oil tank. Farrington stood up and took a few pictures before they all walked outside into the windy, frozen air. They spoke freely, but in hushed tones.

"We have to assume all of the structures are bugged," Farrington said.

"Yeah. I just wonder if someone is watching us right now," Petrovich said.

"We need to assume this is the case and get our job done here. We can upload photos and any data from somewhere down the road, just not here," Sergei added.

They turned their heads at the sight of Dusty and Andrei jogging toward them.

"Anything interesting?" Daniel said.

"Nothing really. I found some recently installed plumbing in two of the rooms, cracked and frozen. They must have a well somewhere close by. There's no way they're connected to a municipal water source, but there's a water pump connected to a pipe that penetrates the flooring," Andrei said.

"Same thing in this building, but there's also a shower. The furnace is new. On demand hot water type and it's hooked into a radiant flooring system, which is also new. I accessed the crawl space from one of the rooms to check it out," Farrington said.

"On the surface it doesn't look like much, but a considerable amount of money and time has been poured into these buildings. The one we examined looked like it might have been their lab center. Andrei?"

"I agree. Nothing there to indicate living quarters. The electrical system is rigged for heavy duty use, with a backup breaker box, which leads me to suspect they ran a lot of equipment in the building," Andrei said.

"There was only one box in our building. I get the impression this was their living quarters. There's an old kitchen that came with the place. Propane stove and space for a refrigerator, not that you'd need one around here now. I see indentations outside where they had probably installed temporary propane tanks," Farrington said.

"I guess the million dollar question is what lies behind curtain number four?" Daniel said, nodding toward the path leading away from the main site.

"Andrei and I will take the trail. You guys finish up any further assessment of the buildings. Let's plan to be back on the road in less than thirty minutes. I like Sergei's idea of uploading all of this shit well away from here," Petrovich said.

"We still need to take a look at the three bodies not far from here. We might find the good doctor with his brains splattered on the ground. I can't imagine Al Qaeda leadership would want him in circulation anymore," Farrington said.

"Fuck. More detours," Andrei said.

"He's right. If Reznikov is dead, then we have no leads and a big problem on our hands," Dusty said.

"We already have a big problem on our hands, if my suspicions are correct," Petrovich said.

"Should we grab the rifles? If someone is watching us, the rifles might keep them from paying us a visit," Sergei said.

"What do you think, Rich?"

"You should really get used to calling me Yuri. You're gonna blow our cover if you can't keep it straight," Farrington said.

"Sometimes the strangest things get under your skin, Yuri."

"I think walking around here with rifles will tip our hand too soon. If someone is watching us, I think it's from a safe distance. They know we're professionals and won't want to take the gamble. At some point they'll call this in, and who knows what we'll be dealing with? A fake roadblock, a small ambush in one of the nameless towns…I think we should keep our ace card hidden for now," Farrington said.

"We have another ace up our sleeves," Petrovich said.

"Yeah, over three hours away. They'll get some nice pictures of our dead bodies. Forget the rifles. Let's get this going and get the fuck out of here. The Russian border isn't that far away, and I'm not in the mood to entertain company," Farrington said.

"Good point. Dusty, why don't you join our group? I suspect you might have a better idea of what Berg expects to find out here," Petrovich said.

"I really don't, but I have a few worst case scenarios in mind," he said.

"So do I, and I really hope I'm wrong."

Ten minutes later, after navigating a treacherous, lightly worn path through several large rock clusters, they descended into a small dip between two hills. The dark structure lay twenty meters ahead of them, and Daniel took a moment to study the building with his night vision scope. A large stone chimney stood at one end of the square building and extended several feet above the flat roof. He didn't see any windows or a door from their slightly elevated position on the trail. He couldn't see anything through the scope that would keep them from approaching the building, so he gave the signal. They proceeded cautiously and quietly, using flashlights to keep them from twisting an ankle or stumbling across a hidden tripwire.

The three men arrived at the front corner of the building and split up. Daniel placed his hand on the brick wall and walked toward the back corner of the building, feeling the brick scrape and catch his gloved hands. The wall spanned about fifteen feet. When he turned the corner and saw the back wall, he felt his heart rate spike. A large metal door sat flush on the brick wall, aligned with the chimney, three feet off the ground. Cut firewood sat stacked against the wall on the other side of the metal door, extending from the frozen ground to a point three quarters of the way to the top of the wall. Petrovich noticed that the roof was constructed of the same brick as the sides. He'd seen something like this before, but it had been a bit cruder.

He stumbled over a few loose pieces of firewood and grasped the oversized metal handle of the door to steady himself. He felt the thick metal door open slightly, and after regaining his footing, he pulled it open. The slightly rusted door creaked open on its hinges, and Daniel directed the beam of his flashlight inside. The metal door spanned two feet by two feet and opened into the immense metal belly of a stove. A thick layer of ash filled the chamber. He shut the door and scanned the nearby area for more ashes. He found two piles measuring three feet high by five feet across. They had burned a lot of wood in a short period of time, he thought. He heard movement near the corner of the building and raised his light, instinctively reaching for the pistol tucked into his heavy coat jacket. He was in full combat mode based on what he had seen so far and wanted to get as far away from this place as possible. His light caught Andrei in the face.

"You need to see this," Andrei said, no longer speaking quietly.

Daniel followed him around to the front of the building. Flashes of bright light filled the entrance, and he couldn't believe Dusty had walked inside that place. There was no fucking way in hell he would set foot in there. More flashes illuminated Andrei, who stood next to the metal door, flashlight in one hand pointed into the building, pistol in the other. Andrei nodded for him to take a look, and Daniel hesitantly moved toward the opening. He could see that the door was thicker than the stove's door, with three oversized external slide lock mechanisms and one large handle. Easy to open with oven mitts. He'd seen it done before.

He poked his head inside and extended his light. Dusty's flashlight lay on the blackened floor, providing illumination while he placed samples of scant material in plastic bags. The room was completely scorched on all sides and constructed of thicker bricks than the outside wall. Heat resistant, refractory bricks, most likely. Though his sense of smell felt compromised by the painfully cold air, the stench of burnt flesh was apparent. He couldn't believe life had pushed him into the path of another human crematorium. A blinding flash caught him by surprise and left large images floating on his retinas when he reopened them.

"Goddamn it, Dusty."

"Sorry, I'm in a hurry…I need to get out of here," Dusty said, rushing toward the opening.

When the door was shut, Dusty grabbed Petrovich's shoulder.

"I have to call our man immediately. There's only one conclusion to draw here. They'd only need a crematorium if they were testing on human subjects," Dusty said, wide eyed and clearly shaken by what they had discovered.

"And they wanted to completely destroy any evidence of the bioweapon. Find out what they discovered in the other building and give him a call. Tell him we're leaving ASAP. We've seen everything we need to see here," Petrovich said.

"Right, I'll…" he stopped and stared at the door again, "I'll get this going. Jesus Christ this is un-fucking real."

"I wish it were. Give me a few minutes down here. I'm going to do a little poking around. I'd like to get an idea of how many people were burned up in Reznikov's experiment," Petrovich said.

"You're planning on digging up skeletons? The ground is frozen, and we need to get the fuck out of here," Dusty said.

"I didn't say anything about digging. If I can find where they buried the remains, I might be able to estimate…without digging. Just a few minutes. Tell the rest of the crew to get ready to roll when I get back. Go with him, Andrei," he said and turned toward his flashlight toward a flat area about twenty meters in front of the crematorium.

Chapter Twenty-Four

1:27 PM
CIA Headquarters
Langley, Virginia

Berg's pager beeped for the second time in the last five minutes, and he waited for the satellite call request window to appear on his computer. He was amazed that the NSA's system could alert him to a satellite call leaving the Kazakhstan search area before the call itself was connected. Dusty had relayed the preliminary information gathered by the team, which confirmed Berg's worst fears. Reznikov and his extremist buddies had likely used the site to create some type of bioweapon. He had no hard proof, but the circumstantial evidence was overwhelming. Regardless of what they created, the presence of a large, recently used crematorium meant that they had conducted extensive human experimentation at the site and didn't want to leave any evidence behind.

Overall, the site had been thoroughly sanitized of any useful evidence, but the team got lucky. Farrington had found small pieces of frozen brain matter jammed under a long wooden bench in a tiny makeshift prison cell. The victim had been shot while lying on the bench, evidenced by the ammonia washed stain still visible at the head of the bench. The cell had been extensively cleaned, based on the overwhelming chemical smell present in the room, but the perpetrators hadn't cleaned the bottom of the bench.

Getting this sample safely into U.S. hands was critical, and he contemplated launching the Predator based on this information alone. He was willing to gamble with the hand he held at this point, but he decided to hold off. Bauer had put her ass on the line arranging the Predator drone, and he didn't want to send the Predator on a one-way trip unless the team was in immediate danger.

The pager beeped again, but no call came through on his computer. Dusty had made the first call en route to examine the dead bodies discovered in the satellite photos. He hadn't expected to hear from Dusty again this quickly, but the kid was jumpy, and he understood why. They had uncovered a major biological weapons conspiracy and strongly suspected that they were under direct surveillance. This was the other disturbing discovery made by the team.

The entire complex had been rigged with high-end listening devices, which meant the Russians had found the site and still hadn't alerted their "allies" in the War on Terror. Muslim extremists had likely been in possession of a bioweapon for over two weeks, and the Kremlin was quiet. Now Reznikov's hometown could not be approached by road from any direction. None of this boded well, especially if the Russians were more interested in covering up their connection to Reznikov than keeping weaponized viruses off the world market.

Once Moscow was awake, he'd place a call to an old friend. Rare coincidence had put the two of them back in touch after many years, and if his former adversary remained the same man he had grown to admire during the Cold War, there still might be some hope of preventing a disaster.

Berg checked his connection to Dusty's phone and saw that all diagnostics indicated an open channel. As soon as he minimized the window, an alert appeared on his other screen. A satellite transmission had been detected in the vicinity of the laboratory site. He opened the alert warning and saw that the signal carried a Russian Federation encryption protocol. *Shit.* Now he had a real problem. If the Russians had gone so far as to place land mines to keep this a secret, then he had little doubt they would try to intercept the team. If he put the Predator up now, they would have coverage for some of their trip back to the main highway. The Predator could escort them far enough north toward Astana to make it unlikely for the Russians to attack them in the open. From that point on, the team could handle itself.

He put on his headset and adjusted the microphone. He clicked on the priority channel to U.S Air Force Special Operations Command (AFSOC), and the computer dialed AFSOC's operations center. The time on his computer read 2:02 PM. Some unlucky crew in Kyrgyzstan was about to receive an early wake up call. With the bird in the air by 1:30 AM, it could be circling over Sanderson's team by 5:00 AM at the latest. An Air Force Major answered Berg's call, and he explained the situation, ready to pass the appropriate encrypted confirmation codes supplied to him by Audra Bauer. These codes would activate a set of protocols that would put an armed U.S. Predator drone over the Republic of Kazakhstan, without that country's knowledge.

Karl didn't envy Bauer's position in this one, but if their suspicions could be confirmed, Bauer wouldn't have to worry about answering to anyone. She would likely earn the right to eventually succeed Thomas Manning as the National Clandestine Service's director…or find herself assigned to an embassy in some remote shithole, if she didn't serve time in federal prison. No guts, no glory is what he used to tell the agents under his charge. Not that he'd ever say this to Audra. She had more guts than this entire floor combined.

Chapter Twenty-Five

6:03 AM
Eastern Kazakhstan Province
Republic of Kazakhstan

Daniel shifted in the front passenger seat of the Toyota Land Cruiser, struggling to keep his eyes open. The SUV sped down the improvised road toward a small, isolated town along their route to connect with Highway A345. The road was in better condition than they had expected, but the constant presence of potholes and washouts kept the Land Cruiser in a seemingly endless cycle of rapid, unexpected maneuvers.

Once they hit A345, the brutal jostling would stop, and they should have a comfortable, straight shot to Astana, followed by a flight out of this Godforsaken corner of earth. Daniel shook his head and refocused on the wrinkled map in his lap. His arm brushed up against the AK-74 assault rifle jammed against the door as he fumbled to keep it steady enough to read.

"We're coming up on Kaynar. The highway is about ten miles beyond that," he said.

Farrington simply nodded in the driver's seat. They all felt the same about getting to the highway and getting the fuck out of Kazakhstan. Whatever the scientists had created and tested on their subjects in the hills outside of Kurchatov, they had wanted to conceal it badly enough to build a brand new crematorium.

They filed their report via satellite and sent all of their pictures with the stationary satellite rig, counting the minutes as the megabytes uploaded. More importantly to the five men in the SUV, "Dusty" had sent detailed routing coordinates to the CIA's operations center, with high hopes that

Berg would launch a Predator drone from the U.S. airbase in Manas, Kyrgystan, to cover their withdrawal. They hadn't run into any trouble so far, but Berg had confirmed that they had been under direct surveillance, and they all expected the worst. At least the Predator had been launched, though they hadn't received any confirmation that it had arrived.

Daniel glanced at the surrounding terrain, as the low structures grew in the windshield. The indomitable steppe lands yielded little in terms of visual interest. They passed a few fissures that spread perpendicular to the road, but beyond that, the town of Kaynar was the only thing that attracted his eye. The road fell away to the right, yielding a crude ditch that they had followed since crossing a stone bridge a few minutes ago. These rudimentary improvements provided the only sign that they might be entering an inhabited area. Daniel couldn't imagine why anyone would choose to live here. The Geiger counters had assured his team that their DNA would likely remain unaltered, but none of them could shake the uneasy feeling that nothing could erase the ill effects produced by nearly fifty years of Soviet nuclear testing in the region.

The sun finally cracked the seemingly endless and featureless eastern horizon, changing the landscape's grayish blue hue to a dull, grayish brown. *Not much of an improvement,* he thought and checked his watch. 0510. They had been driving for three hours in the dark, through some of the shittiest roads he had ever experienced. Sunlight was a welcome sight. A tiny reflection of sunlight from Kaynar caught his eye and before he could react, Farrington jammed the steering wheel to the right, spilling everyone to the left side of the cabin.

The SUV skidded to a halt in the side ditch, throwing everyone against their seatbelts just a fraction of a second before the road ahead of them erupted into a geyser of dirt and rocks. The blast's concussion rocked the vehicle, but left the SUV undamaged. Daniel opened the passenger door and spilled out into the ditch as earthen debris rained down on them, pelting the SUV's thin metal roof and hood in an unsteady hollow rhythm. The sharp crack of supersonic bullets immediately followed, adding to the unspoken urgency of their situation. He grabbed a backpack from the vehicle and yelled into the back seat at their CIA liaison.

"Get your pack and get the fuck out of here!" he said, as the front windshield shattered, followed by the repeated hollow popping sounds of bullets puncturing the steel hull of the Toyota.

He didn't need to tell the rest of his team what to do. They had started to bail out of the vehicle before it had come to a complete stop, and he could already hear the distinctive pounding of their Russian assault rifles. Several long bursts, mixed with semi-automatic fire. His team was on auto-pilot and would require little direction at this point. He glanced toward Kaynar, but couldn't make an immediate assessment of the situation. The cloud of dust and dirt caused by the explosion on the road still obscured the view between their position and the village, which would give them a few more precious seconds of concealment. His first priority was the satellite phone.

Dustin Bremer was still in the SUV fumbling with gear when Daniel drew even with his door. He reached inside and grabbed Dusty by his collar, yanking him out of the vehicle. He made sure that the CIA agent kept a grip on the bag that contained their satellite phone.

"My rifle!" Dusty yelled, trying to reach back into the Land Cruiser.

"Fuck the rifle, Dusty. Your job is to get the Predator here...we're fucked without it!" Daniel said, pushing the young CIA agent forward.

"Suppressive fire! Shift to the other side of the road!" Daniel screamed.

Farrington lay prone near the crest of the road, firing extended bursts from his AKS-74 at the village 150 meters away. Sergei, Andrei and Leo sprinted across the road, throwing themselves to the ground on the eastern side. Although the eastern side of the road didn't fall off into a ditch like the western side, it was raised high enough to give them adequate cover from the automatic weapons fire that poured out of the town. The western side of the road was exposed to the majority of the town's structures, and Daniel could already tell that a majority of the opposing gunfire emanated from the structures and low stone walls on that side of the road. They would have been open to a systematic pulverization if they had instinctively stayed with their SUV.

He shoved Dusty across the road amidst the snap and crack of a dozen near misses before kneeling next to Farrington.

"Nice parking job!"

"I could have parked us on top of that IED!" Farrington replied, quickly changing rifle magazines.

Daniel immediately saw what Farrington meant. A smoldering crater now covered the left side of the road less than fifteen meters ahead of them, created by an explosive force ten times more powerful than a rocket propelled grenade. By swerving right and taking them below the level of the road, Farrington had shielded the entire vehicle from the fragmentation effects of the Improvised Explosive Device (IED). Farrington continued to impress Petrovich.

"I'm glad you didn't. We're in a bad way here!" Daniel said.

The road around Farrington and Petrovich started to explode with the impact of bullets and the distinctive crack of near misses filled Daniel's ears, barely competing with the prolonged bursts of thunderous fire from Farrington's rifle. A few seconds later, Farrington's rifle fell silent and one of the assault rifles on the other side of the road picked up the slack. Farrington started to reload again, but Daniel slapped him on the back.

"Get across, I'll cover," he said and dropped to the road next to Farrington, shouldering his own AKS-74 toward the village.

Through his Trijicon 4X ACOG, he lined up a target partially obscured by one of the buildings on the left side of the road and pulled the trigger twice, absorbing the recoil in his collarbone. He wanted to clear as many of their attackers from the eastern side of the road as possible so they could fully use the elevated road as cover. Anyone firing at them from the eastern side of the road would be able to shoot right down the exposed axis of his team. Focused on his new job, he barely noticed Farrington scoot over his legs and dive for cover among the group on the other side of the road.

He saw the figure he had just shot stumble into the open and crumple to the ground. Satisfied that the ACOG scope was sufficiently zeroed for this range, he started to systematically acquire and shoot any targets that presented him with enough surface area for a clean shot. He didn't require much of a commitment in terms of exposure at this range. At roughly 150 meters, if the enemy gave him three quarters of a human skull for more than a second, he could remove most of it.

Two quick shots, one second of silence. He repeated this three more times, silencing four more shooters on the eastern side of the road before the intense volume of fire concentrated on Daniel's location forced him to vacate his overly exposed position.

He rolled off the road and righted himself, searching around for Dusty. The CIA agent lay huddled against the shallow road bank, assembling the team's satellite phone for mobile use. Daniel turned toward his team, all of whom were frenetically engaging targets with semi-automatic fire.

"Start moving up the road. Keep one weapon up for suppression. We need to close the distance to the village. If our air support shits the bed, we won't last long out here. Fuck! Crossing! Take them down!" he screamed and stood up to shoot at several figures sprinting across the road.

Every weapon on the road and in the village started to unleash long sustained bursts of automatic fire at his team, as the enemy tried to suppress their efforts to gun down the squad sent to cross the fifty-yard stretch between the western and eastern sides of the village. Despite the incredible volume of incoming fire, Petrovich's team held steady and concentrated all of their fire on the ten men trying to cross the road. Each man in his team crouched low, reducing their exposure to enemy fire as much as possible, while keeping their rifle optics trained on the erratically moving targets over a football field away.

Daniel put the ACOG sight's red arrow tip a few notches ahead of the lead runner, and squeezed the trigger twice, briefly seeing a dusty red aerosolized cloud erupt behind the soldier. He tracked another target and fired twice, sending the man into a momentum fueled tumble across the gravel road. The intensity of fire was unbearable, and Daniel could barely hear the sharp cracks of his team's rifles over the hisses and snaps from hundreds of incoming rounds. He ducked down further and took his eyes off the scope to assess the damage they had done to the squad sent on the suicide mission.

Through the cloud of dust, he saw several lifeless clumps spread out along the road, confirming the massacre. He started to lean back into the scope when he saw Andrei's head snap back, followed by a dark red shower that stained the grayish brown dirt in an arc five feet behind the body. Daniel's eye was back on the scope before Andrei's body hit the ground.

Daniel resisted the urge to check Andrei and squinted through the scope at the lone soldier who had succeeded at crossing the murder zone. The man threw his body over a low stone wall that ran parallel to the road and straightened up for the short run to the safety of a one-story cinder block building. Petrovich put the tip of the scope's red arrow one notch over from the moving figure and pulled the trigger, stopping the soldier in his tracks. The red arrow quickly found the soldier's now stationary head, and the reckless charge across the road ended unceremoniously.

"Keep moving forward and don't let anyone cross that fucking road," Daniel said. "Do you have the Predator?" he yelled to Dusty.

"I don't have shit yet. I can't get through to the Ops center!" Dusty screamed desperately.

"Are you shitting me? Fuck! Is the Goddamn thing working?"

"It's working. Nobody is answering…"

Three smoke trails arched lazily out of the western village, deceptively slow at first, until they passed the team's position and raced about twenty meters past them toward the vicinity of the Land Cruiser. One of the rockets skipped off the road, unexploded, and sailed at a forty-five degree angle skyward. The other two exploded on the western bank of the road, presumably destroying their truck. Although they didn't see the rockets hit the SUV, one of the vehicle's side view mirrors landed in the middle of the road, confirming the assumption.

"Keep trying and stay with the team. Pick up Andrei's rifle. He's gone," Daniel said and jogged back to his team.

Farrington and the two remaining combat operatives directed their fire at the soldiers in and around the houses on the western side of the village. Dozens of bullets skipped off the road, kicking up dust and pelting their exposed faces with stinging bits of rock that caused them to frequently shield their eyes behind their weapons.

Another round of rockets sailed out of the western village, heading toward their position, and Daniel could immediately tell that two of the 85mm high explosive warheads would fly harmlessly overhead. The third had frightening potential. He was pretty sure it would slam into the road bank on the western side, but knew from experience that these things never flew a completely straight path.

"Down! Down!" he screamed, and the team slid below the top of the road.

Everyone ducked except for Farrington, who sat firmly in position against the road, firing continuously at targets as the warhead exploded against the steep road bank opposite the team. Daniel popped back up and followed one of the smoke trails back to its point of origin. He stared through his scope and found a team of two men reloading the RPG-7. This was the first time he took a few moments to study their attackers.

Dressed in local garb, neither of the two men would have attracted his attention from this distance, beyond the fact that they were reloading a Soviet-style rocket launcher. He had half expected to see Kazakhstan Special Forces, but their presence would have indicated a major problem.

His team's visit to the area wasn't openly approved by the Kazakhstan government; however, through back channels within the Interior Ministry, they had been assured that no organized military or local interference would become a problem, as long as they were relatively discreet.

Daniel zeroed in on the shooter's upper chest and started to squeeze the trigger when he noticed an earpiece with a thin microphone. He paused for a second to confirm the microphone set, which meant they were dealing with a more sophisticated force than he had originally suspected. None of this was a good sign. He confirmed the presence of a similar communications rig on the man reloading the rocket tube and returned the scope's view to the man holding the tube. Two quick shots and the man crumpled out of sight behind a stone wall. The second shooter disappeared.

"Keep going! We need to get into those buildings! Let's go!" he said and signaled for Dusty to close the gap.

They started to make some gains toward the buildings ahead of them, passing the crater from the roadside bomb meant for their truck. The crater still hissed and smoked from the sizable explosive and was large enough to accommodate at least one of his men. He considered stuffing Dusty in the hole, where he'd be safest, but didn't want to separate any members of his team under the circumstances, especially the one carrying their satellite phone. Not that it was doing them any good at the moment.

The four men moved in teams of two, one team rushing forward ten meters, while the other fired at targets of opportunity in the village. Using this hasty method, they closed the distance to the village to fifty meters, but they also didn't hit any targets along the way. They had sacrificed accuracy for speed, which wasn't the only bad news. The drop-off on their side of the road had gradually faded, forcing them to press their bodies into the dried mud and low-crawl toward the village. Daniel knew they had gone as far as they could go like this. He felt high velocity rounds slice through his backpack with regular frequency, and if they crawled any further, these rounds would start to strike home in his back. He squirmed back until the backpack was protected by the lip of the road.

"Stay put!" he yelled to Farrington.

"No shit…that fucker better get Langley on the line, or this is going to end badly for us," Farrington said.

Farrington was right. They were out of fresh options. Like the enemy soldiers that had tried to cross the barren stretch of road a few minutes ago,

Daniel's team wouldn't make it halfway to the buildings forty to fifty meters directly ahead of them. He counted roughly fifteen shooters still operating in the western village, some firing from positions closer than seventy-five meters away. They'd be dead or bleeding out within a few seconds of standing up for the run. He rolled over onto his side and twisted his body so he could see Dusty. The CIA agent looked terrified and shook his head slowly, staring into Daniel's eyes with a look of extreme regret. He didn't need to ask. No air support.

"Fuck. No air support guys. Any ideas?" Daniel said.

Sergei spoke for the first time since the SUV slammed into the ditch. "We spread out along the road and trim their numbers. They might withdraw at some point. Maybe the fucking Kazahk army will show up and finish this for us."

"They aren't making the same mistakes anymore. It's getting harder and harder to hit any of them. We'll run out of ammo long before any sizable Kazakh force arrives," Farrington replied.

"We're pretty much fucked. I'm down to two mags," Leo added, tapping one of his two remaining thirty-round magazines against the front hand guard of his weapon before inserting it.

"I'm down to one," Farrington stated, between rapid trigger pulls.

Daniel reached into one of his cargo pockets and removed two additional magazines, tossing them at Farrington.

"We'll be down to pistols in less than ten minutes," Farrington stated matter-of-factly, casually retrieving the ammunition magazines from the dirt.

"We could try to get back to the Land Cruiser. We have a couple of marking grenades stashed in the rear. Doesn't look like they detonated with the RPG hits. Might get us across," Sergei said.

Daniel gave this a few microseconds of thought, but dismissed it just as quickly. The wind swept east to west and would not laterally cover their north to south route. Plus, the marking grenades didn't generate the same amount of smoke as a standard screening grenade. It would put out enough red smoke to be easily spotted by a passing aircraft, but would not adequately obscure their passage. Still, it might come to this. Daniel ran the remaining option through his head. None of them looked good.

In all of the noise and confusion, nobody lying along the road heard the armed MQ-1 Predator drone pass overhead. It also went unobserved by everyone inside the village.

ঞ

Major David Adler pulled back gently on the joystick, sending "Crabby Girl" upward to gain another 1000 feet of altitude for its initial attack run. Everyone in the Ground Control Station (GCS) in Kyrgyzstan was nervous about this flight. First, the fact that they had been abruptly awoken at one thirty in the morning and handed a last minute CIA mission didn't sit well with any of the three Air Force personnel. Learning twenty minutes later that the Predator drone had been fitted with two AGM-114 Hellfire missiles made them even more nervous. Nobody inside the air-conditioned, camouflaged metal box sitting next to the main runway had previously flown a live armed mission.

The crew stationed at Manas had previously flown routine reconnaissance missions in support of Tajikistan/Afghanistan border tightening measures. Major Adler hadn't even been aware that the base stored Hellfire missiles. To put it mildly, the "pucker factor" was high in the GCS, and Sergeant Juan Salazar had almost walked off the mission when they were given the initial flight path vector: north into Kazakhstan airspace. Only one of Staff Sergeant Kelly McIntyre's patented pep talks kept him in his seat.

All of them nearly stormed out of the GCS when the flight's operational commander, CIA Assistant Counter-Terrorism Director Karl Berg, gave them the final coordinates of the Predator's "bullpen." The holding area was located 535 miles into Kazakhstan airspace. In another 30 to 40 miles, "Crabby Girl," named affectionately in honor of Salazar's opinionated six-year-old daughter, would cross its Point of No Return.

The drone had a maximum range of 675 miles and needed to return to base shortly if it were to be landed safely. Clearly, this was not part of the CIA's plan. Now they'd be the "crew" that lost a Predator drone. None of them needed this kind of shit, but they didn't have the authority to abandon the mission. The door to the GCS was sealed, and Berg had been given legitimate command over the mission by their superiors. They all settled in for the steaming shit sandwich they had been served, which only seemed to get tastier every time Berg's voice came over the secure communications link.

"Do we even know who we're firing at?" Tech Sergeant Salazar said.

"It doesn't matter," McIntyre replied, adjusting the laser designator's screen resolution.

She wouldn't have a lot of time to acquire the best target cluster to help the friendly ground unit, so she opened the aperture for the multi-spectral targeting system. This would give her a wide view when the Predator reached the apex of Hesselman's climb and started to descend.

"Exactly," Hesselman said, "the friendly unit is under fire. We're under orders to provide them with close air support. Here we go, coming out of the climb…and, three, two, one…over the top."

McIntyre studied the screen and immediately switched to thermal imaging, once she had positively identified and marked the friendlies. Any other thermal signatures were valid targets. She just hoped the firefight had cleared the village of any remaining innocent bystanders.

❧

Daniel risked a glance at the western village and saw several slightly exposed targets. With well-aimed shots from his rifle, he knew he could hit them. Unfortunately, the incoming rifle fire had become extremely accurate, preventing him from raising his AK-74 above road level to fire anything more than a hastily aimed burst. He hunkered back down along with the rest of the team. Even Farrington wouldn't risk more than a quick shot. They had lost what little initiative they had managed to muster in the face of a sudden ambush and had stalled out along the road, unable to press forward without certain catastrophic casualties. Daniel had started to reconsider the marking grenade option, when a shattering explosion rattled the ground and sent a shock wave over the road.

"Something big hit them…let's go!" Farrington yelled and wasted no time starting to sprint toward the structures directly ahead of them.

A second massive explosion rocked the outskirts of the western village, just as Daniel started to sprint with the rest of his team. Amazingly, Dusty managed to sprint past him before they closed half the distance to their destination. The volume of incoming fire dropped to nothing as they expended all of their remaining energy and lung capacity reserves to reach the concrete structures.

By the time Daniel's shoulder slammed against the closest wall, Farrington and Sergei had started firing single, well aimed shots through the red dot sights on their assault rifles. They quickly spread out through the cluster of crudely built, Soviet style bungalows. Leo had bent over one of the dead attackers that Daniel had killed minutes earlier.

Daniel slid along the wall to Farrington's crouched figure and swung his rifle around the same corner, staying upright. Their attackers had rallied quickly after the massive explosions, and there was no time to scan the sky for their air support. It didn't matter anyway, since they all knew that the Predator only carried two missiles. Still, if they could get in touch with the operator, they might be able to get some live intelligence about the attacking force. They were in much better shape now that they had reached the cover of these buildings, but they were far from being out of the woods.

Daniel spotted a target issuing hand signal orders and placed the illuminated red arrow tip at the base of the man's face. He pulled the trigger twice and saw the rust colored mist fill the air behind the man. He rapidly sighted in on another exposed soldier several feet to the left of the fallen squad leader. Before the soldier could react to the gruesome death that had just transpired a few feet away, Daniel fired again, hitting him center of mass and sending him sprawling into the dirt. The next target he found through his ACOG scope took multiple hits to the upper torso before Daniel could squeeze off a shot.

"Quit hogging shots," Daniel said, as a half-dozen bullets slammed into the concrete corner, spraying them with sharp fragments.

"Quit running your suck hole and keep shooting," Farrington replied, without the slightest hint of comedy.

He sighted along the low wall that had housed several shooters before the Hellfire missile impact and found the top of a head several meters down from the smoldering gap caused by a single AGM-114 Hellfire. The head stayed low, bobbing slowly back and forth…barely visible through Daniel's scope. He took a deep breath and exhaled, steadying the scope's red targeting arrow just a hair above the head. He didn't consciously squeeze the trigger. His right index finger had instinctively and uniformly removed nearly all of the trigger's pressure as the red arrow floated where Daniel thought he should take the shot. He never registered the command to continue squeezing the trigger, it just happened as naturally as taking a breath. The 5.45mm bullet took less than a tenth of a second to cross the gap and missed the top of the wall by less than a half-inch, reaching the man's head unhindered. He saw the head rise quickly and drop out of view.

"Nice shot. That fucker's been driving me crazy," Farrington said.

"More than welcome. Keep an eye on the situation. I need to figure out what the fuck is going on around here," he said and took off for Leo, who had nearly stripped the corpse naked looking for signs or clues to indicate what they were facing.

Daniel made sure they were not exposed to any obvious enemy fire and kneeled down next to Leo.

"What do we have?"

"Russians. Standard special forces comm set. Hidden harness with spare magazines, frag grenades, pistol…silencer. My best guess is regional Spetsnaz. Border response team maybe. Something like our Rangers. Probably assigned to the Western Siberian Military District based out of Novosibirsk a few hundred miles from here. Why would the Russians put a reinforced platoon of special forces guys on our asses?"

"That's another million dollar question. Anything else you can tell me?"

"Not really, though I'd like to know how they got here. By my rough estimate, we're looking at thirty plus guys…"

"Hold on, Leo…fuck, do you hear that?"

Amidst the sharp reports of sporadic rifle fire, Daniel heard a deep rhythmic sound that made him shudder. He grabbed the bloodied pair of binoculars next to the dead Russian and wiped the lenses enough to see through the red smeared glass. Scanning the horizon, east to north, he spotted them almost due north. Three helicopters coming in low.

"Motherfucker! Grab an RPG if you can find one and take cover," he said and ran toward Dusty, who sat against the same wall next to Farrington, holding the satellite phone with a grin on his face.

"What is it?" Leo yelled at him as he ran.

"Helicopters!" he said, without looking back.

"Are you fucking kidding me? Shit," Leo said and started scrambling toward more of the dead bodies.

Petrovich reached Dusty, whose grin had faded at Daniel's single word.

"Is that Berg?"

"Yeah…they had some technical difficulties. He—"

Daniel swiped the phone from his hands. "Nice to finally hear your voice."

"Look, you have no idea what I've gone through to put that drone over your head, and from what I can tell—"

"I'll thank you later…right now we have a bigger problem. I have three helicopters headed my way. We were hit by Russians, so I assume this is their ride back over the border."

The satellite phone fell silent for several seconds, and Daniel raised the binoculars to examine the three ugly objects growing on the northern horizon, racing toward the village at 150 miles per hour.

"You still there? Or are we experiencing technical difficulties again?" Daniel said, shifting his gaze to Farrington. "Rich, we need to get across the street and find some RPGs. Mix in a little closer with their ground forces and make it hard for those helicopters to engage. What do we have left over there?" he said, with the satellite phone still jammed to his ear.

"Five or six guys. Maybe a few more. Dug in pretty well. They're not going anywhere," Farrington said and snapped off three shots.

"Scratch one more," Farrington added.

"Berg! You there? Fuck, this guy is killing me."

Berg's voice came back through the phone.

"Daniel, the Predator drone has no remaining ordnance. They can remain on station to—"

"Watch us get killed? What do we have coming our way? They're coming in too low for me to get an ID," Daniel replied.

Leo came into view around the corner of one of the houses with an RPG launcher and a backpack containing three shaped charge warheads. Farrington watched the remaining Spetsnaz troops and the open roadway through the village to ensure there would be no surprises from that direction.

"We're in business!" Leo yelled, and Daniel gave him a "thumbs up," anxiously waiting for Berg's reply.

"Predator control has two 'Hip' Mi-8 transport helicopters…and one Havoc Mi-28 attack helicopter," Berg continued, his voice trailing off with the sound of dread.

"Say again, last helicopter type," returned Daniel, reverting to formal military communications protocol.

"Mi-28 Havoc. One minute outbound…hold on, Daniel, I still might be able to help you out. I need to work on something…"

Petrovich threw the phone back at Dusty, who looked despondent, as the deep, ominous pounding sounds of heavy rotor blades grew louder.

"Stay close to me and put that phone in my ear the second he comes back on the line," he said, then turned to the rest of the team assembled behind the building.

"We need to get as close to their perimeter as possible. We have a Havoc inbound…no time for a plan. Move fast, shoot, use grenades. Don't drop the RPG," he said and smiled at Leo.

"Yeah, fuck you too," Leo responded with a grin, and they sprinted across the street.

⁂

Technical Sergeant Juan Salazar listened to Karl Berg's voice over the secure communications speaker while shaking his head slowly. He made eye contact with Staff Sergeant Kelly McIntyre and half mouthed-half whispered to her.

"No. No. This is fucking out of control."

McIntyre watched her screens intently, simultaneously zooming in on the three helicopters and the "friendlies" now dashing across the road.

"Friendlies just repositioned to western side of the village," she added to the conversation between Major Adler and Berg.

"Mr. Berg, with all due respect, you better have our asses covered on this," Hesselman said.

"Major, no need to hide something that never happened…and let me reiterate for everyone at your station. This never fucking happened. Get this done, Major. They're running out of time."

Major Hesselman moved the joystick left until his camera view showed three helicopters in formation, moving south down the road toward Kaynar. He increased the throttle setting, and the Predator drone accelerated into a dive exceeding the unmanned vehicle's advertised maximum speed of 135 miles per hour.

"I can't believe we're doing this," Salazar muttered.

Kelly McIntyre stared at her main screen with utter amazement as the "Havoc" filled the grainy scene on the monitor. No matter how fast she zoomed out, the Russian helicopter continued to grow until the screen went dead.

"Scratch one Havoc Mi-28 attack helicopter," she said and glanced at Salazar, who looked at her like a disapproving mother, with folded arms and a slowly shaking head.

❧

The first salvo of 30mm cannon fire from the Havoc tore through the buildings they had just passed like paper. Unfortunately, their CIA liaison chose to invest in the deceptive safety of the first building that they encountered after crossing the open road. Daniel had reached out to pull him along, but the terrified agent crouched solidly against the concrete wall. Petrovich had no intention of slowing down long enough to try and physically dislodge him. Just as Petrovich cleared the structure, the house exploded from the near simultaneous impact of several dozen high velocity projectiles, and Dusty disappeared in the maelstrom of concrete chunks and wooden splinters.

Another burst of cannon fire tore into a house ahead of the team, shattering the structure and indicating to him that the Havoc gunner had temporarily lost track of them. They were split between two closely bunched houses, in groups of two. Leo and Farrington were a few houses ahead, loading the RPG. He knew there was little hope of taking this helicopter down. He figured it was a few hundred yards away, well out of reliable RPG range. The Havoc's targeting system rivaled the U.S. Army's AH-64 Apaches, and their little game of hide and seek in the village wouldn't last much longer.

Even if Leo managed to miraculously land a clean shot with the RPG, Petrovich wasn't convinced the rocket would have any effect. The Havoc was heavily armored like the Apache, a virtual warhorse in the sky. Their only hope was to hide close to the Spetsnaz and pray the Havoc crew didn't use rockets. He wasn't very hopeful. With the 30mm cannon providing suppressive fire, they couldn't effectively keep the Spetsnaz in place, and without the Spetsnaz nearby...they'd be rocket fodder. He raised his right hand and delivered a potentially suicidal hand signal to Farrington.

A devastating explosion filled Daniel's ears, and for a split second, he thought the Havoc crew had fired a salvo of 127mm rockets. Instinctively, they all flattened against the ground, but when the rockets didn't instantly tear through any of the structures around them, they executed Daniel's silent order. All of them burst forward from their cover, sprinting between houses in the direction of the massive detonation.

When Petrovich rounded the corner, he grinned wickedly as the burning Havoc banked sharply left and plummeted rapidly out of sight. Before he could visually reacquire the mortally damaged attack helicopter, a second, larger explosion sent another shockwave through the village, momentarily heating the cold Siberian air and sending burning metal fragments deep amidst the buildings. No one in Daniel's team said a word, as they raced to find new firing positions to engage whatever might be left of the Russian force.

Upon reaching the northernmost house several seconds later, he saw two flaming metal wrecks twisted together on a flat area of land barely fifty meters from the edge of the village. The out of control Havoc apparently veered directly into the Mi-8 transport helicopter that had landed to extract the remaining Russian ground forces, exploding both fuel tanks.

The second Mi-8 helicopter hovered where the Havoc had been moments ago, fighting the sudden air flow instability caused by the drastic temperature fluctuations radiated from the conflagration of aviation fuel to its immediate right. Leo wasted no time pushing Daniel out of the way and leaned against the house to steady the RPG launcher. He took a few seconds to gauge the distance to the wavering helicopter and fired the rocket without warning. The rocket's explosive booster charge caused a crunching overpressure among the group, bathing them in a toxic cloud of grayish dust dislodged from the ground.

Petrovich saw the rocket motor engage and propel the 93mm warhead toward the Mi-8's cockpit. The helicopter spun at the last moment possible, causing the rocket to miss the cockpit and detonate against the rear cargo hatch area. His team immediately retreated behind the two closest houses and reloaded the RPG, unsure if the Mi-8's pilot would commence a gun run against them. Though the helicopter didn't carry anything as sophisticated as the 30mm "chain gun" found on the Havoc, nobody on the team wanted to stick around to test the skills of a Special Operations helicopter pilot.

He heard the heavy whining sound of turbo-shaft engines and risked a look at the helicopter. He saw the Mi-8 headed due north at high speed, trailing thick black smoke over the road. When the helicopter passed their own smoking SUV and didn't alter course, he knew they were safe for the moment.

"It's headed north. Nice shot," he said and something caught his immediate attention.

Four Spetsnaz soldiers crouched in the open, watching the helicopter abandon them. Daniel raised his rifle and dropped one of them with a headshot. The remaining three commandos raised their hands as the four Black Flag operatives rapidly fanned out to approach them.

"I want solid intel out of these guys. Kill one if you need to motivate them to talk. I need to see if the satellite phone still works," he said.

Daniel sprinted back through the village and found the wrecked mess of concrete chunks and wooden pylons that served as Dusty's ill-conceived cover from 30mm cannon fire. The repeated bursts had leveled the house, and he struggled to tear the debris clear of a boot that he spotted in the monochromatic heap of shoddy building materials. He lifted a sizable chunk of concrete off the boot, exposing the top of the shin, which was no longer connected to a body. Sheared off below the knee, a jagged piece of bone protruded from the dust caked end of the outer limb. He didn't look forward to digging through the rest of this pile.

A single gunshot echoed through the village, and Daniel wondered exactly how long Farrington had tried to get information before blowing one of their heads off. It really didn't matter, none of those soldiers would leave here alive, and his team needed to be back on the road immediately, though he wasn't sure what they would use for transportation. He kept digging through the rubble, finding a severed hand and what looked like intestines. The phone suddenly rang, and Daniel realized it sat ten feet away near the road. Dusty's last act must have been to toss the phone out of the carnage exploding around him.

He jogged to the phone, and pressed "receive."

"Did my little gift arrive?" the familiar voice said.

"I can't imagine anyone will be happy about losing that drone," Daniel replied.

"A simple thank you would suffice."

"I'll thank you over coffee, once you get us the fuck out of here."

"The Predator control team said there were a few vehicles located at the southernmost point of the village. Most, if not all of Kaynar's inhabitants appear to be herded into an area west of the village, in a depression over a small rise. One hundred plus bodies. They had full thermal signatures, and control saw plenty of movement among the group. It looks like they're all alive," Berg said.

"I don't think the Russians had enough time to properly dispose of the villagers, and I'm pretty sure they didn't expect us to survive the IED blast. The helicopters didn't approach in any sort of attack formation. I think they cruised in low to pick up the Spetsnaz, operating under strict radio silence. It's the only explanation."

"What happened to the helicopters?"

"The Havoc crashed into one of the transport helicopters thanks to your Kamikaze drone. We hit the other with an RPG, and it hauled ass back to Russia. This is fucked, Karl. Something doesn't add up here."

"The picture is still developing, but we might have another lead and a possible explanation for the Russian response. I need to send your team north of St. Petersburg to investigate some bizarre rumors that our signals intelligence team has processed. Nearly the entire Kola Peninsula has gone dark, and we've detected a massive military deployment to the area. Nothing can get through the highway running between Murmansk and Kandalaksha. Russian military has it shut down tight. The only major city along that route is an industrial dump called Monchegorsk, and there might be a link. We have nobody on the ground in the vicinity, and your team has the special talents needed to find a way in."

"Sounds like fun. I assume Sanderson has signed off on this one too?"

"You can give him a call. We've already spoken. You need to get the hell out of there before the Russians decide to carpet bomb that town. Based on this new information and the fact that they have a small army dead within Kazakhstan borders, I wouldn't make any long term investments into the future of Kaynar."

"We'll grab a vehicle and continue to Astana. Can you run any diplomatic interference if we are picked up by Kazakh forces?"

"Negative. You need to reach the airport terminal as originally planned. A U.S. military transport will start moving you toward your next destination. I need to work on an infiltration plan and equipment drop for your team, so if you don't mind, I'm going to let you go. Bring Mr. Bremer with you on the plane. He's compromised in Kazakhstan."

"Dusty didn't make it. Neither did Andrei."

"Shit," he said and paused, "stuff their bodies in the trunk of whatever you find. I'll have someone take care of it from the airport. How bad are the bodies?"

"We'll have to bag up Dusty. He did pretty well under the circumstances," Daniel said.

Two more rifle shots filled the air, causing Daniel to look around.

"We're on the move. I'll call once we're on the road." The Black Flag operatives appeared between two of the buildings, jogging toward Daniel. Farrington shook his head as they approached.

"They didn't know anything useful. They were roused from their barracks and loaded onto the helicopters for an anti-terrorist operation. What happened to Dusty?"

"Dead. We need to bag up as much of him as possible," Petrovich said.

"With what? The truck is gone," Sergei said, pointing at the burning metal hulk down the road.

"He looks like the rest of them. We don't have time to fuck around with this," Farrington said.

"Fine, but we need to bring Andrei with us or throw his corpse in with the rest of them," Daniel countered.

"We toss both of them in one of the fires. Last thing we need on the road is a corpse in the trunk," Farrington said, and they all nodded in agreement.

"Ditch the rifles. Pistols only from this point forward. We need to reach Astana and put this as far behind us as possible. Berg says we'll find vehicles at the southern edge of the village...and since you learned the finer skills of hotwiring cars, the honor is all yours," he said and slapped Farrington on the back.

"Does Berg have any idea why the Russians would take this kind of risk to kill us?" Leo asked.

"He's sending us up near Murmansk to investigate a possible link and explanation. If he knows, he didn't feel like sharing. Let's get moving," Daniel said.

He tasked Leo and Sergei to move Andrei's body to the burning wreckage while he dug around for Dusty's body parts.

Chapter Twenty-Six

7:25 PM
CIA Headquarters
Langley, Virginia

Karl Berg closed the communications circuit with U.S. Air Force Special Operations Command and took a deep breath, exhaling slowly through his nose. A fairly routine, straightforward operation had just gone sideways on him. He leaned back in the plush black leather chair and stared at the ceiling for a few seconds. He had several phone calls to make, and none of the recipients would be pleased to hear from him. His first call had to be Bauer. He could use the operation center's phones for that one. The others would have to be made on one or two of his "burner" cell phones. He had no idea what he was going to tell Bauer, but he suspected that Bauer would be prepared for this. He'd called her about four hours ago to let her know that the drone was airborne. She concurred with his decision to launch, especially based on the Monchegorsk information.

The Russians had sealed Highway M18 at points several miles north and south of the city, effectively cutting off access to Monchegorsk. The roadblocks had also sealed off Olenegorsk, a small town ten miles to the north. Intelligence assets from Murmansk had managed to interview members of several families that escaped Olenegorsk just before Russian Federation Army units arrived. All of them relayed stories of sickness and mayhem in Monchegorsk. Although none of them had seen it firsthand, reports of a violent army crackdown had been enough to send them fleeing in the direction of the regional capital, Murmansk. So far as they could tell, the sickness hadn't spread through Olenegorsk, though the hospital had been filled with patients from its sister city. Strange stories of violent, uncontrollable behavior in these patients sealed the deal and sent them driving in the middle of the night toward Murmansk, against an endless stream of Russian Federation Army vehicles.

The coincidence was too strong for either of them to ignore. Reznikov had poisoned the city somehow and was still at large. The presence of three dead Al Qaeda agents on a side road in Kazakhstan fit the pattern. Reznikov had apparently escaped the crematorium flames that consumed the rest of his laboratory staff and targeted his hometown for the debut release of his designer virus. Berg would send Sanderson's team to Monchegorsk to assess the full scope of the virus's potential. They would have to build a rock solid case against Reznikov before Audra brought this up the chain of command. Berg dialed Bauer's cell phone, which rang for longer than expected. He was about to hang up, when she answered.

"Sorry about that. I'm still in a meeting here. Good news? Aside from the fact that I'm going to have to explain the temporary loss of an armed Predator drone? I have a retrieval team on standby."

"Audra, retrieval is no longer an option. The team was ambushed by a reinforced Spetznaz platoon outside of Kaynar," Berg said.

"Jesus. How bad?"

"Do you want the good news or the bad news?"

"Skip the games, Karl," she said.

"The Predator drone launched both Hellfire missiles at ground targets, then crashed into a Russian attack helicopter."

"Crashed?"

"I ordered the flight crew to crash the drone into the attack helicopter. Two of the Russian helicopters were destroyed by the impact," he said.

"How many helicopters did the Russians send?"

"Three. One Mi-28 Havoc, and two transport helos," he answered.

"So, right now I'm looking at a Predator drone crashed among two burning Russian helicopters?"

"There was no other way. The Havoc was cutting our team to pieces," he said, anticipating Bauer's fury.

"I'm not suggesting there was. I trust your judgment. Please tell me that our team escaped?"

"Four of them. Our CIA liaison is dead, along with one of Sanderson's crew. The good news is that they still have the samples. I'm connecting them with someone from our embassy in Astana, so we can transfer the samples in an emergency diplomatic package. I'd like to have it in a friendly lab within twelve hours."

"I'd like it there sooner than that, but I think our best option is to get the samples back to the States. We don't have any facilities in Europe that we control."

"We're looking at twenty-four hours if we fly it back here," Berg said.

"I should be able to get it here faster on a priority Gulfstream charter. I'll contact the embassy in Astana and arrange for the samples to be transported directly to the Edgewood Chemical Biological Center. This will cost a fortune, but I can't keep the Predator thing quiet for very long. We have to prepare a response, and the White House will need to be notified at some point very soon. I'd like to have those samples analyzed by the time I have to walk this down the hall. Any further word on Monchegorsk?"

"Nothing new. I'm sending Sanderson's team up there to conduct reconnaissance. We might as well keep their momentum rolling. I'll fly them into Helsinki and figure out how to get them into Russia. They'll probably have to approach on snowmobiles. Monchegorsk is roughly 150 miles from the Finnish border, so it won't be a difficult trip."

"All right, I'll activate the necessary protocols with our people in Finland. They'll get full support on the ground there," she said, "unless I get shut down here."

"I don't think we'll hear a word from the Russians. They lost two helicopters and possibly a full platoon of Spetznaz soldiers on Kazakh soil. They won't be interested in drawing any attention to that problem. With any luck, the remaining pieces of the Predator are burned beyond recognition in the helicopter wreckage. Our most immediate problem is that they know someone else is looking for Reznikov. Our team will need to be careful, and so will we. They'll be actively scanning the ground and air for information."

"Well, there won't be much for them to pick up. Since this is still in my pocket, there isn't much electronic chatter out there. They'll be in the dark for a while, unless they identify Sanderson's team. I hope they were discreet getting into Astana."

"They were, but I need to get them out of there on the next flight, and I would be surprised if they weren't identified upon departure. Kazakhstan is crawling with Russians."

Bauer muffled a laugh, which made Berg feel more comfortable. He had never seen this side of Audra, though he had heard rumors. There was a reason that she sat in the deputy director's seat.

"Here's what we need to do. Start looking for Reznikov. While the team works Monchegorsk, we need to find this guy. He may be our only link to the Al Qaeda network that hired him, or he might have stiffed them and taken all of the virus. The three dead bodies back at the lab give me some hope," she said.

"And if not?"

"Then we can't keep this quiet much longer. If the terrorist network figures out that Reznikov released the virus, they might get panicky and pull the trigger a lot earlier than anyone anticipates."

"That's what I was thinking. I'll get this rolling. I may ask Sanderson to activate some of his European assets to augment the current team if we get a lead on Reznikov," he said.

"Doesn't cost us anything at the moment, so go ahead. Look, I have to get back into this meeting. I'll keep this phone immediately accessible all night. Don't hesitate," she said.

"You know I won't," he said and hung up the phone.

It was still too early in Moscow to make the call he desperately needed to place.

Chapter Twenty-Seven

7:40 PM
The Jacksons' Residence
Fredericksburg, Virginia

Darryl Jackson had just brought the perfectly tenderized and sautéed steak tip to his eagerly awaiting mouth when one of the cell phones on the kitchen island started to play Darth Vader's "Imperial March" theme. He looked over at his wife, who raised an eyebrow and almost imperceptibly shook her head. He placed the fork back down on his plate, into the reduction sauce, and excused himself from the table.

"Shall I pack you a small bag? Toiletries, underwear…maybe some cigarettes you can trade with the other prisoners?"

"Very funny, Cheryl. Probably nothing. This shit's off my reservation, so I'm not worried."

"You look worried," she said and took a bite of her own steak.

Jackson mumbled the entire way to the kitchen, still looking back at his wife. He didn't need to glance at the caller ID. Darth Vader's theme had been chosen specifically for his friend, Karl Berg.

"Good evening, Karl. I was just enjoying a wonderful dinner of steak tips with a red wine reduction sauce, rosemary garlic mashed potatoes and my wife's legendary spicy green beans. Brevity would be appreciated," he said.

"Oooh…the green beans? I haven't had those in ages. Tell her I'll bring a rare Bordeaux if she invites me over. Cheryl's cooking is to die for. Sounds like a celebration. Did I miss an occasion?"

"Not really. We're just celebrating my two year anniversary of not going to jail on your account, so you can stop with the lube job. I wasn't expecting to hear from you for another three to four hours, so this sounds like it could be my last supper," Jackson said, walking into his den.

"It's not that bad," Berg said.

"I'll be the judge of that. What the fuck happened this time?"

"Let's just say that your group in Astana won't be getting their weapons or night vision gear back. My team was ambushed, and their truck was destroyed. They ditched everything at the ambush site," Berg said.

"What? Goddamn it, Karl. Those weapons are traceable back to Brown River. The magical arms dealer fairy didn't fucking wave her magic wand and make that shit appear at their compound. It's all categorized and licensed with the Kazakh government. The CIA better be hiring middle-aged African Americans with no foreign language skills," he said.

"The weapons won't be traced back to Brown River. My team was hit by a platoon of Russians using similar weapons. They threw them into the burning wreckage of one of the helicopters that was shot down. There are thirty or forty AK's scattered among the dead Russians. Nobody will be comparing rifle serial numbers."

"Jesus H...helicopters? I don't want to know. Sounds like you're in over your head over there."

"Still treading water. I'm sorry about the weapons and the hassle you'll go through explaining their loss, but they couldn't risk travelling with them anymore."

"No big deal. Pain in the ass, but I had expected worse," Jackson said.

"From me? That hurts my feelings."

"You don't have any feelings," he said, and they both laughed.

"But I have a soft spot for you...actually it's your wife's cooking. I guess this will put off my invitation for another year or so?"

"Another year? Shit, you're still serving time for the last disaster. Thanks for the heads up, Karl. I have to get back to the table, or you won't be the only person she won't invite to the dinner table."

"Sorry to interrupt. Talk to you later."

"Look forward to it...I suppose."

Daryl closed the phone, walked back into the dining room, and sat down to a sardonic look on his wife's face.

"I don't know why you still take risks for that guy. He almost sent you to jail two years ago," Cheryl said.

"He saved my life, honey. I'll never be able to repay him for that. Karl's a good man, better than most I've ever met. He didn't have to help me in Afghanistan, but he was the only man in a room full of spooks that couldn't watch us die. Can you imagine that? One man…I'm just glad he was in charge of the Predator flight, or we would have all died that day. He's worth a little heat. To see you and the kids again? Well worth it."

"I understand, hon. Let's just try and keep you out of federal prison so you can spend the time productively."

He nodded and smiled, staring into her deep brown eyes. He wasn't worried about going to jail as much as he was worried about losing his high-paying job and the ability to continue funding his two daughters' private college educations. Unfortunately, much of the kids' reserve college fund had been trickled to an overseas contact in order to pay back the sudden loan needed to clean up Berg's debacle two years ago. In the grand scheme of things, it was a small sacrifice to be sitting at this table, with the woman he had loved for nearly thirty years.

Chapter Twenty-Eight

6:40 AM
FSB (Federal Security Services of the Russian Federation) Headquarters
Lubyanka Square, Moscow

Alexei Kaparov smashed his fourth cigarette of the morning into the impossibly full ashtray on his desk and dumped the precariously balanced contents into the dented gray trash bin to the right of his desk. The bin was emptied every evening, by someone eager to prevent another trash bin fire caused by his hastily extinguished Troikas. On the day that one of the fires spread to the paperwork on his desk, nearly engulfing the entire desktop in flames, his staff decided to empty the over-stuffed incendiary pile themselves. Kaparov chuckled at the pile of ashes and cigarette butts in the empty can. For two years he couldn't get the cleaning staff to empty the can on a regular basis. He had to nearly burn the building down to get it done. He started to wonder what he might need to do to have hot coffee waiting for him in the morning.

He lit another cigarette and returned his attention to the emails he had been following. Something was going on, but he couldn't put his finger on it. He was slowly being removed from the loop regarding Reznikov, relegated to providing background information and further field data analysis. In reality, this was his section's job, but Kaparov didn't like being marginalized in cases that directly involved possible WMD threats, and this one had the potential to be the biggest in years. The search for Reznikov was in different hands, but as the deputy director for Biological and Chemical Weapons of Mass Destruction, he needed to be directly involved with the case.

Lab results from samples taken at the Kazakhstan site had not arrived at his desk, and all of his attempts to secure the results had met with stalling. Kaparov was an expert in the field of withholding information and knew better than anyone when he was on the receiving end of these tactics. The fact that the findings were being actively withheld from him was an ominous development.

At least he wasn't the only one falling out of the loop. Information regarding Monchegorsk had also slowed to a trickle at every level. Reports had hit his section's desk with a fury the other day, triggered by every search parameter his analysts had programmed into the system. An infectious outbreak resembling a pandemic flu had filled Monchegorsk's hospital within the span of a day. Follow-on reports suggested strange symptoms, involving uncontrollable patients and citywide violence.

Patients had been sent to Murmansk for further testing, and within forty-eight hours, the roads leading out of Monchegorsk were secured. Only military traffic travelled into or out of the city. He had hand delivered his assessment to the director of Counter-Terrorism, which included the high likelihood of a link to Reznikov's recent activities. Since this delivery, information regarding the situation in Monchegorsk had become scarce for everyone. Now there was a new development.

Kaparov arrived at work early by most FSB agents' standards, but this morning he found parking to be an unusual challenge. His reserved place in the garage had been occupied, forcing him to drive to a space far from the entrance door. A minor inconvenience, but the significance hadn't been lost on him. He recognized many of the cars crowded into the coveted parking spaces. FSB Special Operations Division (SOD). He had placed his bare hands on a few of the car hoods and found them to be cold. Something important had dragged over twenty SOD personnel into headquarters in the middle of the night.

He had walked directly to their operations center, but had been politely turned away upon exiting the elevator. This wasn't unusual, but confirmed that a live operation was underway. He could only assume that it was related to Reznikov, but wouldn't be able to confirm it until the operation ended, when a sea of loose lips spilled out into the rest of the building. He had several good friends in the Special Operations Division and would find out soon enough, unless it was a Vympel or Alpha Group operation. If that was the case, he might have to rely on Prerovsky's female liaison. She had already provided more information than either of them had expected, and Kaparov was more than happy to fund another night on the town for Prerovsky and his lady friend.

His desk phone erupted, breaking the silence, and he glanced at his watch. 6:45. A little early for phone calls. He considered letting it go to voicemail. It certainly wasn't a courtesy call from the Special Operations Division with an update on their operation. He stared at the phone for a few more seconds and picked up the receiver out of curiosity.

"Deputy Director Kaparov."

"Alexei Kaparov. I can't believe you've lasted this long. I expected one of those ambitious youngsters to have taken your job by now," said the familiar voice in passable, academic Russian.

"The younger generation doesn't have what it takes to topple someone like me or you. Field work today doesn't build the same steely resilience. Sounds like you and I must have done something wrong back in Berlin. We're both chasing the same thing these days," Kaparov said.

"It wasn't what I did wrong back then. I think we both played the game pretty well."

"Indeed we did. To what do I owe the honor of a call from an old friend? I must admit that I find your timing a bit…shall we say, coincidental?"

"I didn't think you were a big believer in coincidences, Alexei."

"I'm not, but the new generation is softer, and I've already been to sensitivity training twice this year."

"Do you have time to talk to an old friend?" Karl said.

"Leave me a number and I'll call you in about ten minutes. I could use some fresh air," he said.

"You're not still smoking those horrible cigarettes?"

"Hey, I've cut down to two packs a day and I'm now considered a style icon. Troika cigarettes are all the rage now. All part of our nation's identity crisis. The youth are reaching back to their communist roots and embracing the worst cigarettes ever produced by mother Russia."

"Let's hope they don't reach too far back," Berg said.

"I'm not too worried. They don't have the stomach for those times. I'll call you when I'm out of here," he said and shuffled to the door to grab his warm wool overcoat.

Ten minutes later he strode across Lubyanka square, fighting a stiff, frigid wind to light another Troika. The wind was no match for the veteran smoker, and he thrust his bare hands back into the warm fur lining of his coat. The temperature had barely crested above freezing this morning, which was unseasonably cold for late April. Kaparov smoked about half of the cigarette, walking the outer edge of the square, gathering his thoughts. Finally, he called his former Cold War adversary, who answered on the first ring.

"So, why are you so eager to call me? It must be late there?" Kaparov said.

"I was hoping you could tell me. It sounds like the FSB or SVR is looking for someone important in the vicinity of Kazakhstan and possibly Monchegorsk," Berg said.

"It sounds like you are very well informed, as always. Unfortunately, I don't have much to add," Kaparov said.

"Won't add, or can't add?" Berg said.

"Neither. I assume we've come to the same conclusions about the 'someone important' you mentioned and his link to Monchegorsk?"

"And the lab site outside of Kurchatov?" Berg said.

"My God, you are well informed. What do you know about the site?"

"Enough to know that Monchegorsk might burn to the ground…if it's not bombed first."

Kaparov stared back at the Lubyanka Building and took a few seconds to process Berg's words.

"You still there, my friend?"

"I am. I am. Something big happened this morning. The lot was full when I arrived."

"What time did you arrive?"

"About six…"

"This morning? You just arrived? Alexei, don't fuck around with me. Do you know what happened in Kazakhstan today?"

Kaparov didn't want to admit that he was out of the loop on the Reznikov case, but he sensed something important in Berg's tone. They had played a brilliant cat and mouse game for three years in Berlin, then two more in Moscow before Berg vanished overnight. After spending five years scrutinizing Berg as a Cold War adversary, he could read the slightest change in tone or facial expression. Right now, Berg sounded truly surprised that he might be in the dark on Kazakhstan.

"Embarrassingly, I've been cut out of the loop, and this is what worries me the most. Tell me about Kazakhstan," Kaparov said.

"A small reconnaissance team of mine ran into a reinforced platoon of Russian Spetznaz in a small village called Kaynar…and a few helicopters. Kaynar is well over one hundred and fifty miles from the Kazakh-Russian border."

"What is the American reaction to the attack?" he said, sensing an impending international disaster.

"None. I'm running this off the books for now, and most of my team survived. Your side is looking at thirty-plus KIA and two downed helicopters. One of them was a Havoc."

"This isn't a joke or some kind of a trick? You've confirmed this?"

"I watched it happen on a live feed. I'm concerned, Alexei. If they're marginalizing you at this point, then we both know where this is headed."

"Straight under the rug," Kaparov added.

"The link back to Russia goes under the rug, and an unknown quantity of virus gets delivered to the United States and Europe, compliments of our radical friends in the Middle East."

"Karl, my hands are tied here right now, but I may be able to push my way back in. I can't threaten exposure or I'll end up in the Moscow River."

"You have to muscle your way back in somehow."

"It won't matter either way. Even if they let me in, I won't have any influence. This will be a joint investigation, involving assets that nobody cares to admit still exist."

"My team is still working this. If your people find Reznikov, it sounds like they'll kill him on the spot. I want a fighting chance to grab him first," Berg said.

"I'm sure they will. Let me put some thought into this. I have a very dangerous idea forming," Kaparov said.

"I like the sound of that. In the meantime, I'll keep you posted on my team's progress. If we work together, we can accomplish both countries' goals and avoid a nightmare. Do you know what type of virus we're up against?"

"Well, you and I have previously discussed what he tried to steal from the lab several years ago," Kaparov said.

"Partially weaponized encephalitis samples?"

"Hmm. Partially," he mumbled, not willing to say everything he had heard recently.

"What am I missing, Alexei?"

"Have you ever heard of the Lithuanian film director Jurgis Meras?"

"No. Dare I ask how this is related?"

"On November 3rd, 1969, Jurgis Meras was found in a park on the outskirts of Vilnius, with his throat slit from ear to ear. He lived with his parents, who disappeared that same night, leaving a ransacked apartment behind. Meras was a popular underground director, who didn't waste his talents producing seditious material like too many others. He stayed off mother Russia's radar for the most part. In early October of '69, one of his films became wildly popular in Vilnius, attracting the wrong kind of attention. According to my sources, the film was named "Ghouls of Vilnius" and it depicted a zombie outbreak. Not surprisingly, Meras was a big fan of American movies and had a sizeable collection of American film magazines to prove it."

"Alexei, I'm sort of following you on this, but I need you to get to the point."

"A lot of people connected to Meras vanished without a trace over the next few days, from Lithuania to Moscow, and it was no secret that the KGB had a hand in it."

"I'm sure he wasn't killed because he violated international copyright laws..."

"Of course not, but word of the movie had spread farther and wider than anyone had expected, and it obviously made somebody very nervous. These were some of the most paranoid times in our history, and our nation's bioweapons program was in full swing.

"Do you know what scientists at VECTOR informally called the weaponized encephalitis virus? Zoja. Zoja is the Russian phonetic military equivalent of your Zulu. I think we are looking at a virus that targets the temporal lobe and causes a rabies-like aggressive behavior. Meras's zombie hit a little too close to home in the Kremlin and triggered a violent response from Lubyanka Square. I'm afraid the government is preparing to do the same with the entire city of Monchegorsk. The initial hospital reports out of Monchegorsk are consistent with this. Starts with a fever and flu-like symptoms, and as the disease destroys the temporal lobe, unpredictable violent behavior ensues. This was the hallmark of certain encephalitis cases."

"This is worse than I imagined. If Al Qaeda is sitting on a stockpile of this stuff, we are all in deep shit, my friend."

"I agree. Unfortunately, I have no eyes on the ground in Monchegorsk, and the analysis of the samples our people brought back from Reznikov's lab is being withheld from me."

"I'm working on a plan to change all of that. I have a sample in the air as we speak, which will be in one of our labs by dawn. I also have a team approaching Monchegorsk. I should have a solid picture of what we're up against by late tomorrow evening my time," Berg said.

"I'll give my idea a shot over here and call you back later this afternoon with some new phone numbers to use. I don't trust anyone at this point. I've come too far along to end up feeding the fish."

"They still have fish in that river?" Berg said.

"The fish are making a comeback. Lots of bodies to keep them fat throughout the winter. I'll be in touch."

Kaparov wondered exactly how robust the FSB Special Operations Division internal security might be and knew exactly who to ask for this information. Then it would be up to Prerovsky. He would have to convince his lady friend to spy on her own people. This might be the biggest long shot he ever played, but it was worth the risk. He had always put mother Russian ahead of his own interests and this instinct had served him well. He wasn't about to make any changes to these guiding principles. He threw the exhausted cigarette stub to the pavement and walked back to the headquarters building, hopeful that Prerovsky wouldn't turn him over to Internal Affairs on the spot.

Chapter Twenty-Nine

6:40 AM
Edgewood Chemical Biological Center
Edgewood, Maryland

Kristin Flaherty checked her watch again and took another sip of her lukewarm coffee. She had been asked by the lab's assistant director to report with another researcher at two in the morning to prepare a biological test panel for an incoming biological specimen. The center's Sample Receipt Facility (SRF) was still a few years away from completion, so they would run the panel in the Biosafety Level Three facility. She knew not to ask questions about the source of the specimen, and given the timing, she knew it must be important.

Gary Pierce had arrived thirty minutes ahead of her, and by two-thirty, they were ready to run a full battery of tests on whatever arrived. Four o'clock passed unceremoniously, stretching to five o'clock, and after two pots of coffee, the clock hit six without any sign of a courier delivery. She started to become annoyed at six-thirty, when a walk to the front lobby to check with the security guard showed sunlight peeking over the trees beyond the empty parking lot. At six-forty, she snapped.

"I think it's time to call the contact associated with the specimen. They should have been here nearly three hours ago," she said.

Gary yawned and nodded.

"Concur. Either way, they need to know it didn't arrive."

She picked up the clipboard with the classified order sheet and searched for the contact number. She was to only identify herself as "Edgewood Laboratory," using a predetermined and secure outside line. The contact would mention "Mount McKinley" in his first phrase, or she was to hang up and call her director. She walked over to the encrypted phone and dialed the number.

"Mount McKinley Dry Cleaning. How may I help you?" the voice answered.

"Good morning, this is Edgewood Laboratory. We have a slight problem," she said.

"Have you identified the sample?"

"No, it hasn't arrived. That's the problem."

"Are you absolutely sure the sample hasn't been delivered?"

"Absolutely. We've been here since one-thirty. Nothing arrived before us."

"Understood. You'll need to standby for instructions from your director."

"Do you know when that might be?" she pressed.

"I'll be in touch with him shortly."

The call was abruptly cut short, and Kristin glared at the phone. How about a little common courtesy?

"We're stuck here, and I get the feeling that we're the least of this guy's priorities right now."

"Wonderful. I'll grab some breakfast at McDonald's if you don't mind holding down the fort."

"Sounds like a plan," she said, "and grab me a large Diet Coke."

⁂

Karl Berg placed his cell phone on the desk.

"Damn it," he muttered.

This didn't bode well at all. The agent assigned to the flight had strict instructions to call him if anything changed regarding the flight's itinerary. He had access to the aircraft's satellite phone and had been issued a GSM enabled cell phone. The eight-hour, direct flight pushed up against the Gulfstream 550's cruising range of 7,500 miles, but they had been assured that the aircraft could continue on to Chicago without refueling. Why the fuck had they waited so long to call him? At least he was in the right place to make some calls.

He had just driven back to the office after a few hours of sleep in his apartment, to monitor the setup phase of the Monchegorsk operation and help Audra prepare a presentation for the National Clandestine Service director. Based on the intelligence passed to them by Sanderson's team, Audra's presentation could be one of the most important threat assessments delivered in CIA history.

Sanderson's team would cross the Finnish/Russian border at first light tomorrow and proceed on snowmobiles to the outskirts of Monchegorsk. The total distance spanned roughly one hundred and fifty miles of infrequently travelled snowmobile trails. They would avoid the common routes used by recreational snowmobilers out of Finland. Once there, they would watch from a distance and wait for dark to enter the city, which would be a long wait. One hundred miles north of the Arctic Circle, the sun wouldn't drop below Monchegorsk's horizon until ten in the evening.

Now, everything hinged on the performance of a rogue mercenary team led by two men at the top of the FBI's Most Wanted list. The irony wasn't lost on him. The sooner Audra brought everything to the National Clandestine Service's director, the better. This had already spiraled well past his own pay grade, and he suspected Audra had started to overreach her own authority. He called up a screen on his computer and picked up his office phone to dial the number provided for AeroStar Global, the charter company that had provided the aircraft. The call was answered within three seconds.

"Anton Moreau, senior vice president for Client Relations. How may I help you today?" a thickly French-accented voice answered.

"Good afternoon, Anton. I'm calling to check on flight Alpha Sierra 310, which carried one of my clients. I'm concerned that the aircraft may have been diverted, since my client is nearly three hours late."

"Ah, yes. I'm afraid we are still trying to ascertain the status of this flight. It is of quite a concern to us, as I am most sure it is to you. The flight departed Astana, Kazakhstan, on schedule at six in the evening. We lost satellite tracking of the flight over Russia, near Volgograd, less than two hours after takeoff. We're doing everything we can to determine the status of the flight."

"The flight vanished six hours ago?"

"That's when we lost our global satellite connection, which isn't altogether unusual. The flight missed both of its check-ins over Europe, which raised alarms, but the rest of the flight transited over the Atlantic, so we couldn't draw any conclusions. For us, a flight more than one hour late is considered missing. Alpha Sierra 310 was declared missing two hours ago. I apologize that you were not immediately contacted, but the contract instructions denied active contact. We were to wait for you to call us," the extremely polite executive said.

"I understand. What is your company doing to locate the jet?"

"Everything. The aircraft is equipped with the latest generation emergency beacon system, and we are working with national authorities along the route to search for the beacon. Unfortunately, if the aircraft was lost over the water, we are unlikely to ascertain its fate. I can't stress enough how sorry I am. Let us pray for the best."

"Thank you, Anton," he said and hung up the call.

He had his theories, none of which he would be able to conclusively prove at this point. He assumed that the Russians had identified the flight out of Astana and had scrambled fighters to intercept the jet. They had gambled on the quick transit over Russia, from Kazakhstan to the Ukraine. A four hundred mile, thirty minute stretch. They couldn't take the flight south of Russia, since they didn't have clearance to transit Iran's airspace. They could have routed it through Azerbaijan and Georgia to break open onto the Black Sea, but Berg had the feeling the result would have been the same. The Russians had no intention of letting that flight land anywhere. He'd like to think the act was simple revenge for the loss of two helicopters and a platoon of soldiers in Kazakhstan, but he knew it was something more sinister. For some reason, the Russians were hell bent on concealing Reznikov's secret. He wondered if Kaparov knew more than he had been willing to reveal yesterday.

His next call would be to Audra. She had planned to meet him in the Operations Center at nine to examine Edgewood's report, so she would probably be awake at this point. Even if she wasn't, this news couldn't wait. The deliberate targeting of flight Alpha Sierra 310 could very well mean it was time for her to make some difficult phone calls.

Chapter Thirty

9:22 PM
Filitov Prospect
Monchegorsk, Russian Federation

Valeria Cherkasov's eyes fluttered open. She could hear some kind of knocking, but couldn't make any sense of the sound. For a brief moment, she had no idea where she was. The sensory details started to return, beginning with her vision. She was in her apartment, or what remained of it. A fading light crept through the shattered window in her living room, exposing the unbelievable amount of damage done to the apartment. A broken chair from her small kitchen table set lay on the floor under the window.

She smelled the smoky remains of a fire and wasn't surprised when further visual inspection of her surroundings revealed that the kitchen table had collapsed on itself, apparently due to a fire. The flames had cracked the bulb and melted part of the light fixture attached to the ceiling, leaving a massive charred area above the destroyed table. Just beyond the smell of fire was something else. It almost smelled like barbeque.

She now noticed that the room was freezing and that she was shivering. The thin wool blanket covering her on the small couch did little to deter the arctic air that freely poured into the room. Why wasn't she on her bed, under her thick down comforter? She heaved her legs over the side of the couch and stood up. All she could think about was getting under that comforter. She glanced at her hands and saw that they were bruised and scratched, dried blood coagulated in several places around the worst cuts. Walking toward the bedroom, she saw several blood smears on the cinderblock walls. *Did I punch the walls?* None of this made any sense to her.

When she reached the bedroom doorway, she realized why she was on the couch. The deeply charred wooden bed frame formed a shell around a large burned mass of mattress springs, feathers, pillows and dark unrecognized material. She didn't like the smell in this room. Some kind of combination of charcoal lighter fluid and meat. Disgusting. She stepped back into the first room and her senses homed in on the sound of knocking at her door. *How long had that been going on? Shit. That was what woke me in the first place.*

She walked over to the door and stared through the peephole, immediately recognizing one of the clinic doctors. She couldn't remember his name, but he was certainly familiar to her. They had dated off and on, until he settled down with a nurse from the hospital. She strained to remember if she knew what had happened to the nurse. She couldn't recall anything. Something was wrong with her detailed memory. She opened the door and registered the look of shock on his face.

"Are you all right, Valeria? I heard that you got out of the hospital. You're lucky you left. Army units showed up and nobody has heard any news from that part of town. What happened to you? You look like you've been attacked."

"I think I need to sit down," she said, straining to remember his name. Nothing.

"That's a good idea," he said, escorting her to the couch.

She wondered what he was doing here. It seemed odd to her that he would show up out of nowhere to check on her. Didn't he have a wife? Or did they ever get married?

She sat down on the far right side and felt a sharp pain in her right thigh. She didn't react to the pain, beyond slowly rising up to see what had happened. The man had turned his back on her, muttering something she couldn't hear. He glanced at the table and walls, furtively looking back at her. She caught this, but pretended to stare out of the window at the fading light. She turned her attention to the couch and her thigh, seeing fresh blood pour out of a shallow cut in her leg. The gleaming blade of a large butcher knife protruded between the cushion and the armrest of the couch. *Now, where did that come from? Oh, yeah. Now I remember.*

She glanced up at her friend, who was slowly approaching the bedroom door. Without thinking, she pulled the knife out of the couch by the flat side of the blade and stared at it. A crusted layer of dark red blood covered at least half of the blade. She hid it along the side of her bleeding leg and stood up slowly.

"Valeria, what in hell happened here?" he said, transfixed by the scene in the bedroom.

"Same thing that's gonna happen to you," she hissed into his ear.

Ten minutes later, after using the rest of the charcoal lighter fluid and most of the wood in the apartment to burn the man's body beyond recognition, she opened a small painted trunk next to the door and took out a warm fur hat and thick, fur-lined leather gloves. She took a moment to adjust everything before taking her favorite gray wool overcoat off one of the coat hooks next to the front door.

She pulled the coat over her bloodied hospital scrubs, wondering why she hadn't changed these yet. It didn't matter. She just needed to get out of her apartment and find a more secure place to stay. She knew the streets weren't safe, but neither was staying in her apartment. Since arriving from the hospital, her windows had been smashed in, and someone had thrown a small firebomb into her bedroom. It was only a matter of time before something more dangerous occurred. She was on the second floor and someone could easily climb in one of the broken windows. Maybe she could find a vacant apartment on an upper floor in her building. Even better, she might find someone that would take her in. She hated being alone.

A gunshot echoed through the open window, startling her. She turned toward the kitchen and walked over to the knife holder, searching for her favorite cutting knife. If she was going out into the darkness, she'd better arm herself. Failing to find the large butcher knife, she settled for the smaller one, which would be easier to hide in the spacious pockets on her jacket. She didn't want to walk around holding a knife. Someone might mistake her for one of the lunatics walking the streets.

Chapter Thirty-One

3:03 PM
MS Tallink Superstar
Tallin, Estonia

Anatoly Reznikov walked into the bar and took a seat at a small booth nestled against the window of the ferry's highest lounge. He glanced out of the window at the city of Tallin, which had taken on a gray pallor from the oppressive rain clouds hovering above the city. Tallin was an ugly city from this vantage point, nothing but a sea of colorless office buildings, punctuated by several shiny mirrored high-rises that represented Tallin's downtown area. He glanced at the other side of the lounge and could see vestiges of Tallin's Old Town. Towering church spires, byzantine-style domes and the red shingled roofs of ancient medieval buildings. He craned his neck slightly and saw a few of the Old Town's intact watchtowers. No wonder this side of the ship hadn't been crowded.

He settled into his seat on the two-thousand-passenger ferry, which looked more like a cruise ship, and signaled for the waitress that stood inside the bar, scanning the lounge's patrons for anyone suspicious. He ordered a double vodka, straight, from the attractive, bored-looking blonde waitress and turned his attention back to the industrial wasteland out his window. He'd love to poison this city, too. He didn't know why, but staring out into the city, he felt powerful, like he held the fate of the entire city in his hands. He had experienced the same feeling last night, right before he had left the hotel in St. Petersburg.

Staring out at St. Isaac Square from an expensive suite at the Ambassador Hotel, he drank the bottle of Rodnik vodka acquired in Nizhny Novgorod and monitored the situation in Monchegorsk via news media and internet sources. He knew sticking around Russia was a major risk for him, but he had taken precautions. He had undergone a series of minor cosmetic surgeries over the past five years, designed to alter his appearance enough that even his closest college friends wouldn't recognize him on first inspection. He had finished with these surgeries two years ago and purchased an expensive set of Russian identity papers. For the right price, everything was for sale in Russia.

Once media sources confirmed that Highway M18 had been closed by the army, he knew the virus had been successful. His elation lasted a few seconds, before an angry desire to acquire more of the virus hijacked him. He had the power to destroy entire cities, but had sold himself short with the terrorists. He should have insisted on taking more for himself, but his position with them had been precarious. He felt lucky to have escaped. They could have shot him at the site, but since he insisted on leaving immediately with the first encapsulated batches, they were forced to pretend that he was free to go. They couldn't afford any problems with the remaining laboratory staff at the time, since they were critical to the preparation of the remaining capsules.

A small shudder brought his thoughts back to the ferry, followed by three short blasts on the ship's horn, which were muffled by the lounge's thick glass windows. He watched as the city started to move out of his view and barely noticed the drink placed on his table. The ferry would take him to Helsinki, where he would take the next available flight to Stockholm. If the Stockholm address didn't provide results, he would move on to Copenhagen, then Germany. Eventually, he would find more of his virus. He had a notebook filled with addresses, all provided by careless, arrogant conversations in his laboratory.

Chapter Thirty-Two

5:25 PM
United Nations Detention Unit
The Hague, Netherlands

Srecko Hadzic stared at his image in the small mirror on the wall of his private cell. He looked like shit. Thick, bruised bags hung under his narrow brown eyes. His eyes were bloodshot and his face looked drained of blood. His stomach growled, adding to the misery and reminding him that his ulcer was acting up again. He hadn't slept or eaten well for nearly three weeks. Ever since his nephew visited with news that the traitor Marko Resja, or whoever he claimed to be, had been discovered in Argentina.

Finding him had been a stroke of pure fucking luck, but he'd take it. A higher power wanted this to happen, and the fact that that whore Zorana had been discovered at Marko's side proved it. Srecko clearly remembered the day that Marko raised her decapitated head out of the gym bag. He even recalled seeing the nose ring through the thick, blackish blood on the head's battered face. Nobody forgot it, especially the cowards that had recounted the story to the war crimes tribunal in exchange for a reduced sentence or their freedom. He'd deal with all of them eventually. His nephew, Josif, kept track of everyone.

He rubbed his eyes vigorously and ran both of his plump hands through thick silver and black hair. He really needed to try and eat something at dinner, but he'd need to visit the infirmary first to see if they could give him some form of stomach medication. Maybe the purple pill he had seen on television. He caught motion in his peripheral vision and turned to the door. One of the guards had just passed the small window located three quarters of the way up the dark green door. He turned to his desk unit and stared at the computer screen. He had forced himself to postpone checking his email account.

As a designated e-Court, the International Criminal Court (ICC) had mandated that each detainee have a computer in their cell, which was linked to a single computer at The Hague Court. Only Srecko's defense attorney had access to that computer, and the communications were designated as privileged. Still, they were cautious when using the electronic link, as neither of them fully trusted the detention center personnel. Pressure to convict high level members of Milosevic's regime had intensified.

He sat at the desk and activated the monitor. He waited a few moments, and typed in the passwords required to access his mailbox. A new message awaited him, titled "Recent Developments." This might be it. He clicked on the message, which was brief.

"Z in BA again. No M. Proceeding at first opportunity. Will supervise video production on site. J."

Srecko realized his fists were clenched. Zorana was alone in Buenos Aires. He'd prefer to grab them both at the same time, but this would work just fine. He could use Zorana to draw out Resja and dispose of them both...after long, unending torture sessions. He felt better knowing that Josif had flown out to personally handle the entire affair. He still had a few trusted Panthers in Argentina, but nothing compared to the comfort he took in knowing that a loyal blood relative had his best interests at heart, and Josif was as capable as he was loyal. He responded to the email.

"We'll need Z to find M. Proceed with filming, but don't terminate production. Expect to watch first cut shortly."

He deserved to watch her suffer for the hell they had put him through. The gang war between Mirko's "Avengers" and his own Panthers had turned Belgrade into a bloodbath. He'd lived like an outcast, running from one safe house to the next, trying to stay one step ahead of Mirko's assassination teams. He should have spent the time figuring out how to escape Yugoslavia and enjoy what remained of his criminal fortune. Instead, the NATO bombing campaign kicked into full gear, and the threat of NATO ground intervention drove Milosevic to accept the terms of a NATO peace plan.

The plan involved the withdrawal of Yugoslavian forces from Kosovo and the presence of peacekeeping forces along the Kosovo border. Since most of his Belgrade staff had disappeared, either killed or gone into hiding, he was forced to travel to the Kosovo front in an attempt to personally order the withdrawal of his paramilitary forces. He had managed to locate the senior field commander and give the order, but Srecko was intercepted by American commandos on the way back to Belgrade. He never saw Serbia again, and Zorana would pay the worst for his forced exile.

He wanted them to work her over using every form of torture and sexual assault imaginable, but he needed her alive to lure Resja out of hiding. He couldn't wait to watch her suffer. Maybe Josif could smuggle a thumb drive into the prison. He had managed to smuggle more than that over the past few years. If not, he was willing to risk having it sent over the computer. The thought of watching Zorana on film stirred something in his pants that he'd suspected had gone dormant over the past two years. Maybe he would add the little blue pill to his pharmacy request. He could imagine watching much of Zorana's movie debut with his pants down. He pressed "send."

Chapter Thirty-Three

3:25 AM
Angels Night Club
Palermo, Buenos Aires

Jessica held both hands high in the air and closed her eyes, letting the deep rhythmic beat pulse through her body. She could still see the lights flashing in sync with the music through her eyelids. The sensation left her excited and slightly dizzy, so she opened them to the same scene. A cloud of synthetic smoke enveloped the dance floor, temporarily adding another layer of anonymity to the darkened, frenetic environment.

She had been dancing in the club for nearly three hours and could keep going all night. She loved the energy, the people, and the free abandon of writhing shoulder to shoulder with hundreds of strangers. She was in her element among the hip, chic crowd at Angels, by far her favorite club off Serrano Square. The music switched between house and techno, never stopping, and she only took the occasional break for a quick drink. As the music shifted speeds, she took this as her cue to take another break and made her way to the sleek bar.

Set toward the back of the club, a layer of low tables and plush chairs shielded the packed cocktail area from the thronging mass of revelers jammed onto the dance floor. She broke out of the chaos and walked confidently through the maze of tables, completely aware of the attention she attracted leaving the relative safety of the pack. Her hypnotic dancing and apparent self-absorbed demeanor on the dance floor kept all but the most persistent or drunk men from bothering her. The bar area was a different story. Most of the club sharks operated in these waters, and despite the fact that she didn't mingle or flirt while refueling with a quick drink, few of them could resist her presence.

She wore a black sleeveless cocktail dress snugged tightly against her athletic body, accentuating her sculpted arms and legs, which gave her an advantage over the endless ocean of gorgeous women in the club. Jessica's daily regimen of running, calisthenics and classroom physical training gave her an unmatched physique among the typical nightclub crowd that dieted and rode machines at a gym in order to squeeze into their slinky outfits. Her organic level of fitness turned heads everywhere, male and female.

She could sense that the shark population had grown around the bar, so she didn't plan to linger for very long. She ordered a shot of high end tequila, which was delivered promptly, compliments of someone watching her at the bar. She downed the shot, skipping the salt and lime ritual, and winced slightly as the tequila burned going down. She felt the warmth radiate outward, pleasantly drifting and buzzing her head. A glass of water accompanied the shot, and she squeezed the lime into the water, gulping half of it down before heading back onto the dance floor. She never glanced around to see which one of her many admirers was vying for a moment of eye contact in return for the shot of tequila.

As she melted back into the crowd of dancers, she picked up the electronic dance beat and started to move, keeping an eye on the bar area. She wouldn't be surprised if a few of the sharks tried to follow her out into the fray, but she was pretty sure that she would be safe for now. 3:30 was still early for Buenos Aires, and the heavy drinking hadn't really started. With Daniel, they never stayed out much later than two in the morning, so she had limited experience in the pre-dawn party hours. She had stayed out past dawn the night before and had found the experience distasteful. She loved to party, but hated fighting off the desperate men during the dreaded final hour around last call. Tonight, she would dance for another half hour and suddenly disappear.

Fifty minutes later, she stole a glance at her watch and decided to walk out. It was later than she had expected, but still too early for Daniel to call. She didn't expect to hear from him until the operation had ended, but remained hopeful that he might sneak in a call to her. Pushing her way through the dense crowd, she broke through near the entrance. VIP booths lined the windowless wall to the left of the club's vestibule, packed with an exclusive-looking crowd. She ignored the blatant stares and a purposeful nod from a man surrounded by champagne bottles and supermodel-beautiful women.

The humid, slightly polluted warm air was a welcome break from the stale, sweaty air inside, but the respite was short lived. The Buenos Aires air was immediately ruined by dozens of smokers, either standing in the endless line snaking down the sidewalk, or huddled in a small designated smoking area on the other side of the entrance. Buenos Aires had gone smoke free in public buildings the year before, which created a gauntlet of smokers outside of most buildings, day or night.

She stepped out onto the street and was treated to the immediate presence of a taxi cab, which was a welcome change from the night before. She had closed a different club, along with nearly three hundred other drunken partiers, at about six in the morning, and taxi cabs must have been in demand across most of the city for the same purpose. Luckily, Serrano Square was within walking distance of their apartment, if you didn't mind a forty-minute walk. Tonight, she wasn't in the mood to walk, and the taxi was her salvation from a long night.

She started with a lavish dinner at ten, followed by a walk around the lively Serrano Square…until the line started to grow at Angels. Seven hours of nightlife, two evenings in a row had taken its toll, and she looked forward to a long sleep. She opened the taxi door and gave the driver her address, drifting away in her thoughts for several minutes as the driver made his way down familiar streets to their high-rise apartment building on Avenida Raul Scalabrini Ortiz.

❧

Dimitrije Gravojac watched the whore walk to the front door of the high-rise building, happy he could play a role in bringing this traitorous bitch closer to her end. He had been driving cabs in Buenos Aires for nearly a decade and didn't know the woman from Belgrade, but his compatriots had filled him in on enough of the details that he wished he could be there when they caught her. He was surprised that they didn't want him to bring her in tonight, or jump her when he dropped her off. He could have easily opened her door in an act of chivalry and bashed her over the head with a blackjack, but they had expressly forbidden it. It didn't matter either way. He had been paid nearly five hundred dollars for this easy job. He had tried the night before, but he couldn't get his taxi to her on the side of the road. There were too many pushy drunks on the street and they eventually forced their way into the cab. This night had been easier, since she left before the masses.

Now they had her address and could follow her more easily. He continued to watch as she used some kind of card to open the front door. Inside, a security guard rose to greet her. *High end apartment*, he thought. He'd pass this information on to his contact along with the address. Headlights appeared on the street behind him, and he decided to get moving. He didn't want to make her suspicious, though if she had turned around, she would have caught him staring at her for way too long. She was probably used to it. Dressed like a whore and all made up…what did she expect? As he applied pressure to the accelerator, he thought about asking his friends if he could be part of whatever happened to this woman. He had a good idea what they had in store for her. As he pulled away, he glanced at his rearview mirror and saw a minivan turn into the ramp leading down to the Bianca Hotel's parking garage.

Chapter Thirty-Four

1:15 PM
Palermo Soho
Buenos Aires, Argentina

Goran Brujic sat patiently at the wheel of the white commercial van that sat several parking spaces back from the intersection at Nicaragua Street. He had long ago stopped the van's engine, opening both passenger windows to air out the cabin. The back of the van was beyond hope for proper ventilation, unless the van was moving. Windowless, except for two fixed windows on the back doors, he had done the best he could to keep them in a shaded spot where he could still survey the sidewalk café. Four men sat stuffed in the back of the van, waiting for a chance to grab Zorana off the street.

The men had been selected carefully for their previous experience with off-street kidnapping. This particular group had worked together for years to supply young women for prostitution rings in several different countries. Snatched off the street, nearly all of the women were exported immediately, bound for Africa or Europe.

The group had been warned to be careful with this one. Careful not to kill her… careful with the takedown. None of the men in the back had ever known her from Belgrade, which gave him the peace of mind that they wouldn't do anything stupid to jeopardize Srecko's wishes.

Josif had assured them that they would be paid handsomely for the capture, and once Srecko was back in circulation, they would be rewarded with high-ranking positions in the wealthy crime lord's new enterprise. This street grab was well worth the risk, though he had been specifically told to back off if any complications arose. There was a backup plan.

He started the van, sensing that she was about to leave. She no longer sipped her coffee and had started to check her watch frequently. The woman placed money on the table and reapplied her lipstick as the waiter came by with the bill, scooping the money up at the same time. Some pleasantries were exchanged, and she stood up from her table in the heart of the seating area. He started the van and pulled it out onto the street, attracting no attention from the woman. The men in the back pulled black ski masks down over their faces and prepared to pour out of the back. Goran had to time this perfectly.

He would get two chances. The first one would take place in a few seconds, right in front of the cafe as she crossed the street to walk in the direction of her apartment. The other would happen on Nicaragua Street. If the timing didn't work out now, he could turn the corner slowly and hope that she moved down Nicaragua Street to a spot that was shielded from the café. He had done this dozens of times in similar situations and knew how to read the scene. If she ducked into the coffee shop, like she was prone to doing, they might have to circle around and wait for their opportunity on Nicaragua.

He gently pressed the accelerator and moved to intersect, pretending not to notice her. Just another rude delivery truck cutting off a pedestrian. Buenos Aires was full of inconsiderate traffic. The woman didn't stop at the edge of the curb and wait for him to pass, which would have put her in the perfect position to be snatched off the street. Instead, she sped up and slapped her hand on the hood of his truck, causing him to apply the brakes hard enough to gently screech the tires and draw a few stares from the café. It didn't matter; they'd still grab her in front of everyone. She glared at him with an icy look, and he prayed that the men in the back weren't visible through the semi-transparent plastic cabin divider. She stepped in front of the stopped van, shaking her head, and Goran decided they would grab her from the other side. As he drove forward, she yelled through the driver's side window in Spanish.

"Cuidado, maníaco!"

He ignored her taunt as she passed the window.

"Stand by," he said to his men.

The van pulled forward, and he prepared to give the command. He knew exactly where she would appear in the mirror when her body had cleared the back of the van. *Right about now*, he told himself and started to press the brakes. Something in his peripheral vision told him that the scene was off. *Fuck!* He turned his head and saw a blue and white striped fiat turn the corner at the intersection. The presence of a thin rack of blue police lights on the car's roof caused him to ease off the brakes.

"Abort. Cops. We'll try it on Nicaragua," he said.

Their flower delivery van cruised past the Buenos Aires Police Department patrol car and stopped at the intersection. A minivan on Nicaragua had the right of way at the four-way stop. Goran took this moment to watch the woman enter the coffee shop on the corner, which meant he would have to circle for a while. No problem. They would have this wrapped up pretty quickly. He activated the right blinker and turned right. They had some time to kill.

❧

The last thing she needed this morning was more coffee, but she felt compelled to duck into the Mama Gracha Café. Jessica scanned the coffee shop for the man she and Daniel had spotted a week ago. He had reappeared two days ago, and Jessica couldn't shake the feeling that she knew him. The man was definitely Balkan, possibly Serbian, but like Daniel had pointed out, this was becoming more and more common in Buenos Aires. Like most Europeans, Serbians enjoyed strong coffee, particularly Turkish coffee, and this shop served one of the best Turkish coffees in Buenos Aires. If strong coffee was your pleasure, you'd end up here eventually.

The driver of the flower truck looked like the same man she had seen in here, but she couldn't be sure. He wore sunglasses and a ball cap, but she had only caught a glimpse of him beyond the sun's reflection in the windshield. Her view of him through the passenger window lasted less than a second, and he didn't turn his head to acknowledge her purposeful insult. She was certain that the man was Caucasian, but beyond that, she had nothing but her instincts to support the theory that he was somehow familiar. She had learned to trust these instincts without question, and this policy had kept her alive for over six years as an undercover operative.

She decided it was time to head back to the compound. She was probably being paranoid, and a vicious hangover didn't help her think clearly, but she and Daniel had discussed the risks inherent with an ever increasing number of Serbian immigrants to Argentina. Between the two of them, they had spent over eight years in Belgrade and had come into contact with hundreds, if not thousands of people. If just one person recognized either of them, they could find themselves in immediate danger. She watched the flower delivery van turn right on Nicaragua and this gave her some relief. She would be headed in the opposite direction and would flag a taxi at the first opportunity. She'd pack up as soon as she reached the apartment and book the next available flight out of town.

⁂

Goran grew more infuriated by the second. He had circled back around, expecting to find her strolling along Nicaragua Street, but she was nowhere to be found. He had scoured the adjacent streets with no luck. At this point, he had driven down every street between here and that bitch's high-rise building on Avenida Raul Scalabrini Ortiz. He knew there was a backup plan, but he didn't like to fuck things up in front of Srecko's nephew. He wasn't sure why the kid was here. He probably wanted to impress his uncle, just like the rest of them. At least he had enough sense to stay out of their way. He respected that, and if placating Josif was the key to securing a future with Srecko, he'd cover the kid's back.

He pounded the steering wheel, glancing desperately around the streets. Losing Zorana on the streets didn't help his position with Josif. There were plenty of other eager players on the scene. Right now, they were probably singing sweet songs of Goran's incompetence to Josif. He turned the car onto Avenida Castillo, after completing a sweep of Avenida Armenia. A few seconds later, his cell phone rang. He recognized the number. Josif.

"I'm almost done with the sweep…she fucking vanished," he said.

"She's headed up to the apartment. Just arrived on the street. We're going with the backup plan."

"Understood. I'm less than three minutes away," he said and threw the phone on the passenger seat.

He floored the van, cruising through the stop sign on Malabia. The next street was Avenida Raul Scalabrini Ortiz.

ぐ∽ର

Jessica walked through the door of her apartment and placed her purse on the brown granite-topped, cast iron foyer table. She glanced in the mirror and noted the puffiness under her eyes. She could see it through the makeup. She had taken full advantage of the ability to stay out later than Daniel usually preferred. He had never been a big fan of the club scene, but had played along with her everywhere they had lived. Two in the morning was the absolute latest she could keep him out on the streets and she never pushed it with back-to-back nights. With Daniel, she treated it like an infrequent indulgence. They had other thrilling and pleasurable ways to spend their time together.

She closed the door and decided to book her flight first. Something that left late in the afternoon and gave her enough time for an indulgent, midday nap. She crossed the shiny marble floor and stopped at the end of the foyer hallway, frowning. She detected a rancid smell that she thought hadn't been in the apartment when she left. She had eaten some leftover Thai food last night, but was pretty sure she had put it away…though she had been fairly intoxicated at the time. She turned the corner and glanced into the kitchen. The counters were spotless, but something else caught her eye and caused her to stiffen. Through the open bedroom door, she could partially see a small digital camcorder set on top of a tall tripod.

Jessica turned for the foyer hallway and sensed movement in the furthest reaches of her peripheral vision. She lashed out at the movement with her right elbow, catching a short, broad-shouldered man wearing a light blue shirt directly in the nose, splattering blood down his face. Halfway out of the foyer closet, he stumbled and tried to bring both hands to his shattered nose. She immediately followed with a solid front kick to his solar plexus. The kick drove him down the foyer and slammed him against the entry door, knocking him off his feet. He grasped for the cast iron table near the door, bringing it down with a hard thud onto the white marble floor.

She reached for the ultra-slim, serrated, four-inch blade concealed along her outer thigh. She managed to hike up her red knee-length skirt high enough to fully grasp the knife, but found herself suddenly paralyzed, struggling to move her hand another inch. She lost all sense of balance and fell to her knees, focused on the incredible surge of pain radiating from the right side of her lower back. She started to topple over against the foyer wall, unable to arrest her continued fall, and watched helplessly as the man with the bloody nose threw the heavy table aside. He walked up to her and spit a mixture of blood and mucus on her face, right before he kicked her in the stomach…harder than she had ever been kicked before. The image of his face grew hazy as he cocked his fist and delivered a crunching blow to her face.

Before her vision returned, Jessica's first instinct was to struggle. She could barely breathe and felt an unbearable pressure under her chin. She reached up with her hands to feel around her neck and was yanked up onto her knees by her head. Her fingers managed to find the source of the excruciating pain. She desperately tried to pull the thin wire surrounding her neck to ease the pressure that prevented her from taking more than a few, shallow gasps of air. She felt fresh blood trickle onto her hands and run down her chest. The pressure tightened, and she took her hands off the garrote, which resulted in a slight reduction in pressure.

Her vision settled on a bloodied figure in front of her. The man looked familiar through the blood pouring out of his nose and down over his mouth and chin. The bloodstains gave him a ghoulish look, like he had just dug into raw meat. She stared at him for a few more seconds, struggling to gain some leverage against the steel wire garrote that was yanked every time she moved. If she fought too much, additional pressure from the wire could cut into her carotid artery. She would bleed out within minutes if this happened…and kept this in mind as an option. She had no idea what they had in store for her, but she was pretty sure that a fast bleed out would be the best alternative.

"Did you really think you'd get away with it, you stupid cunt?" the bloodied man uttered.

"Get away with what?" she rasped.

"Stealing all of Srecko's money. I remember you from Belgrade. Whore. Zorana Zekulic. Queen of whores…until she started fucking Resja. Then she was demoted back to simple whore."

She started to answer, but a quick flick of his head caused the man behind her to pull on the garrote, cutting off her response.

"Your filthy mouth opens when I ask you a question. Nod if you understand."

Jessica nodded and looked around the room. Details of her apartment blurred, as she directed all of her mental energy to the men surrounding her. The man standing next to the brute with the bloodied nose stood with his arms crossed. A poor choice in any situation, but he obviously felt pretty confident. Jessica wasn't going anywhere, as far as he could tell. Another man stood outside of her peripheral vision. She had heard him grunt. Four men, none visibly armed, which gave her some hope. She had to make her move now, before they tied her up. She had no delusions about their intentions.

"We're going to ask some questions about the money and about Marko Resja. If you answer them quickly and truthfully, I'll kill you mercifully. If not, this will be the longest day of your life. Srecko's nephew, Josif, flew into town to personally document your end. He told me Srecko is running out of movies to watch in his cell. He requested a twenty-four-hour documentary on raping and torturing whores. I guess it's a new passion of his. Josif is setting up the film studio as we speak. Are you ready for her yet?"

Josif Hadzic appeared in the doorway, and Jessica strained to turn her head so she could fully see him. He stood there dressed in white coveralls and finished pulling on a pair of matching white rubber gloves. He was young, in his mid-twenties, with long, thick, black hair. He looked clinically psychotic in the stark white outfit.

"Almost ready. I just need to bolt one more end of the harness sling to the floor," he said, turning his attention to Jessica.

"This should be a whore's dream come true," he said, then turned his attention back to Miljan.

"When will the rest of the men be here?"

"They should be pulling up any second," Miljan said.

"Good. Ten men and no real hurry. Should be a fun time for this whore. Once everyone's sick of fucking her, we'll start the real work," he said and disappeared into the bedroom.

From the bedroom, she heard an industrial screwdriver attached to a small air compressor. She'd heard the same sounds when they were using nail guns and heavy duty hand portable equipment at the compound.

"I don't think I could ever get tired of sticking it to this one. Lots of holes to fill," the man with crossed arms said.

"I'd avoid the hole with teeth. This is a feisty little bitch," the man grasping the wire around her neck said.

"We'll just have to knock all of her teeth out," the man retorted.

Miljan leaned in close to her face and spoke softly. "If I were you, I'd start the beginning of your documentary with a little disclosure. We want to know where the money is located and how to access it. Then we want to know where to find Resja. Tell me this and I'll cut your throat right now. Josif might not like it, but his uncle is a rational man. He wants his money back, and I can always make him another snuff film. I need your answer before you walk through that door. Understood?"

She nodded again and decided it was now or never. She knew there would be no merciful deal on the other side of that door. Srecko didn't deal in mercy, and neither did any of his henchmen. Miljan Jendzejec had been a ruthless enforcer for the Panthers' organized crime syndicate, and she had steered clear of him from the start. Even the endless supply of Russian prostitutes in Belgrade eventually learned to give him a wide berth in the city's clubs. Too many women disappeared in his company.

She gently slipped her right hand to her thigh, while pulling on the wire with her left. The struggle would hopefully provide enough of a distraction for her to remove the knife and cut the man's right forearm muscle to the bone. She could follow up with a quick jab to his groin, which should cause him to release the garrote. Once free from the piano wire noose, she would have a fighting chance. Not much of a chance, but she'd rather go down fighting than be chained to some kind of sick contraption. Her hand reached the scabbard, and she was yanked skyward.

"Looking for this?" Miljan said.

Jessica strained through blurry vision to focus as her knees settled back to the floor. Both of her hands were desperately clawing at the wire tightened dangerously around her neck. She felt a warm trickle cascade down her chest, filtering through her sticky fingers.

"I guess I have your answer," he said and lowered the hand holding her knife.

All of the men in the room laughed, and she made her decision. She closed her eyes and thought of Daniel. This was all her fault. She knew this would devastate him and wished she could change everything. Change all of this. At least she could count on him killing every last man in this room. It was a terrible consolation, but it gave her the strength to force a smile, as she prepared to fight ferociously against the wire that dug less than a few millimeters away from her carotid artery.

"Get her to her feet," Miljan said.

She heard a sharp crack, and the wire suddenly loosened. Jessica opened her eyes and saw that everything had changed. Miljan's light blue shirt was covered with bright red splatter and dark bits of tissue. Shock was plastered on his brutal face. She noticed that his right arm hung precariously by a few strands of exposed ligament below the elbow. Jessica understood what had just happened. A bullet had passed through her strangler's head and hit Miljan's forearm. The room froze, until her knife clattered against the marble floor, released from Miljan's useless grip. Without warning, she sprang forward with a single focus. *Survival.*

ஒ

Jeffrey Munoz tossed the van keys in front of the empty ice bucket next to the coffee maker and heaved his black backpack onto the bed. Melendez tossed the oversized blue gym bag on the other bed and headed for the bathroom. He unzipped the backpack and removed a pair of binoculars and a spotting scope, placing them on the small table pushed in front of the balcony sliders. He opened the balcony door and pulled the curtains all the way to the side, opening the room to a wide view of the city, which was mostly blocked by a high-rise apartment building. He moved the table directly in front of the opening and plucked a small tripod from one of the suitcases jammed against the corner wall. Once unfolded, he attached the 15X spotting scope to the tripod and placed it on the table.

The Petroviches' apartment sat on the eleventh floor of the high-rise in front of the Bianca Hotel and occupied the right front corner of the building. From their surveillance nest on the fourteenth floor, they could see into most of the apartment, although they had trouble seeing the back of the kitchen or the foyer. The apartment consisted of a combined kitchen-living area, and a dining nook space that occupied two thirds of the space directly in front of them. The entire front held ceiling to floor glass and several sliding doors that led to a balcony connecting the living areas with the bedroom, which comprised the remaining third of the apartment. A small white table and two chairs sat on the balcony in front of the living area.

Munoz situated the tripod on the table and angled it slightly downward before staring through the eyepiece, roughly guessing that it was aimed into the apartment. He was slightly off, and the bottom of the patio table filled his view. He gently corrected the scope until it was centered on the open patio door. What he saw froze him momentarily. He shot up from the scope and snatched his backpack from the bed, moving rapidly toward the door.

"Melendez!"

"What!" he heard from the bathroom, followed by a flush.

"They've got Jessica! Get on the gun and engage targets immediately! Don't wait for me! Channel eight on comms!"

Munoz had already slammed the hotel room door shut by the time Melendez charged out of the bathroom. He sprinted down the hallway to the elevator. If the elevator car was near his floor, it would ultimately be quicker than taking the stairs. It would give him time to attach a silencer to the Steyr TMP machine pistol buried in his backpack. He glanced at the illuminated numbers above the elevator doors. Sixteen and five. He hit the "down" button, and stared at the numbers, ready to hit the stairs. The sixteen changed to fifteen. Fucking beautiful.

He reached into the backpack for the compact radio and headset, figuring that if he put this on first, people would be less likely to question his counterfeit Buenos Aires Police credentials and the evil-looking submachine gun that he would be readying in the elevator. The door opened, yielding an empty elevator. He jumped inside and jammed the button to close the door. He prayed that it went straight to the parking garage.

The hotel door slammed shut and a blanket of panic settled over Melendez. He had no idea what was happening, and for the first time since he joined the Black Flag program, he was on his own. What the fuck had happened? Munoz had told him to start shooting and bolted through the door. That was it. While he tried to process the confusion, he shifted into autopilot and started mechanically running through his mental checklist. It was his best defense against the stress that had suddenly engulfed their situation. He didn't spend any time thinking about what he might see when he put his eyes to the scope. Right now, he needed to put rounds downrange as quickly as possible. Munoz's voice left little confusion about that fact.

He yanked the black RPA Rangemaster Standby 7.62mm sniper rifle out of the bag and grabbed the nylon ammunition pouch containing four additional ten-round magazines. While passing the second bed, he reached into Munoz's backpack and retrieved the other radio set. He threw this onto the table and shoved the spotting scope out of the way. After rapidly unfolding the rifle's stock and securing it into his shoulder, he opened both lens caps on the Schmidt and Bender 3–12 x 50 scope and extended the bipod. Finally, he rested the rifle on the table and canted it toward the eleventh floor of Jessica's building, methodically searching for the targets Munoz had assured him would appear.

The variable power scope had been set for 8X magnification and required no elevation adjustment in this case. The distance from the end of the rifle's barrel to the apartment was seventy-three meters, a calculation he had digitally assessed on their first day in the room with a laser rangefinder. At such short range, only a serious wind would affect his bullet. All of the flags on nearby balconies stood motionless.

As he settled into the scope, he detached the magazine already inserted into the rifle and replaced it with a different one from the small nylon pouch. The rounds in the new magazine were specialized bonded core bullets, specifically designed for shooting through glass obstacles. The only downside to the 180-grain bullet was that it would pass through its target, even after penetrating glass. At less than 100 meters, the bullet would strike its target at 2,600 feet per second and could easily kill someone in an adjacent room after passing through a human target.

He removed his hand from the rifle and switched the radio on, removing the headset from the compact unit. He glanced over to confirm that the orange LED read "8." Back on the scope, he continued to breathe slowly and searched for targets.

The scope's wide field of vision gave him a view of the entire room, which allowed him to immediately assess the situation. He could see Jessica on her knees behind a man that was actively struggling to keep her down. The man's hands were visible on both sides of his hips, tightly gripping and pulling backward. He was clearly strangling her. Three more men stood in the room, and he made quick mental notes to help prioritize his shots. The man close to the front window, on the far right, cradled an automatic shotgun in his arms. The man facing him, directly in front of Jessica's attacker, pulled a knife from behind his back. His face looked bloodied. The guy to his immediate left stood with his arms folded, laughing. Strangler, Shotgun, Knife, Chuckles…in that order.

He pulled the bolt back and chambered a round, steadying the scope at the highest point on the back of Strangler's neck. He started to depress the trigger, watching the crosshairs drift ever so slightly with his shallow breath. He found the drift's natural rhythm and removed a little more pressure. Any additional pressure would fire the weapon. As the scope's center dot eased into place on a point directly aligned with the man's spine, he barely activated the muscles in his finger, and the rifle kicked into his shoulder. He vaguely heard the glass shatter on Jessica's balcony, before reloading another round. He was in a different world right now, where all of his attention was focused on the mechanics of shooting. The fear and panic that had tried to overtake him less than a minute ago had vanished, replaced by an eerie, detached calm.

&

The man to Miljan's left started to reach behind his back. Jessica instantly closed the gap and executed a hinged high kick to his throat, sending him back against the foyer wall next to the hallway closet. Both of his hands instinctively reached for his own neck. The rest of her body hinged with the kick toward the floor, allowing her to grab the knife. From the downward position, she placed the serrated knife behind Miljan's knee and reversed the hinge, using most of the momentum to sever the hamstrings of his right leg. Miljan screamed and collapsed, falling into the crook of Jessica's knife arm. Bracing him against her body and keeping him upright, she slashed the blade viciously across his neck, feeling the knife's serrations tear through the tracheal cartilage. At the same time, she reached her left hand toward the small of his back and found the handle of a pistol.

As the knife came free and her slashing arm swung outward, she continued to spin into a stance facing the man she had just kicked. He had begun to gain some sense, but both of his hands were still occupied with his rapidly swelling neck. At point blank range, Jessica fired the semi-automatic handgun several times into the man. Her final shot sprayed brains and other dark matter against the closet door.

She ducked and spun, aiming the pistol with her off hand at the next target she could find. She didn't have much time to process the scene. The strangler's body lay face down in a massive crimson pool, centered on what remained of his head. Josif stood in the doorway with his mouth and eyes wide open, a pistol held limply in his right hand. Her main problem appeared to be the man aiming a Saiga semi-automatic shotgun at her head.

The shotgun erupted a fraction of a second after the wall behind him turned red. She felt a sharp stinging pain in her pistol hand and saw that Josif's white coveralls were now stained by a bright red lateral slash. The man with the shotgun fell to his knees; a powerful fountain of blood sprayed from his neck onto the ceiling as his body continued down to the floor. Jessica's left hand didn't respond to the electrical impulses ordering it to fire the pistol at Josif, despite the fact that it was aimed directly at his chest. She didn't waste any time trying to figure out why. In one easy motion, she threw her knife at Josif.

Despite its undeniable usefulness as a hand-to-hand weapon, her Spider knife had been designed as a throwing weapon. She had special ordered a serrated set from the company and found that the serrations barely affected their ballistic performance. She could accurately place the knives in a six-inch diameter circle at thirty feet, and Josif stood well within that range. The knife buried itself in his upper right arm and prevented him from raising the pistol. She watched him dash to the right and disappear behind the wall.

Both hands slick with blood, she pried the pistol from her damaged left hand and fired at the thin wall between the two rooms. The remaining several bullets in the gun formed a tight pattern on the wall, three feet above the floor, and two feet back from the doorway arch. If Josif had opted to hunch near the wall and wait for her to charge forward, he would have taken those bullets in the head or groin, depending on his choice of stance.

She tossed the weapon back and dragged Miljan's corpse into the foyer with her good hand. She could safely use the foyer wall as cover, since the dishwasher in the kitchen on the other side of the wall provided an additional layer of solid material. She turned Miljan over, looking for spare pistol magazines. Blood continued to pump out of his neck, connecting with the red tide expanding from the bullet riddled body slumped against the closet door.

ꟷ

Melendez chambered another round and started to center the scope's crosshairs on the man who appeared in the bedroom doorway, but he disappeared from sight before he began to remove any slack from the trigger. He had planned to target the guy with the knife next, but could tell from the scope's wide field of vision that Jessica had already turned that side of the room into a slaughterhouse. Several gunshots shattered the momentary calm, and he used the scope to scan the living area for more targets. Covered with blood, Jessica pulled one of the bodies behind the kitchen wall.

He heard loud voices down on the street and rushed forward to investigate. He watched as five men sprinted into the building, followed by a single gunshot from below. Fuck, she was about to have more company, and he didn't have any way to communicate with her. He got behind the rifle and found Jessica through the scope.

She had just finished reloading a pistol, holding the weapon upside down between her knees. He could see that her left hand was a mess and wondered how she would chamber a round. Amazingly, she flipped the pistol between her knees with her good hand and pulled back the slide while keeping the weapon anchored between her legs. The pistol was up and aimed around the corner in a flash.

He aimed the rifle back toward the window and looked for any shot that might have a chance of reaching the man he had seen in the bedroom doorway. He knew Jessica wouldn't back down from the situation and feared the worst. There could be more than one more attacker in the bedroom, and she wouldn't stand a chance bursting through the doorway.

Even if she survived, she'd soon be up against five more men, unable to quickly reload her pistol.

The bedroom's windows were covered by thick shades that gave him nothing. He decided that he would fire blindly through the windows until she breached the doorway. It might distract whoever was left in the bedroom long enough for her to get the job done. If she survived, he might be able to keep the new arrivals pinned down long enough for Munoz to finish the job.

He took his hand off the rifle and jabbed at the radio, putting it to his ear. "Munoz?"

"Just hit the street. Tell me she's still alive."

"Miraculously, but five men just hauled ass into the building. You're about twenty seconds behind them. There's one more confirmed target in the apartment, but I don't have a shot."

"Do what you can until I get there," Munoz said.

"Understood," he said and focused on the scope.

Jessica was tensed, and he could tell she was about to make a move. He placed the crosshairs in the center of one of the bedroom sliders and fired. He saw Jessica sprint toward the bedroom before she could have possibly heard the rifle shot. Melendez chambered another round and fired hastily into the ceiling to floor bedroom window farthest from the wall that separated the two rooms. It was up to Jessica at this point.

&

Goran Brujic ran up the stairs with his pistol drawn. He knew they would all be physically spent by the time they arrived on the eleventh floor, but he didn't plan to take any chances with an elevator. He had no idea what had gone down in the apartment, but he was pretty sure that several rapid gunshots was not part of Josif's plan. He had no intention to step out of the elevator into an ambush. They would catch their breath at the top of the stairs and move cautiously from there.

He reached the door and kneeled beside it. Most of his team slid into place behind him with their pistols drawn while they waited for Jovan to move his oversized carcass up the stairs. The man was at least a half a floor behind them and carried a shortened pump action shotgun. As Jovan slammed into the concrete stairwell wall, out of breath, Goran opened the door slowly, peering into the elevator foyer. He didn't see anything out of place and decided to move into the lobby with his gun aimed forward. A man and woman turned the corner and gasped at the sight of five armed men in the lobby. Goran pulled a counterfeit Buenos Aires police badge out of his back pocket and flashed it at the couple, signaling for them to go back to their apartment. The man tried to speak, but Goran put his finger to his lips and shook his head. Whether they believed the five Caucasian men were police officers didn't matter. Goran heard a door slam and knew they wouldn't be a problem.

He peeked down the hallway leading to the Petroviches' apartment and found it clear. Whatever had happened was confined to the apartment. He told the men to hurry and ran down the hall to the door. He pulled out one of several key cards that had been made for his team by the doorman this morning and waited for everyone to fall into place around the door. Once Jovan's sweaty, heavily breathing body settled in, he inserted the card and removed it quickly. The light turned green, and he opened the door quietly, sliding into the room with the gun aimed forward.

He edged down the foyer hallway, amazed by the amount of blood covering the floor. He saw two bodies, which he immediately recognized. Something had gone terribly wrong in here. He suddenly heard a desperate scream from deeper inside the apartment. He kept still, listening and scanning for clues. The scream was followed by sobbing and repeated begging, which ended in what sounded like a slap. He took a few more steps forward and froze. The sliding glass door in the middle of the living room lie shattered in pieces on the shiny marble floor and concrete balcony. *Sniper?* He wasn't going to take any chances. He glanced around for a few seconds, seeing an opportunity that would buy him some time.

❧

Melendez tried not to pay attention to what was happening in the bedroom. Jessica had plunged through the doorway opening and opened the shades less than a minute later. Behind the curtains, he saw the man in white coveralls strapped into some unusual contraption on the floor next to the bed. He watched, slightly confused, as she adjusted a camera that had been knocked down by their scuffle. What she did next made him uncomfortable and he was relieved to turn his attention back to the foyer. He loaded a new magazine into his rifle and settled in to wait.

He heard a primal scream and expended considerable restraint from looking into the bedroom. He needed to focus on the impending arrival of the remaining attackers. A few seconds later, he saw light reflect off the marble floor in the dark recess of the foyer. Someone had opened the door, and he knew for a fact it wasn't Munoz. Munoz had followed the Serbians up the stairwell, trailing them by five floors, careful not to alert them to his presence. He had just checked in with Melendez from the stairwell.

From this angle, he couldn't see more than a quarter of the way into the foyer, so he placed the crosshairs at the furthest point along the foyer floor and waited. A foot slowly appeared, followed by another, as his next target moved cautiously down the hallway. He sighted in on the man's left knee and started to settle in for a shot. The man had stopped, which made his job easier. He started to apply pressure to the trigger, when the man suddenly bolted out of the foyer. His crosshairs found the man standing in front of an intact window, and suddenly, the view was obscured by a dark brown curtain. The curtain continued rapidly across the entire front of the living area, stopping a few feet from the wall separating the two rooms. Since he couldn't shoot effectively, he grabbed the radio. Everything relied on Munoz.

❧

Goran pulled the curtain as far as he could bear and moved toward the bedroom doorway. He heard another scream filled with Serbian expletives, followed by a female voice speaking Serbian.

"Smile for your uncle, Josif. He doesn't want to see unhappy faces in prison."

"Fuck you, you miserable bitch. I'll carve your eyes out for this and force your husband to eat them!" Josif yelled.

Goran realized that she hadn't heard the curtains. He had tried to be as quiet as possible, which was quite a feat given the amount of slippery blood on the floor. Fuck, this was perfect. He would kill Zorana and rescue Josif on camera. Nothing could solidify his future with Srecko more solidly. He hated to deprive Srecko of the fun they had planned for Zorana, but they needed to get out of here immediately. The neighborhood would be crawling with police in a few minutes.

"Did you hear that, Srecko? Your precious nephew is somehow going to cut my eyes out. Doesn't he look so cute strapped into this thing? I know this wasn't the video you were expecting, but it'll have a few things in common. I'll just leave out the rape and sexual defilement, though some of the toys they brought along might spice up the show for you."

Goran stepped into the room, leading with the pistol. The sight of Josif writhing in the harness momentarily distracted him. Josif's white coveralls and undergarments were sliced open and pulled away from the center of his body to expose his entire torso. The act of splitting the clothing down had left numerous slashes extending from the top of his chest to his penis.

"Kill this fucking bitch!" Josif screamed.

Goran tried to aim the pistol at Jessica, but she had already ducked behind Josif, placing her knife across his throat and jamming her head right against his. He wasn't a good enough shot to hit the sliver of her face that remained exposed.

Goran saw her pistol on the bed and knew he could make this work. If he could get close enough to her, he could shoot her through the head. She would never cut Josif's throat and sacrifice her only leverage. Unfortunately, he didn't dare venture any further into the room with a sniper watching the apartment. He'd wait for the rest of his team and charge her while someone else closed the curtains.

"Jovan, Predag…let's go!" he yelled and looked back.

His men emerged from the hallway and he knew this would be over quickly. Jessica crouched behind Josif, and Goran hoped she'd go for her gun. She wouldn't make it halfway across the room. He glanced back at his team and found it odd that they had all slipped and fallen at the same time. The thought was interrupted by a sudden, intense pain at the top of his neck. What the fuck? He reached up, and his left hand hit something solid. None of it made any sense. He glanced toward Jessica and saw her crouch back down next to Josif. *I'm gonna kill this bitch!*

Movement in his peripheral vision brought his attention back to the other room. A stocky Latino guy dressed in jeans and a dark blue windbreaker stood near the foyer, aiming a silenced submachine gun at his chest. Goran heard a staccato popping sound and was hammered to the floor in front of the bed. He watched helplessly as Jessica leaned over him and pulled the knife out of his neck. She grinned as she wiped the blade clean on her red skirt. His attention drifted to the thick black cylinder that hovered inches from his face.

༺༻

Munoz changed the selective fire setting on the TMP to semi-automatic and pulled the trigger once, putting the Serbian out of his misery.

"We need to go, right now," he said, glaring at her.

"I just need a minute alone with him," she said.

She looked half crazy, and Munoz wondered how in the hell they were going to pull this off. She needed immediate medical attention, as far as he could tell. Her left hand was mangled, showing bone through the torn flesh on at least two of her fingers. She pressed the bleeding hand against her breast, thoroughly soaking her white blouse down to her abdomen. Not that he could be sure this was the source of the blood stain. Cuts and abrasions across her neck slowly seeped dark red streams down her upper chest. If that wasn't enough, she had taken a massive blow to the face, which had cut her right cheekbone and left a swollen, red mark the size of a baseball on the right side of her face. He spotted something that might help them get her out on the streets without attracting too much attention.

"We need to be on the street in less than a minute. Melendez is packing up and expects us to be walking south on Loyola. Change your shirt. Something black. And wipe off as much of that blood as possible from your arms and legs," he said.

"I'm not done with the video. This piece of shit hasn't put on his best performance for the camera," she said.

Munoz watched in sheer amazement as she turned her back on him and walked toward the writhing figure strapped into some kind of sadomasochist bondage harness. He figured this contraption was meant for her and could understand her anger, but they didn't have time for this. He gripped the TMP with both hands and lined the sights up on the man's forehead. The weapon coughed twice, and a large red stain hit the wall behind the man's head.

"What the fuck? I wasn't done with him," she said.

"If you want to see Daniel again, we need to be out of here in sixty seconds. I can hear police sirens. You need to make a choice, Jessica. One way or the other, I'm leaving in sixty seconds," he said.

"All right. Let's get out of here," she said.

She placed her face in front of the camera. "You're a fucking dead man, Srecko," she said and ejected the small tape in the camera.

Munoz found a few packets of Celox powder among the supplies spread out on the floor next to the bed. Celox was used on the battlefield to stop bleeding and could even be used to treat a severed artery. He'd have her wash as much of the blood off her skin as possible before she applied the powder. With a change of clothes and some makeup, they should be able to pull this off. When he turned to check on her, she grabbed the Celox packets out of his hands and pointed to the bedroom door.

"A little privacy," she said.

Munoz walked through the door, which slammed shut behind him. He glanced at his watch and swore to himself that he'd walk out the door in forty-five seconds.

&

Melendez spotted them hopping down from a wall on the left side of the street, fifty meters ahead of his van. He had parked and vacated the driver's seat while they worked their way through several yards and alleys. From the back of the van, he watched several police vehicles form a roadblock at the corner of Avenida Loyola and Avenida Rual Scalabrini, which was one hundred meters back down Avenida Loyola. On his police scanner, he monitored the most active police channel he could find and determined that the police had found the murdered doorman. Once they found the apartment, the entire police department would swarm the area. The sooner they got out of here, the better. He pulled the van onto Avenida Loyola and cruised over to pick them up. Once Munoz and Jessica were in the van, they would call General Sanderson. He imagined this wouldn't be a pleasant phone call.

Chapter Thirty-Five

2:17 PM
Nuequen Province
Western Argentina

Terrence Sanderson stood on the covered deck of the headquarters lodge and shook his head. This was exactly the kind of publicity he had strived to avoid for the past two years. He opened the screen door and walked inside. Parker looked up from his array of three laptop computers, which were stationed around one end of the large conference table.

"Parker, we have a problem."

"Shit. Don't tell me the Russians know they're coming?" Parker said.

"No. Possibly a bigger problem."

He placed his satellite phone on the table and sat down next to Parker, exhaling for dramatic effect. Parker raised an eyebrow and stayed silent.

"The Serbians found their apartment in Buenos Aires..."

"Daniel's?"

"Exactly. They grabbed Jessica in the apartment, right in front of Munoz and Melendez. Jessica is fine, but she needs medical attention. We have ten dead Serbs in what Munoz described as a slaughterhouse. He said he'd never seen this much blood in one place, ever. The Petroviches kept the apartment sanitized of any identifying documents, so we have no concern there. The apartment is leased through a dummy corporation in Panama and has been prepaid for three years. All untraceable."

"Cameras?"

"That's the real problem. Daniel chose the apartment because of its security. The key cards are changed upon request and the place is loaded with cameras. The doorman was shot dead, so maybe the cameras were disabled when the Serbs broke into her apartment. Either way, I'm sure the police will have pictures of Daniel and Jessica very shortly. Probably Munoz and Melendez, too. Eventually, they'll figure out the ballistics, and locate the hotel room across the street. Once the pictures hit circulation, the Argentine Police will be able to identify them. Their cover identification will be ruined, and it won't be easy to move them around."

"Maybe we should move them out of the country now," Parker said.

"It doesn't sound like Jessica would fit in very well on a commercial flight. I'm sending them to a safe location outside of Buenos Aires, where Jessica can get in-house medical treatment. Munoz said most of her wounds were superficial and shouldn't require her to be in place for more than a few days."

"Do you want to get word to Daniel?"

"Negative. I need him focused on Monchegorsk. If Monchegorsk is as bad as Berg suspects, then the CIA will have enough evidence to start convincing the right people that U.S. interests are in imminent danger. Berg is also working on a Russian contact that may be willing to help us find Reznikov. If we can bag Reznikov and get him to talk, we might be able to leverage the information."

"Leverage?"

"I don't plan to work in the shadows forever. If we can get information from Reznikov that can prevent other attacks, I think we'll have more than enough leverage to get this group an immunity deal. It would be a win-win situation for our government. Fast results. Complete deniability. Zero cost to the taxpayer. Seamless integration with the CIA and a few other spook agencies. It would be perfect."

"What if they say no?"

"We don't lose if they call our bluff. Reznikov won't be our last opportunity. The world is a dangerous place and our services can't be ignored forever. Did Schafer arrive in Finland?"

"He met with Berg's guy and escorted the crew north. They're geared up and waiting in Oulu for first light. They'll cross the border south of Salla and stick to the less popular trails. Farrington wasn't very happy with the equipment provided by Berg's CIA contact."

"Will it get them to Monchegorsk?"

"He wasn't complaining about the transport. He said the weapons were sixties era Kalashnikovs, apparently part of a Cold War era weapons cache recently discovered thanks to a former KGB defector. The night vision equipment consisted of a few civilian model handheld scopes."

"He's starting to sound like Petrovich. As long as the weapons function, I don't give a shit. They're on a reconnaissance mission and shouldn't need weapons if they do their jobs correctly. Make sure to remind them of that. They need to figure out what happened in Monchegorsk and get the fuck out."

"Understood. I'll reemphasize your point."

"Thanks. I need to get in touch with *señor* Galenden. He shouldn't have any exposure to today's events, but if Daniel and Jessica are identified as the Russos, then authorities will be able to track them back to the airport in Nuequen, which he owns."

"We should send someone to the airport to retrieve their jeep. One less link to worry about," Parker said.

"Good call. Galenden won't be happy, but this is the first issue we've had in two years. From this point forward, all traffic goes in and out of our private airfield. Let me know when our team hits Russian soil."

"They should be underway in about nine hours, scheduled to arrive in the vicinity of Monchegorsk roughly four hours after that. They'll enter the city when it's dark. I'll keep you advised. Good luck with Galenden."

Sanderson nodded and grabbed the satellite phone. He'd take a walk in the woods and give Galenden the bad news. He couldn't imagine any conceivable circumstance that would cause Galenden to pull the plug on his operation, but he had learned never to make major assumptions. The Black Flag program was at a key juncture in its life cycle, and Sanderson wanted to avoid any major interruptions.

Chapter Thirty-Six

11:55 AM
Outskirts of Monchegorsk
Kola Peninsula, Russian Federation

Daniel stood against a tall pine tree and programmed his GPS unit with the snowmobile hide site's coordinates. He was the last member of the team to complete this task, and once he finished, they would set off on skis toward Monchegorsk. The hide site was located deep within the woods of a small hill overlooking the city. They were still several kilometers west of the nearest city structure, which should have been enough distance to keep the whine of the snowmobile engines from drawing any attention in the city.

Daniel confirmed that the waypoint had been accepted and placed the GPS receiver in one of the front lower pouches on his gray-white camouflaged, military style harness. Another pouch contained a digital camera capable of taking high resolution pictures and video. Most of the lower pouches held ammunition for the forty-year-old AK-47 assault rifles slung over their shoulders.

Farrington carried a similar camera and the team's satellite radio, their only link to Sanderson and Berg. He also carried a suppressed PPS submachine gun, which would serve as their only covert weapon beyond the knives strapped to their legs. Sergei commented that the PPS had probably been produced in a Soviet factory before any of them had been born. In all reality, all of the weapons had likely been buried in Finland before any of them were born. The team had spent a few hours removing the thick storage grease that had covered the weapons, inside and out. Once the weapons had been thoroughly cleaned, they tested each weapon's action and picked the five most reliable rifles. None of them cared to dwell on the viability of the ammunition found with the weapons.

They were all dressed in expensive, mobile cold weather clothing, covered by old Soviet Era winter camouflage and relatively modern harness gear. White wool watch caps with gray and brown camouflage specks topped each of their heads, along with simple black ski goggles. If they ran into a Russian patrol, they might actually pass for some twisted version of cold weather Spetznaz.

Once Daniel nodded, they conducted a communications check, speaking quietly and acknowledging each other. Each man wore a sophisticated throat microphone, with an invisible earbud for communication. The throat rig didn't require them to speak above a whisper, since it absorbed vibrations directly from the speaker's vocal cords through the neck. It also cut out almost all background noise, allowing them to talk under windy, extremely noisy conditions, like a firefight or snowmobile ride. The communications gear and cameras were the only items they carried that appeared to have been produced within the past two decades. Even their Telemark skis looked like ancient castaways, rivaling the age and condition of the snowmobiles provided by South Kola Limited.

Their CIA contact from the embassy in Helsinki had arranged everything and had stressed that they were lucky to get the snowmobiles. South Kola Limited had balked when he asked for maps of Russian trails leading to Monchegorsk and a covered sled to pull behind the snowmobiles. Though nobody at South Kola Limited's shop would speak of it, the CIA agent got the distinct impression that they knew Monchegorsk was off-limits, and as one of the premier snowmobile outfitters in the area, had been warned not to send anyone into the Kola Peninsula. An exorbitant amount of money had secured a waiver in the form of South Kola Limited turning a blind eye. The cost of this blind eye turned out to be the shittiest equipment in their inventory. Apparently, they weren't expecting any of it to return.

Gunshots echoed through the hills as the scene unfolded in the distance. The city of Monchegorsk was a stereotypical Soviet Bloc city, dominated by rows of ugly, tall, rectangular apartment buildings. Gray dominated every street, building and common area below them, all merged together perfectly by a blanket of dirty snow. A low cloud cover smothered the city and almost swallowed the tops of the several dozen smokestacks located northwest of the city. The faded red and white warning pattern painted on Norval Nickel's vast array of spires provided the only color he could find in the city, aside from an orange blaze consuming one of the apartment complexes. The industrial plant's tall stacks stood dormant against the sky. More gunshots drifted their way, and they searched for the source.

A dark green BTR-80 Armored Personnel Carrier raced onto one of the main boulevards followed by two GAZ 2975 'Tiger' Jeeps. The Tiger resembled an up-armored U.S. HMMWV (Humvee), but retained some of the boxy features normally associated with an armored car. Gunners on each of the vehicles fired at a three-story office building as the drivers formed a rough semi-circle around the southern end of the structure. Chunks of concrete exploded from the building's facade as 14.5mm projectiles from the BTR-80's turret tore into the cheap Cold War era construction. The 12.5mm heavy machine guns mounted on the Tigers concentrated on the ground level of the building, shattering glass and splintering wood frames.

After several seconds of continuous heavy machine-gun fire, heavily armed soldiers wearing green camouflage uniforms and helmets poured out of the vehicles. Several soldiers from the furthest Tiger disappeared out of sight around the back of the building, and a fierce firefight erupted out of Daniel's view. Successive explosions just out of view showered the Tiger in dust and debris. Soldiers huddled near the BTR-80 reacted swiftly. They stopped firing into the building and sprinted to the rear corner of the bullet-riddled building. From the cover of the intact corner, the soldiers fired at targets somewhere behind the building, most likely in support of the squad that had just disappeared. Through his binoculars, Daniel watched as figures emerged from the smoke.

The squad that had originally deployed behind the building carried three wounded soldiers toward their hastily drawn perimeter. The gunfire intensified and one of the pairs struggling toward the nearest vehicle suddenly dropped to the ground. More soldiers rushed forward to retrieve their wounded comrades.

"Looks like a rescue operation," Daniel remarked.

"Rescue from what?" Farrington replied.

A smoke trail raced out of the southern-facing wall and tore through the thin roof armor of the Tiger closest to the engaged troops, detonating inside. The gunner firing the heavy machine gun mounted on the Tiger disappeared in a fireball that shattered the truck and caused every soldier in sight to drop into a prone position. The BTR-80 started to back up, and Daniel sensed that they were about to withdraw. Heavy machine-gun fire intensified against the side of the building that had been used to fire a rocket propelled grenade at the platoon, and the Russian Federation soldiers scrambled to reach the two remaining vehicles. Simultaneously, everyone in Daniel's group heard the faint sound of helicopter blades. They exchanged uncomfortable glances. Far over Monchegorsk, two helicopters appeared, flying low.

"Two Havocs. Fuck. Seeing one up close was enough for me," Leo muttered.

"We'll have to be extremely careful at night. They'll be equipped with the latest thermal imaging equipment. Same with the armored personnel carriers," Farrington said.

They watched as the armored vehicles, jammed beyond their advertised troop carrying capacity, lurched down the road at top speed. All binoculars turned to find the helicopters, which grew in size as they approached, barely missing the tops of the tallest gray structures in the downtown area. Daniel lowered his binoculars and took in the entire scene.

The helicopters slowed to a hover several streets away and formed up side by side. Once the rear helicopter pulled up next to the lead Havoc, both helicopters fired dozens of unguided rockets at the building the soldiers had just left. The rockets slammed into the unobserved side of the building, followed by thunderous detonations that reached the side they could see. Most of the windows on the second and third floor of the building blew out onto the street, followed by flaming internal debris. Daniel saw at least two bodies sail out of the building among the flaming wreckage.

The Havocs fired another salvo that tore completely through the second floor and brought half of the third story down, raising an impenetrable cloud of concrete dust and smoke. They watched more smoke trails arc into the haze from the helicopters, followed by successive detonations that shook the forest floor. Daniel couldn't tell what happened, but it felt like an earthquake tremor. The helicopters started to drift toward the structure, falling back in a line as they intersected the main road recently travelled by the surviving Russian Army vehicles.

"They aren't fucking around. The entire building just collapsed," Leo said.

Daniel's attention drifted to several figures that emerged from the expanding wave of dust. They moved slowly, helping each other cross the street in front of the destroyed building. At least two members of the group carried assault rifles and wore the same camouflage uniform as the soldiers. Instead of helmets, they wore black watch caps, which were covered with the gray dust from the building. The two helicopters cruised up the street, and Daniel saw puffs of smoke trail the lead Havoc's forward mounted 30mm cannon. The cannon's projectiles ripped into the group on the street before the sound reached Daniel's ears. The extended burst of cannon fire dropped all but one of the figures trying to reach the cover of smaller building across the road. The lone survivor of the Havoc's gun-run picked up one of the dead men's rifles and fired at the helicopter as it cruised overhead. The shooter disintegrated into a bloody mound of twisted limbs and exposed bone as the sound of the second helicopter's cannon washed over Daniel.

"They're not fucking around one bit," Petrovich reinforced.

"Did the local army garrison turn?" Leo said.

"It certainly looks that way. Berg said the garrison's base is fed by several wells and isn't connected to the city water supply. This is mainly a local unit and a majority of the personnel have families that live in Monchegorsk or nearby towns. He suspects that Russian leadership would try to simplify things and lump the entire garrison into any kind of quarantine effort. This doesn't look like your typical quarantine."

"More like an extermination," Leo said.

"Exactly. Like Parker said, we stick to the basics on this mission. Get in, figure out what the virus does and document as much evidence as possible. Our job is to get as much information to Berg as possible. The Russians are playing the containment game, and everyone else is in the dark. Berg wants enough evidence to crack this wide open," Petrovich said.

"All right, we'll approach the southwest end of town, stash the skis and set another GPS point," Farrington added.

They set off on skis as the two helicopters banked left and raced back toward the center of Monchegorsk. A loud explosion rocked the hills, and they turned in time to see another fireball reach skyward from a building several kilometers into the city, far from the two attack helicopters. They continued to follow the lightly travelled snowmobile trail that had brought them this far and would bring them to a point concealed in the forest, less than a half kilometer from a series of industrial buildings. They'd hide among the pine trees and wait for dark.

Chapter Thirty-Seven

10:45 PM
Outskirts of Monchegorsk
Kola Peninsula, Russian Federation

Petrovich sprinted for the rear corner of the building closest to the cluster of trees that had served as their final approach point to the outskirts of town. He reached the rusted metal edge of the prefabricated structure and stopped to scan the area beyond with his night vision. He listened to the area around the buildings, and after spending a few minutes of studying the green images produced by his handheld scope, he signaled for the rest of the team to join him. Sporadic distant gunfire drifted through the maze of structures, masking the direction of its origin.

From what he could tell, none of the action was focused on this part of town, which should simplify their approach to the apartment buildings on the southwest edge. Their main risk involved crossing Highway M18, which carried a steady stream of military traffic and patrols. There would be ample opportunity to cross unobserved, but it still made Daniel nervous. Unfortunately, every approach from the west crossed M18, but this route provided the cover of several lifeless buildings that were unlikely to attract any attention. Most of the windows were missing, and they saw no signs of recent human activity from their hide site in the forest. As the rest of the group stacked up along the concrete wall, Daniel checked the area again.

"We'll move up together through the buildings and approach the highway. We can watch a considerable stretch of road from ground level on either side. Once across, we'll hightail it to the abandoned gas station on the other side. Our goal is to find a way into one of the apartment buildings less than a mile from the station," he said and took off without warning.

The team worked its way through another five hundred meters of neglected gray buildings, dodging large heaps of scrap metal and discarded industrial materials. They moved as quietly as possible through pitch-black expanses, stopping momentarily to scan for sentries or anything out of place that might signify an early end to their trip.

By consensus, they had agreed to focus their attention on a block of several closely clustered five-story apartment buildings in the western suburbs of Monchegorsk. By day, the apartments looked like they might have been thoroughly evacuated, but as night descended, they picked up hints of light with their night vision through the thin curtains of several windows. They'd close in on the nearest building and find a place to observe the area for a while.

If they could see lights inside the apartments with second generation civilian night vision scopes, the Russians could see them, too. Russian units would be equipped with fourth generation night vision optics, thermal imaging equipment and infrared detection gear. Based on what they witnessed all afternoon, the Russians were scouring the city with no rules of engagement.

Upon reaching the last building before the highway, Daniel signaled for them all to hold at the corner. He lowered his body and crawled through the dirty snow along a row of dead bushes to the front of the building. He raised his head far enough to see down the road to the south and did the same for the north. Nothing. No illumination or signs of movement. He pulled out his night vision scope and took a look in each direction.

The green image didn't reveal any hidden surprises, but it emphasized the limitations of their night vision gear. The persistent, thin haze blanketing Monchegorsk during the day remained at night to reduce the effective visual range through his scope. For longer distance spotting, they would be better off using the naked eye. The Russians wouldn't have this problem with the newer generation low-light technology. Daniel's team would have to be extremely cautious when making decisions based on long-range detection capabilities.

"One person at a time will crawl up. Stay low. If a vehicle approaches from the south, this wall will be exposed, but you should have enough cover. When you get to the corner, watch the road for a minute to be sure it's clear, then sprint across. Rally point is behind the gas station."

He heard the rest of the team whisper their acknowledgment and glanced down the road in each direction. All clear, he hoped. Daniel was on his feet in a flash, sprinting in the direction of the gas station. He crossed the road diagonally and skirted the edge of the station's parking lot, headed straight for a large trash dumpster behind the small building. He reached the back wall and slammed his left foot into the door, which gave slightly. He stepped back and kicked it again, splintering the door frame and sending the door inward. He unslung his rifle and moved quickly to the outside corner of the gas station.

"All clear at the station. The back door is open. Rally point inside," he said.

A figure appeared across the street, barreling in his direction. A few minutes later, they huddled inside the frigid gas station. Sergei was the last to arrive.

"I didn't see anything on the road. I think we're good," he said.

"All right. Let's move out. Schafer, you'll bring up the rear. Stay back far enough to watch over us and provide cover if anything pops up," Daniel said.

Schafer gave him a thumbs up that he could barely see in the dark.

"We all need to be on the lookout for snipers. If you hear a snap or see a flash…sprint for three hundred and sixty degree cover. Whatever you do, don't stay in place. I hunted groups like this for two years, and the only thing that ever saved my targets was an immediate panicked sprint for cover."

"I thought you didn't miss," Farrington said.

"I don't. I was talking about the only response that kept me from killing everyone in the group."

"We need to get moving," Farrington said.

"I'll take point. Farrington, Sergei and Leo bring up the middle. Schafer, you know what to do."

"You're never going to call me Yuri, are you?" Farrington said.

"Probably not. Move out," Daniel said and disappeared running.

Fifty minutes later, Daniel walked slowly through a small children's playground. An apartment building loomed overhead, yielding no signs of life. He scanned the windows, aiming the rifle where he looked. It looked dead, but they knew better. He slowly approached a door on the ground level and squinted intensely at the dark gray and blue image provided by the naked eye. He could barely see twenty feet in front of him.

"Do you see anything on the ground level?"

"Negative. I still have a few windows on the third and fourth floor with activity," Schafer said from his over watch position in the distance.

"Roger."

He reached the door and leaned against the concrete wall to its right, extending his right hand to test the door handle. It didn't budge, but he could tell that the door opened inward, which was a good thing if they had to use brute force. Daniel removed both of his thin gray Nomex gloves and stuffed them into cargo pockets. He retrieved a small zippered kit from his backpack and started using the contents to open the door's lock. He tried several combinations of small tools until he felt the tumbler move. He squeezed the thumb mechanism on the top of the handle and pushed inward on the door, which moved effortlessly on its hinges. Perfect.

"We're in. Move the team up."

Daniel moved into the apartment, and noted that the temperature inside didn't improve much from the outside. The rancid smell of decomposition hit him suddenly, which sent a few waves of panic through him. He was in the dark with dead bodies. He put his gloves back on and took out a small flashlight. He turned it on and pointed it down the hallway. He saw dead bodies stacked floor to ceiling against the front doors of the building. Something yanked the flashlight out of his hand.

"Are you fucking crazy?" Farrington said. He turned the light off and handed it back to Petrovich. "Use your night vision."

The rest of the team assembled inside, except for Schafer, who would watch the building from the outside and provide early warning if the Russians approached. Using his night vision scope instead of a flashlight, Daniel could now see that this was the custodial level and contained no apartments. Large pipes attached to the ceiling ran the length of the hallway. The doors they could see would likely lead to large boilers or furnace equipment.

"We'll head up those stairs to the third floor and hit two rooms at once. Third door and eighth door on the right. I'll stack up with Leo on the far door. Yuri and Sergei take the closer one."

"If we have the doors right. Could be two or three windows per apartment," Leo said.

"We'll figure it out. We need to find what we're looking for in this building. The gunfire is increasing out there," Daniel said.

"I heard helicopters," Farrington said.

That was all anyone needed to say. The team jogged toward the staircase on the northern side of the building and opened the door. The staircase contained no windows, so Daniel flashed his light up the stairwell. Empty. They quietly climbed to the second floor and approached a door. Daniel peered through the window and saw nothing but darkness. He opened the door several inches and took another look with his night vision scope. He saw trash and assorted debris, but no bodies. They hadn't detected any signs of life on the second floor from the outside, and it looked to be no different on the inside.

"Clear," he whispered.

The team continued to the third floor, hugging the walls and keeping their weapons focused on the door leading into the third floor's main hallway. They had counted at least six sources of light on this level, so they approached the door cautiously. Daniel moved his hand to the door handle and pulled it gently, but it didn't move.

"Locked," he whispered.

Farrington moved to the other side of the door, followed closely by Sergei, who glanced up into the darkness of the stairwell toward the fourth floor. Farrington edged his head closer to the door's window and peeked into the hallway, pulling it back immediately. He shook his head and removed his night vision scope, placing it against the glass. He used his right hand to signal for Daniel to work on the door's lock. Daniel removed the same kit he used earlier from one of the pouches on his vest and started to use the two tools that had opened the ground level door. He knew exactly what he needed to do to manipulate the lock's tumblers.

As soon as he felt the tumblers move, the door slammed inward, knocking both Farrington and Petrovich to the concrete floor of the stairwell. Blinding lights and screams filled the stairwell from every direction, and Daniel felt himself ripped off the floor, onto his knees. Someone kneeled on the back of his legs, holding them down, and his arms were quickly pinned behind him. The only thing he didn't hear was gunfire, which for the moment was a good thing.

He was too stunned to react and tried to look around before a dark bag was placed over his head. He felt hard metal press against the side of his skull and figured there was no point in trying to flip the guy restraining his arms. He hoped the rest of his team came to the same conclusion. If they had been captured by civilians, they had a good shot at surviving. When the yelling and struggling calmed, a thick, authoritarian Russian voice emerged.

"You'd all be dead by now if this one hadn't spoken English downstairs," the voice said.

"Even as you approached the building, a few of my people didn't think you were Russian. Who are you?"

"American Special Forces," Daniel said, in Russian.

"Now you speak Russian?" he said and ripped the hood off Daniel's head.

Someone aimed a flashlight directly in Daniel's eyes, partially blinding him, but he had seen enough to know that the rest of his team was on their knees with bags over their heads. Roughly a dozen loosely uniformed men crowded the stairwell landing. Most of them were occupied with restraining his team. A large man stood in front of him, wearing Russian Army camouflage and a large brown fur hat with side flaps. He held an AKS-74u fitted with a bipod and holographic sight. A large night vision rifle scope was tethered by a D-ring to a loop on his camouflage jacket.

"That scope should be attached to a rifle," Daniel said.

"Wouldn't do this crew any good on a rifle. You don't look like Special Forces. This rifle is older than you are and most of your outer gear is old Russian Army issue. What is your mission here?" the leader said.

"To assess and report. We suspect whatever happened here is linked to a rogue Russian bioweapons engineer," Daniel said.

The man exchanged glances with a few of his men and walked over to confer with a man standing halfway up the stairs. He asked a question from the stairs.

"Do they think this is contagious?"

"No. We think this is a form of weaponized encephalitis. Most likely delivered directly through the city's water supply."

"Encephalitis? Whatever it is, it's making people sick in the head. Half the city went crazy. What are you supposed to do with the information?"

"Transmit immediately via satellite and leave."

"You have a satellite phone?"

"Phone with high bandwidth rig," Daniel said.

He heard Farrington start to yell, but the operative was quickly muffled.

"We'll need to take that phone. The world needs to know what happened here. What our government is doing."

"How about we come to an agreement?"

"An agreement? We're in the position to be making demands, not the other way around," the man said.

"More or less true, but the phone isn't on either of us, and it'll disappear if we don't reach an agreement."

An excited voice yelled down the stairs. "Helicopters!"

"Where is the phone? With the other guy outside?"

"He's listening to this entire exchange, so I recommend we cut the shit. We're on the same side," Daniel said.

The man spoke into a small radio he had kept concealed in his camouflage jacket and listened for the faint reply.

"Fuck! Your man bolted. What do you want?" he said and issued orders down the stairs.

"I need to know exactly what happened here and I need tissue samples. Preferably a live sample," Daniel said.

"You want to take someone back with you?" the man said.

"Someone that can move on their own. One of your soldiers," Daniel said.

"These aren't all soldiers, but we have plenty of candidates for you to take back," he said. He cocked his head and listened to the radio. "Fucking helicopters are inbound. You need to get your guy into this building immediately. He won't last very long out there. Thermal imaging. 30mm guns will chew him up and spit him out," he said.

"Do we have a deal?" Daniel demanded.

"What do I get in return?"

"I'll give you the satellite rig."

"Can it scan documents?" the man said.

"It comes with a digital camera for that purpose. I can hear the helicopters now. We need to wrap this up and get my guy inside. He has the satellite phone," Daniel said.

"I'll need you to help me get documents," the man said.

"What kind of documents?"

"The kind you can only find in a command vehicle," he replied.

"You have plenty of soldiers for that," Daniel said.

"The soldiers I have are military police reservists. Most of the men and women fighting in the city are civilians. I need Special Forces types to take down a command BTR."

"Release my men immediately and return their weapons. Then we have a deal," Daniel said.

The man ordered their release and Daniel struggled to his feet.

Farrington immediately got in Daniel's face. "We don't have time for diversions or passengers. We need to take tissue samples, interrogate the locals and get the fuck out of here," he said.

"Hold on. Schafer, can you get back to the building without exposing yourself to the birds?"

"I'm on my way back. The sounds are still muffled. I should be fine. ETA, one minute."

He returned his attention to Farrington. "Yuri, it's too late for that. A deal's a deal. It's not like we had a lot of negotiating power. How long do you think it would have taken them to find the phone?" he asked, patting Farrington's chest.

"You were bluffing me?" the former soldier said.

"Not really. Schafer has the high bandwidth rig. Where do we go from here?"

"Out of this building. We moved our headquarters here earlier in the day, but it appears that we have attracted enough attention to bring them into the area."

"When are we getting our weapons back? They took them upstairs," Farrington demanded.

"You're not getting those rifles back," the man said.

"What the fuck? It was part of the deal and—"

"Those rifles are shit. We have better weapons for you…unless you want your forty-year-old Kalashnikov back. You should keep the PPS though. We can make use of that," he said.

Several armed civilians descended the stairs and stacked several weapons and new equipment along an empty wall on the landing. They continued down the stairs amidst the yelling and chaos of a general evacuation. Daniel spotted Schafer on the stairs, pushing his way through a mass of armed men flowing to the lower levels of the building. The man directed them toward the weapons and harness gear.

"Take your pick. Just make sure to swap out your rifle magazines. None of these will fire 7.62mm. Hurry up. I want to clear out of this building in a few minutes. The helicopters won't fire on the buildings before the ground troops arrive, unless they're fired upon first."

"We saw them take a building down about a mile from here. Earlier in the day," Farrington said.

"That was my fault. I had sent a squad to that neighborhood with the hopes of drawing their attention away from our headquarters move. The squad took it upon themselves to shoot up a foot patrol and got stuck in the building. We saw the building collapse from the rockets. Our squad never returned," the man said.

"They were all killed," Farrington said, grabbing a fully rigged AKS-74u.

"Along with everyone in the building. The government has switched from evacuation to extermination mode. Not that there was ever really a difference," the man said.

"What do you mean? Do you have any suppressors for these weapons, or long-range night scopes?" Daniel said, lifting a thick-barreled AK-74 from the stockpile.

A young man standing near the stairs answered. "No suppressors. We didn't have anything like that in our armory. We were lucky to have advanced sights for the weapons. I can get you a scope. I'm Sergeant Malyshev. One of the few regulars assigned to the battalion."

He walked over and extended his hand to Farrington, who shook it, followed by Daniel. After shaking the man's hand, Daniel became concerned. In the scattered light of several flashlights, he could see that the man's face was drained of color and his eyes were bloodshot. He coughed softly into the crook of his elbow.

"Sergeant Malyshev has been a blessing to the battalion. One of the few regulars with combat experience to ever be assigned to our unit…and the only regular to stay behind. He saw extensive combat in Chechnya. I'm assigning him to your group."

"We don't need any additional manpower," Daniel said.

"Trust me, you'll be glad to have this soldier backing you up. He knows the streets…and he can fight like the devil. You're taking him with you when you leave. He's your live sample."

It all made sense to Daniel now.

"How far along are you?" Daniel said, flashing his light in Malyshev's face.

"I'm still a day or so away from having real problems. Right now I just have flu symptoms. That's how it starts," he said.

"How did he get infected?" Sergei said.

"Many of the men refilled their canteens when we took to the city. Nobody at the base was initially infected. We're not on city water. Some got sick, some didn't. Maybe some houses had already flushed out all of the bad water and others hadn't. Bad luck? Who the fuck knows? I'm Maxim, by the way. Captain Maxim Sabitov. I commanded the 332nd Reserve Military Police Battalion…still do I guess.

"On Saturday, April 7th, most of the battalion remained overnight for our monthly drill. It's mostly administrative work this time of the year, so we let a number of the men return to their families off base on Saturday night. They all got sick over the course of the next week. The men who stayed on base that night were fine."

"How many men did you have under your command?" Farrington said.

"Three hundred and fifty-six. Forty-three went home that night. Forty of them got sick. About thirty complied with Russian Army Command's order to abandon the base, leaving me with roughly two hundred and eighty men."

"Abandon the base?" Daniel said.

"Of course. The situation in Monchegorsk had deteriorated significantly by then, and Moscow had three hundred armed soldiers assigned to the base. Most with families living in Monchegorsk. They didn't want us sticking around town to cause trouble, so they ordered us north. Only the unmarried soldiers obeyed. We made sure to secure the armory from the very outset. Most of us knew what was at stake here."

His radio chirped again and he put his hand on Daniel's shoulder. The deep, rhythmic thud of helicopter rotors intensified and passed, replaced by the steep whine of the twin turboshaft engines. The entire building vibrated as the helicopter passed overhead.

"We need to get moving. I don't want to be responsible for bringing another building down on their heads," Maxim said, pulling Daniel toward the stairs.

"How many civilians are still around?" Farrington said.

"Hard to say. A few thousand maybe. Scattered everywhere. The Russians have started block by block sweeps to the northeast."

"That's a lot of people. Why doesn't the government just evacuate them?"

"Because nobody believes the government is actually evacuating them. From the very beginning, rumors have circulated that they just truck everyone over to the nickel pits and shoot them. Based on what I've seen in the city, I wouldn't be surprised. The other problem is that half of the people I've seen are violently insane and unpredictable. They can't effectively restrain the sick ones. You'll see what I mean. It's fucking crazy out there. Especially at night."

&

Lieutenant Colonel Grigory Zadornov stood in a circle with his battalion's leadership. He had three infantry company commanders and an assortment of infantry and armor platoon commanders. The sound of throttling diesel engines competed with the chatter going back and forth among the men.

"Cut the chatter," he barked, and they immediately quieted.

"I've just received orders to move the battalion four miles through the city to an area here. Helicopter and Spetznaz surveillance reports indicate a heavy concentration of armed civilians among the buildings," he said, pointing at a map held up to his chest.

"Too many weapons in one place to be another disorganized gaggle. We know the insurgents moved their headquarters earlier today, so we're going to hit this area in force, with helicopter support. Nighttime rules of engagement are in place. Shoot anything that moves. Conserve ammunition during the transit and make sure to deploy your troops as soon as you make contact. We lost two vehicles last night to some kind of bullshit improvised explosives that were placed on the vehicles by hand. Nobody should be getting close enough to touch one of our vehicles. Infantry commanders and vehicle commanders need to work together. I better not lose another vehicle to a Semtex sticky bomb. We move out in five minutes. All orders and rally points have been transmitted to your mobile battlefield feeds. Mark your maps and standby to depart."

He turned and stepped through an open side hatch into his vehicle, a command variant of the BTR-80 armored personnel carrier, easily identifiable by two large whip antennas protruding from the top rear corners of the troop compartment. The air inside was considerably warmer than the wind-whipped arctic air flowing down the street through his column. One of the infantry captains had remained behind to chat.

"What if we have more civilians trying to surrender? The orders last night weren't clear with the men," he said.

"No prisoners. Anyone on the streets is to be shot. It sounds harsh, but the water supply to the city has been poisoned. At this point, my commander has determined that anyone remaining in the city is likely to be infected and will eventually transform into one of the abominations we've been dealing with all over the city. Our government is fighting desperately to keep this outbreak from spreading to other cities. Unfortunately, we're on the shit end of that fight. Get your company ready for heavy contact. I expect this to be a long night," Colonel Zadornov said.

Once the captain left the vehicle's rear opening, he turned back to his command center to review the maps and any new orders that might have come through on his mobile battlefield terminal. The command center barely qualified as anything more than four square feet of table space on the right side of the BTR. With the mobile battlefield terminal (MBT) affixed to the hull above and to the left of the table, alongside a row of radio receivers, the setup gave him enough room to use half of a map. He could simultaneously scour the MBT for updates from his various subordinates, and if he didn't like what he was seeing or hearing, he had three radios at his disposal to remedy the situation.

A harness seat had been bolted to the deck at one end of the table, allowing him to stay at the command center, while the BTR scrambled from one location to the next. Cold weather clothing, issued harness gear, weapons and ammunition were crammed into every other conceivable space in the back and would spill everywhere once they started moving.

His operations officer would stuff himself somewhere among the four soldiers riding in back, who had been assigned to defend the vehicle. He would fight for space around the command center to advise Zadornov. Even under the best circumstances, it was organized chaos, and whenever possible, Zadornov would ride in the turret. Especially when they came under fire. The rear compartment shrank with the sounds of small arms fire knocking against the hull, and he hated the thought of helplessly waiting for a rocket propelled grenade to tear through the thin armor.

He lifted one of the radio handhelds from its receiver and transmitted an order to the battalion.

"This is Zovra Command. Three minute warning for the scout elements. Stick to your assigned routes. No variations. Over," he said and listened for all of the individual units' acknowledgments.

He wondered what the young captain had really thought about the battalion's orders. It didn't take a university degree in science to realize that command's supposed fear of an outbreak was utter nonsense. If they were dealing with a contagious epidemic, the troops would have been issued biological suits…at least masks. They had arrived with all of that gear, but his commander had been told not to issue it. Rumors about the water supply had spread through the battalion like wildfire, reinforced by strict, repeated orders not to drink from indigenous water sources.

For Zadornov, it didn't really matter. Something had infected the population and turned them into stark raving lunatics. He'd seen every form of depraved behavior, from gang raping in the middle of the streets, to children jumping from the rooftops. Everyone in the city was psychotic on some level. It was impossible to predict when a seemingly normal person might pick up a rock and try to bash your head in.

He didn't like the order to shoot on sight, but after spending five nights patrolling the city, he didn't see any other choice. He just hoped that when this was over, the government didn't decide to drag his entire battalion over to the nickel pits. He didn't want to know what the Internal Ministry Troops were doing in the industrial sector of town to the northwest.

His seat rumbled as the driver revved the engine in anticipation of the assault. All around him, vehicles sprang to life and started to move forward. His operations officer, a young infantry captain, hopped through the side hatch and issued an order to the rest of their crew. Within a minute, the troop compartment of the BTR was crowded with soldiers and all hatches were sealed. The BTR lurched forward, knocking everyone around the metal compartment and spilling gear everywhere. Zadornov reminded himself to find another driver for tomorrow.

❧

Daniel Petrovich stepped out into the darkness and scanned the neighborhood. The crescent moon provided enough ambient light to outline the large hulks of more than a dozen apartment buildings, all tightly stuffed into an area Sabitov had called Katayev Prospekt.

They had met for a few minutes in the basement to discuss Sabitov's plan, which involved moving the bulk of his fighters to this development. From there, his fighters would put up a brief fight and disperse. Their goal was to occupy all of the Russian Army's attention, while Daniel's group tried to pull off the impossible.

"You ready for this? Walk in the park for Special Forces, right?" Sabitov said and slapped him on the back.

The rest of the team joined him and listened silently. They could hear rumbling in the distance and the distinct thud of helicopter rotors.

"Armor is moving in this direction, but the helicopters will track my people. Everything will be shifted to the Katayev Prospekt. I expect the entire Russian force to be concentrated on that area. Fifteen apartment buildings. Much larger than the one we left," he said.

"The helicopters don't shoot people on the streets?" Sergei asked.

"Not yet, but I suggest we move as discreetly as possible," Sabitov said.

"Lead the way," Petrovich said.

The group of nine men set off in a northeasterly direction, led by Major Sabitov and Sergeant Malyshev, who both carried loaded RPG launchers. Three additional soldiers had been added to the group to help Sabitov create a diversion. The soldiers were dressed in civilian clothes and carried additional rockets. Like Sabitov's sergeant, they didn't sound very healthy. As long as they could do their jobs, Daniel wasn't concerned.

Daniel's team, which included Malyshev, would assault the vehicles. Daniel had made it clear that if the command BTR didn't take the bait, they would depart Monchegorsk immediately. Sabitov was convinced that the information found in the battalion commander's vehicle would be worth the risk. Daniel traded looks with Farrington as they sprinted off into the darkness. They were both thinking the same thing, but Daniel had no intention of double-crossing Sabitov. The man had stayed behind against overwhelming odds to protect his family, which was something Daniel could relate to.

They weaved their way through a maze of smaller buildings and snow-covered yards, occasionally ducking behind walls or kicking in doors to hide from the Mi-28 Havoc that screamed overhead. The helicopter was loud enough to hear from a distance, and they had no shortage of places to hide.

Soon enough, they'd come up on an open area leading to a small cluster of apartment buildings and would have to carefully time their transit. Gunfire picked up to their front, punctuated by the loud crack of RPGs exploding. Sabitov listened to his radio.

"They've just ambushed the recon elements of the armor battalion. We wait here and see if they take the bait," Sabitov said.

"How far ahead are they?" Daniel said.

"Less than a mile. My teams will pull back to Katayev Prospekt and draw them into the area around the tall buildings. We'll have to time this carefully. We need to—"

A sudden growl stopped his sentence, followed by a horrifying scream and mumbled voices.

"What the fuck is that?" Leo said.

The Russians exchanged worried glances just as three screaming figures charged between the two structures behind them. They closed the short distance quicker than he'd expected, and he couldn't identify them in the darkness. Several gunshots exploded, and the attack stopped as quickly as it started. They heard demented laughter off in the distance.

"They must have followed us," Malyshev said.

"Who followed us?" Petrovich demanded.

"The sick ones. This is what happens," he said, kicking over one of the bodies.

Petrovich stared at a young woman's dead body, focused on the blood encrusted butcher knife near her hand. She was dressed in an unbuttoned gray overcoat, which covered blood-splattered, light green hospital scrubs. "Dr. Cherkasov" was embroidered over the left breast pocket.

"Don't ever be fooled. They're all armed with crazy shit like this. Mr. Petrovich, would you take one of your men back to those buildings with the PPS and scan the street for any additional followers? I can hear them," Sabitov said.

Daniel tugged at Leo's jacket, just as Farrington tossed the silenced PPS at them. Leo snatched it out of the air, and they both walked briskly between the buildings with their weapons held ready. He reached the end of the building and risked a peek around the corner. Through the darkness, he could see someone repeatedly stabbing another person about twenty feet down the street. Movement in his peripheral vision alerted him to the presence of two figures emerging from the shadows of the buildings on the other side of the tight road. The Russians appeared to be the least of their problems at the moment.

"Two more walking down the middle of the road, dragging something behind them. Looks like half of a body. Fuck," Leo whispered.

"Take them down first, then hit the two across the street."

Daniel raised his rifle and turned the corner, immediately finding his target through the Russian made 3X PN23 night vision scope. He quickly centered the red dot on the side of the attacker's head and shot him. He heard several muffled shots from the PPS and shifted his rifle to the two figures across the street. Both targets appeared in the scope, and he chose the man to the right, who stood with his mouth open, twitching. The second man charged them, and Daniel shifted his scope to the runner, preparing to fire.

"A little help with this one," he said and took his eye off the scope to fire an unaided shot.

The PPS coughed an extended burst, and the man tumbled to the street, his riddled body feeding a rapidly expanding dark shadow in the snow. Daniel sighted in on the man across the street, who hadn't moved since they started shooting. He watched a line of bullets stitch across the man's chest, knocking him back into the shadows. Daniel picked up movement on the street from several directions at once.

"We need to get the fuck out of here," Leo said.

"Agreed. Farrington, inform Major Sabitov that we can't stay here," Daniel said.

His earpiece crackled. "Understood."

Daniel raced back to the group, and Sabitov informed them that the entire armor formation was headed toward Katayev Prospekt down one of the main roads. He predicted that the battalion would split up into three groups, about three hundred meters before reaching the large cluster of buildings. He'd watched them employ this same strategy three nights in a row and the command BTR always joined the group on the left flank. Last night, the BTR broke off on its own and drove one block to pursue a group of looters. The two GAZ-2975 Tiger jeeps assigned to escort the command BTR followed closely. He watched the three vehicles fire point blank into a group of several civilians and could barely believe his eyes when the soldiers in the BTR dismounted to check the bodies. He told them that their success hinged on the Russians' opening the BTR's hatch.

As they all started to run, Daniel grabbed Farrington. "How will they get the Russian commander to open up the hatch? If they come under attack, they'll stay buttoned up in the APC's. I think it might be time to pull the plug on this," Daniel said.

"I don't think the three soldiers will be returning with the rest of us," Farrington said and sprinted to catch up.

Daniel thought about this for a few seconds, until a maddened scream from the street behind him spurred him into action.

&

Lieutenant Colonel Zadornov studied the MBT screen and cross-referenced points on the map spread out on his compact table. The attack helicopters had confirmed that a large insurgent force had arrived in the vicinity of the Katayev Prospekt apartment development, and his reconnaissance vehicles had been viciously attacked near Katayev, forcing their withdrawal after the loss of one Tiger. The insurgents were desperately trying to keep his battalion away from the development, which led him to conclude that this was their headquarters. He could put an end to the armed resistance in Monchegorsk tonight, if he maneuvered aggressively and killed the insurgency's leadership. To keep the insurgents busy while his battalion approached, he ordered the two Mi-28 Havocs to conduct gun runs to engage targets moving into the area. Within seconds, he heard the distinctive, rapid bark of a 30mm cannon above him. The helicopters' gunners had wasted no time finding targets.

He glanced at the map one more time before issuing his final deployment orders, which would split the force into three groups along Troika Street. The battalion would push into Katayev Prospekt from three directions, looking for a weakness in the insurgent deployment. He might even consider using the Havoc's rockets to topple a few of the ten-story apartment buildings. If he crashed the buildings on the left flank, he could roll right into the middle of the battle, without fear of a lucky rocket propelled grenade puncturing the top armor of his BTR.

The tall buildings presented a unique challenge, as evidenced by the loss of a Tiger earlier in the day. One well aimed shot from the six or seventh story of those buildings had the potential to turn any of the battalion's vehicles into a flaming coffin. There were simply too many windows in each building to cover adequately from the ground, so the infantry would have to clear them, room by room, before the bulk of the vehicles could move forward. Or, he could flatten a few of the buildings. He also had the availability of four Su-25 "Frogfoot" ground attack jets based out of the airbase in Murmansk. Two of the Frogfoots, each armed with eight 500-pound bombs, sat on the runway ready to take off. He could have them over Monchegorsk in less than fifteen minutes.

The BTR rattled and tried to throw the men out of their seats, as the driver swerved to follow Alpha Company's vehicles to the far left flank of the Katayev Prospekt. Zadornov moved into the turret and took a look at the scene through the vehicle commander night scope. He saw tracers arc upward into the buildings from the lead vehicles, while return tracers tracked down toward the street, ricocheting in every direction upon hitting the pavement. The lead BTRs and Tigers of his column deployed their troops, which consisted of a reinforced infantry company. Chaos erupted as one hundred and thirty-five soldiers scrambled for cover from the incoming small arms fire and pushed to rally with their squads for the infantry assault into Katayev.

One of the Havoc gunships roared overhead, firing an extended burst of 30mm projectiles into the closest building. Shell casings ejected from the gun rained down on the vehicles, clanging off the hatches and armor, reminding Zadornov of the thin top armor on his BTRs. To him, the shell casings' impacts sounded like rocks thrown against a corrugated tin shack. He took another look through the sight at Alpha Company's deployment. From his vantage point fifty meters back along the street, he could see most of the company's BTRs and Tigers, sixteen vehicles arrayed in a staggered formation along Yumashev Street. They didn't have much cover from the towering apartment buildings, but at this range in the dark, RPGs were not a major threat. In a few minutes, a few of the BTRs would move forward to support the infantry assault. That's when he expected to see the RPGs.

Just as he ducked down from the turret, a sharp ping echoed off the left side of the vehicle, which struck him as odd, since the Katayev apartments didn't face the left side of the vehicle. His driver had stopped the BTR on the far right side of the road, hoping to take advantage of the cover provided by the homes and businesses crowded together near the road. Another ping sounded from the left side, followed by the pounding sound of his escort vehicles' open mounted 12.7mm heavy machine guns.

He popped back up into the turret as it swung to the left. "Is that small arms fire hitting us?" he asked the gunner.

"Three guys standing in the middle of the street. One of them is firing a rifle. Hold on, sir."

The 14.5mm turret gun rapidly recoiled and shook the entire BTR, flinging smoking hot empty shell casings against the inside metal hull of the turret. The casings cascaded down into the body of the BTR. The sounds of the heavy gun's blasts were mercifully diffused by the BTR's airtight seal. He heard several bursts of fire from assault rifles and figured the troops in the escort Tigers had deployed.

"Did you hit them?" he said to the gunner.

"Negative. They scrambled off the street too fast."

"Sir, we could pursue the group. Looked like a couple crazies with a rifle. I saw three guys in civilian clothes," the vehicle commander said, a wide-eyed, ruddy-faced senior sergeant.

Zadornov thought about his request for a moment and moved to one of the left side viewing ports. He swiveled a metal plate upward and stared through the thick glass into the darkness, which was useless. It was pitch black outside. Only his driver and gunner had vehicle-installed night vision optics. A flash caught his eye, followed immediately by another ping against the BTR's armor, which caused him to flinch. The 14.5mm cannon fired another salvo, which was immediately joined by the two Tigers and several infantry soldiers surrounding the vehicles.

"They're fucking around near one of the buildings on the corner of the next street. We could roll them up pretty easily," the senior sergeant said.

He closed the viewing port's armor shielding and took a seat at his table. He read the most recent updates from his platoon and company commanders. All ground units were moving toward the apartments under heavy small arms and machine gun fire, but the sheer volume of fire from the battalion's vehicle mounted guns and attack helicopters kept the insurgents from concentrating fire on their advance. Two more pings sounded through the BTR, and he heard a scream from somewhere outside. A speaker next to the MBT came to life.

"Sir, we have a casualty from Tiger One. One of their soldiers was hit in the legs. They pulled him back into the vehicle. Do you want to relocate the vehicles away from the shooters?"

Zadornov was annoyed by the vehicle commander's insinuation that he didn't plan to take action. He was in the middle of a major operation and didn't have time to chase three lunatics through the streets. The BTR's 14.5mm gun roared to life, jarring him out of his thoughts.

"Fuck me. Look at this!" the gunner yelled.

Zadornov jumped out of his seat and opened the top hatch of the BTR to take a look for himself. He was greeted by the bright orange light of flames and the smell of burning gasoline. Several guns fired at a slumped figure on the ground near the corner of a small hardware store, shattering the front window and tearing the body apart. A large patch of flames burned in the middle of the street, dancing in the wind and dying quickly. He knew what had happened as soon as he took it all in. One of those nutcases had tried to throw a Molotov cocktail bomb onto his vehicle. A bullet ricocheted off the turret armor, no more than three feet from his head, causing him to duck back inside and slam the top hatch closed. Son of a bitch!

He grabbed the radio handset and ordered the command vehicles into pursuit. He typed a message on the MBT, notifying his subordinate commanders that he was breaking off to pursue a small group of civilians. The vehicle pulled forward and took off down the street with the Tigers alongside. As soon as he pressed "send" on his message, all hell broke loose at Katayev Prospekt and reports started streaming in through all of his radios. If he had stayed in position on Yumashev Street, he would have seen at least a dozen rocket propelled grenades arch down from the buildings reaching for his vehicles.

❧

Daniel watched the three armored vehicles move down the darkened side street that intersected with the road in front of him. Farrington had been right. The three soldiers dressed in civilian clothes had no intention of returning from this mission, and he could barely blame them. After seeing the results of Reznikov's virus on the streets, he'd want to end his own life as quickly as possible. The two remaining soldiers huddled between buildings on the other side of the street and waited for the vehicles to round the corner.

The battle at Katayev Prospekt intensified when the command BTR reached the halfway point down the side street, just as Sabitov had promised. With the entire battalion occupied, their ambush might go unnoticed long enough for them to avoid clashing with more Russian units. The vehicles approached the turn onto their street, and Daniel slid his body along the roof of the building to the front right corner, careful to stay out of sight. Somewhere below him, the rest of his group waited. He heard someone yell from the street and poked his head over the short concrete lip that kept him concealed.

The street exploded with heavy machine-gun fire, and green tracers poured from the vehicles into the two men, who were caught in the middle of the street. The onslaught of heavy caliber firing continued as the vehicles approached, sending ricochets in every conceivable direction, shattering building windows and causing Daniel to hug the roof until it stopped. He heard the deep rumble of the BTR-80's powerful diesel engine as it approached a point across the street from his building.

He poked his head over the edge and saw all three vehicles in a line less than twenty meters away, with the BTR centered on the two dead bodies. The BTR's devastating 14.5mm gun was aimed down the street, which relieved Daniel. Even a near miss from one of those shells could put him out of action. Soldiers exited the rear hatches on the Tigers and fanned out to form a hasty perimeter. Daniel kept his head pressed against the lip, tilted sideways to expose as little of him as possible. The gunners on the Tigers swiveled their night vision equipped 12.7mm machine guns in a vigilant attempt to keep watch over the formation.

The BTR-80's side hatch opened and extended into a two-step ramp between the second and third tire on the side exposed to Daniel. Two soldiers scrambled out of the hatch, followed by an officer.

Daniel pushed himself up to his knees and swung the rifle over the lip, bracing it against the concrete. He centered the scope on the officer's face and fired a hasty shot. His next shot spun the rear Tiger's gunner out of the swivel mount and onto the ground behind the vehicle. Before he could engage another target, two RPGs popped through the windows below him and slammed into the Tigers. At this point, Daniel's only job was to keep anyone from closing the BTR hatch.

He stared intensely at the scope's green image as bullets cracked overhead and skipped off the concrete. He ignored the furious firefight between the Russian soldiers and his own Black Flag team. A body filled the hatch, and Daniel squeezed the trigger, causing the figure to tumble out of the BTR onto the snow-covered pavement. An arm and head appeared, stretching to reach the hatch. Daniel centered on the top of the arm, and fired. The soldier immediately dropped to the deck of the BTR and was pulled out of sight before Daniel could fire a bullet into his torso.

He fired two shots through the hatch, to discourage anyone else from trying to close the hatch. He hoped the rounds didn't ricochet and destroy any equipment they might need to examine. Through his left eye, he saw the BTR's turret start to turn in his direction, just as two figures scrambled toward the hatch from the street. He was fairly sure they were part of his team.

"Petrovich displacing," he announced, so the team would know he was no longer covering them.

"Breach team in," he heard, followed by the sounds of muffled gunfire from the street below.

He sprinted for a few seconds and dove into the snow, glancing backward. His previous position behind the concrete rooftop lip disappeared in a series of explosions that showered him with sharp fragments. The pounding lasted a few more seconds and suddenly stopped.

"Breach team is in control of the BTR. Send Malyshev," he heard through his earpiece.

Daniel picked his bruised body up off the debris strewn roof and sprinted back to the edge of the roof. He saw Malyshev sprint toward the open hatch, under heavy small arms fire from a group of soldiers huddled near the rear Tiger. Leo fired into the soldiers from somewhere below him, dropping one of them and scrambling the rest. Daniel picked up movement out of his peripheral vision, just as Malyshev jumped into the BTR and closed the hatch. A soldier climbed onto the damaged lead Tiger and jumped behind the 12.7mm gun.

The gun started to swivel, and Daniel aimed through his scope, barely beating the turret. He squeezed the trigger, punching a 5.45mm steel jacketed projectile through the soldier's Kevlar helmet, just as a grenade flew from the building into the Tiger. The rocket's detonation penetrated the Tiger's armor and exploded it from the inside, catapulting the body in the turret several feet into the air. When the explosion settled, Daniel noticed that all he could hear were sounds of small arms fire on the street and in the distance. He couldn't help but wonder if the last grenade had attracted any attention from the soldiers engaged in battle near the Katayev Prospekt.

"Breach team needs to move fast. Have Malyshev monitor communications. The last RPG blast might have attracted some attention," he said.

"Understood. We're accessing the MBT. Keep the infantry off the vehicle," Farrington said.

Daniel leaned over the edge, searching for more targets. He saw a soldier firing from a position behind the remaining Tiger and snapped off a quick shot at his head. He saw the soldier crumple to the street, his helmet spinning in the snow on the pavement. He spotted another soldier creeping between the Tiger and a partially shattered glass storefront window, trying to approach the BTR. A short burst from Leo's assault rifle knocked him back through the remaining glass. The firefight died on the street after the last burst.

The lead Tiger burned furiously, sending a column of superheated smoke and sparks skyward. There was little chance of the ambush going unnoticed for very long, and he suspected a few of the vehicles' soldiers had disappeared into the neighborhood, headed back to the infantry company deployed less than 1000 meters away. Sabitov had told them that his soldiers would expend most of their remaining rockets to provide a diversion for the ambush. There would be no second volley to distract the battalion. Daniel scanned the air for what they all feared the most. He spotted one of the Havocs hovering less than a mile away firing cannon shells into one of the center buildings, which now burned brightly. Every building in the Katayev Prospekt apartment development had caught fire at this point, illuminating the area around the buildings.

He heard motors rumble in the distance, and a Havoc helicopter suddenly appeared from behind a tall building down the street.

"Leo, get the RPGs to the roof, but stay in the stairwell. Yuri, get Malyshev on the BTR's cannon. We have a Havoc moving up the street, fifty meters above the buildings. It's moving slowly. Scanning."

He dashed back to the stairwell and ran inside, closing the door behind him. The sound of the rotors grew thunderous as the Havoc drew within a few buildings of the wrecked vehicle formation.

Leo and Major Sabitov raced up the stairs with loaded RPG launchers. Daniel reached out to take Sabitov's.

"Ready?" he said.

Leo stared at him with an incredulous look and nodded.

"Is Malyshev on the gun?"

"Affirmative. He's very familiar with the BTR," Farrington said.

"We're going to try and hit it with a double RPG salvo. You pound away with the gun. We have to get the Havoc to withdraw. More vehicles are inbound."

"We just heard on the radio. Let's get this over with," Farrington said.

"Roger. Here we go," he said and cracked the door open.

The only thing he cared about was the direction of the 30mm gun. It was aimed down the street and to the left, so he pushed the door open and stepped out far enough to make room for Leo. He aimed at the Havoc's center through the crude sight and depressed the hand trigger. The rocket's booster detonated, shooting the projectile out of the launcher. Less than a half second later, the rocket's motor fired and propelled the 85mm high explosive grenade toward the Havoc at nearly one thousand feet per second. Daniel heard the second RPG fire and ran back toward the door, pushing Leo and Sabitov down the staircase.

The first rocket missed the Havoc's right weapons pylon by less than a meter and struck the helicopter's rotor blade arc, failing to detonate or cause any disruption to its flight stability. Leo's rocket struck the underside of the helicopter, just behind the landing gear, bucking the helicopter, but causing no structural or mechanical damage that would end its flight.

Daniel and his accomplices tumbled over each other past the second floor when the first of the 30mm projectiles started to tear the roof apart. They dumped the rocket launchers at the bottom of the staircase and pulled Sabitov out of the back door as the ceiling above the ground floor started to disintegrate in successive blasts. They turned right and ran along the back of the stores, in the direction of the helicopter. They heard the BTR's 14.5mm gun start firing and Sabitov yelled to them.

"One more round for the RPG!"

The major held up one of the launchers they had dropped and reached behind him for the last rocket, which rested in a specialized munitions backpack that had been previously carried by one of the infected soldiers. Leo and Sabitov scrambled to load the rocket while Daniel rushed toward the street between the nearest two buildings. As he approached the street, he could hear the BTR's 14.5mm rounds strike the helicopter above. The cracks against the helicopter's metal were answered by the deafening bark of the Havoc's 30mm cannon. He poked his head around the building's corner in time to see several 30mm rounds puncture the BTR, exploding its fuel tanks and flattening all of its oversized tires. The Havoc hovered over their side of the street and fired another burst of projectiles into the BTR and the building behind it.

"Over here!" he screamed back to the men.

Leo rushed down the opening to join him, just as the Havoc moved forward above the buildings. The helicopter's rotor wash scattered the snow between buildings, lifting it into a painful frozen mist that engulfed the small space. The helicopter slowly appeared above them, and Leo aimed skyward. The rocket's blast instantly cleared the tight alleyway, and they saw the rocket explode behind the under mounted 30mm gun, just below the cockpit. Neither of them waited around for the result. They ran back though the alleyway and sprinted down the back of the buildings as the sounds of the Havoc droned off into the distance, replaced by the rumble of diesel engines. Daniel stopped them as they reached an open area.

"You're on your own, Major. Sorry it didn't work out for you. I need to be on my way out of Monchegorsk within thirty minutes. Farrington gave me the phone, so we can still make the calls you wanted. I'll take care of this once we've reached a safe distance," Daniel said.

"That wasn't part of the deal," Sabitov said.

"Neither was losing most of my team."

"The deal is still on! Keep moving! Half the Russian Army just turned the corner!" Farrington said, emerging from the same opening in the alley they had used just seconds earlier.

Farrington, Sergei and Schafer caught up to them, and the entire group sprinted across a soccer field to the next neighborhood, praying that the second helicopter didn't make a sudden appearance. A few streets into the neighborhood, they heard several massive explosions, and Daniel turned to see the second helicopter fire dozens of rockets into the lower floors of the centermost apartment building in Katayev Prospekt. The explosive impacts lit up the night sky and showered burning chunks of debris down from the mortally damaged structure.

A second salvo of rockets raced toward the building and exploded inside, blowing chunks of flaming orange fragments out of the back of the building. Daniel watched as the ten-story building tipped forward and slowly collapsed out of his view. The ground shook beneath his feet, rattling the buildings around him. He turned to leave and ran right into Major Sabitov, who stared at Katayev Prospekt in disbelief and listened to the hiss of static on his radio.

"You've done everything you could possibly do for these people. Keep moving," he said; his hand on Sabitov's shoulder.

The sound of diesel engines died out as they plowed ahead at full speed toward Grozny Prospekt. As they ran, Daniel thought about Malyshev. The sergeant had sacrificed himself so they'd have a chance to escape with the data from the BTR. There was no way he was going to screw Sabitov after that.

They'd return to the original apartment building on the outskirts of Monchegorsk, if it was still safe, and transmit the data wherever Sabitov chose to send it. At the snowmobiles they would take the time to file a report with Berg. He wished they could find another live volunteer to return with them, but he wasn't optimistic about finding another early-stage infected civilian willing to leave.

As they crossed another bleak, windswept street, he caught some movement a few houses away, followed by nonsensical muttering. He slowed to a walk in the middle of the street.

"You need the PPS?" Farrington asked, several steps ahead.

Daniel's hand gripped the razor-sharp combat knife strapped to his leg. "No. I should be fine."

He pulled the seven-inch serrated blade from its sheath. Maybe he could find something a little more compact to carry back to Finland.

Chapter Thirty-Eight

7:50 PM
CIA Headquarters
Langley, Virginia

Karl Berg shut his laptop and looked up at Audra, who was rubbing her temples and staring at one of her two flat-screen monitors. It was nearly eight o'clock on Sunday evening, and the two agents had been working in her office since nine in the morning. They had put most of the final touches on the package that Audra would bring to the National Clandestine Service's director, Thomas Manning, as soon as he arrived on Monday morning. Berg would meet Audra here a few hours before the director's usual arrival time and add the laboratory evidence they expected to receive from Finland.

"I wish I could be there to see the looks on their faces. It's not every day that someone delivers a cooler stuffed with a severed head," Berg said.

"I don't like to think about it. Brilliant overall, considering what we suspect…but gruesome," she said.

"They don't seem to be constrained by the same psychological processes that keep the rest of us in check. I don't know where Sanderson finds these guys, but he certainly does his homework."

"I hate to say it, but we need people like this on our side."

"I couldn't agree with you more. I'm calling it a night. I'll be in at 3:30 to make sure the lab reports are available for your report. I'm keeping the team in Helsinki for now, just in case," he added.

The embassy in Helsinki had arranged for priority handling of the team's biological sample at the Division of Infectious Diseases in the Helsinki University Hospital. They felt confident with Sanderson's team moving the sample. The location of the Gulfstream's wreckage remained a mystery, and she didn't expect the Russians to disclose the location. Damage from an air-to-air missile was nearly impossible to hide from seasoned investigators. With the Russians playing hardball, anything was possible. The team was expected to arrive in Ouru, Finland, within three hours and would be placed on a commercial flight leaving at 11:30 AM, local time. They both doubted the Russians would shoot down a Boeing 717 flown by Scandinavian Airlines.

The evidence gathered in Monchegorsk would be the tipping point. Audra expected their package to make its way to the White House immediately after the meeting. From that point forward, it would likely be out of their hands. Pictures of the Russian Army Mobile Battlefield feed had also been sent to Reuters in London, and nobody could predict the fallout that would ensue from worldwide exposure of the Russians' siege in Monchegorsk.

Russian military authorities had been careful with their wording of the orders, and Berg saw no mention of an epidemic in any of the digital images taken from the battalion commander's MBT. The word "insurgency" was used in place of "epidemic", and the infected were called "insurgents." Russian military orders to shoot insurgents on sight would provoke international outrage, and the United Nations would demand an investigation, but the Russians weren't likely to bow to this pressure. Berg didn't think that the world would discover the true scope of Monchegorsk's tragedy within a useful timeframe, so with Kaparov's help, Berg still planned to send Sanderson's team after Reznikov.

He didn't trust the speed at which the White House bureaucracy would react to the threat. Their only hope of quickly discovering the true implications of the Kazakhstan laboratory remained with the Russian scientist. There was little doubt that he had poisoned Monchegorsk, with cataclysmic results. At this point, Reznikov's link to Al Qaeda was purely circumstantial and in most cases, anecdotal. They needed time sensitive information that couldn't wait for weeks of sleep deprivation and waterboarding in a secret location. If the virus had been mass produced for Al Qaeda, which he suspected, the West might be looking at days, instead of weeks, before a massive coordinated biological attack. He needed Sanderson's team to find Reznikov before the Russians silenced him.

Chapter Thirty-Nine

10:25 AM
U.S. Embassy
Buenos Aires, Argentina

Special Agent Susan Castaneda examined her computer screen again, absorbing the details of the email sent by her lunchtime friend in the Argentine Federal Police. She had heard rumors of a particularly nasty murder scene in Palermo Soho involving Serbian nationals and had placed a call to Agent Federico Mariano. He had clearly anticipated her call because an email appeared while they chatted about their next lunch date. After opening the attached digital pictures, food was the furthest thing from her mind.

The crime scene photographs had taken her breath away, along with her appetite. Agent Castaneda had never seen that much blood and carnage in one place, even in the movies. Dark red blood covered most of the white marble floor in the living room, sprayed against the walls and kitchen cabinets. She counted at least eight bodies crumpled in various positions on the floor. The bedroom was the real shocker, and she couldn't help but gasp and stare at the pictures, trying to make sense of them.

The bright white bedspread was splattered with dark red clumps and brighter blood stains. A body lay slumped on the floor in front of the bed. It took her a few moments to figure out what had happened to the other body. A half undressed, badly slashed man had been strapped into a steel and leather harness contraption that suspended him a few feet off the floor in an extremely vulnerable, belly up position. His unsupported head tilted back and downward, above a pool of blood. She didn't envy the coroner's job on this one.

She finished reading Agent Mariano's assessment and dialed Agent Sharpe.

"Special Agent Ryan Sharpe," he answered.

"Ryan, it's Susan Castaneda from the embassy in Buenos Aires."

"Hi, Susan. Great to hear from you! Thank you again for the information you passed along. I can't go into details, but it proved to be extremely helpful."

"I'm really glad to hear that. I miss investigative work. Not much in the way of that down here. Hey, I ran across something this morning that might interest you. A bunch of Serbian immigrants and a few Serb nationals were found dead in a high end condominium high-rise yesterday. Strange circumstances to say the least."

"Another sponsored attack like the others?"

"My contact doesn't think so. I just sent you an email with all of the details and some pretty nasty crime scene photos. The condominium was owned by an Argentinian couple. Security cameras in the lobby show that the wife was staying there alone this weekend. The lobby is occupied by a security concierge twenty-four/seven and the night shift guard confirmed that she was alone. The day guard was killed during the attack. Bottom line, we have ten dead Serbs in the apartment. Federal Police are investigating the possibility that a sniper fired into the condominium. A few of the windows facing a hotel across the street were shattered and at least two of the men were hit by rifle caliber projectiles. Weapons found in the room fired 9mm. Security cameras caught a man and woman leaving through the back lobby door shortly before police arrived."

"You have pictures of them?"

"Yes. The last six pictures were taken from the security cameras and the pictures labeled 'Russo' were taken by security for visual identification reference. The building had decent security. Nobody gets in or out, unless their identity is confirmed."

"Sounds like a lot of unauthorized people got in that day," he said. "Here it is. Russo."

The line went silent for several seconds.

"Everything all right?" she asked.

"Uh…yes. Susan, do me a huge favor and keep these photos out of circulation. I need to make an urgent phone call. Thank you again. Sorry to be abrupt…I have to go."

The line went dead in Susan's ears.

"That was strange," she muttered.

She opened the digital pictures of the Russos and arranged them side by side. Natalia Russo was stunningly beautiful, but not really her type. Glamour girl for sure. The earrings looked like they could cost more than her entire outfit. She liked the confident expression on Natalia's face, though. Almost cocky. Susan liked women with attitude. Dario Russo was handsome in every traditional way, but in a different league than Natalia. Still, they made an attractive couple. She studied Dario Russo's picture for a few more seconds. For some reason, he looked familiar to her. She closed her eyes and concentrated.

"No way," she whispered.

She navigated through the FBI intranet on her second monitor for several seconds, until a face filled the screen. She compared the two images.

"No shit," she said out loud.

Dario Russo's picture identically matched Daniel Petrovich, also known as Marko Resja. Wanted for several counts of murder and domestic terrorism? She scanned a list of known associates and saw the name of his wife, Jessica Petrovich. Her picture appeared on the screen and she compared it to Natalia Russo. Another exact match. She was wanted for assaulting a federal agent and conspiracy to commit murder. She was also classified as a domestic terrorist. No wonder it sounded like Agent Sharpe had swallowed his phone. She'd give Sharpe some time to formulate his own response before she passed the discovery on to her boss back in D.C. They'd make the call on what to do with the information.

The next picture she examined was the best shot taken from the security camera and showed Natalia, bloodied and bruised, in the lobby with a man that clearly wasn't Dario Russo. Interesting. She closed the file and sat back in her seat, wondering if she should send the picture of the man in the harness contraption to Agent Dan Bailey. It might curtail his extracurricular activities and restore some dignity to the legal attaché's office in Buenos Aires. She laughed out loud at the thought, after deciding it would probably only serve to give him another bad idea.

Chapter Forty

8:32 AM
FBI Headquarters
Washington, D.C.

Frederick Shelby pressed the blinking red button on his office phone. "Agent Sharpe, good to hear from you. Things are shaping up nicely on my end. Nothing I can share with you at the moment, I'm afraid. Margaret said this was important?" he said.

"Very important. I just received several digital photos from our legal attaché in Argentina. The photos confirm that Daniel and Jessica Petrovich are living in Buenos Aires," Sharpe said.

"These are recent photos?"

"The Petroviches went by the names Dario and Natalia Russo. Ten Serbians were found massacred in their high-rise condominium. Jessica managed to escape the carnage. We don't think Daniel was in town at the time of the attack."

"Who attacked whom?"

"That's unclear at the moment, though I'd put my money on the Serbians attacking Jessica."

"She killed ten men by herself?"

"No. She had help. I have a picture of her being escorted out of the building by Jeffrey Munoz."

"Sweet lord. This seals it," the director said.

"That's what I thought," Sharpe said.

"Keep this quiet for now. In a few days, it won't matter. The last thing we need right now is for Daniel's picture to be linked to this mess. Interpol will attach a red flag to Russo's passport, and I guarantee Sanderson will be notified. We don't want to give Sanderson any reason to pack up and vanish. I'll handle the legal attaché in Buenos Aires."

"Understood. We'll keep digging into the finances. You should already have an email from me, with the Legat's assessment and the pictures."

"Thank you, Ryan. This will help ease some minds on Capitol Hill. I'll be in touch," he said and hung up the phone.

Frederick Shelby immediately opened the pictures, which filled his screen.

"Christ, that's a lunch killer," he said, minimizing the image of Josif Hadzic's suspended body.

Chapter Forty-One

8:45 AM
CIA Headquarters
Langley, Virginia

Thomas Manning interlocked his fingers and turned away from the forty-two-inch flat-screen monitor mounted to his office wall. Audra waited for him to speak. Surprisingly, she hadn't been nervous about this meeting. The potential disaster looming over the United States and its European allies dwarfed the potential issues raised by the breaches of protocol and procedure she had authorized. If Manning chose to focus on these aspects instead of a confirmed bioweapons threat, there was nothing she could do about it. She didn't know Thomas Manning well enough to make a personal assessment of how he would respond, but he had a solid reputation for being practical. Still, nobody rose to the rank of National Clandestine Service director without a solid foundation in political maneuvering. This was the only facet of Thomas Manning that concerned her.

"We have a serious problem on our hands. Don't make any plans for the day and cancel any meetings you have scheduled. I expect to walk this up to the director's office within the hour. From there, we'll be on immediate standby to meet with the national security advisor. I can't imagine the Helsinki lab will sit on these results for very long, and if Reuters can confirm any of the story passed to them from Monchegorsk, this will break wide open. The White House will want to stay slightly ahead of this, if that's even possible at this point."

"The lab assured me complete discretion. I reinforced the need for that discretion with some scary-looking operatives and cash, which was accepted."

"I'm not even going to ask any questions about who you have running around Europe," he said.

"You really don't want to know," she said.

"I bet I don't," he said and paused before continuing. "Excellent work on this, Audra. All of it."

"Thank you, sir," she said.

"Now that I got that out of the way, I needed to know about the Predator drone as soon as you requisitioned it," he said.

"But you wouldn't have authorized an armed Predator drone for this mission. Nobody would have, based on the scant information available at the time," she said.

"And your initiative in the case still falls under the 'excellent work' category. Still, I should have been notified when it was used to attack Russian forces."

"We still don't know they were Russian. The helicopters were unmarked and the ground forces were dressed like locals. If they were Russian, the Kazakhstan government should be happy that we defended their sovereign borders."

"Luckily, the threat you uncovered far overshadows things like unauthorized Predator strikes or illegal invasions on Russian soil," he said.

"A simple snowmobile trip to the Kola Peninsula. It's a popular destination this time of the year," Audra said smoothly.

"Most tourists don't return with a severed head in a cooler. I assume they avoided customs?"

"Presumably," she said, smiling.

"When the dust settles, I'm sure we'll…I mean you'll have to answer some questions, along with your partner in crime, Karl Berg. I'm promoting him to the position of assistant deputy director. Effective immediately."

"I didn't know that position existed."

"Everyone complains that we lack the resources to fight the War on Terror. I've just enhanced our capabilities…and when we talk to the White House, I need this to look like a consolidated effort by the National Clandestine Service. "

"He'll be happy to hear that."

"Don't count on it. Karl Berg likes to operate in the shadows. In many ways, he's most effective on the fringes, just out of sight. Give me a few minutes to process all of this and stay close. We could be walking down the hall at any minute," he said.

Chapter Forty-Two

6:23 PM
FSB Headquarters, Lubyanka Square
Moscow, Russian Federation

Alexei Kaparov closed the small window on his desktop monitor and tapped another cigarette out of the pack he now kept in plain view on his desk. If the Internal Affairs Division monitored his smoking habit, they would have noticed that he had started smoking three packs a day since the beginning of the weekend. That alone should have alerted them to the fact that he was up to no good.

Agent Prerovsky's friend in Special Operations had turned out to be more than Kaparov had expected. Lucya was a senior analyst in the division, with a computer software engineering degree from Moscow University. Far from the desk clerk that Kaparov's prejudiced mind had imagined. She had access to the Special Operations Division's (SOD) inner sanctum, often serving as lead data technician for live operations. She was in the perfect position to feed them information, and after several expensive, romantic dinners, she had agreed to help them.

Fortunately, the two had started dating well before the Reznikov fiasco had surfaced, or he would likely be sharing a cell with Prerovsky on charges of treason. She had responded well to his request, especially when he told her the truth about Monchegorsk. Even within the Special Operations Divisions, the situation had been described as a violent political revolt, sustained by an armed insurgency. Everyone with the Operations Center knew this sounded like nonsense, but early details about Monchegorsk had been suppressed.

The window he had just closed was fed by a direct link engineered by Lucya. The Foreign Intelligence Service (SVR) was deploying Spetznaz assets to Stockholm, Sweden, where they would wait for further instructions. She felt confident that they didn't have a specific address or location for Reznikov, but she sensed they were getting close to a breakthrough.

The deployment of SVR Spetznaz on foreign soil was a risky venture under any circumstances; a decision never taken lightly by the Special Operations Division. Given the serious, yet sensitive nature of the mission, Kaparov had little doubt which assets they would use. SVR leadership would activate "Zaslon" operatives from Directorate S, the Foreign Intelligence Service's "Illegals" division. Comprised of deep cover operatives living abroad, Zaslon Spetznaz were considered to be the most elite and specialized covert operations group ever produced by the Russian Federation. The group was all that truly remained of the original Cold War era Vympel Spetznaz and its existence had never been acknowledged by Russian authorities.

He flipped open his cell phone and punched in a text message that would reach halfway around the world in less than a minute.

❧

Karl Berg felt his cell phone vibrate against his chest. He reached into his sport coat and pulled the phone out of the inner breast pocket. He stopped halfway up the stairwell that emptied onto Audra Bauer's floor. He had been summoned to meet with her quite suddenly, and she had asked him to "dress it up" a little. She also informed him that he would probably be out of the office for most of the day, which left him a little concerned. He just hoped that he'd be allowed to return with a job. She hadn't said a word about her earlier meeting with Thomas Manning.

He read the text.

"Recommend a visit to Stockholm. Very pleasant to visit this time of year, but can be a little crowded. Make sure to properly outfit. Be ready to jump at some of the early attractions."

He dialed a number kept on speed dial.

"How can I help you, Mr. Langley?"

"Very funny. Move your team to Stockholm immediately. They'll need to be ready to roll at a moment's notice. We don't have a specific location, but I'm getting real time information. You should assume they'll be up against Vympel Spetznaz. Our team has to move fast. We need Reznikov alive," Berg said.

"Our team? There might be hope for you after all, Karl."

"Call it sucking up. I might be on a flight to Argentina later today if my next meeting doesn't go well. I hope you can use a former CIA agent with a considerable worldwide network of contacts," Berg said.

"I can't guarantee the pay to be better," Sanderson said.

"Somehow I doubt that. I'm on the way to meet with my boss and I suspect we'll be taking a trip across the Potomac a little later today. This will go straight to the top, very quickly."

"You should keep our names out of this for now," Sanderson said.

"You think? I didn't plan to unveil our relationship in front of the national security advisor…on account of the fact that every name I might mention is on the FBI's most wanted list. Let me know when the teams are in place, and if you need any help with equipment."

"I'll handle the equipment this time."

"What, your team didn't like having to rummage around a trunk full of Cold War era Spetznaz goodies?"

"Not really. I recommend that you contact the team directly with Reznikov's location when you get it. Success in Stockholm might come down to seconds. Calling me will waste precious time that they won't have. You have their satellite phone number. I'll make sure the team is ready to roll," Sanderson said.

"Sounds good. I'll touch base with Petrovich," Berg said.

The call went dead.

❧

General Sanderson clutched the phone in his hand and jogged from the armory to the headquarters building, one hundred meters away at the edge of the woods. The dirt path led up a gentle incline that didn't give him the slightest pause. By the time he had reached the log and beam structure's covered porch, his heart rate had just started to rise, ever so slightly.

Sanderson could be considered a physical machine at any age, but for a man in his early fifties, he was an anomaly. He stayed in top physical shape out of pure habit forged by over twenty plus years in the U.S. Special Forces.

He started out as an infantry officer in 1973 after graduating from the United States Military Academy at West Point and was quickly identified a few years later as a candidate for the recently formed 1st Ranger Battalion. His superior performance and reputation within the battalion earned him a spot on the ill-fated rescue attempt of the American embassy hostages in Iran. Captain Sanderson watched in horror as Operation Eagle Claw unraveled.

From his distant position at the westernmost roadblock, he felt the heat from the fireball that engulfed a C-130 transport plane and crashed one of the RH-53D Sea Stallion helicopters at the "Desert One" landing site. Unaware at this point that the mission had been aborted, Sanderson scrambled back to the site for information. His radios had been rendered useless by the sand.

He nearly knocked over Colonel Charles Beckwith, who suddenly appeared out of a sand cloud kicked up by the nearest surviving helicopter. Beckwith had created Delta Force, America's brand-new counter-terrorism group, less than a year before Operation Eagle Claw. Sanderson had never heard of the unit before he had been assigned to the rescue mission. Colonel Beckwith informed him that the mission had been aborted and that his Rangers would board the last C-130 along with his Delta Force operators.

Sanderson stared with disbelief at the remaining helicopters. To him, it looked like they still had what they needed for the rescue operation. Beckwith put his hand on the captain's shoulder and said, "Son, it's not our call to make." By the time the C-130 had landed at their staging base at Masirah Island, near Oman, Captain Terrence Sanderson had been personally invited by Beckwith to attend the next 1st Special Forces Operational Detachment-Delta "selection course."

Sanderson spent the next eleven years with Delta Force, eventually emerging as the unit's commanding officer. His plans for the Black Flag program had been born while in the Delta ranks, and by the time he had finished his tour as Delta's commanding officer, the first round of selectees had been assembled at the primary training site in Colorado. Colonel Sanderson was assigned to a "ghost" billet at Joint Special Operations

Command (JSOC) and promoted to brigadier general. He promptly disappeared from the radar, along with millions of dollars funneled to his "non-existent" program.

Black Flag had been his vision to address the greatest shortfall he encountered while serving with Special Forces: a costly reliance upon the CIA for nearly all human intelligence. Costly in terms of lives and wasted resources. In his experience, CIA operatives lacked a specific military focus in their deep cover intelligence gathering, which limited the value of information flowing to the real operators. Rivalry between the Pentagon and Langley often resulted in situations where no intelligence was shared and devolved to the point where the Pentagon rarely trusted what the CIA finally produced. In Sanderson's view, the system for acquiring the useful, mission critical information necessary to conduct special operations had ceased to exist. The Black Flag program was his solution to the problem, and it was embraced by the top Pentagon brass…behind closed doors.

He opened the door to the lodge and stepped inside. Parker looked up from his workstation at the large conference table.

"Things are shaping up on all fronts," Parker said.

"Indeed they are. I just spoke with Berg. Move Petrovich's team to Stockholm. Set them up in a central location just outside of the downtown area. Good access to major roads. Berg's contact in Moscow said the Russians are sending assets to Stockholm. They'll be in a race with the Russians to get to Reznikov, and we'll likely be a few minutes behind. Let Petrovich know that Berg will contact them directly with Reznikov's location. Send some additional operatives up from mainland Europe."

"We have two more readily accessible to Scandinavia. Hubner and Klinkman."

"I don't want Klinkman in on this. We still haven't figured out what happened to Navarre, so we need to be careful with Klinkman. People like Navarre don't disappear without making deals with federal prosecutors."

"I'll send Hubner to meet them in Stockholm. He can arrange the transfer of weapons from our cache in Poland. I don't think he'll have any problem getting the weapons into Sweden via fast boat, with the right crew and a ton of cash, of course."

"Get everyone and everything to Stockholm as soon as possible. No rules of engagement on this one. We need Reznikov, period."

"I'll make sure they understand," Parker said.

"All right, let's get this moving. The Russians could come up with an address at any time."

As he opened the door to step back outside, he could barely contain his excitement about the future. His plans were shaping up nicely. They just needed to grab Reznikov before the Russians. He'd call Berg and see if the CIA had anyone that could be trusted to make a move against Reznikov in the event that the address was uncovered prior to Petrovich's arrival in Stockholm. If the location was disclosed soon, the Russian team wouldn't be in place either. A quick CIA grab might be an option, though he loathed the thought of relinquishing control of Reznikov. In the grand scheme of things, it probably wouldn't matter, as long as Reznikov didn't fall into Russian hands.

Before calling Berg, he needed to reach out to *señor* Galenden and assure him that the situation was under control in Buenos Aires. The massacre at the apartment dominated headlines and pictures of the Russos had been leaked everywhere. So far as Galenden's police contacts could tell, their passports had not been flagged, which was a temporary blessing.

Dario Russo had been identified in the media as being out of the country on business and, according to Galenden's source, was not being treated as a suspect. Natalia Russo was wanted for questioning in the case, but no warrants for her arrest had been issued either. The Argentine Federal Police were still trying to make sense of the killings. Either way, these identities were compromised. Sanderson felt comfortable letting Daniel use Dario's passport to enter Sweden, but beyond that, Sanderson would arrange new temporary papers for both of them. It wouldn't be long before the FBI stumbled across the striking resemblance between the Petroviches and the Russos.

Chapter Forty-Three

5:15 PM
Odengatan
Stockholm, Sweden

Daniel closed the door to the third-floor apartment and nodded for Sergei to shut the curtains. The rest of the team dropped the four suitcases on the floor between the dining room table and the light brown sectional couch that faced an aging oak entertainment center.

"Let's break out the gear and stage everything we need for a quick departure. We'll use the duffel bags to move the weapons into the vehicles. Pack one for each. Body armor will be worn at all times. I want to be out the door within ten seconds of receiving the call. Assault rifles go with the van. Load weapons, check gear and prep your bags," Daniel said.

The team descended on the suitcases, opening them at the same time and stacking their contents on the shaky dining room table. When the suitcases were finally empty, the dining room table was stacked with high end weaponry and equipment.

"Perfect selection, Konrad. MP-7's go to the assault team. Like Daniel said, rifles go to the support van," Farrington said.

Konrad Hubner reached forward and grabbed one of two G-36C assault rifles, locking the bolt open to examine the chamber. He depressed the bolt catch button just forward of the trigger guard, and the bolt slammed forward. He depressed the trigger on the empty weapon, and they all heard a click. The G-36C was a compact, futuristic-looking weapon fitted with a Zeiss RSA-S 3x Reflex Sight. It fired 5.56mm steel-jacketed projectiles from a 30-round detachable magazine and could be concealed under a three-quarter-length jacket. Hubner and Schafer would be equipped with the two rifles for use against any Russian operatives preventing the assault team's extraction from Reznikov's location.

The assault team, comprised of Daniel, Farrington, Sergei and Leo, would be armed with Heckler and Koch MP-7 submachine guns (SMGs). The German-designed weapon fired a unique 4.6X30mm solid steel projectile, capable of penetrating Kevlar body armor at two hundred meters. Smaller than the G-36C, they retained the handling and concealment characteristics of a small SMG, but could match the power of a modern assault rifle at shorter ranges. The four MP-7s on the table were fitted with Zeiss 1x Reflex Sights and a side rail-mounted flashlight. Daniel saw a sizeable stack of 40-round magazines for the submachine guns and four six-inch-long suppressors.

Suppressors were mandatory for the assault team. He had no idea what they would encounter as they pulled up to Reznikov's address in their rented Volvo sedan, but he knew they would need every spare second available to grab Reznikov and move him safely away from the site. Berg's source told them that the Stockholm police response would vary, depending on the location and reported problem. A report of automatic gunfire would generate a massive response. The longer they could delay a concerned citizen's call to the police, the better their chance of avoiding a confrontation. He just hoped the Russians were playing by the same rules.

Six waist level bulletproof vests, equipped with front and back ballistics plates, sat stacked on the chair at the head of the table.

"Vests first. Get used to wearing these under your expensive jackets. Ballistic plates stay in. I guarantee the Russians won't be playing around with full metal jacketed bullets. Expect the same ammunition we're using," Farrington said.

Everyone grabbed a vest and stripped off their jackets. The jackets had been purchased at a designer boutique on the way to the apartment. Their distinctly Russian brands stood out at the airport, and Hubner shook his head in disgust and embarrassment as the group emerged from their rental vehicles to help him offload the suitcases from the boat. Several thousand dollars later, they looked "acceptable" for Stockholm, according to Hubner.

"Will these plates stop armor-piercing rounds?" Leo said, knocking on the front of his vest.

"You're looking at Enhanced Small Arms Protective Inserts. Should defeat most engineered hard core ammunition, up to 7.62mm AP. I figured the Russians would be equipped with PP-2000s firing their new 9mm AP rounds," Hubner said.

"They don't know we'll be right on their asses, so their load out might be a little lighter than usual," Daniel said.

"Don't count on it with Vympel Spetznaz. They wrote the book on this type of operation," Farrington said.

"Hopefully we won't have to test these plates," Daniel said. "Who wants Thai food? There's a takeout place right down the street," he added.

He heard some complaining.

"Pizza might be easier on the stomachs. Move the gear into one of the bedrooms, and I'll call a place that delivers. I'll run down to one of the corner markets to grab some instant coffee. It's going to be a long night."

Before he opened the phone book, he unfolded the map of Stockholm given to him by Hubner. He spread it out on the kitchen counter and removed a portable GPS from his coat pocket. He folded the map to show the immediate suburbs of Stockholm and pinpointed their location on Odengatan. The apartment was situated one block north of the Stockholm School of Economics, within view of the National City Park. From this location, they could access major roads leading in any direction.

Their placement in the city, just like that of the Russians, would decide who arrived first at Reznikov's location. Luck would play a bigger role than usual. Given their similar objective, Daniel wouldn't be surprised if the Russians had chosen a similar location nearby. He wondered if Berg's Moscow contact would pass along the Russians' location.

Possession of this information could help shape their strategy when Reznikov's location was disclosed. Although tempting, he didn't think a preemptive strike against the Russians would be a wise move. Too many variables and their inside intelligence suggested the possibility of facing more than ten Russian operatives. Ultimately, it might not be his decision, but he liked the idea of surprising them on the street better than trying to strike a fortified location.

Chapter Forty-Four

6:25 PM
Sveavägen
Stockholm, Sweden

Major Stepan Eristov studied the city map of Stockholm with their local contact, Dmitry Solomin. Solomin worked for Gazprom's Stockholm branch and had been chosen to provide the assembled Zaslon team with a suitable city location and detailed information about traffic patterns and city routing. He had been recruited by Russia's Foreign Intelligence Service in 1993 and had lived in Stockholm as a Gazprom executive for the past eight years, facilitating SVR operations in Scandinavia with the help of several other Gazprom "employees."

Captain Georgy Rusnak and Master Sergeant Ivan Zhukov joined them standing around the dining room table. The rest of the team, consisting of seven additional "illegals" from northern Europe, sat around watching television or reading magazines. Their weapons and gear had already been checked, double checked, and stuffed into small individual backpacks that sat with each man. They were ready to leave the apartment within seconds.

"I assume major traffic through the downtown area is limited to the typical morning and afternoon hours?" Eristov said.

"If you need to travel south of the downtown area at any time of the day, make sure you link up with the Klarastrand well north of the lower Stockholm interchanges. Any other direction from this location will carry the typical traffic patterns. Morning is always crowded, but unless the target location is south, you should move along nicely. The afternoon could be slower as everyone heads to the suburbs," Solomin said.

"The traffic won't matter getting to the target location. I'm more concerned with extraction. We have orders to try and remove the target, if feasible. Either way, we won't be returning to this apartment. Control has given us a location north of the city in a rural location," Eristov said.

"I know it well," Solomin said.

"Then you should try your best to forget about it," Captain Rusnak said.

"Understood," Solomin said.

Eristov regarded Solomin with caution. The fact that Directorate S trusted him to be in the same room with Zaslon operatives had spoken volumes about the operative, but his participation would go no further than helping them with the last second routing and staying behind to sanitize the apartment. He had already fielded a few questions about Solomin's fate from members of the team, none of whom would have been surprised if Eristov had told them he would be killed and stuffed into the bathtub. Zaslon operatives didn't exist according to Moscow.

Most of them had ceased to exist on the active SVR rosters within the past ten years, and despite the fact that they were assigned military ranks, the ranks were meaningless in the traditional military sense. For the Zaslon operatives, ranks were determined by time in service and operational experience, which translated into a meritocracy-based leadership structure.

They had all served with various military and SVR Spetznaz units prior to their assignment to Zaslon, but Major Eristov didn't hold a university degree or family connections over Sergeant Arkady Greshnev, who sat on the couch sharpening a small knife. Seven years of operational experience separated the two men, which signified a world of difference as an "illegal" operative living abroad.

"We'll sleep in shifts determined by vehicle assignment. The call could come at any time. From what I understand, they're close to making a connection," Eristov said.

"I'll keep the coffee going all night," Solomin said.

"No sleep for the wicked," Zhukov added.

Wicked indeed, Eristov thought. The men gathered in this apartment had been chosen carefully for Zaslon. Life abroad as an "illegal" required a unique psychological profile that would leave most behavioral health professionals stunned. Unlike the KGB "illegals" of the Cold War era, who melted into their surroundings and remained inactive for decades, Moscow had higher expectations for the newer breed. Candidates were carefully screened for the mental resilience required to live under a false identity and the moral flexibility necessary to carry out Moscow's orders.

Eristov had operated in Poland for fourteen years and had spent most of his time tracking and watching industrial sector contacts, both Russian and foreign. A considerable amount of time was spent on the surveillance of Russian business contacts. Several times a year, he participated in an operation similar to this one, but never with this many operatives.

He never received any specifics regarding the target's background, and like every mission prior to this, he wasn't told why the target needed to disappear. He suspected that Reznikov was significantly more important to Moscow than the rest of the targets Eristov had been assigned in the past. Reznikov had been assigned "capture/kill" status, which was rare. Most of them were designated "kill," but for some reason, Moscow wanted them to try and bring this one back. This made Eristov feel better about their mission. Lately, he had grown weary of assassinating businessmen that had somehow aggravated the wrong billionaire crony in Moscow.

"Make sure the drivers are familiar with the major routes and have their GPS systems programmed with several waypoints. Solomin will help them determine points within several neighborhoods, along multiple routes. We'll fine tune the routes on the way to the target," he said and slapped Captain Rusnak on the back.

"Ruslan, Greshnev, let's take another look at this map, eh?" Captain Rusnak said.

Greshnev slid his knife back into a small sheath along his ankle, hidden under his brown corduroy pants, and stood up from the couch with Sergeant Ruslan Ekel. Ekel would drive the Mercedes Benz Sprinter van that would transport Reznikov north of the city. He would also provide over watch support during the assault team's breach of the residence. Greshnev would drive the Volkswagen Passat that carried the assault team.

The van would arrive first and deposit the support team at various locations along the street. Once the van was parked, the Passat would bring the assault team as close to the residence's primary entrance as possible. They would all attempt to park legally if possible, double parking only if necessary. They wanted to avoid drawing any law enforcement attention to the location, though the support team was equipped with non-lethal means to deal with limited police interference. Ultimately, it would be Rusnak's call regarding how the support team responded on the street, to either civilian or police interference. Moscow had made one thing clear. They should let nothing stand in the way of success on this mission.

Chapter Forty-Five

1:30 PM
Acassuso Barrio
Buenos Aires, Argentina

Jeffrey Munoz closed the door behind the doctor and walked back to Jessica, who had propped her arm up on the couch. Her eyes looked glassy from the sedatives and local anesthetic used to keep her from jumping off the portable medical table. Sanderson had arranged for a team of medical specialists to treat her superficial injuries, but most importantly, to repair Jessica's left hand. They had done most of the work yesterday, and from what the doctor could tell, she would regain full, unrestricted use of the hand.

The indirect shotgun blast had mangled three of her fingers, bending them at odd angles and stripping away a considerable amount of skin. Luckily, most of the raw material needed to reset the fingers and close up the wounds was still present. The finished work wouldn't be pretty, especially without sophisticated skin grafting and plastic surgery, but it would suffice for the moment. Once Sanderson stabilized the situation, Jessica could seek further medical treatment at a private reconstructive surgery center. Her hand was wrapped in several layers of bandages and gauze, which the doctor would change regularly over the course of the following week, while checking on the hand's progress.

Jessica had been unusually quiet since they arrived at the private house, far north of the downtown area. Munoz would have preferred getting further out of Buenos Aires, but Jessica's hand was in bad shape and the injury to her neck looked frightening up close. Driving their minivan into the gated courtyard of this house had been a blessing in disguise for all of them. They had desperately needed somewhere to stop and regroup their thoughts.

Now it appeared that they would spend the next week here with Jessica. At least she had apologized repeatedly before being hit with the sedatives. She hadn't been too coherent since the surgery, rambling on about nothing he cared to hear about and insisting on calling her husband. What choice did he have but to listen to her? They were trapped in this house, and he had no intention of letting her out of his sights. He especially had no intention of letting her use a phone to call Daniel.

Sanderson had been specific about that, so he had disconnected the landlines and enabled passwords on their cell phones. He didn't trust Jessica any further than he could throw her and wouldn't be surprised to find out that she was pretending to be wacked out on painkillers. He'd removed every possible weapon, with the exception of the table legs and remote controls. He considered zip tying her legs together; to discourage an escape attempt, but Sanderson had made it clear that she was not to be restrained. For now, he just needed to make sure she didn't vanish.

According to Sanderson, Daniel and his team were stacked up against nearly impossible odds, which was why he didn't want the two of them communicating right now. Daniel couldn't afford the distraction.

He watched her lean her head back against a cushion and close her eyes. He knew she'd been through a lot in her life. Before yesterday. Before Daniel. Maybe she deserved a second chance, or was this her third? He had no idea. He just hoped Daniel made it back alive. He couldn't imagine what she might do if Daniel was killed.

Chapter Forty-Six

11:10 PM
USS DECATUR (DDG-73)
Pacific Ocean off Chilean coast

EW1 (SW) Robert Wegner studied the AN/SLQ-32(V)2 display screen again and checked the entire console. He'd done this several times over the past fifteen minutes and nothing had changed, except for the number of personnel lurking over his shoulder. It had started out with his chief, division officer and department head, which was bad enough, and had quickly expanded to every officer standing watch in the Combat Information Center. The crowd's seniority culminated with the presence of the ship's executive officer, Lieutenant Commander Shelly Davis, who would report Wegner's assessment to *DECATUR*'s commanding officer and await permission to transmit the report to mission planners onboard the *USS BOXER*. At least Captain Higgins had stayed on the bridge. The last thing he needed was *DECATUR*'s commanding officer breathing down his neck too.

"Everything still looks clear, Petty Officer Wegner?" Davis said.

"The scope is clear, ma'am. I have a few commercial maritime radars, but these are typical for the fishing vessels in these waters. Nothing land based or airborne," Wegner said.

"What are the effective ranges for the radars you've detected?"

"24 to 48 nautical miles...best case scenario. In this visibility, they'll probably have the radar picture set to a modest range...maybe 12 nautical miles. Signal strength confirms low output associated with reduced power transmission settings. They won't be able to detect *DECATUR* at any range with those radars. *BOXER* is a different story. Nothing stealthy about that ship, ma'am."

"That's why we're here first. I'll let the captain know the area is clear of any contacts of interest," she said.

DECATUR would loiter in the area, scanning for radar signals with its AN/SLQ-32(V)2 Electronic Warfare Suite, while at the same time employing a time tested, low budget method of surveillance. Lookouts. On this particular night, *DECATUR* employed three times the normal number of lookouts, all equipped with powerful night vision optics to spot vessels far out on the horizon. Just thirty nautical miles from the Chilean coast, this section of ocean needed to be clear of maritime traffic at 0200, when *BOXER* arrived to launch the strike force. The radar invisible destroyer had a few more hours to ensure that the *BOXER* would arrive undetected.

Chapter Forty-Seven

7:21 AM
Obolons'kyi District
Kiev City, Ukraine

Feliks Yeshevsky knocked on the thin wooden door and waited with a cracked smile on his face. To the right of the door, his partner pressed up flat against the wall with a retractable metal baton held tightly along the side of his black trousers. Feliks listened for movement inside the apartment. Nothing. For a few desperate seconds he wondered if Mr. Kaluzny had somehow slipped past them on the street. Dragging him out of his office downtown would be less than optimal given their time constraints.

He couldn't see how they had missed him. They had seen his wife exit the aging apartment building with their six-year-old daughter. They had walked hand in hand down the street toward the local primary school. Mrs. Kaluzny was dressed formally and carried a large handbag, so they didn't expect her to return to the apartment. They had waited fifteen minutes before entering the apartment building's unlocked main door.

He knocked on the door again and heard a voice from inside the apartment. He widened his smile and saw the light behind the peephole disappear.

"Can I help you?" Vanko Kaluzny said.

"Do you mind opening the door? I'm one of your neighbors from a few floors up. I saw something strange yesterday when your wife and daughter were walking into the building," Yeshevsky said.

He heard the deadbolt slide open, followed by a small click from the doorknob. He reached behind his back, underneath his thick wool coat, and gripped the compact Makarov pistol tucked into his belt. The door opened a few inches.

"I'm sorry. What exactly did you see happen to—"

Yeshevsky didn't allow him to finish the sentence. He kicked the door as hard as he could into Kaluzny's face, knocking the man several steps backward into the apartment. The man hidden along the wall sprang forward through the door and hit the stunned man squarely on the head with the metal baton, adding to the confusion and pain suddenly thrust into his life.

Mr. Kaluzny barely made a sound when hit, which was odd in Yeshevsky's experience. His partner shoved the man to a sitting area in front of an old television and forced him down onto a flimsy wooden chair. Yeshevsky locked the door behind him and removed a bulky silencer from one of his inner coat pockets. He started to screw the silencer to the Makarov's threaded barrel as he walked over to Vanko Kaluzny.

"What in hell do you want? Is my wife all right? My daughter?"

"That all depends on you, Mr. Kaluzny. We're interested in your university roommate, Anatoly Reznikov. We need to know where to find him."

"I don't know where he is. I haven't seen him in years," Kaluzny said.

Yeshevsky nodded imperceptibly and his partner's arm flashed, bringing the metal baton down on Kaluzny's left shoulder. The man screamed.

"Hold on! Hold on! I don't understand. Who are you? Russian Federal Security? You have no jurisdiction to—"

The baton crashed down on the man's collarbone, audibly cracking it. The force from the blow nearly collapsed the chair under Kaluzny.

"Fuck! Stop! Stop! Why are you doing this? I haven't seen him in several years," he said, exasperated from the pain.

"That's not what your mother told us."

"You visited my mother?"

"She's fine, for now, but she's not very fond of Mr. Reznikov. Said she found some false identity papers while snooping around his things. Isn't that why she refused to let him stay there? She could never understand why the two of you were such good friends," he said, tightening the silencer on the pistol.

"Look, I don't know what he's doing or—"

"But you know he can't travel under his real name?"

"A lot of people from Russia seem to have that problem nowadays."

"Maybe we'll ask your sister next. Your mother said the two of you were close. Following in your footsteps were her words. I have a few nice pictures of her on my phone. Sent to me this morning. She was on the way to classes at Volgograd State University. Would you like to see them? Maybe my colleagues should yank her out of class for a chat."

"You people are crazy," Kaluzny whispered, staring at the floor.

"Not crazy. In a hurry. I was really hoping that you would help us right now. I won't be in such a good mood if I have to wait around all day for your wife and daughter to return. Especially if I'm cooped up all day with your rotting corpse. Just the thought of their screaming and crying at the sight of your bloated body puts me in a foul mood. I've never been good around kids."

Kaluzny flinched at the baton's movement and glanced up at Yeshevsky. "He gave me a forwarding address in Sweden. I forward maybe two packages a year for him. 22 Bondegatan, Apartment 3B, Stockholm. Please don't hurt my family," he pleaded.

"Is he at this address right now?" Yeshevsky pressed.

"I really don't know. I haven't heard from him in over a year. I passed a few packages on to the address several weeks ago. 8x10 padded mailers from Novosibirsk. Looked like an air shipping company name. Something with aviation in the title."

A few weeks before, FSB agents had found three men murdered at the Nizhny Novgorod airport. Two Chechen mobsters and a guy who ran a VIP transportation business out of Novosibirsk. It was enough to keep Vanko Kaluzny alive for the moment. Yeshevsky signaled for his partner to leave, and they both walked briskly toward the door of the apartment.

"That's it? Are you going to kill me?"

Feliks Yeshevsky stopped and turned his head. "Do you want me to kill you?"

"No. I just—"

"Then quit trying to talk me into it. We know where you live. Where everyone you care about lives. If you fucked us over with this address, we'll kill all of them in front of you. If you somehow miraculously remember a phone number for Mr. Reznikov and try to call him, I will personally arrange the rape, mutilation and live incineration of your entire extended family. If I were you, I'd call in sick at Cragnia Biotech and head to the hospital to have that collarbone examined. Once the shock of our visit wears off, the pain will become unbearable."

Yeshevsky followed the other SVR agent out of the apartment and closed the door behind him. He quickly removed the silencer and placed it back in his jacket. Screwing the silencer onto the pistol in front of the suspect almost always produced immediate results. As they walked toward the staircase, he pulled out his cell phone and placed a call to Moscow.

Chapter Forty-Eight

6:26 AM
Sveavägen
Stockholm, Sweden

Major Stepan Eristov slapped his cell phone shut and turned to Captain Rusnak. "22 Bondegatan. Apartment 3B. No guarantee he is there. I want both vehicles moving in less than twenty seconds," he barked.

"The van goes first," Rusnak said.

All of the men scrambled to put on their jackets, which would conceal the weapons attached to specialized slings underneath. The slings allowed them to covertly carry their weapons "hands free," tightly along their torsos until they needed them. In one swift, practiced motion, each member of the team could put their weapon into action at a moment's notice.

Most of the team carried the latest Russian PP2000 submachine guns. Compact and futuristic-looking, it fired the new 7N21 armor piercing 9mm projectiles at a rate of 800 rounds per minute. Each weapon was loaded with a 20 round magazine for initial concealment, but each team member carried several 40 round magazines on their internal harness rig.

Two members of the support team would carry AKS-74u assault rifles, which would be stashed within easy reach inside each of the vehicles. The assault rifles would give them additional stopping power and range in the unlikely event that the operation blew up in their faces. Major Eristov and Captain Rusnak also carried silenced Makarov pistols, which would be the only suppressed weapons used by the team. Zaslon training had stressed the importance of minimizing the use of suppressors, which often served to encourage the inappropriate use of firearms during an operation. Eristov envisioned using his silenced pistol to compel Reznikov's compliance with their abduction, or if that failed, to kill him.

As the operatives piled out of the apartment, Dmitry Solomin grabbed Eristov. "Bondegatan is south of Stockholm in the Sodermalm district. Get over to the Klarastrand immediately. Head south on Sveavägen and take a right onto Radmansgatan, then a left onto Dalagatan…"

"We have maps, Dmitry. I'll call you when we're finished," Eristov said.

"Bondegatan is a one-way street headed east. Tight quarters with plenty of cafés and stores. You'll need to be very careful."

"We'll take that under advisement," he said and shut the door on the SVR agent.

Chapter Forty-Nine

12:29 AM
CIA Headquarters
Langley, Virginia

The National Clandestine Service's Operations Center was fully staffed and buzzing with activity in anticipation of the impending covert operation in Stockholm. They had no idea when or if the operation would proceed, but most of the CIA personnel currently locked into the glass chamber wouldn't see daylight until it was finished, or the mission was abandoned.

Similarly, a small private chamber in the White House Situation Room was manned by the most trusted members of the national security advisor's inner circle, along with a similar group aligned with the Secretary of State. They had access to a live, classified feed of the operation. A CIA operations technician ensured that none of the data fed to the White House directly compromised CIA operatives in the field. The White House would see a slightly watered down version of what was seen and heard in the Operations room.

Bauer and Manning had managed to convince White House bureaucrats that any premature release of information to European allies could be intercepted by the Russians, with horrifying results. Any sniff of a western intelligence agency alert in Stockholm had the potential to cut off their inside source at the FSB. Without Reznikov's address, the Russians would dispose of the rogue scientist, leaving them with no leads to chase down the deadliest bioweapon ever mass produced. The White House agreed to give the CIA team one shot at recovering Reznikov before bringing the rest of Europe into the fold. The CIA was gambling everything on the success of Sanderson's team.

Berg glanced over at the bioweapons specialists assembled around one end of the table. They had borrowed a few scientists from the Edgewood Chemical and Biological Center to analyze the lab results from Helsinki. The scientists had been asked to stay in the Operations Center to provide technical support to the team in Stockholm. None of them had any idea what they might find in Reznikov's apartment. Manning had suggested they stick with Edgewood personnel for now, until the next phase had been decided. The scientists were assigned to the U.S. Army and much less likely to slip away for a private phone call than their Center for Disease Control colleagues.

The scientists had stressed the serious implications of the laboratory examination performed on the intact brain sample retrieved from Monchegorsk. The subject's temporal lobe showed multiple localized lesions, in addition to a generalized neuropathy throughout the entire brain. The severe damage to the limbic system, specifically the temporal lobes, explained the erratic and violent behavior seen by Petrovich's team on the streets. The CIA's chief psychiatrist had added her own assessment and explanation of the bizarre behavior witnessed by Petrovich's team and confirmed as widespread by Major Sabitov.

In her opinion, the encephalitis virus had been genetically modified to mimic the behavior of the Herpes Simplex Encephalitis (HSE) virus, which was the only form of encephalitis known to localize in the limbic system. She explained that the temporal lobes were critical to the mediation of aggression. Psychiatric literature strongly suggested that patients with severe temporal lobe damage frequently exhibited a tendency for marked destructiveness and impulsiveness. It was not uncommon for patients to look emotionless or unresponsive, followed by sudden, unpredictable fits of uncontrolled motor activity and aggressive behavior. She called it intermittent explosive disorder (IED), but one of the scientists from Edgewood called it the ultimate weapon.

He suggested that the virus may have been engineered to maximize the impact of the symptoms described by the psychiatrist. Untreated, Herpes Simplex Encephalitis (HSE) resulted in rapid death in roughly 70% of cases. Lab analysis suggested that this strain had been modified to reduce lethality. They wouldn't know for sure until they could get a sample to Edgewood, but the implications of this modification were frightening.

Even among patients immediately treated with high-dose intravenous Aciclovir, fatality rates hovered at thirty percent and less than three percent ever regained normal brain function. An effective, widespread attack with this virus would be devastating. Unlike nerve agents or traditional biological weapons, the effects of this bioweapon would expand far beyond the original target. It would create a pocket of sick, uncontrollable patients that would require massive resources to manage effectively.

With the frightening potential to transform entire cities into violent playgrounds filled with irreversibly brain-damaged citizens, the world would never recover from the psychological damage caused by the release of Reznikov's virus. The resources required to house and treat the mentally disabled survivors would serve as a constant reminder to the public. In his opinion, the Russians had taken the easy way out in Monchegorsk.

The most frightening aspect of the entire situation stemmed from a casual comment made by one of the Edgewood scientists. In passing, Berg heard him tell one of his colleagues that he highly doubted the virus had been genetically modified in some "half-ass laboratory trailer in the middle of Kazakhstan." Berg didn't pursue the comment, but kept it in the back of his mind. It might explain why the Russians wanted to find Reznikov so badly. Maybe their biological warfare program hadn't died on the front lawn of the Novosibirsk facility in 1978, along with Anatoly Reznikov's father.

He started to walk over to Audra when his cell phone rang. Berg took one look at his BlackBerry's screen and nodded at Thomas Manning. The bustling conversations within the operations center ceased instantly, and every face stared at Karl Berg as he raised the phone to his ear.

"Berg here," he said.

"Reznikov's address in Stockholm is 22 Bondegatan, apartment 3B," a deep Russian voice said.

"22 Bondegatan. 3B," he said to the operations analysts.

Berg didn't pause before speed dialing Petrovich. "22 Bondegatan. Apartment 3B," he spoke into the phone and paused to scan the screens.

"South of the city. Stay on the line and we'll get you there as fast as possible. I have a CIA employee on the ground within ten city blocks of that location. She'll provide us with live intel," he said.

"Patch her voice into the center! I want to hear everything she says!" Berg said.

He glanced up at the main screen in the Operations Center, which displayed a city map of Stockholm, resized to encompass two locations. The team's starting point on Odengatan and the ending point on Bondegatan. The street was one of Stockholm's notoriously tight one-ways.

"Tell them to get over to the Klarastrand. They'll have to backtrack a bit off of Odengatan, but it's the fastest route. Traffic should still be light at this time of the morning. Tell the team to watch the pedestrian traffic on Bondegatan. Lots of cafés doing brisk coffee business. Still too early in the year for permanent outdoor seating, so it should be relatively clear of any crowds," said an analyst from their Scandinavian Section.

Berg nodded and relayed all of the information to Petrovich, who acknowledged it and informed Berg that he would be in receive only mode until they were on the road.

"How long to get there?" Berg said.

"Fifteen minutes with no delays," the analyst said.

This promised to be a long fifteen minutes.

Chapter Fifty

6:48 AM
Sodermalm District
Stockholm, Sweden

Farrington guided their Volvo V60 sedan out of the South Way Tunnel onto Folkungagatan, accelerating the car through traffic toward the yellow traffic signal ahead. The intersection was crowded with people headed for the Metro station entrance at the far left side, and Daniel cringed as their car narrowly missed a cluster of pedestrians leaning into the street. The signal turned red a few moments before they entered the intersection, clearly visible midway down the front windshield. Daniel looked around for any police cars and marveled at their luck.

"Take it easy, Rich," he said and glanced behind them.

"Fuck, they stopped at the light."

"We don't slow down. They'll be there for us," Farrington said.

Daniel didn't respond. He picked up the radio and spoke to Schafer in the van.

"We're proceeding to the target. Take the first right after the light. Bondegatan is the third street on your left. Stop the van just out of sight before the street. Schafer, I want you on foot covering us from the street corner, just like we discussed. Hubner, be ready to move that van in front of the apartment. It's on the right side of the street."

"Roger," Schafer replied.

"Berg, what are we looking at?" Petrovich said.

The car turned right and was now less than two hundred meters from the turn onto Bondegatan.

"Stand by," Berg said.

"Fuck, we're almost at the turn. Slow down," Petrovich said.

He felt the sedan decelerate as the cell phone in the center console burst to life with Berg's strained voice.

"The van is parked on the right side of the street, thirty meters back from the target entrance. It's a white Mercedes Sprinter Van. The other vehicle is parked a few spaces ahead of the entrance on the right. Silver four-door Passat. Daniel, they're already on the street. Three men between the target and the van and two beyond the target down the street. All male, wearing dark, mid-thigh-level jackets. One of them is leaning against the van on the sidewalk. She says they're easy to pick out from the others."

"Others?" Daniel said.

"Five more are at the door. Where the fuck are you?" he yelled.

"I'll call you when this is over."

He stuffed the cell phone in one of the pockets on his jacket and cradled the MP-7 in his lap, disengaging the safety. This was moving way faster than he had expected. He needed to bring it all under control and issue final orders. For Daniel, time slowed down significantly as he formulated a last second plan. They would hit the men at the door hard and let Schafer provide enough cover fire for them to get into the apartment. His plan relied upon taking down at least half of the Spetznaz in the first few seconds of firing. Beyond that, the random nature of combat would decide who lived and who died within the next few minutes. If he made it into the apartment alive, he would readjust their plan accordingly.

"Safeties off! Leo and Sergei. Get down as low as possible!" he said. "Lower! Lower!"

Daniel felt the engine surge as the car started to turn onto Bondagaten.

"Keep the car moving at a normal speed. Stop when you come parallel with the target door. As soon as the car stops, Leo, Sergei and I will engage targets in front of the apartment. Rich, you'll immediately engage targets forward of the car, up the street. Everyone storms the apartment once the Russians are down!"

As the car completed the turn, the situation described by Berg's street contact materialized in deadly detail. They were about to purposefully stop their car in the middle of a three-way crossfire.

He spotted the white Mercedes van immediately and picked out one of the Spetznaz on the opposite side of the road. He leaned against a yellow wall next to a large café window, pretending to read a newspaper. He couldn't see the second or third operative on this end of the street, but knew from Berg's report that one of them was hidden from view by the van. That one probably had access to an assault rifle. He kept the handheld radio out of sight below the window and pressed the radio transmit button. He could see the team of Spetznaz assembled in front of the apartment building entrance.

"Schafer, one target in the open on the left side of the street. Dark brown hair, black jacket, gray pants. Second target obscured by white van. Careful with that one."

"Roger. We're through the light and moving fast to your position," the radio crackled.

The car pulled even with the white van and Daniel spotted the second operative with his peripheral vision. He fought the urge to look.

"Stay low, guys. Almost there."

He counted six men near the entrance to 22 Bondegatan. The entrance consisted of a dark brown, windowless double door, surrounded by a salmon-colored facade. The building towered five stories above the cramped street and connected seamlessly with the other apartment structures lining the one-way concrete boulevard. One of the Spetznaz operatives stood to the right of the target door, in front of several weather-beaten bicycles, apparently keeping watch over the two operatives furtively working to breach the apartment. A second lookout stood on the other side of the door, glancing casually at their car as it approached.

Directly across the street, a red and white checkered awning covered two small tables occupied by locals. A woman dressed in a gray business suit emerged from the café and adjusted an oversized dark red bag hanging from her right shoulder. She glanced across the street and momentarily locked eyes with Daniel before turning left to walk up the street.

Time slowed to a crawl as the car pulled up to the space in front of the door. Another operative stood less than ten feet away on the curb, his head turned toward the apartment building. He had his left hand stuffed into the right side of his jacket and started to bring his head around to face the sound of the sedan. The Volvo stopped suddenly, jolting everyone forward.

Major Eristov sensed that something was off. He heard a car motor, which wasn't the first to pass since they emptied from the Passat sedan. It was something about Sergeant Greshnev. With the lock pick tool still in both hands, he turned his head to glance at Greshnev, who appeared unusually tense and focused. The sergeant's left hand drifted toward the PP2000 hidden under his jacket, and Greshnev considered turning to look at the car. His thought was stopped by an intense, sharp pain in his upper right back. Greshnev's sinister-looking submachine gun emerged from beneath the sergeant's jacket in a blur of hands and black steel. *Shit!*

Eristov pivoted his body and reached inside his jacket to grab his PP2000. Before the lock pick tool clattered to the ground behind him, his left hand had already reached the front grip of the submachine gun and started to pull it forward. Out of the corner of his eye, he saw two bursts of machine-gun fire flash from the car. One of the bursts tore through him, arresting his turn and slamming him into the thick wooden door. He heard Greshnev's PP2000 shatter the morning silence, followed quickly by another loud staccato burst from somewhere down the street. With his head still cocked toward the street, he saw the inside of the car turned bright red as Russian bullets found targets. Oddly, he felt no pain.

*

Most of the Volvo's windows shattered simultaneously as Daniel's team fired extended bursts from their suppressed weapons, catching most of the Russian operatives by surprise. Daniel's first burst cut straight through the stomach of the operative standing on the curb, passing straight through to strike one of the men working on the door. Several bullets stitched across both of the men huddled in front of the entryway, as Daniel instinctively shifted the MP-7's reflex sight to the man standing to the left of the door and fired another burst, striking the man in the upper chest. The armor-piercing rounds punched through him a mere fraction of a second after the Russian put his own PP2000 into action against Daniel's team.

The Russian's hastily fired burst struck the car's rear door, easily penetrating the sedan's thin metal. Two rounds impacted with the ballistic plates inserted into Sergei's vest and one passed through his right leg, spraying the compartment with arterial blood. Simultaneously, a concentrated burst of fire from the Spetznaz operative standing in front of the bicycles struck the upper rear corner of the Volvo. The bullets effortlessly entered the car's passenger cabin and passed through Sergei's skull, turning most of its contents into a red aerosolized mist that instantly obscured the remaining intact windows. One round continued unhindered and shattered Farrington's driver side window.

Hot arterial blood pumped through the space between the headrest and seat, splashing Daniel's neck before he opened the door and charged through the space between two cars.

ẟ

Leo's head slammed into the top of the driver's seat when Farrington hit the brakes, but he still managed to rise quickly and find his first target through the rear window of the Volvo. He fired a suppressed burst at a man leaning against the apartment wall about ten meters down the street, crumbling the car's safety glass into a thousand pieces and striking the Russian operative in the neck and head with several armor-piercing bullets. Through the Reflex sight, he saw the body instantly drop to the pavement, leaving the sight's bright green dot centered on a red-stained wall.

He swung the MP-7 inward along the apartment wall and started to acquire a second target, but was hit by a hot spray that covered his face and obscured his Reflex sight. Undeterred by the fact that his best friend's brains had just coated his face, he fired two extended bursts without the Reflex sight, relying on his practiced ability to aim instinctively down the barrel. He saw the shooter stumble backward, toppling over several bicycles.

He looked past Sergei's useless body and assessed that all of the targets in front of the apartment building were down. Farrington's MP-7 clattered and the front windshield turned opaque. Blood still pumped furiously from Sergei's leg wound, splashing the car's gray interior. A loud staccato burst echoed from the street, followed instantly by the hollow impact of bullets against the Volvo's metal shell. Time to move.

He opened the door halfway and slid out of the sedan, staying low. Farrington had made the same decision, and they both stepped onto the street at the same time. Leo charged along the rear side of the Volvo, but was stopped in his tracks by a well-aimed burst of 5.45mm projectiles from a shooter near the Russians' white Mercedes van. Three of the four bullets struck the Enhanced Small Arms Protective Insert of Leo's tactical vest, protecting the vital organs of his chest from instant jellification. The fourth bullet hit a few millimeters above the hardened boron carbide plate and passed easily through the softer level IIIA material. The hardened steel core projectile shattered his right clavicle and exited through the top of his right arm. The near simultaneous impact of all four bullets dropped Leo to the pavement, which saved his life. Another burst of assault rifle fire peppered the door he had just opened.

&

Farrington slammed on the brakes and raised his MP-7, searching for one of the targets he had identified as the car approached the front of the apartment. He braced the MP-7 against the steering wheel and centered the Reflex sight's green dot on a man running across the street about 50 meters up the road. He fired a short burst and the entire front windshield shattered without falling, effectively obscuring his view of the street. Through the small hole punctured by the tight burst of 4.6mm projectiles, he could see that his target had stopped in the middle of the street. Aiming through the tiny opening in the opaque, bluish white windshield, he fired a long burst at the stationary man, but couldn't see the results. Without warning, the inside of the car erupted in a warm spray that painted the windshield red and coated the dashboard with a thin pinkish-red film. He didn't need to turn his head around to figure out what had happened. He heard muffled bursts of fire from the remaining MP-7's and decided it was time to hit the street. Out of his peripheral vision, he saw Daniel open the front passenger door.

As he stepped out of the car, he immediately saw that his target had collapsed into a motionless heap in the middle of the road. A fraction of a second later, the sound of heavy caliber gunfire reached his ears, followed by shattered glass and a sharp pain in his upper left arm. He reacted swiftly and dove to the concrete roadway, as several bullets penetrated the open back door and slammed into the space he'd recently occupied. He squeezed off a hasty burst at a shooter located across the street from the van, causing the man to duck inside a doorway. He noticed that Leo lay bleeding on the pavement next to the Volvo's right rear tire. He wanted to help him, but made the decision to get off the street as quickly as possible.

He jumped to his feet and sprinted around the front of the Volvo, staying low as bullets followed his path, knocking out the rest of the Volvo's front windshield and peppering the silver Renault parked along the curb. He slid over the Renault's hood and landed on the sidewalk, searching for targets ahead of them. Thirty meters up the street, he spotted a man crouched low on the sidewalk next to a white sedan. The man fit the general description of the Spetznaz operatives, but Farrington didn't fire. The man looked panicked and appeared more interested in keeping his head low.

&

Hans Schafer hit the pavement running when the van stopped. He held the compact G-36C assault rifle under his coat, well aware that the barrel extended a few inches below the bottom. He was several meters from turning the corner onto Bondegatan when the shooting erupted. Instinctively, he knew that the sound of unsuppressed automatic weapons fire meant one thing. The team was in deep shit. He pulled out the assault rifle and sprinted to the corner, praying that he wasn't too late to help. The red light had fucked them over. Hubner wanted to run it, but by the time the van would have entered the intersection, there would be little doubt in any police officer's mind that they had just run a red light. The last thing they needed was a police escort to Reznikov's apartment, and he didn't have time to scan the full three hundred and sixty degrees around them to make a decision. Schafer had put his hand on Hubner's shoulder and told him to wait. He assured him that they'd arrive in time. As he turned the corner, his initial impression was that he had been badly mistaken.

He walked casually between two cars parked near the corner, careful not to draw any attention from the Spetznaz operative shooting from a concealed doorway along the sidewalk. Once past the cars, he ducked low and moved swiftly down the street. He saw Leo lying face down on the pavement, trying desperately to claw his way under the Volvo. Automatic fire erupted from behind the Mercedes van where he had been told to expect another Russian, followed by a deafening extended burst of fire from the shooter in the recessed doorway. The bullets hit the cars parked in front of the doorway, ricocheted off the concrete facade of the building and splintered the dark brown doorway to Reznikov's apartment. He saw Daniel and Farrington pop up from a position between the two parked cars and fire suppressed bursts at the Russians, who responded immediately with a fusillade of their own gunfire.

Schafer knew what needed to be done. He stayed low, sprinting along the cars, until he drew even with the Mercedes van. The recessed doorway was located ten additional meters down on his side of the street. He rose to a full stand and aimed through the window of the van, finding the Spetznaz operative's head through his 3X Zeiss RSA-S Reflex sight. He fired a quick burst through the van's window and turned to acquire the doorway shooter. As he placed the green dot on the next Spetznaz operative's forehead, he had time for a quick thought before he pulled the trigger. Fuck that guy was fast.

Schafer's 5.56mm bullets struck the Russian between the eyes, but not before the operative returned the favor with a well-aimed burst to Schafer's upper chest. Two of the bullets struck Schafer's assault rifle, shattering it. The third bullet passed through his neck, causing irreparable damage and severing his carotid artery. Schafer staggered forward, aware that he was fatally hit. He let the assault rifle fall to the concrete and raised his hands to his neck. He stared at his blood-soaked hands for a few seconds and moved his gaze to Reznikov's apartment. He watched Farrington and Petrovich fire point blank into one of the doors and kick it in. The last thing he saw before falling unconscious to the street was their van speed around the corner.

❧

More than a dozen bullets snapped overhead, striking the concrete behind Daniel. Leaned against the front bumper of a compact white Fiat, he felt several bullets impact against the car's metal frame. One projectile popped through the hood and barely missed his right arm. He scooted backward, bumping up against Farrington, who had also decided that the tight space between the Fiat and bullet-riddled silver Renault was the only safe place on the street. A burst of gunfire shattered the momentary calm, and another fusillade of bullets skipped off the pavement near Farrington's feet. Daniel risked a peek through the Fiat's partially shattered windshield and saw Schafer running down the street, hidden from the gunmen by the line of vehicles on each side of the road.

"Our backup just arrived," Daniel said.

"About fucking time," Farrington muttered.

Daniel heard a burst of fire from Schafer's G-36C, followed immediately by a tight burst from one of the Russian submachine guns. He popped back up to fire at the shooter in the recessed doorway, but the Russian had already fallen from view. A dark red stain covered the yellow wall next to the alcove, evidence of the Russian's death. His eyes shifted to Schafer, who stood motionless for a moment in the middle of the street. Blood pumped furiously out of Schafer's neck.

"Schafer's hit," he said to Farrington. He pulled out his handheld radio and turned to the door, pushing Farrington onto the sidewalk. "Get those bodies out of the way," he said, before speaking into the radio. "Move the van to the target doorway. You'll need to figure out a way to move the Volvo."

"Tell Schafer to move it. I'll be there in a few seconds."

"Schafer's dead. Farrington's the only other survivor," he said and stuffed the radio back into his jacket.

"Leo's still alive," Farrington said.

"He'll figure that out on his own," Petrovich said, kicking the remaining Russian away from the blood-showered door.

"Try the lock pick set?" Farrington said.

"Are you fucking kidding me?" Petrovich said, aiming his MP-7 at the doorknob.

Farrington backed up and leveled his weapon at a similar point. Both weapons kicked furiously as the operatives poured several dozen armor-piercing projectiles into the area surrounding the doorknob. The bullets tore through the handle and obliterated the solid wood next to the door frame. Petrovich kicked the door with the bottom of his foot, and it gave no resistance.

"You want to knock on Reznikov's door?" Daniel said.

"No, I'm gonna use you as a battering ram."

Daniel smirked and darted inside the splinter-filled foyer, searching for the staircase. He found it just past a small set of stairs leading into a lobby.

"Up there," he said.

&

Reznikov's eyes flashed open. He thought he'd heard gunshots. He tried to figure out where he was, but nothing made sense to him. His head started pounding immediately, and he tried lazily to lift his head from the table. His face felt numb and moving his head required too much effort. He started to pass out when two staccato bursts of gunfire jarred him back into the moment. His head shot up and he slid one of his heavy arms out along the table, knocking an empty bottle of vodka to the hardwood floor. The bottle shattered, and he tried to focus his vision with little success. The light pouring into the kitchen was overwhelming, and he squinted, which brought a temporary clarity to his sight.

He heard yelling and screaming from the street below and had the strange thought that he might not be in Stockholm anymore. He recognized the kitchen, so he must still be in his apartment. What the fuck was going on? He saw another empty bottle of cheap vodka teetering on the edge of the table next to a small leather-bound notebook. Dozens of crumpled pages lay scattered on the table, partially concealing a small black revolver.

He suddenly remembered why was sitting at the table, where he had apparently passed out from drinking. He had planned to kill himself, but admittedly the details were still hazy to him. He knew he should grab the pistol and put it to his head, but two bottles of vodka had erased much of the argument leading to this decision. He smiled. As a scientist, he would have to work through the process again and empirically prove that he must kill himself. He wondered if there was a shortcut, since he wasn't sure he'd be close to sober by nightfall. Several more bursts of gunfire echoed from the street, followed by screaming, which spurred him to grab the revolver. Someone was coming for him. If it was those dirty Jihadists, he might be back in business. Unfortunately, he didn't think he could effectively stand up from the table. A small detail to work out.

❧

Daniel took two stairs at a time until they reached the third floor. He yanked open the stairwell door and quickly poked his head in and out of the opening, checking both directions. The hallway was empty. A polished brass placard on the wall in front of him indicated the direction they would take to apartment 3B. Daniel and Farrington turned right and slithered along the wall, aiming their weapons forward. They paused at the door to 3A and examined it. Daniel pushed on the thin door, testing it before he whispered to Farrington.

"Staggered hits until we're in. I'll go first," he said, and Farrington nodded.

They arrived at 3B, noting that it faced the street. Reznikov would undoubtedly be ready for something. They listened for a second and heard nothing. Daniel nodded, and they both backed up to the other side of the hallway. Petrovich barreled forward, tucking the MP-7 low and slamming into the door with his right shoulder. He felt the door buckle significantly and shifted left to clear out of Farrington's way. Farrington struck the door with his left shoulder and continued through the splintered door frame, rolling out of Petrovich's way.

Daniel braced his weapon against the doorframe and aimed at the figure sitting at the table. Reznikov fired his revolver three times at the open doorway, before placing the gun to the side of his own head. A single shot from Daniel's MP-7 struck the revolver and knocked it out of Reznikov's hand onto the kitchen floor, along with a few of his fingers. They both charged the Russian scientist, who knocked the table over trying to stand up. Farrington arrived first, grabbing Reznikov by the collar of his shirt and yanking him facedown into the table. Petrovich took a pair of zip ties from his jacket and secured his hands. They had Reznikov up on his feet in a matter of seconds. Farrington spoke to him in Russian.

"Do you have any of the virus here in the apartment?"

"It's all gone, you see. That's why I'm still here. They didn't do it…and now I have nothing…I can't even know this…"

"He's fucking drunk," Petrovich said.

"The notebook didn't lie…they just changed the game," Reznikov said, as his head wobbled and his eyes lost focus.

Petrovich punched Reznikov in the face twice before Farrington could react.

"What the fuck are you doing? We need to get out of here and I don't need him unconscious. Bag up that notebook and the crumpled papers. Ten seconds and out. I'll get him to the van," Farrington said, dragging the moaning scientist to the door.

Daniel turned around and got down on his knees to collect the scraps of paper knocked onto the floor. He dropped the MP-7 and started stuffing the papers into his pockets. The notebook was small enough to fit into one of the inner coat pockets. He glanced around for anything else that he could grab in the few seconds he had remaining. Under a metal frame desk parked against the hallway wall, he saw an open topped cardboard carton overstuffed with folders and loose papers. He grabbed his submachine gun and pulled the carton out, partially ripping the cardboard due to the weight of the papers inside. He didn't have time to dig through it. He jammed the MP-7 into the carton, and lifted it by the two handles.

He caught up with Farrington and Reznikov at the bottom of the stairwell and saw that Farrington had resorted to punching Reznikov to keep him moving. The scientist was bleeding from the nose and mouth now, and Farrington looked like he was a second away from slamming the scientist's head against the wall. Maybe he already had. Petrovich kicked the stairwell door open and ran through the lobby onto the sidewalk. The Volvo was gone, jammed against a sedan a few spaces down on the other side of the street. His view of the café across the street was blocked by their white VW Transporter van. Hubner stood in front of the van with his assault rifle ready. Police sirens grew louder, echoing through the tight streets. He could see light blue flashes from a police car two blocks from the entrance to their stretch of Bondegatan.

"Throw a smoke down the street," Daniel said and nodded toward the turn they had taken onto Bondegatan.

Hubner reacted immediately and reached into his jacket pocket to withdraw a soda can sized gray cylinder. He ran to the back of the van and rested his G-36C against the bumper. In one motion, he pulled the pin from the smoke grenade and hurled it as far as he could down Bondegatan. It landed a few meters past Schafer's body and exploded in a thick, billowing white cloud. The effect was immediate and completely obscured the entrance to this stretch of Bondegatan.

While Hubner took care of the smoke screen, Daniel heaved the carton of papers into the van and took off back into the building to help Farrington. He had seen Leo propped up in the back row, barely conscious. His entire right shoulder had been covered with a pasty red mixture of Celox and blood. From the brief glance he managed to steal, it looked like the hemostatic powder had stopped the bleeding.

He caught up with Farrington at the lobby stairs, and together they manhandled Reznikov into the van. Daniel heard tires screeching beyond the persistent, thick smoke, coupled with piercing sirens. He figured these were first responders and wanted to discourage any heroics.

"Drop a smoke next to the van, and get us out of here," he said, furiously unscrewing the silencer on the MP-7.

While Hubner pulled the pin on another smoke grenade, Daniel removed the silencer and changed magazines. He pointed the unsuppressed weapon out of the van's open side door and fired most of the forty rounds into the silver Renault. Screaming ensued from several locations on the street, and he heard tires screech beyond the smoke as the lightly armed police officers presumably thought better of keeping their cars exposed to automatic gunfire.

He slammed the door shut and turned to get into the front passenger seat. Reznikov's body stiffened and arched like he was trying to get up. Farrington tried to shove him back into the bench seat, but Reznikov's body didn't budge. Petrovich punched him in the groin and his eyes rolled back into his head. He went into convulsions as the van lurched forward out of the smoke.

"Fuck, I think we're losing him," Farrington said.

"Just keep him in his seat until we're clear of this mess. Hubner, take your first left and head north back into the city."

Daniel pushed his way past Farrington and dropped into the passenger seat. He grabbed one of three remaining smoke grenades and lowered his window. Glancing out of the open window, he saw something he would never have expected.

❧

Senior Sergeant Daniil Karev furtively watched the operatives shove Reznikov into the van. He was the lone surviving member of his team, mainly because he had decided at the outset of the ambush to serve as Moscow's insurance policy. The street battle had lasted less than thirty seconds. As the gunfire died, he was confident that he had made the right decision. Their mission had been clear. Capture or kill Reznikov. If he'd opted to fight, there was little doubt in his mind that his blood would have filled the Stockholm sewers. Restraint kept him alive, and he'd have one more shot at completing their mission.

A long burst of automatic gunfire filled the street with more sounds of civilian panic. Close to him, he heard a stifled scream from the woman that had hidden herself in a recessed doorway. He stood up and turned his back on the van, which had started to move up the street. He passed the sobbing woman, who was huddled against the dark green door in the shelter of the concrete alcove. She clutched a red handbag and appeared startled by his sudden appearance. Karev took a few steps past the doorway and gripped the PP2000 in both hands. He was fully prepared to spin around and fire several well aimed bursts of armor-piercing bullets into the van. He kept walking as the van's engine grew louder. One more second and…

His chin was yanked backward, followed by an incredibly intense burning across his neck. His knees buckled and the PP2000 was yanked from his hands. A strong forearm kept his head back, and he felt three painful sharp jabs to his lower back, followed by a complete release of the pressure locking his head back. Unable to control his legs, he fell to his knees and toppled onto his left side as the van sped by. Through his fading vision, he saw a blonde woman wearing gray walk quickly up the street. She tossed his PP2000 under a car and readjusted her oversized, red leather handbag.

❧

Daniel locked eyes with the woman in the gray suit again. Considering what he'd just seen her do to the Russian operative, he wanted to stop the van. They could use someone like that to help them get out of the city. Just as the thought emerged, she broke eye contact and leaned over to dispose of the submachine gun she had cut loose from the Russian's body sling. He dropped the grenade as they approached the turn. If they could get off Bondegatan unobserved, the smoke screen would confuse police units long enough for them to escape.

Currently, no police units would have a detailed description of their vehicle. Civilian emergency calls might identify a white van, but they had just passed four white vans parked on this street alone, not to mention the Russians' van. As traffic picked up in Stockholm, there wouldn't be enough police in all of Scandinavia to stop and search every white van on the streets. Hubner took the left turn at Bondegatan and Farrington slammed against the van door.

"Take it easy! Daniel, he's not breathing."

Daniel turned around in his seat and saw that Reznikov indeed looked like he had gone into cardiac arrest. Leo had spilled out of the rear bench onto the floor. His eyes fluttered open and he grimaced, which was a good sign. He turned his attention back to the road and grabbed one of their maps, unfolding it.

"I need to concentrate on getting us out of here, or we're all fucked," he said.

"His heart is racing like crazy! If Reznikov dies, we're most certainly fucked," Farrington yelled.

"I'm working on it!" Petrovich said.

"Working on what?"

Petrovich ignored him and concentrated on the map. He located what he was looking for. "Take a right onto Folkungagatan, then your first left on Renstiernesgata," he said.

"Got it," Hubner replied.

As they stopped at their first cross street, he saw a police car approach the intersection from the right and reached back with his left hand to grab his MP-7 from the cardboard carton behind his seat. Hubner expeditiously accelerated the van through the intersection and Daniel dropped the map to adjust the side mirror so he could see behind the van. He watched the police car turn left at the intersection and speed the wrong way down the one-way road. Another police car followed a few seconds later. They were clear for now. He wondered how long it would take them to figure out that they weren't still sitting in front of 22 Bondegatan. The smoke screens would start to clear in a few minutes.

They passed one more road and approached Folkungagatan. Several police cars and a formidable-looking van sped through the light, followed by two additional police cars that turned on their street, forcing them to squeeze the van as far over as possible to let them pass. Once the police cars sped through the bottleneck, Daniel smiled at Hubner, who raised his eyebrows.

"Take a right here," Daniel said.

"Maybe we should take him to a hospital. We can take hostages and hold off the police until we can get some information out of him. I don't give a fuck if we're captured. Once we get the information, the Swedes won't care about any of this," Farrington said.

"He has a point," Hubner added.

"Left here," Daniel said, "and keep your eyes peeled for a Metro station up on our left. Slussen Station."

"The Metro?" Farrington said.

"I have a plan," Daniel said.

"You have less than a minute to put your plan into action, or we're storming the nearest hospital."

The van turned left after burning up nearly twenty seconds of Daniel's allotted time. He could sense that Farrington was close to snapping on him.

"Give me that minute when we hit the Metro station," he said.

"I'll give you thirty seconds. If you're not back in the van, we're leaving you," Farrington said.

They cruised through another green light before the road eased left onto a wide road that overlooked Stockholm's old city waterfront. The distance ahead of them on the road looked vast.

"Where the fuck is this Metro station? His heart is going haywire!" Farrington said.

"Just ahead. Trust me on this," Daniel said.

As the van pulled past several modern buildings on the right side, the Metro station entrance suddenly appeared.

"There it is! Slussen Station! Double park and keep an eye out for police."

The van pulled even with the covered Metro entrance, and Daniel burst out of the door, sprinting through traffic for the escalator. He pushed past several civilians and reached the Metro floor, glancing around. He found what he was looking for near the turnstile, along the wall next to a bank of telephones. He just hoped Farrington didn't hold him to thirty seconds. He was already well past that deadline. Less than twenty seconds later, Daniel emerged from the ground and ran to the van. He tossed the bright yellow plastic Automated External Defibrillator over the front passenger seat at Farrington and hopped in the van as it took off toward downtown Stockholm.

"Bring him back to life while Hubner gets us through Stockholm. I need to make a call."

Chapter Fifty-One

1:07 AM
CIA Headquarters
Langley, Virginia

The wall-mounted communications LCD flashed a number that was immediately recognized by Berg.

"It's the Stockholm team. Patch the call through on speaker," Berg said.

"This is Berg. You're on with the entire Ops center. What is Reznikov's status?"

Daniel's voice filled the room. It was obvious from the background static and white noise that they were on the road.

"Barely alive. He had some kind of fucking seizure. His heart started doing all kinds of shit. We have him hooked up to a portable AED, but I don't know how much longer he's going to last. The thing's already shocked him three times."

"Keep him hooked up to the AED. What about the rest of your team?" Berg said.

"One of my men is seriously wounded and requires immediate medical attention. We left two others dead on the street. We just headed north on...what the fuck is...Birger Jarlsgatan? These street names are killing me."

"Understood. What happened to the Russian team?"

"Ten of them. All dead. We need to transfer vehicles immediately. Possibly split up," Daniel said.

"Did you recover any of the bioweapon?"

"Negative. We grabbed some papers. We didn't have time to search his apartment," Daniel said.

"Send him to the Ostermalm district. Tell him to take his next right," the operations watch officer said.

Berg glanced at the main screen above him and searched the Ostermalm district for an icon representing one of the replacement vans that had been activated.

"I have a van close to your position. Take your next right."

"I assume the van isn't white?" Petrovich said.

"It's blue," the watch officer reassured him.

"After the transfer, I need you to make your way north to E18. I'll direct you to a safe house in a quiet place called Viggbyholm. We're sending a discreet medical team to the same location. Keep Reznikov alive until you get there."

"It's all up to this machine. How far away is the safe house?" Petrovich said.

The route suddenly appeared on the wall monitor, extending from the current location of the transfer van to a location well north of the city.

"Seventeen kilometers. Twenty minutes without traffic. I'm estimating thirty to forty minutes for you right now," the watch officer said, reading what had been typed into a visible data field on the screen by their Scandinavian analyst.

"We'll get him there. Make sure there are enough medical personnel on scene to treat my guy at the same time. We just turned right on Sturegatan."

"Take your second right onto Linnegatan. The van is headed your way. It'll meet you in less than a minute at the corner of Linnegatan and Nybrogatan," the watch officer said, nodding at Berg.

"I understand your priorities," Berg said.

"Let's just make sure the medical team understands them," Petrovich said.

"Our van is parked in a handicapped space in front of a dark green awning that reads 'Gold and Silver,'" the watch officer said.

"Copy. We just turned onto Linnegatan. I'll be in touch shortly," Petrovich said.

The call went dead, and Berg looked over at Audra Bauer and Thomas Manning.

"We just need to keep them away from the police," Berg said, walking over to the two of them.

"That would certainly put a halt to this show," Manning said.

"That's the problem. This crew won't let a few police cars get in their way. They just took down an entire Spetznaz team. Probably a Zaslon team. The best in the business."

"Who exactly did we get involved with?" Manning said in a lowered voice.

"The only people who stood a chance of snatching Reznikov away from the Russians. I'd consider us to be extremely fortunate," Berg said.

"Let's just do everything in our power to guide them safely to Viggbyholm," Audra added.

The watch officer, a dark-haired, stiff-looking man dressed in a navy business suit, interrupted them. "Director Manning. The White House Situation Room."

"All right. I better take this. I'll have to brief our director after that," Manning said and stepped away.

"Nice job handling the team," Audra said to Berg.

"You should expect nothing less from your assistant deputy director."

"I'll have to keep a close eye on you. With a performance like this, I could easily be replaced," she said.

"I don't think you have anything to worry about. When they figure out the team belongs to Sanderson, I have a feeling I'll be looking for employment…if I don't get rendered in the middle of the night to some oil rig in the middle of nowhere."

"I'll be joining you," she said.

"No. I got your back on this one," Berg assured her.

"Maybe you could go to work for Sanderson," she joked.

"Trust me; I've given it some serious thought. Either way, we're not out of the woods with this op yet. A lot could go wrong in the next hour. I just hope they can get some actionable intelligence from Reznikov."

"Me too. This is just the tip of the iceberg."

Chapter Fifty-Two

1:10 AM
White House Situation Room
Washington, D.C.

Frederick Shelby shifted uneasily in his high-backed leather chair. Operation Bold Scimitar's strike force was less than twenty minutes from touching down inside Sanderson's compound, and half of the room was still missing. He couldn't imagine what might be more pressing at 1:10 in the morning, but much to his surprise fifteen minutes ago, three of the key players in the room left suddenly after Miss Kestler took a phone call. The White House counter-terrorism director, along with the national security advisor and secretary of state, left without saying a word. At least the secretary of defense didn't leave. He had stayed glued to his laptop computer screen, probably shifting between the live camera feeds received from the assault force.

The two massive flat-screen monitors at the end of the room displayed a helmet camera feed from the SEAL force's commander, Lieutenant Commander Scott Daly; and a nose mounted feed from the lead helicopter, a Special Forces HH-60H Rescue Hawk from the Firehawks squadron. They had all watched the green images in silence as the darkened Chilean coast filled the screen and the strike force went "feet dry" over Chile at 12:37. Less than twenty minutes later, Operation Bold Scimitar lost half of its audience.

He stared at the empty seats around the far end of the conference table and directed his attention toward Lieutenant General Frank Gordon at the head of the table. The general's purposeful eyes were glued to his own laptop. He felt slightly disconnected without the same information feeds seen by the secretary of defense and the commander of U.S Joint Special

Operations Command, but this was more a function of feeling left out than operational necessity. He was along for the ride as a courtesy and didn't want to overstep his boundaries.

The flat-screen monitor mounted on the side of the conference room showed the strike force's progress on a detailed topographic map and displayed a bunch of information on a side window that nobody had bothered to explain to him. A digital clock featuring three time zones counted away the seconds toward the strike force's proposed 3:30 AM local time arrival at the compound. He turned to his least favorite person in the room to ask a question.

"How does everything look, Gerry? On schedule?" he said.

Gerald Simmons, assistant secretary for Special Operations and Low Intensity Conflict Capabilities, regarded him with a thinly veiled annoyance, pretending to examine Shelby's laptop, which relayed no additional information beyond what the FBI director could already see for himself on the room's screens.

"Looks like they might arrive ahead of schedule. The flight commander made the decision to fly directly over a low mountain range instead of snaking through a few lower canyons, so they picked up a few minutes and saved some fuel. This might come in handy if they have to loiter around the Sand Box. You don't have this on your…uh…never mind," he said.

"Sand Box?" Shelby said, wishing he could rip the computer away from Simmons and bash it over his head.

"That's the informal name the SEALs gave to the LZ Alpha. Sanderson. Sand Box. They like to keep things interesting for us," Gerry said.

Shelby was pretty sure that most of the SEALs and marines on this mission would smash a beer bottle over this prick's head if they ever ran into him in a dark bar. He glanced down the table at Brigadier General Lawrence Nichols, who had caught Gerry's comment about the SEALs and looked like he was having the same malicious thoughts. Nichols made eye contact with Shelby and shook his head.

The door to the room opened suddenly, and two serious looking Secret Service agents walked in, appraising the dozen or so people occupying seats. After a few seconds, one of them spoke into a handcuff microphone, and the missing members of the room filed back in, followed by the president of the United States.

"The president of the United States," was announced by someone, and everyone stood.

"Please. Don't let me interrupt," he said in a southern accent and motioned for the national security advisor to sit closest to General Gordon.

The president rolled an empty chair from the wall and tucked himself just behind and between General Gordon and Brigadier General Nichols. He shook hands with both of them and exchanged a few pleasantries. Several seconds later, he locked eyes with Director Shelby and stood up, motioning for him to come over. Director Shelby stood up from his chair and made his way through the small crowd that had followed the president's entourage into the room.

"Mr. President. Always a pleasure. What brings you down for our little operation?" he said, gripping the president's hand in a vigorous shake.

"Busy night, Frederick, and the pleasure is all mine. Fantastic work on this. Only God himself knows what Sanderson is capable of. Your diligence helped put a dark chapter behind us. I'll be relieved when he's off the grid," the president said.

"My sentiments exactly, Mr. President."

"I'm told we might be a few minutes ahead of schedule. I guess it's in the capable hands of our nation's finest," he said and patted General Gordon on the shoulder.

"This is the most sophisticated Special Forces strike package ever assembled, Mr. President. In seventeen minutes, Sanderson will be on his knees, zip tied in front of that monitor," General Gordon said.

"Grab a seat," said the president, motioning for one of the Secret Service agents.

Within seconds, he was sitting next to the president, with a bird's-eye view of the entire operation. This was much better, he thought, though he still couldn't shake the feeling that something big was going on without his knowledge. On his way to their conference room, he saw that every station on the Watch Floor was occupied, which struck him as unusual this late at night, even during a major operation. At least one of the smaller conference rooms had been in use, which was also unusual, and the primary conference room was clearly being reconfigured for a major operation. All an unusual amount of activity outside of daytime hours, which made him wonder what he didn't know. As the leader of the nation's domestic law enforcement and intelligence arm, he didn't like to be out of the loop.

Chapter Fifty-Three

1:20 AM
CIA Headquarters
Langley, Virginia

"Ms. Bauer, you have a call from the White House Situation Room. Line eight," the operations watch officer announced.

Audra walked over to one of the semi-private computer stations near the wall that separated the Fish Bowl from the rest of the operations center and picked up the phone handset, pressing the button for line eight.

"Audra Bauer."

"Audra. It's Alex. Any word on Reznikov?"

"He's still alive. They're still about twenty minutes from arriving at the safe house. The team collected some scraps of paper that look like they were torn from a notebook belonging to Reznikov. The scraps contain cities and addresses in Europe. One right in Stockholm. Reznikov is still unconscious, so we can't get an explanation. We're compiling a list of these addresses right now for the White House."

"All right, I'll pass that information along. They're reconfiguring the main conference room here to handle the situation as it expands. Hey, thanks a lot for the warning about our VIPs. I looked like a crumpled bag of shit when the president walked in. I didn't even have a sport coat."

"The president monitored the operation?"

"Along with the national security advisor and secretary of state. I almost fell out of my chair."

"Kestler didn't give you a heads up?"

"She's been popping in and out of here all night like this is some kind of side show. She dashed in here with the big three a few minutes after we got Reznikov's address. They all vanished as soon as the team hit the road in the transfer van. There's some kind of big military operation going on. I saw a bunch of Special Operations brass earlier, including Lieutenant General Frank Gordon, JSOC commander. Oddly enough, Frederick Shelby was chumming around with them."

"The director of the FBI?"

"The one and only."

"He's there?"

"Unless he left. It was about ninety minutes ago."

"You didn't assign another liaison for a second operation?"

"No. I was not aware of another operation that required CIA support. Shit, I hope I didn't miss something. I've been preoccupied with the Stockholm op."

"I didn't see a bulletin, so I don't think you missed anything."

"Let me do a little poking around. I'll call you right back," Alex said.

"You know where to find me," she said.

Alex Holstein had served as the CIA's senior White House liaison for three years and spent a large portion of his time in the White House Situation Room. The fact that he was at a loss to explain the presence of General Frank Gordon and the director of the FBI at one in the morning in the White House Situation Room left Audra with a strange feeling that she was missing something. She checked on Berg's progress compiling Petrovich's list of addresses. They were a few minutes away from having a complete list. So far, the locations presented no particular pattern, aside from the fact that they were clustered in central Europe, the United Kingdom and Scandinavia. Eighteen addresses had been identified from Reznikov's writing.

Three minutes later, the watch officer announced another call from the White House.

"Audra Bauer," she answered.

"It's Alex. I confirmed that Kestler is preoccupied with another operation, but I couldn't get any more information from the Watch Floor. I don't have the same rapport with the night shift, and their new tiered seating arrangement doesn't allow for the same easy, over-the-shoulder access to their monitors. I did manage to see which time zone locations are being actively monitored. Washington, D.C., Stockholm and Zapala. The last one stumped me. I just checked, and it's in the Nuequen Province of western Argentina."

Audra Bauer felt her chest tighten and her pulse quicken. It all suddenly made sense to her.

"Thanks, Alex. I'll get right back to you with that list," she said and hung up before he could respond.

She pulled a small paper day planner out of her suit jacket and opened it to the first page, which contained two hastily written satellite telephone numbers. She picked up the phone again and selected an encrypted line. She entered her telecommunications security code, which would allow her to place a call out of the center. The call would be flagged for the watch officer and recorded. Once the line went live, she dialed the number and waited. She let it ring for a minute and tried the second number with the same result. No answer.

"Are you talking to the team leader?" she yelled to Berg, careful not to use Petrovich's name, though she suspected it wouldn't matter soon.

"Yeah," Berg said.

"I need to talk to him immediately," she said, and her tone attracted the attention of Thomas Manning.

"Something wrong?" he said, walking over to meet her near Berg.

"Possibly. Thomas, I'm going to need some privacy."

He looked at her quizzically.

"For your own protection," she added.

"I think we're well past the point of plausible deniability. I just authorized and witnessed a covert operation that left twelve dead bodies on a city street in Stockholm. I think I'm fully vested in whatever mess the two of you have created, though I get the distinct impression that this would have gone down with or without my approval."

"Fair enough," she said and took the phone from Berg.

"This is Audra Bauer. National Clandestine Service deputy director. Have you talked to your boss recently?"

"I briefly spoke with him less than five minutes ago. We've been a little preoccupied if you haven't noticed."

"I just tried both of his satellite numbers, and he didn't respond."

"Then have Berg call. He may not pick up unknown numbers. Especially government lines."

"I have reason to believe he might have company at the compound very soon. It's possible that he's already entertaining them," she said.

"He sounded fine to me. What has you so spooked, if you'll pardon the expression?" Daniel said.

"I just learned that the president of the United States and pretty much his entire National Security Council just went into a sealed situation room with the director of the FBI and JSOC's commanding general. One of the time zone clocks somewhere in the White House Situation Room is set to a small town named Zapala. Ever been there?" she said.

"I need to make a call," he responded.

"You need to promise me you'll see your current mission through to the end, no matter what happens to your boss."

"I'll get Reznikov to the safe house alive."

The line went dead, and Audra handed Berg the phone. "He'll try to reach Sanderson. This couldn't be happening at a worse time. We need these operatives focused on Reznikov. I'm worried they'll go rogue if Sanderson is apprehended or killed."

"General Sanderson? Holy shit. These are Sanderson's people? The people you were supposed to be helping the FBI find?" Manning said, shaking his head in despair.

"Sanderson's team got us this far, which is way further than we could have gone with our own assets. We just need to keep Sanderson out of custody until we can take possession of Reznikov. The Russian holds the key to figuring out exactly who else has possession of this virus. He mass produced this stuff in Kazakhstan for someone. Probably Al Qaeda. With the right motivation, he should be able to help us start to unravel this plot," Berg said.

"I suppose we need Sanderson's men to apply the proper motivation?"

"Unless you want to wait for a covert interrogation team to fly into Sweden," Bauer said.

"Looks like all of our eggs are in Sanderson's basket," Manning said. "Do you have any other way to get in touch with him?"

"No. He normally picks up our calls immediately, regardless of the time. Let me try," Berg said.

"Well, I hope he's out sleep walking. Preferably several miles from wherever this compound is located. How did we not know about this operation?"

"Frederick Shelby didn't agree with Karl's assessment of what happened two years ago at the Georgetown safe house and several other aspects of the CIA's involvement. He pretty much shut us out of Agent Sharpe's ongoing investigation, which I had become convinced was going nowhere," Bauer said.

"Clearly we're not the only ones that can keep a secret. I just hope you're not keeping any more from me," Manning said.

Berg looked up from his cell phone and shook his head. "Nothing," he said and started to dial another number.

"Did you get a hold of him?" Berg said into the phone.

Karl Berg listened to the reply carefully before speaking.

"Daniel, just get Reznikov to the safe house and I swear to you we'll help you find her. She's not going to disappear. You have my word."

The phone call ended and Berg glanced at Audra. "Maybe this is a good time to tell Thomas who we have escorting Reznikov to our safe house."

Chapter Fifty-Four

3:27 AM
"Hellfire 11" HH-60H Rescue Hawk
Nuequen Province, Argentina

"Thirty seconds!" the crew chief screamed over the artificially created wind storm buffeting the inside of the helicopter.

Through the AN/PVS-14 night vision system attached to his Kevlar helmet, Lieutenant Commander Scott Daly saw the helicopter gunners energize their GAU-17/A miniguns. He could even hear the electric whine of the barrels over the turbulence created by their 140 mile per hour dash to LZ Sand Box. He knew the same scene was visible to a select group thousands of miles away. He'd grown accustom to the presence of this distant audience, as recent advances in technology had put most of their high profile operations on large screen monitors in several locations back in the United States. He rarely thought about the small night vision capable camera mounted next to the AN/PVS-14 system.

He edged closer to the crew chief, holding the starboard side overhead bar tightly with both hands. The cabin doors were wide open, and he didn't want to exit the bird prematurely while the pilots maneuvered them into position.

Daly glanced over his shoulder and saw Chief Petty Officer Warren Inderman take the same position on the port side. He couldn't see Inderman's face, but he knew the chief would be the first on the rope out of the door. He knew everything his men would do until they secured the armory. After that, it depended on how their situation developed. This was how they managed to work in complete darkness. By memory and instinct.

As he moved toward the starboard side door, his feet and knees bumped up against the coiled fast-rope, which took up a considerable amount of the space in the already cramped troop compartment.

Already attached to a cabin anchor bar that extended one foot beyond the door, the one-and-three-quarter-inch-thick, sixty-pound rope would be muscled through the hatch by Petty Officer Jake Ellison as soon as they settled over their designated insertion point. Daly would wait for the crew chief to confirm that the rope hit the ground before giving the order to deploy. The helicopter generated a significant static electricity charge in flight, and despite the fact that their ropes had been specifically designed as non-conducive, it remained standard procedure to let the rope hit first. Design variances in ropes had led to some unpleasant surprises in the past. Surprises that Lieutenant Commander Daly's SEAL's couldn't afford tonight.

He stared through the troop compartment into the cockpit and strained to make any sense of the view through the cockpit window. He thought he saw the dark field of pine trees change to a lighter view. Bright white sparkles resembling several simultaneous flashes caught his eye. From experience, he knew these were reflections off water, probably the river next to the LZ. He raised the AN/PVS-14 night vision from his face and prepared for the inevitable.

"Stand by!" the crew chief screamed.

He edged forward with the crew chief, leaving enough room for the coiled rope to be pushed out by Petty Officer Ellison. Three men competed for room in the ridiculously small space offered by the open cabin door. The GAU-17A took up half of the space, leaving barely enough room for one fully equipped SEAL to pass through. He was eager to get out of the bird, but knew the crew chief had a job to do. He backed off far enough for the crew chief to poke his head out of the door. The helicopter descended suddenly and flared its nose upward, settling into a stationary hover.

"Deploy ropes!" the crew chief screamed, and Daly repeated the command into his own headset.

He felt the massive rope coil slam forward, hitting his leg on the way out. Two seconds later, he heard the crew chief scream "Go!" There was no need to utter any commands. He reached out and jumped forward at the same time, gripping the rope solidly as he started to descend below the helicopter. The powerful rotor wash pushed him down the line, and he braked by squeezing his hands. He didn't need to see the ground to know when he was close to reaching the bottom. He had practiced this fifty-foot descent so many times, he could literally do it blindfolded. He slid for a few seconds and braked a little more, slowing his descent. He was rewarded when his boots gently hit the soft valley floor.

He quickly moved out of the way and hoisted his Mk18 Mod1 rifle, scanning the tree line for targets through the rifle's sensitive AN/PVS-24 night vision scope. He heard a soft thud, followed by scrambling footsteps, and knew that Ellison was headed toward the armory twenty meters away. He didn't need to look to know that Chief Petty Officer Inderman was crouched in a similar position to his left, also scanning the tree line. The rotor wash created a dirt storm around the SEAL commander, pelting his goggles with fine river rock and obscuring his view of the tree line. He felt comfortable knowing that Hellfire 1-1's gunner was scanning the same area unhindered and could deliver a withering fusillade of 7.62mm projectiles if his SEALs came under fire.

Several tense seconds passed before he felt a tap on his shoulder, which meant that the last of the eight SEALs had hit the ground. He ran forward to stay clear of the area underneath the helicopter. Both fast-rope lines would drop in a few seconds, and he didn't want to get hit with sixty pounds of braided nylon rope. He never heard the ropes hit the ground over the scream of the helicopter's twin turbo shaft engines, lifting their ride into the darkness above. The rotor wash intensified for a second and suddenly abated, leaving him feeling exposed.

Watching the tree line through his rifle scope, he sidestepped toward the armory as Hellfire 1-2 and Hellfire 1-3 disgorged the rest of the support platoon onto a wide flat area between the river and the trees. The sixteen SEALs would rush to positions along the tree line and provide cover for the arrival of the main assault force. He reached the corner of the armory and lowered himself to one knee. He heard a small explosion behind him, followed by a report that the armory was secure and that most of the weapons appeared to be present. This was good news for his assault force. If the armory had been empty, he would have been extremely concerned about what awaited his men. He felt another tap on his shoulder.

"I've got it from here," Chief Petty Officer Inderman said, who nudged Daly out of his position along the wall and assumed watch over the area between the trees and the armory.

Daly lowered his helmet-mounted NVGs and turned around to head toward the armory door. The armory sat at the northernmost point of the compound, at the end of a dirt road that paralleled the river. Situated on a slight rise, it overlooked the "inhabited" portion of the river valley. A light machine gun barrel protruded from the darkened doorway. As he approached the door, he saw four SEALs sprint across the road toward the compound's garages closer to the river.

"Renegade entering the armory," he whispered into his headset seconds before stepping over the barrel.

Through his night vision, he saw Petty Officer Sonny Abregon squatted down next to the doorway, monitoring Daly's command net through combat headphones. Abregon scooted down the wall, giving him a position at the door to observe the entire operation. Daly was momentarily distracted by what he saw inside the spacious room. Along the back wall, beyond a few picnic tables that were likely used to sit and clean weapons, sat unlocked racks filled with automatic rifles, light machine guns, sniper rifles, shotguns and pistols. The only difference between General Sanderson's armory and his own at SEAL Team Three was that Sanderson had a wider variety of foreign weaponry. Daly was impressed by what he saw and now he was even more relieved that most of the rack spaces were still occupied.

"Renegade Two and Three deployed. Hellfire 1-2 and 1-3 outbound," he heard through his own headset as the two helicopters ascended.

Their rotor sounds were quickly drowned out by the ground-shaking power of the two CH-53 Super Stallions that descended to take their place. The powerful transport helicopters didn't hover like the Rescue Hawks. Instead, they landed on the dirt road fifty meters apart, with their ramps down. Thirty marines from 1st Marine Special Operations Battalion poured out of the back of each helicopter and sprinted toward the tree line, forming into four separate teams of fifteen marines.

The CH-53s lifted a cloud of debris and pebbles that obscured the entire LZ as the marines ran straight through the SEAL support positions toward their objectives within the woods. Two MH-60Hs flew into the valley from the south, following the river until they reached their assigned over watch positions in the valley behind the SEALs. They hovered, their gunners scanning for targets.

"Green Machine 1-1 and 1-2 outbound. Hellfire over watch in place," he heard from Lieutenant Dan Simons, his support team commander, who was mixed in with SEALs along the tree line.

"Wild Eagle units formed and moving into breach positions," he heard from the marine commander.

Major Raymond Strout, the Marine Special Operations commander, would screen reports from his marine units under the call sign Wild Eagle and relay them to Lieutenant Commander Daly. Strout's marines constituted the bulk of the assault force that would systematically breach the compound's structures, starting with Sanderson's suspected headquarters. The first of the marine teams reached their positions alongside the closest structures. None of the units had reported any enemy activity, which suited him fine, but they needed to start the breach phase immediately.

"Back Yard ready. Positive identification on all four rear structures."

He now had all of the strike force units in place for a coordinated strike on the buildings. The second SEAL platoon had fast-roped into a tiny forest clearing two hundred meters behind the compound and had moved into positions behind the structures furthest from the river.

"All units. Breach targets. I say again. Breach targets!" Lieutenant Commander Daly yelled.

ᘏ

Staff Sergeant Peter Gibson crouched against the timber wall next to the door and watched his team leader closely. Captain Tony Polidoro pressed against the wall on the other side of the door, his M4A1 SOPMOD rifle pointed at the door. The captain turned his head and whispered something behind him. A marine carrying a sleek black shotgun materialized from the shadows of the porch. Captain Polidoro leaned in front of the screen door and grabbed the handle next to the staff sergeant's face. As he pulled the screen door open, he whispered to Gibson, "Breach this fucker."

Gibson reached out to test the inner door handle, prepared to immediately yank his hand out of the way if it was locked. Sergeant Manuel Rodriguez had his M1014 Joint Service Combat Shotgun aimed at the handle, and Gibson didn't want his hands anywhere near the business end of that gun. The shotgun was loaded with Lock Busters, which would impart all of their kinetic energy into the locking or hinge mechanism, instantly disintegrating it. If the door didn't open cleanly after Rodriguez finished his job, Staff Sergeant Gibson would swing a small portable battering ram at the door. This combination of brute force rarely failed to open even the most stubborn doors. Strangely enough, the doorknob turned, and he was able to push the door slightly inward using just his hand. He barely got his hand off the door knob before Captain Polidoro charged through the door, followed swiftly by the five marines stacked along the wall behind him. Rodriguez and Gibson were the last two marines to enter Sanderson's suspected headquarters.

Gibson had mentally prepared himself to rush in against a hail of gunfire, but by the time he got through the door, he had already heard most of his team members pronounce their appointed cardinal sectors to be secure. Powerful beams of light rapidly swept the two-story room, exposing every potential hiding spot. Gibson directed his rifle-mounted LED light around the front of what appeared to be a comfortable wilderness lodge. Glowing embers in the fireplace were the only sign of recent activity in the entire building. His beam swept across a large wooden table and stopped. Another beam found what Gibson had just noticed.

He moved quickly to the table and lowered his rifle, taking a smaller flashlight off of his tactical harness. The softer light brought everything into better focus. A glass of milk sat next to a plate of cookies in the middle of the table, along with a remote control placed above an 8.5 x 11 sheet of paper. Further down the table, he saw what looked like a small teleconference device with wires extending over the edge of the table. A few spare wires lay coiled next to the machine. He could see writing on the top half of the note and leaned in to read it.

"Fuck me. Captain, you need to see this right now," he said, trying to remain calm.

ര്യ

Lieutenant Commander Scott Daly had a sinking feeling in the pit of his stomach. He had expected to hear multiple shotgun blasts as the marines and SEALs forcibly breached all of the structures. Instead, he watched marines disappear silently through all of the doorways, followed by a brilliant green light show as they searched the structures.

"Renegade, this is Back Yard. It's a bust. Nobody's home."

"This is Renegade. Copy your last. Assume Back Yard over watch."

"This is Back Yard. Roger. Out."

Daly leaned against the armory's door frame and scanned the visible structures with his rifle scope. Marines had started with the largest of the structures, which they had assumed would house the largest number of targets, and moved to the smaller ones. At this point, every structure had been breached, and there had been no report of resistance. He needed a status report from Major Strout.

"Wild Eagle, this is Renegade. Have your teams found anything? Over," he said into his headset.

"This is Wild Eagle. Negative. I'm receiving reports from the last structures breached. They all report no personnel on site. Over," Major Strout answered.

"Understood. Assemble all Wild Eagle units for immediate extraction."

"Roger. Out."

"Back Yard, this is Renegade. Collapse toward extraction point and cover Wild Eagle. Over."

"This is Back Yard. Roger. Out."

He turned off his transmitter and pounded his fist on the wall inside the armory.

"Mother fucker," he muttered and turned to his radio operator.

"Sonny, get the birds back in for extraction. Make sure they know we're empty-handed. Send the abort code back to *BOXER*."

He'd personally seen thermal satellite imagery confirming targets on site just hours before the operation launched. How the fuck had they screwed this one up? He had to be careful with his verbal criticism since he was still on candid camera, though he'd be sure to deactivate his camera for the ride back to *BOXER*. He could control his own comments, but there was no way he'd be able to censor any of his SEALs. He was just thankful that he wouldn't be riding with the marines. He could only imagine what they might have to say about this navy-sponsored operation.

"Renegade, this is Wild Eagle. Marines in the suspected headquarters building found something you need to see immediately."

"This is Renegade. I'm on my way. Extract birds are inbound. Over."

"Understood. Out."

He grabbed Petty Officer Obregon, who was already packed up and ready to move and patted Petty Officer Ellison on the shoulder as he slipped through the doorway with Obregon.

"You're last out, Chief. See you at the bird!" he yelled to Inderman, who signaled his acknowledgement with a thumbs up.

Daly arrived on the lodge's porch and opened the screen door. Upon entry, he saw that most of the marines were dispersed tactically throughout the structure, guarding entrances. Captain Polidoro and Staff Sergeant Gibson stood in front of the table, flashlights aimed down its surface.

"What do we have here, Captain?" he said, striding up to the table.

"We've been made, sir."

Daly leaned in to read the note. He'd wanted to shake his head, but he was painfully aware of his long distance audience. Fuck them. This was their problem now. His only concern at this point was getting the strike force back to *BOXER* intact.

Chapter Fifty-Five

1:33 AM
White House Situation Room
Washington, D.C.

Frederick Shelby couldn't believe this was happening. National Reconnaissance Office satellite imagery confirmed humans at the target at 10:30 PM local time and had supposedly watched the site right up until the landing. He just saw General Gordon examine a satellite image showing the damn helicopters at the site. How in hell could this be right? Did they check under the beds? He wanted to yell this question to the officers in the room, but knew the comment would land him squarely in Gerald Simmons' camp.

"Can you get Renegade to focus on the note?" General Gordon said into his headset.

A few seconds later the helmet cam steadied on the note, which was illuminated by flashlights.

Greetings warrior brethren,

It's an honor to have so many brave men and women pay us a visit. I am truly humbled by your presence. You have my word that you are in no danger from my organization at this site. Please use the remote control to activate the monitor on the wall above the table. I urgently need to speak to the men and women watching from the White House and Pentagon about the situation developing in Europe.

Your most humble servant,
General Terrence Sanderson, USA (Ret)

P.S. The cookies are delicious. I won't tell if they go MIA.

General Gordon turned to the president of the United States. "I recommend we get our people out of there immediately. If he wants to talk to us, he can fly up here and meet us in person," Gordon said.

"I concur with the general," Shelby added.

He knew from the depths of his soul that Sanderson was up to no good and that everyone in the room would regret the decision to turn on that monitor.

"If he's connected to the situation in Europe, we need to know how. I can't see the harm in it. The helicopters have enough fuel to loiter for a few minutes," the national security advisor said.

"I'd feel more comfortable getting the marines and SEALs airborne. The longer those birds linger over the area, the more potential for trouble," Brigadier General Nichols said.

"Sir, we need to figure out how he's connected," Sarah Kestler insisted.

"Sanderson is a slippery character. You don't want to open Pandora's Box," Shelby added.

"I'm not sure we have a choice. A situation has developed in Europe that took a messy turn thirty minutes ago. We're looking at a very likely WMD deployment scenario in Europe and the United States. If Sanderson has any light to shed on the situation, I'd like to hear it. Tell Lieutenant Commander Daly to switch on the monitor. How will Sanderson hear us?" the president said.

"We'll take care of the patch, Mr. President. We'll be talking in real time with the team in the room. The SEAL commander's radio operator has a sophisticated communications rig and should be able to transfer the audio to that teleconference machine."

Shelby wondered about Europe. WMDs on U.S. soil. He couldn't imagine why this had been kept from the FBI. Based on the president's comment, he envisioned a very busy day for the J. Edgar Hoover Building.

They all watched the green image on the right screen, which showed a hand reach out and grab the remote control. A few seconds later, the green image intensified, and they could no longer make out details in the room.

"Have Lieutenant Commander Daly remove his helmet cam's night vision attachment," Gordon said into his headset.

The image shook and became obscured for several seconds, which prompted a few gasps in the room.

"He's fine. Just working on the camera," General Nichols reassured them.

The green image changed to a regular color scheme and shifted again. The new image settled in on the monitor, and they all saw General Sanderson sitting in front of a small lamp, his face beaming a grin that Shelby could only interpret as smug.

"Your radio operator should find the cable he's looking for on the table. It's the left one. I wasn't sure if I'd be dealing with a SEAL or Marine Advanced Communications System. If you'd also power up the teleconference device, we should be able to chat," Sanderson said. "While I have your undivided attention, let me welcome you to my humble compound. I commend all of you for an incredibly efficient operation. Commander, you had your task force offloaded in eighty-four seconds. That's a record in my book. I would have ordered an immediate surrender if the compound had been occupied."

Shelby didn't like the sound of this and registered the concerned looks from the military leadership around the table. Sanderson was watching the assault force, which didn't bode well.

"I assure you we have no intention of harming any of the assault team. Barring any unforeseen mechanical difficulties, you'll bring everyone back, Commander."

General Gordon gave the president a thumbs up and pointed to the microphone on the table, which flashed a green light. Shelby shook his head, indicating that he thought it would be a bad idea to start out with the president. They needed to treat Sanderson like a terrorist, and terrorists didn't get to speak with the president of the United States.

"General Sanderson, this is General Frank Gordon. I'm in charge of this operation. We're working on a very limited timetable here, so if you would make your communication brief, we would appreciate it."

"Frank, always good to hear your voice. JSOC is in capable hands," Sanderson said, nodding on the screen.

"I wish I could say it was good to hear your voice, Terry."

"I understand and assume you're not alone in that spirit. I'll be brief. I want to discuss the terms of an immunity deal in exchange for critical information related to the recent bioweapons attack on Russia and possible subsequent attacks throughout Europe and the United States. I'm seeking informal presidential immunity for my organization. This will be a wide-scoped agreement, encompassing the activities of all of my operatives, past and present. I'd also like to discuss reactivating the Black Flag program."

Shelby shook his head and looked at the president, who leaned toward the microphone. *Please don't do this,* he thought, and briefly considered pulling the president back in his seat, which would have been a career limiting move. He heard the national security advisor tell one of his aides to get a hold of the president's chief of staff. He caught a whisper about the attorney general and lawyers. He really hoped they weren't going to give this any consideration.

"General Sanderson, this is the president of the United States. Please explain the nature of the information in your possession. I have no inclination to negotiate with you."

"I appreciate your tough stance, but I have detailed information about the attack on Monchegorsk and specific information about the locations of impending attacks in Europe. I assure you that this information is worth sweeping my past and present activities under the rug."

"We can't just sweep terrorist activity under the rug," Shelby whispered and received a scornful look from the president.

"General, I already possess this information. I'm not sure how the information came into your possession, but I have to seriously question your involvement in the plot. There will be no immunity deal, and we have no need for your rogue operatives. I will never entertain the idea of sanctioning one of your programs. We can get the work done without you."

"Really, Mr. President? Who do you think got you the information from Stockholm? CIA operatives? Special Operations assets? Two of my people sacrificed their lives on Bondegatan Street to capture Reznikov and provide the CIA with that information. Another is critically wounded. I lost another man in Kazakhstan, alongside a CIA operative, while tracking Reznikov. I gave you this information."

"What is he talking about?" General Gordon said.

There was a general murmur in the room, especially among the White House staff. Shelby was at a complete loss, which was a rare and uncomfortable feeling for him.

"My team is several minutes from delivering Reznikov to a CIA safe house north of Stockholm. Should I send them somewhere else?" Sanderson said.

"These are your operatives?" the president said, then whispered to the national security advisor, "I thought this was a CIA team?"

The national security advisor shook his head and shrugged his shoulders. An argument escalated between the two of them when the national security advisor suggested that this couldn't be construed by the public as their fault. Shelby couldn't believe what he was hearing. It didn't matter who knew what. The president was ultimately responsible, and he had unknowingly used terrorists to pursue terrorists on European soil. This was a disaster of epic proportions for the administration and all of them. Their leverage had just evaporated.

"Terry, you're a better man than that!" Major General Bob Kearny yelled from down the conference room table. "I can't believe you would withhold information that could save thousands of lives, just to save your own ass!"

"Is that you, Bob?" Sanderson said.

"Damn straight it is. Up until right now, I still respected you on many levels. Tell me I'm mistaken here with my new assessment of your character," Kearny said.

There was a long pause.

"I have no intention of stealing away with Reznikov. I just wanted to drive home the point that you need the kind of capabilities my organization can provide," Sanderson said.

"We have plenty of assets suitable for these operations," General Gordon said.

"And they're all wrapped up in red tape, constrained at every turn. How long would it have taken to put a Delta team in Stockholm? If we hadn't been in place, the Russians would have captured or killed Reznikov, flushing all of your links to the bigger plot down the toilet."

"General, I appreciate your gesture and will rely on General Kearney's previous assessment of your character to ensure that you carry through on your promise to deliver Reznikov. If you have no further information to offer, I'd like to bring General Gordon's people home," the president said.

"Reznikov's yours, but I think you're overlooking my main bargaining chip."

"If you take action against the assault force, I'll bring to bear the full resources of the United States to hunt you down. They'll find you holed up like Saddam Hussein," the president said.

"I'd rather die myself than endanger these brave warriors, but I have no problem causing irreparable damage to your administration. Compliments of a very well connected businessman here in Argentina."

"Ernesto Galenden," Shelby said.

"Yes, thanks to Galenden, I'm holding some very hard to come by telephone numbers. The Chilean and Argentinian Defense Ministers for starters. Better yet, I have a direct line to the 31st Electronic Detection Group's commanding officer. Coincidentally, the group commander picked tonight for quick reaction drills. It was a last minute decision. I'm told that their Boeing 707 Condor is fueled and can be airborne in five minutes. I have arranged for several phone calls to be placed, all alerting the base to a large formation of low flying helicopters just north of Villarica. I probably don't need to remind you that the Condor carries the Phalcon radar system. 200 nautical miles of three hundred and sixty degree coverage, both in the air and on the surface. I'm pretty sure they'd pick up your birds as soon as they leveled off over the airbase in Puerto Montt. I might be wrong about the helicopters, but I can't imagine they would miss the *BOXER*."

"That action could endanger the strike force, General," the president said.

"I can't imagine it would lead to a military scenario, Mr. President. It will, however, lead to the second worst day of your presidency. An armed incursion violating the sovereignty of our two strongest allies in South America? The secretive deployment of U.S. warships off the coast of Chile. All to capture me? I think the international community might be a little more forgiving if the mission involved capturing Osama Bin Laden or some other high level member of Al Qaeda. But a lowly General Terrence Sanderson? What did he do—other than run a controversial covert operations program in the nineties—that the U.S. government would apparently do anything to keep quiet, including invade other countries? See where I'm going with this? Maybe it's time to let the public decide whether they need the Black Flag program. Maybe they need to know why they're not all dying from encephalitis in National Guard tents…or lighting their own children on fire in a virus-induced rage. Why? Because General Sanderson believed so wholeheartedly in what he was doing, that he personally funded the creation of a new covert operations program. A program so successful, that it singlehandedly derailed Al Qaeda's plot to attack the West with a weaponized version of the encephalitis virus. A virus that has already wreaked havoc on the unsuspecting city of Monchegorsk. I'm sure the fate of Monchegorsk will start generating some attention once Reuters breaks the story."

A contemplative silence descended on the conference room, followed by fierce whispering between the president and his present cabinet. The door opened, and the White House chief of staff entered, followed closely by a serious-looking woman in an impeccable black business suit. She carried a small laptop computer under one arm and a briefcase in the other. Shelby assumed she was the most senior legal counsel present at the White House. He had hoped to see someone from the Justice Department walk through the door, though he was fairly certain that some very unhappy lawyers were receiving phone calls at this very moment.

"We'll need some time to discuss this," the national security advisor said.

"I also have some nice, high definition video of the entire operation at the compound. It would be pretty hard to deny that these were American helicopters or American service members. The word MARINES and the U.S. emblem is pretty clear on my screen. Right next to the zero seven designation. I'm giving you two minutes to sort this out. Immunity gets your helicopters back undetected and buries the digital evidence of your landing."

Shelby heard just about every type of comment as he sat there, feeling completely irrelevant. There was no way the president could grant this man immunity. He would not permit it…though admittedly, there was nothing he could do about it. The comments continued to stream.

"He just tagged one of the Super Stallions loading our marines."

"He has eyes on the LZ."

"I don't see any other options. This will not go well if they put the Condor up. I don't know how we missed that."

"There's nothing we can do about the Condor. It might even pick up the *DECATUR*."

"Giving him a pass is the best option right now. He can blow the lid on this whole thing. Keep in mind that we lost an armed drone over Kazakhstan. Nobody over there has figured that one out yet, but he has witnesses."

"I agree with the national security advisor. We need to focus on the developing Al Qaeda threat. The last thing we need is a full blown international incident shattering our credibility," the secretary of state whispered.

The president pulled General Gordon away from his seat, and Shelby overheard snippets of a discussion about the possibility of the helicopters slipping under radar. The HH-60Hs flown by the Firehawks squadron had been reconfigured with stealth composite material that drastically reduced their radar cross section, but they came nowhere close to matching the stealth capabilities of the custom built Special Operations Black Hawk helicopters that had just entered service in support of Tier One assets like Delta Force and SEAL Team Six. The two CH-53 Super Stallions on the mission had been given a basic Special Operations reconfiguration that paled in comparison to the HH-60Hs. Gordon didn't sound optimistic, unless they could employ some sort of active jamming from *DECATUR*.

~

Five hundred meters away from the compound, deep in the woods on the opposite side of the river, Jared Hoffman stared through the ATN Mars 6x Night Vision scope attached to his OM 50 Nemesis sniper rifle. In experienced hands, the Swiss-made .50 caliber rifle could support a consistent three-inch shot grouping at 900 meters. Hoffman had considerable experience with this weapon, and at less than 500 meters, he could tighten that grouping to less than two inches.

Lying next to him in a specially-constructed hide site, Dhiya Castillo watched three helicopters land along the long stretch of road in front of the compound. She confirmed the range to the rear helicopter for Hoffman. They had waited for several hours in the hide site, shielded from satellite detection by the thick earthen ceiling. The hide site sat slightly submerged in the ground, allowing Hoffman to comfortably rest the sniper rifle on its bipod within the structure. His headset echoed Parker's voice, and he whispered to Dhiya, "Here we go. Confirm range again."

He could see that the helicopters had finally settled in as SEALs ran from covered positions to their transportation.

"Four hundred and sixty meters," she said.

He wouldn't need to make any adjustments to the night vision scope. He started to breathe slowly and centered the orange crosshairs on the last helicopter's tail rotor assembly, removing some slack from the trigger. He let the crosshairs settle and removed the rest. The powerful rifle pummeled his shoulder and created a muffled crack. The ridiculously large, custom made suppressor reduced the .50 caliber explosion to a sound that could still wake a person out of a dead sleep. However, with three helicopters roaring on the road, nobody would hear the shot. He sighted in on the tail rotor again, ready to send another armor-piercing projectile through the rotor. Five seconds later, he heard Dhiya's assessment.

"Tail rotor just ripped itself to shreds. Nice shot."

❧

Frederick Shelby heard commotion from the SEALs through the microphone attached to the helmet recording device. The helmet had been placed on the table facing the screen so Lieutenant Commander Daly could do his job while the White House Situation Room watched General Sanderson on the screen. A few seconds later, General Frank Gordon stopped in mid-conversation with the president and asked for a confirmation of something that had just been passed to him over his headset. Shelby wished he could hear what was going on.

"Mr. President, I've just been informed by the SEAL commander that one of the helicopters is grounded at the LZ. Hellfire 1-3 experienced a catastrophic tail rotor failure and had to shut down."

"Can they fix it?" the president said, already shaking his own head with the answer.

"Negative. The rotor shredded itself, along with the rotor housing assembly. I'm afraid it's not going anywhere," he said.

"Shit," the president muttered, "so now he has one of our helicopters to show the Argentinians and the rest of the world. Can they destroy the helicopter and render it unrecognizable?"

"They can turn it into a smoldering hulk, but he has video of the entire operation. It won't be hard for anyone to put two and two together here."

Sanderson's voice boomed over the speakers.

"Mr. President, my observer reports that one of your helicopters is inoperable. I'd be glad to take care of this mess for you, in exchange for a deal. Otherwise, you'll see footage of that helicopter on the *Today Show*," Sanderson said.

The president consulted with the woman who had entered with his chief of staff. She referenced a thick document taken from her briefcase and nodded. He turned back toward the conference table.

"Turn the microphone back on."

"Mr. President, please tell me you're not going to give this criminal immunity. This is blackmail. Any immunity deal signed today could be challenged in court as produced under duress."

"I'm well aware of the circumstances, and if my immunity deal is indeed challenged by any of the courts, I'll know where to come looking first. General Gordon."

The commander of the Joint Special Operations Command flipped a switch next to his computer, and the LED under the microphone turned green. He nodded at the president.

"General Sanderson, I accept the terms we've discussed and offer you the immunity you seek. It'll take some time to produce the documents and have them reviewed by counsel. In the interim, may I have your assurances that the helicopters will not be hindered during their withdrawal to *BOXER*?"

"If you provide me with a readily accessible email address or fax number, I'll be happy to send you a copy of the document I have prepared, along with contact information for my lawyers, who are standing by as we speak. Pardon me for highlighting the fact that I am somewhat of a Cold War relic, but I follow the mantra 'trust but verify.' I'll give you twenty minutes to get a signed agreement into my lawyers' hands. It's not a lengthy document."

"It sounds like you were prepared for this moment," the president stated.

"I'm prepared for every contingency, Mr. President."

"Apparently. General Gordon has the information needed to send your document to the Situation Room. We'll have it to your lawyers within twenty minutes, as long as it doesn't contain any surprises."

"No surprises, Mr. President. I just want to assure and protect the liberty of the selfless men and women that have served in my program. I did add a small presidential pardon to the document. One of my operatives was picked up by Customs last February, while en route to pay last respects to his recently deceased grandfather. He may or may not have been convicted of a federal customs crime. Either way, he's disappeared and I want to make sure he reappears a free man."

"I don't have a problem with that. General Gordon, let's get this done. General Sanderson?" the president said.

"Yes, sir?" Sanderson responded.

"I'm sorry for the loss of your men."

"Thank you, sir."

"Based on the circumstances, we won't be able to retrieve them properly."

"I understand, sir. Nature of the business."

"Unfortunately. We'll be in touch," the president said and stood up.

Director Shelby had to use every ounce of restraint he possessed not to launch into a tirade. This had been a set up from the start. From Victor Almadez's arrest to this very moment. All orchestrated to provide Sanderson with the leverage he needed to get a presidential immunity agreement. Despite the fact that he'd been warned directly by the president, he wouldn't rest until this conspiracy was unraveled. Someone in this room had helped facilitate this entire fiasco and he'd get to the bottom of it.

His money was on one of the generals or admirals, though he couldn't quite shake the notion that Gerald Simmons was involved. For all he knew, they were all in on this. Sanderson was one of theirs, a member of this tightly knit group of Special Operators, or whatever they liked to call themselves. The only one he really trusted was Major General Bob Kearney. He hadn't spent a single day of his entire career as one of these "shadow warriors." Hopefully, Kearney would help him uncover the traitor in this group. At the same time, he'd do some poking around the CIA. He'd love to know how Sanderson got hooked into the CIA. If he couldn't prosecute any of Sanderson's crew, maybe he could do something about the criminals running illegal operations out of Langley.

Director Shelby stood up when the president's departure was announced. Unlike General Gordon and the rest, he was done here for the evening. He planned to drive home and get a few hours of sleep before facing tomorrow's uncertainty. He dreaded calling Special Agent Sharpe. Like Shelby, the man had made it his personal mission to bring Sanderson down. He would be crushed to know that he had unwittingly participated in a plot to restore Sanderson's legitimacy. He waited a minute for the Secret Service agents to clear the hallway outside and walked out of the conference room without saying a word to anyone.

Chapter Fifty-Six

8:25 AM
CIA Safe House
Viggbyholm, Sweden

Daniel opened the back door to the modest one-story home and stepped out into the backyard. He needed some fresh air after spending a tense hour hovering between Reznikov and Leo, both of whom required close medical supervision. According to the physician provided by the CIA, Reznikov had almost slipped away twice before they could finally stabilize him. The doctor didn't think he would last through the next night, unless he was taken to a major hospital, which wasn't an option until they were certain that Reznikov had told them everything. Given the Russian's delicate condition, he wasn't very optimistic about Reznikov surviving the kind of interrogation required to guarantee full disclosure. The physician anticipated that Reznikov would be ready for a light interrogation by the early evening. Daniel didn't bother to ask when he'd be ready for a hard interrogation.

Barring any unforeseen complications, Leo would survive, though without immediate reconstructive surgery, it appeared unlikely that he would fully recover the use of his right shoulder. His collarbone had been shattered, and the doctor couldn't repair it. He had managed to stop any major internal hemorrhaging and close both the entry and exit wound. Daniel had already spoken with Berg about moving him out of the country to a discreet hospital facility.

He took in a deep breath of crisp spring air and closed his eyes for a few seconds. He had a number of loose ends to tie up, the first of which was to contact Sanderson. Audra Bauer's abrupt phone conversation had weighed heavily on his mind as they raced toward the safe house. He understood the implications of her cryptic message and had tried no fewer than ten times to get through to Sanderson and Parker. If U.S. Special Forces units had raided the compound, Jessica could be on her way to Guantanamo Bay, or even worse, some unknown military prison in Central America or Africa. His chances of seeing her again, if she survived the attack, would be nearly nonexistent.

Sanderson's capture meant that they would have to leave the safe house immediately. He didn't believe for a second that Berg or this Audra Bauer could guarantee their safety. Once the White House figured out who the CIA had used to capture Reznikov, Berg and Bauer would be lucky to emerge from the scandal without serving a jail sentence. All of this had the potential to be an awful waste. He just hoped the information provided by Reznikov's journal entries would be enough to continue the investigation.

He was tempted to grab either Farrington or Hubner to investigate the Stockholm address found on one of the pieces of crumpled paper, but figured they were better off waiting for Reznikov to come around. He had a feeling that Reznikov already knew what they would find in Stockholm, if they chose to pursue the address. The scientist had nearly drank himself to death and put a gun to his head when they kicked down the door.

Daniel stared out into the backyard at the thick screen of uneven pine trees that formed a natural private barrier in the quaint neighborhood. He sat down at a small stone table and placed his satellite phone on the cold, rough granite surface. He weighed the options if Sanderson didn't answer. Fuck it. They had delivered Reznikov to the United States at the cost of three operatives, which was more than anyone could possibly expect from them, given their status as fugitive terrorists.

He dialed Sanderson's number, fully expecting to walk back into the safe house and gather his men for an immediate departure. Sanderson answered on the first ring.

"Daniel! I have good news."

"I don't. Where the fuck have you been?"

"I had to entertain a few guests. About a hundred or so."

"You sound in good spirits, so I assume they didn't stay."

"They departed about fifty minutes ago. SEALs and marines from the *USS BOXER* Expeditionary Strike Force. A remarkable show of force I must say. Unfortunately for them, nobody was home."

"Thank God. I was worried about Jessica. I haven't been able to get in touch with her."

"Jessica wasn't here. She's in Buenos Aires. I need to tell you something that I purposely withheld from you earlier. I didn't want you to be distracted."

"Somehow, I have the distinct feeling I'm not going to like what I hear."

"By the end of this conversation, you'll be very pleased. Trust me. First, Jessica is fine, but Srecko's people found her."

"What?"

"She's fine, but she went through one hell of an ordeal and will need some time to recover. They grabbed her in your apartment. I had you and Jessica under twenty-four-hour surveillance in Buenos Aires. Call it a training exercise. Munoz and Melendez barely got her out of there."

"I need to talk to her immediately."

"She's in a safe place. Her left hand was damaged, but she'll be fine. We have the best people looking after her," Sanderson said.

Daniel stayed silent for a few seconds. When the expected tirade from Sanderson about how their trips to Buenos Aires had jeopardized the Black Flag program didn't materialize, he jumped back in the conversation.

"I'm glad they were there to help her. Two of the best we have. I owe them big time. Did she sound all right?"

"Still groggy from the pain medications. They had to do some work on her hand. You know how she is. I'd expect a full recovery."

"Yeah. She's surprisingly resilient," he said. "So, what was the good news you were so eager to share?"

"I thought you'd never ask. I'm holding a verified and legally binding immunity agreement from the president of the United States. We're no longer fugitives from the law."

"You've got to be shitting me. How the hell did you pull that off?"

"A combination of many factors, which included the fact that they had to leave one of their helicopters behind due to a mechanical failure…caused by a .50 caliber armor-piercing bullet. The administration wasn't very keen on having this raid exposed to the international media. Doesn't look good when you're caught trying to erase all evidence of the covert operatives you just sent on a shooting and kidnapping spree throughout Europe."

"You're a diabolical genius. Is this really binding? We can return to the U.S. without any repercussions?"

"It binds the federal government. The individual states typically respect the terms of these agreements, but I wouldn't plan any trips to Maryland or Maine any time soon. Beyond that, you're free to return under your original identity."

"That's simply amazing."

"How is Leo doing?" Sanderson said.

"He needs reconstructive surgery. Berg is working on a way to move him out of the country. Other than that, he's shaken pretty badly, but he'll be fine. Reznikov is the one I'm worried about," Daniel said.

"When will he be ready for an interrogation?"

"Probably not until late in the afternoon. He's a fucking mess. Alcohol poisoning and atrial fibrillation. Not a good combination. I've passed everything in the notebook to the CIA. My plan is to interrogate Reznikov for further leads. I found a crumpled note with the words 'German distribution company' on it. I'm willing to bet he knows more about this company."

"Do whatever it takes to get this information," Sanderson said.

"Is that an order from you or the CIA?"

"From me, though I plan to formally hand over control of your team to Berg at some point in the day. If my instincts are correct, our services won't be dismissed in the middle of this crisis, and I intend to continue delivering results."

"You really think they'll officially bring you back into the fold?" Petrovich said.

"I don't want them to. That's the quickest path to destruction. I learned that the hard way. We all did. I'd prefer to keep running this in the shadows and give them the illusion of plausible deniability. They can use us when they need us. The last thing I need is an office in the Pentagon with a placard announcing our presence."

"I don't think you'll get a warm and fuzzy reception at the Pentagon after Farrington's stunt."

"Oh…I wouldn't be so sure about that. Daniel, you've exceeded my expectations again, which is now something I've come to expect. Pass on my congratulations to the rest of the team and my condolences for the loss of Sergei and Schafer. We paid a high price for Reznikov."

"I'll make sure Reznikov was worth that price. How do I get in touch with Jessica?"

"I'll give you the number. It's still early here, so give her some time to rest. Call me when the interrogation is finished."

"Understood."

Daniel looked back at the house and wondered if the doctors had something they could administer right now to bring Reznikov around. The quicker he finished this interrogation, the sooner he could be on a flight back to Argentina.

Chapter Fifty-Seven

7:15 AM
CIA Headquarters
Langley, Virginia

Karl Berg rested at one of the computer stations with his head down. He just needed about fifteen minutes to reboot his brain. He'd been racing in overdrive for the better part of forty-eight hours and it had finally caught up with him. Reznikov's capture had kicked off a series of events that kept them trapped in the Operations Center. Twelve European addresses were found on the scraps of paper collected by Petrovich. Ramblings in Reznikov's notebook had implied that these were locations mentioned by the Al Qaeda operatives at the Kurchatov laboratory. Apparently, Reznikov could understand Arabic.

They had spent the last five hours coordinating with the intelligence services of eight different European countries to direct the simultaneous raid of the addresses gathered. Less than forty minutes ago, law enforcement agents in France, Germany, Sweden, Denmark, Italy, Netherlands, Spain and the U.K. had kicked down doors to find the locations abandoned. The apartments had been left spotless, with the exception of the Copenhagen and Stockholm flats, which had been trashed. Berg now agreed with Petrovich's assessment of Reznikov's suicidal mental state.

The crazed Russian had probably gone to each of the Scandinavian locations with the intention of stealing some of the virus back from Al Qaeda. Copenhagen was an easy seven-hour drive from Stockholm. Now it was obvious that Al Qaeda had changed their game plan, which pushed the investigation into the next desperate phase. They would have to rely on

Black Flag's interrogation to uncover another link. The most promising lead appeared to be Reznikov's reference to a German medical supply company.

The Edgewood scientists agreed that this represented a serious threat. If the terrorists had someone on the inside at this company, the weaponized encephalitis samples could be packaged as harmless diagnostic specimens. The illicitly disguised cargo could then be sent overnight using FEDEX, and if the company used to send the samples had a reputation for violation free shipping, there was very little chance that the packages would be inspected. Reznikov's virus might already be in the United States, which changed everything.

Half of the Edgewood scientists had departed a few hours earlier, presumably to meet with administration officials to advise them on a national response to secure the U.S. water distribution system. The CIA's source at Reuters said the news organization was a few hours from breaking the Monchegorsk story, which would include speculation that the city's water supply had been attacked. This was their own speculation, since Petrovich had ensured that the insurgent army major's transmission to Reuters didn't include any reference to a biological attack. The transmission only exposed the Russian government's brutal extermination of the Monchegorsk population. Still, combined with reports of widespread illness, it didn't take an investigative superstar to reach this conclusion.

Once the Reuters story hit the wires, U.S. and European governments would have a short period of time to react and demonstrate that appropriate measures were being taken to protect their water supplies. He wouldn't be surprised if the U.S. deployed the National Guard to achieve this task.

All of this was on top of the potentially explosive political pushback against Russia. Every nation in the West faced a possible biological attack by Al Qaeda, and it would become crystal clear that Russia had known about the possible threat for weeks. Not only had they known about it, but they had tried to cover up their connection to the information. His mind wandered back to what the Edgewood scientist had said about the unlikeliness that the initial virus had been created in a makeshift lab within Kazakhstan and his minded swirled uselessly. He really needed about fifteen minutes to shut his eyes.

"The director of the CIA is on his way to the Operations Center," the seemingly tireless watch officer announced.

He lifted his head and sighed. He'd have to get some rest later, if he still had a job. He wondered if Sanderson's immunity agreement extended to Audra and him. He stood up and put on his suit jacket, brushing it with his hands. Thomas Manning checked out of the Fish Bowl to meet General Copely.

"This should be fun," Berg said.

The watch officer raised his eyebrows, which was the extent of the emotion Berg had seen displayed by the man. At least it was something. Audra looked infinitely more confident than he felt.

"We'll be fine," she said.

"Maybe I'll get another promotion."

"I wouldn't go that far."

A few minutes later, the director of the CIA walked through the Fish Bowl doorway. General Robert Copley looked pleasant enough given the circumstances. He wore a dark blue U.S. Air Force service dress uniform, adorned with four stars on each shoulder epaulet and a thick board of multi-colored ribbons on his chest. He was the sixth active duty officer in CIA history appointed to the position. The director pushed his wire rim glasses up by the bridge of his nose and stopped to regard the Operations Center. The room had fallen quiet upon his entry.

"Congratulations on a job well done. All of you. It's been a long night and I'm afraid the day has only begun. The president and I count on your continued diligence and success. Mr. Harcourt, you can direct your people to make noise again. I think they work more effectively that way."

"I agree, sir," the watch officer said and started whispering commands into his headset, which brought the din of the room back to a normal level.

"Thomas, may I speak with you and your deputy director in private?"

Berg started to slide back into the room.

"And as Ms. Bauer's assistant deputy director, you're no longer working in the shadows, Mr. Berg. Please join us."

Shit. This couldn't be good, in his opinion. All four of them left the Fish Bowl for a small conference room on the other side of the Operations Center.

"Take a seat," Copley said. When everyone was seated, Copley began. "The president was not pleased to have his back put against the wall by Sanderson today. Sanderson's play was a complicated and brilliantly orchestrated event that the White House brought down upon itself. Still, the president did not deserve to be blindsided by the fact that Sanderson's agents had been critical to the recovery of Reznikov...and had been shooting their way across Europe. It put him in the untenable position of having to admit that the U.S. had operated terrorists on foreign soil. Not to mention the fact that his own Central Intelligence Agency had kept Sanderson's location a secret from the FBI and Interpol. Director Shelby was sitting right next to him when Sanderson exposed this dirty little secret, and he has a long memory. We'll all have to watch our backs for quite some time.

"This was an important operation, and I can't commend all of you enough for the results, but if you decide to use questionable assets in the future, I need to know about it, so I can whisper in the president's ear."

"The use of Sanderson's people was my doing. I was contacted by Sanderson immediately after the HYDRA investigation fiasco two years ago. He told me to keep his new organization in mind for any operations too sensitive for the direct use of American assets. This one fit the bill. I should have involved Thomas and Audra from the start. This is really my fault," Berg said.

"Don't be so quick to fall on your sword, Karl. I can't fault you for outsourcing the operation. I just need to be kept in the loop. Understood? Let me determine whether the CIA informs the president. That's what I get paid for."

"Sanderson's team is preparing to interrogate Reznikov. We expect this to happen within the next few hours. We'll keep you posted through Thomas," Audra said.

"That won't be necessary. I'll monitor the progress of the operation through a direct link with the Operations Center. Sanderson's operatives are now part of an officially sanctioned covert task force. The president was thoroughly impressed with the efficiency of this joint collaboration and wants Sanderson's assets to prosecute any leads generated by the interrogation, in direct cooperation with the CIA. You'll also reach out to Major General Bob Kearny at the DIA. He runs the Defense Counterintelligence and Human Intelligence Center and should prove to be an invaluable source of information. He might even be able to provide hard support in the form of operatives from their Strategic Support Branch."

"We'll make sure Mr. Harcourt immediately establishes a link for you to monitor," Manning said.

"Excellent. I won't hold you up any longer," Copley said.

"Has Sanderson been informed of his participation in the new task force?"

"No. That's your job. And you need to stress that this is a non-negotiable, temporary arrangement. I don't think he'll have a problem with this. The president sensed that this was more important to him than the immunity agreement."

The director shook their hands and turned to depart. He stopped and turned his head. "You still haven't heard from your Russian contact?"

"No, sir," Berg said.

"That was a brave thing for him to do."

"He's a brave man. I'm sure he'll be fine."

"Let me know if you hear anything," Copley said and walked toward the exit station.

Berg turned to Manning and Bauer, hoping to cut off any further speeches.

"I suppose I should break the good news to Sanderson," Berg said.

"When you're done, I'd like to hear the whole story about how you and Sanderson first formed this alliance," Manning said.

"Unless the president's immunity agreement extends to me as well, that's a story better left untold," Berg said and opened the door to leave.

Chapter Fifty-Eight

3:30 PM
CIA Safe House
Viggbyholm, Sweden

Petrovich and Farrington sat on simple dark wooden chairs dragged into the bedroom from the dining room. They waited for the doctor to finish making adjustments to the IV bag's drip chamber. After checking the peripheral IV line inserted into Reznikov's right hand, he turned to the operatives.

"Fifteen minutes at the most. I'll be right outside the door if there is an emergency," he said, in Swedish accented English.

"You might feel more comfortable watching some television with your staff. We'll come running if there's a problem," Farrington said.

The doctor regarded him cautiously and glanced back at Reznikov, who now looked more aware of his surroundings. The gray-haired physician nodded in resignation, clearly not comfortable leaving them alone with the Russian.

"I understand," he said.

After the doctor shut the door, Farrington walked over and locked it. Both of them walked right up to Reznikov's bed to examine him.

"Why am I restrained? You are not Russians," Reznikov said, lightly pulling at the metal handcuffs attached to the hospital bed.

"I'm glad you're feeling well enough to ask questions," Farrington replied, in Russian.

"My heart is racing. What did he put into my IV?"

"Epinephrine. It's a slow drip designed to keep you focused and alert for questioning. The doctor warned us that we could spend no more than fifteen minutes with you, or the effects of the epinephrine could be fatal," Farrington said.

"Fifteen minutes is going to feel like an eternity. Trust me," Petrovich said, in much less polished Russian.

"The old good cop, bad cop routine, eh?"

Farrington's hand flashed across the hospital bed and cut a shallow two-inch line across Reznikov's forehead. The Russian screamed and tried to yank his hands up to reach the wound, but found them shackled to the metal frame of the bed. Farrington raised the small serrated blade above his shoulder and tensed his arm.

"No. No. Don't do this," Reznikov stuttered.

"Just so we're perfectly clear. There is no good cop in this room."

Blood streamed down the sides of his face onto the bright white pillowcase. Daniel grabbed a gauze pad from a neatly stacked pile of assorted medical supplies on the bedroom dresser. He padded at the thin cut on Reznikov's tight forehead.

"Why were you trying to drink yourself to death?" Daniel said.

"Two bottles of vodka can't kill a proper Russian. I had the pistol for that, but I passed out...after spending most of the night with it pressed against my head," Reznikov said weakly.

Farrington watched Reznikov's vitals on a monitor behind the IV pole. 132 beats per minute and settling, for now. The doctor had given him a minimal IV dose of epinephrine, but warned them that the administration of adrenaline could put him right back into ventricular tachycardia. The doctor further warned them not to excite Reznikov, which would cause further spikes in his heart rate. He had just watched the Russian's heart rate spike to 169 BPM in response to the knife slash. He couldn't imagine where it would go if they had to resort to real torture.

"Let me rephrase the question. Why were you trying to blow your brains out? And before you answer, let me make something clear. I won't rephrase any more of my questions. You need to focus on the goal of surviving the next fifteen minutes. Dead or alive, we turn you over to the good doctor," Petrovich said.

"I want a guarantee of safe passage to America, where I'll seek political asylum. I have interesting information for the American government," Reznikov said.

"Then you'd better start answering our questions. If you survive the next...thirteen minutes, you get a one-way ticket to the United States. Otherwise, we push you out of a van onto the side of a road somewhere north of here."

"I worked in the Russian bioweapons division," Reznikov stated.

"We already know that. Why were you trying to kill yourself?"

"You're not listening to me," Reznikov said.

Farrington placed the tip of his blade against the Russian's left eye socket and pressed until it broke the skin.

"And you're not listening to either of us," Farrington hissed.

"I heard what you said. We'll get to that."

"Time for two knives." Petrovich withdrew a spring-loaded folding knife from his back pocket and popped it open above the bed.

"The addresses were vacant," Reznikov said.

"Why were the addresses important to you?" Petrovich said, moving his knife along Reznikov's thin hospital gown toward his groin.

"They were taking the virus containers to these locations. I wanted to get a hold of more," Reznikov said.

"Who was taking the virus to these locations?" Farrington said.

"You don't know? Al Qaeda, or a splinter branch...I'm not exactly sure. I overheard them talking about plans. I speak Arabic."

"So we've surmised. They spoke openly about their plans?"

"Yes and no. They were an arrogant bunch, but they weren't sloppy. Sometimes they talked while I was around, but I also had a few surveillance devices installed during the reconstruction of the lab."

"What happened to these devices?"

"They're still at the site. I committed the data to memory and wiped the recordings. Your government will want to know what I heard," Reznikov said.

Farrington wondered how much of his memory had been transferred to the notebook they recovered.

"Did you keep a record of this information? Nothing was recovered at your apartment. We left in a hurry after slaughtering the Spetznaz team sent to murder you."

"No need for records. It's all up here," he said and tried with futility to point to his head.

"I'd feel a lot more comfortable if you had kept a record. You haven't exactly been preserving your brain cells," Farrington said.

"There is no record. We can get my mind cleared up and I'll be able to tell your people everything."

Farrington glanced at Petrovich, who seemed focused on the man's vitals. 172 BPM. He didn't need to see this to know the man was lying. The notebook might be all of it, though he'd be surprised if Reznikov hadn't reserved some of the information in case the notebook was discovered. Either way, he'd have to reserve a few of his questions for the end. If Reznikov realized that they possessed the notebook, he would never talk to them about the German distribution company.

"You worked in the Russian bioweapons division. Recently?"

"I should be talking to your scientists about this," he said.

Petrovich slashed his knife across the top of Reznikov's upper thigh, squirting blood over both legs. The Russian's screams pierced their ears, as his body rattled the hospital bed. Farrington pushed down on his forehead with one hand and pushed the knife against Reznikov's left eyelid.

"You'll start by talking to us. We'll determine if you get to fly back to speak with our scientists. This is your last warning."

"Okay. Okay. I'm sorry. I didn't mean to...I left Vector Labs a few years ago. I worked on several of their bioweapons projects. I was fired for trying to smuggle virus samples out of the lab. They tried to kill me for it, so I disappeared."

"The Russians have an active bioweapons program? Is this what you're telling me?" Farrington said.

"Yes. That's why they've been trying to find me."

"But you had already successfully smuggled samples of a genetically modified encephalitis virus out of the lab. Right? You were caught on a subsequent attempt to steal more," Petrovich said.

"How could you know that?" Reznikov said.

Farrington saw his heart rate shoot up to 182 BPM. They were entering dangerous territory.

"Our scientists examined samples of brain tissue that I personally recovered from Monchegorsk. They didn't think that you could have done the required genetic work in your makeshift lab outside of Kurchatov. You grew enough to weaponize it at the lab. Is this right?"

"Yes."

"How much did you weaponize? We assume you enclosed the virus in tablets that would protect the virus, but rapidly dissolve. How many tablets did you produce?"

"Enough."

"Enough to poison eleven cities in Europe? Twelve including Monchegorsk," Farrington said.

Reznikov's eyes widened, and Farrington realized that the easy part of the interrogation was drawing to an end.

"How could you…?"

"Two canisters for each city. Twenty-four total. How many more canisters were produced?

"You couldn't know this…unless…"

"Unless we have your notebook? What is the name of the German medical distribution company? Is this how they plan to ship the virus overseas to the United States?"

"Too many questions to answer at once. I need time to process this," he said, clearly trying to buy time that wasn't for sale anymore.

"By my watch, you have eight minutes. Let's start with the German company," Farrington said.

He nodded toward Petrovich, who picked up the fully recharged Automated External Defibrillator they had stolen from the Metro station. Farrington sliced open Reznikov's thin white gown and tore it open, exposing him from the chest down to his genitals. Petrovich started to attach the AED's pads to his chest.

"What are you doing?" Reznikov said.

"I plan to make this the longest eight minutes of your life. I just want to make sure you're here for every second of it," Daniel said.

He moved one of the electrical pads to Reznikov's genitals, which caused the Russian to shriek.

"Sorry. We'll save that for later."

"Now that you've had some time to organize your thoughts, let's start out with the name of the German company," Farrington said, increasing the pressure on the knife poking the man's eyelid.

Fifteen seconds later, the screaming began. It continued for another six minutes, which was longer than Farrington had expected the scientist to last.

Chapter Fifty-Nine

12:32 PM
Acassuso Barrio
Buenos Aires, Argentina

Jessica savored the sun on her face. She took a sip of raspberry infused iced tea and set the glistening glass down onto a wicker end table. She leaned back into the thickly cushioned, dark rattan chaise lounge and stared out at the small, private backyard. The terra cotta patio extended another fifteen feet beyond her chair, which was pushed up against the house. A lush green lawn bordered the patio on all sides, meeting with a thick layer of ferns and low palms that concealed most of the six-foot-tall stucco wall surrounding the backyard. The back of the house faced north, which provided constant sun exposure to the generous windows facing the enclosed yard and the French door leading to the patio.

"Jessica, you have a phone call," she heard from inside the house.

"Can you bring it out here for me?" she said, not budging from the chair.

"You got shot in hand, not the legs," Munoz replied.

She heard him muttering inside, which caused her to laugh. She had wondered how long it would take them to revolt against her constant demands for iced tea, warm towels and snacks. I guess this was it for Jeff. Maybe Rico would continue to wait on her. She'd have to play this one right.

"Enrique, can you help me out and bring the phone?" she yelled.

"Don't you dare move, Rico," Munoz said. To Jessica he called, "You want to talk to your husband, or shall I tell him to call back later?"

Jessica used her good hand to lift herself up and out of the chaise lounge and walked through the open patio door to the darkened interior. Jeffrey Munoz was talking on the phone.

"She's doing really well, man. Seriously…I'm glad we were there. Driving us fucking crazy, but what else is new, right? Here she is," he said and held the phone out to her.

"Amazing how fast you can move when you want to," he added.

"Hey, this is like a four star vacation for you guys," she said, taking the phone.

"This is the only vacation I've ever been on where you're locked in a house, waiting hand and foot on the Queen of Sheba," he said.

She walked back out onto the patio and breathed in the perfect seventy-five degree fall air.

"Danny, it's so good to hear your voice."

"I've been waiting all day to call. Had a few loose ends to tie up here that required my full attention. Sorry I didn't call earlier."

"I heard about your morning. The story made the headlines throughout Europe and the U.S. Sorry to hear about Sergei and Andrei. Schafer, too."

"Frankly, I'm not sure how we pulled it off, but somehow we did."

"I think that's becoming your specialty," she said.

"Impossible missions? I hope not. I need a break from Russian attack helicopters and Spetznaz. What's the weather like out there?"

"It's a beautiful day, honey. Just like the last weekend we were here together. I miss you," she said.

"I miss you even more. I would give anything to be there with you right now. Sanderson was smart not to tell me what happened to you. I would have been on the first flight out of Helsinki. How is your hand?"

"Luckily, it's my left. It'll be fine. I'll probably need some cosmetic surgery later. You know, to make it look a little less claw-like," she said.

"I'll love you just the same. Claw or no claw."

"You're always so romantic," she said.

"That's what gloves are for anyway," he said.

"Now that's not exactly nice. I suppose you'd buy me a mask if I had been shot in the face?" she teased.

"No. Then you wouldn't be allowed to leave the house and even then you'd have to wear a bag over your head inside the house…unless you're showering, I suppose."

"I'll make you pay for that one," she said.

"Promise?"

"I'm not sure I can do all of those things one handed," she whispered.

"I suppose we'll have to wait anyway. I'm headed to Germany to investigate Metzger Labs. Reznikov identified the company as a possible shipping point for the virus. The company specializes in live research samples for institutional and corporate use," he said.

"Wouldn't that be a task better suited for the German police?"

"Not if you want to have a candid conversation with one of the employees, or an after-hours tour of the facility. Hopefully, I'll have this wrapped up in a few days and will be on a plane back to Argentina. Does the house have a pool?"

"Hot tub. I've been told to stay out of it due to the painkillers. Whatever. I really wish you didn't have to go to Germany," she said.

"This should be a quick operation. They're already working on accessing the employee files. If we can get our hands on the right shipping manifest, we'll be able to determine where the virus is headed. We don't have the time to mess around with interagency politics on this. I'm technically working for the president of the United States now. Can you believe what Sanderson managed to pull off?"

"Not really. I'm not jumping to make travel plans any time soon. I'll let Sanderson test the waters first."

"I hear you there. Hey, I'm getting that impatient stare from Farrington. We need to be at the airport soon to catch a flight to Frankfurt. I'll call you when we get there. I love you so much, Jess."

"I love you more than that. Hurry back. I don't think Bert and Ernie here will last much longer," she said, raising her voice.

"You got that straight!" Munoz yelled from inside.

"Take it easy on those guys. I owe them everything," he said.

"So do I, which is something I think we need to talk about when you get back. I don't want to leave Sanderson's program anymore. I think this is our home now," she said.

"You might be right. We'll have to talk about this later. Love you."

"Love you more," she said and hung up.

"You can have the phone back!" she yelled.

"Don't push your luck, princess," Munoz replied.

Chapter Sixty

11:25 AM
FBI Headquarters
Washington, D.C.

Special Agent Ryan Sharpe sat facing Special Agent Frank Mendoza in the small reception office outside of the director's conference room.

"So, did you get me in trouble or something?" Mendoza said. "Because I just started my new job and I haven't been there long enough to piss off the director yet."

"This might have something to do with Sanderson. That's all I can say. Honestly though, I'm purely speculating. Sounds like you've hit the ground running in your new position. I'm hearing good things."

"It's different than following the money trail, that's for sure. The investigative focus is a lot broader, and field activities are a shit ton more intensive," he said, and they both glanced up at Shelby's secretary.

"Sorry, Margaret," Frank said.

"You two aren't the first potty mouthed FBI agents to sit in those chairs," she said, without taking her eyes off the computer screen.

"The financial background is indispensable, even if it's only one aspect of our terrorism investigations. I used to think terror financing was the center of the universe," Mendoza said.

"Cut off the funding and there is no terrorism. At least not from extremist groups like Al Qaeda. The people don't hold jobs here in the U.S., unless you count mosque employees or the rapidly expanding sea of Imams. Your average terrorist cell here couldn't scrape up enough money on its own to buy the nails needed to fill a suicide vest."

"The director will see the two of you now," Margaret interrupted.

"Thank you," Sharpe said.

Mendoza and Sharpe stood up and walked toward the conference room door and opened it. Once inside, they each had silent doubts about their own immediate job security. Half of the conference table was occupied, which had taken Sharpe by surprise. He had been expecting another private visit with the director, possibly to thank Mendoza and himself for laying the groundwork that had led to Sanderson's capture. Now that he saw the players seated around the conference room, he was no longer so optimistic.

Keith Ward, director of the Domestic Terrorism Branch within the Terrorism Financing Operations Section was present, along with his former boss, Gregory Hill, who still commanded the Radical Fundamentalist Financial Investigative Unit. A past and present boss in the same room was never good news. Frank Mendoza's direct supervisor within the International Terrorism Operations Section One sat at the table, next to the Counter-Terrorism Division's director and assistant director. This put four assistant directors in the room, along with the executive assistant director for the National Security Branch and her associate executive assistant director. They all sat around Director Shelby at the far end of the conference table.

"Agents Sharpe and Mendoza. Please take a seat," Shelby said in a grim tone.

Two seats, side by side, were offered to them on the right side of the table. The appropriate nods were exchanged between all of them, which made Sharpe feel a little better about the situation. He was pretty sure they'd be kept standing if they were to be fired, and he highly doubted anyone would smile or nod at them. As soon as they were seated, the video monitor on the wall opposite to them came to life. The assistant directors on the other side of the table swiveled their chairs to view the screen.

A map of Argentina appeared next to a satellite photo dated April 25th, 2007. It was a close up of Sanderson's river valley compound and was centered on the road that ran parallel to the river. A lone helicopter sat on the road. Sharpe wasn't sure what to make of the photograph. The picture had been taken today, during the daytime. Now Sanderson had a combat helicopter at his disposal?

"At approximately 1:27 AM, Eastern Standard Time, a force of ten special operations helicopters landed nearly one hundred marines and SEALs at this compound in western Argentina, with the intent of putting an end to General Terrence Sanderson's rapidly growing terrorist organization. Unfortunately, Sanderson had been tipped off, and the entire operation was a complete failure. The compound was empty. This is one of the helicopters that had to be left behind due to a mechanical failure. Likely related to a high velocity projectile. The whole thing was a set up from the start."

Sharpe shook his head with a look of disgust.

"Special Agent Sharpe's investigative efforts got us to the compound, only to be thwarted at the last minute."

"We'll get another crack at Sanderson," Sharpe said.

"Unfortunately, this is only half of the story. At 12:49 Eastern Standard Time, completely unknown to me, a rogue Russian bioweapons expert was snatched from a Stockholm street by one of Sanderson's foreign operations teams. The team, working on behalf of the CIA, left ten dead Russian Spetznaz operatives in its wake, along with two of their own. Apparently, everyone wanted to get their hands on this Russian scientist."

"What is the connection between the two locations?" Sharpe asked.

"Sanderson is the connection…and he now works for the United States government."

"What?" Sharpe said. "He's still at the top of our terrorist list."

"Not any more. His organization has been granted unlimited immunity from prosecution. Including, but not limited to all activities past and present. This extends to all personnel that have been involved in these activities."

"Petrovich and Farrington?" Sharpe said, incredulously.

"We can't touch any of them, and it's quite possible that we will be working with some of them very shortly. Information acquired from the Russian scientist indicates the high possibility of an imminent WMD attack here in the United States. We'll work with Homeland to coordinate a response. As it stands, the threat appears to be a genetically modified, weaponized form of encephalitis, primarily designed to be delivered into a municipal water supply. The effects of this virus have been confirmed by Sanderson's team. Apparently, this scientist poisoned Monchegorsk, a city of 50,000 in northern Russia, before he was captured. Petrovich himself covertly entered the city and documented the effects. It's a worst case scenario. Those that don't die within the first week of exposure end up going aggressively insane from focalized temporal lobe damage."

"This is headed our way? Why am I the only one asking questions?" Sharpe said.

"Everyone here has already received this briefing except for the two of you. This is definitely coming our way. We just don't know how. The scientist, Anatoly Reznikov, was funded by Al Qaeda, or an organization very similar. He produced over sixty canisters of viral tablets, two of which were used by him in Monchegorsk. That leaves fifty-eight missing. Twenty-two of the canisters were originally slated for attacks on European cities, but all of the sites listed by Reznikov have been raided, yielding empty apartments previously occupied by Arabs...or people that looked like Arabs.

"The CIA is investigating a German medical supply company in Frankfurt. The company was identified by Reznikov as a possible distribution point for the canisters. This is our only direct lead at the moment. There was something else mentioned, which is why the two of you are here."

Director Shelby nodded at Carol Whitman, head of the National Security Branch, who stood up to address them.

"Reznikov told interrogators that he heard the Al Qaeda operatives mention a domestic terrorist group within the United States. This was a one-time conversation overheard by Reznikov in the laboratory. Unbeknownst to his benefactors, he speaks fluent Arabic. He told Sanderson's team that Al Qaeda had arrived at some kind of agreement with American ultra-nationalists. We think Al Qaeda might have entered into some kind of partnership with one of our domestic terrorist groups, which is why we want to appoint the two of you to lead a task force with the express purpose of investigating this possibility. Do we have a domestic terror organization that would consider working with Al Qaeda? It sounds like an awful stretch," she said.

"I'd start with True America. They have the most extensive physical network, and wouldn't have any religious objections to using Al Qaeda to achieve their goals. We haven't scratched the surface of their network, but they're rumored to have penetrated every level and walk of life in the U.S. We can start by focusing on known members employed in the Public Works sector, specifically anything having to do with state or local water systems. We might get lucky."

"If this shipment is inbound or already here, we'll concentrate on known fundamentalist cells near the True America members you initially identify. They'll have to come together at some point," Mendoza said.

"I assume that the canisters will be shipped to the Al Qaeda operatives. They wouldn't trust anyone outside of their own network to receive the bioweapon. If the CIA can get a shipping manifest soon, we might be able to intercept the shipments and roll up Al Qaeda operations in the U.S. before they make a handoff," Sharpe said.

"Sounds like we picked the right people to head this team. Pick your personnel from both sides. Finance and Operations. This has the highest priority, as agreed by everyone in the room. The task force will fall under the direct control of Carol Whitman. Any questions?"

"You mentioned that we might be working with Sanderson's people?"

"I was hoping you had forgotten that comment," Shelby said.

"It's hard to forget considering what he did two years ago," Sharpe said.

"Sanderson has operatives trained specifically to penetrate Arab fundamentalist groups like Al Qaeda. Arab-Americans capable of complete immersion…"

"It's too late to try and insert a deep cover operative," Mendoza said.

"I understand that, but they could be used to interface with True America. Possibly mimic one of the Al Qaeda cells. Our capacity to do this is extremely limited," Shelby said.

"Sanderson's people aren't exactly the kind you can restrain. We'll have to weigh this option carefully," Sharpe said.

"Maybe a little less restraint is necessary in the face of this kind of threat. This is ordered by the president, so let's figure out how to use them constructively. If you start to lose control of them, Carol needs to know immediately. I need to know. Don't think this isn't distasteful for me. We won't be parading them around headquarters or any of the field offices. This will be the most secretive aspect of the task force. Are we clear on that?"

Everyone sounded their agreement.

"Let's get the ball rolling. This is a twenty-four seven investigation, starting right now. Sharpe and Mendoza, start assembling your team," Shelby said.

"Forward your requests to Assistant Executive Director Gilmore. They'll be processed immediately. I expect this task force to be up and running by tomorrow morning," Carol Whitman said.

"That'll be all for now. Good luck, Agents. You're going to need it," Director Shelby said.

Mendoza and Sharpe left the conference room and didn't say a word until they were far outside of the executive wing of the J. Edgar Hoover Building.

"Looks like we're going to be up all night piecing this together," Mendoza said.

"I'm looking forward to it. We'll have to buy another leather chair for you. I foresee many long nights ahead of us," Sharpe said.

"I'll see about dragging a couch into your office. Damn, Sherry's gonna kill me. I'm supposed to be on a trip to the Mayan Riviera in two weeks," Mendoza said.

"Hope you bought trip insurance," Sharpe said and slapped him on the back.

"I always do," Mendoza replied.

Chapter Sixty-One

5:35 PM
Nuequen Province
Western Argentina

General Terrence Sanderson stared out at the HH-60H Rescue Hawk sitting in the middle of the dirt road outside of his headquarters lodge. The matte black helicopter was shadowed from the setting sun by the pines blanketing the foothills to the west. The grounding of this helicopter had pushed the president over the edge. Most of Sanderson's plan had been a bluff, with the exception of his threat to expose the helicopter and video evidence of the raid. Even that had been a bluff on many levels, since it would have achieved nothing for his organization. The helicopter was his trophy for now, until the U.S. government figured out how to insert a team to repair it. He imagined they would fly out using the same route and land it on one of their radar invisible destroyers. What a pain in the ass that would be for the U.S. Navy.

His satellite phone rang inside the lodge, and he opened the screen door to walk back inside. The plate of cookies still sat on the table, with one missing upon their return to the compound. He had found his note turned over, with a scrawled message at the top:

Expect resume shortly, LCDR Daly.

Parker knew Daly well from his time in the SEALs and said he'd make an excellent addition to their training or headquarters staff. He could possibly serve as a recruiter for more direct action operators. Now that Sanderson's people could come and go as they pleased, he was only limited by his imagination. He might even consider moving the training compound, though he was very comfortable on *señor* Galenden's property. He picked up the phone, recognizing the number.

"Bob's Used Helicopters...lightly flown and gently landed," he answered.

"Clever. I was going to wait a little while to get back in touch, but apparently we'll be working together, effective immediately."

"I heard the news about an hour ago. The rest of my group is on their way to catch the next available flights to Germany. Including the four already in Europe, that'll give them fourteen operatives to shake things loose over there. What a day this has been. I can't thank you enough for all of your help over the past couple of years. I'll buy you a proper drink when I get back to the States."

"I'll take you up on that. Until then, I'm working on a plan to find your organization a permanent home...or at least an official slot on someone's organizational chart."

"Don't do anything that's going to jeopardize your career. You've done enough for me already," Sanderson said.

"This is different. There's some serious talk about permanently assigning Special Operations assets to our spook friends. Langley has their own people, but the group is fairly small and highly compartmentalized. The National Clandestine Service has started to informally ask the Pentagon for help. Naturally, there's a lot of resistance from SOCOM. They don't like to give up operational control of their units, especially to the CIA...the two barely function together as it is. This might be a nice fit for you, and a chance to expand the program."

"This sounds exactly like the service we're already providing," Sanderson said.

"My thoughts exactly, and SOCOM wouldn't have to give up control of any assets. If things go well in Europe, you might just slide into this role without any help from your fan club in D.C."

"Thank you again for everything. I'll never forget this."

"It was my pleasure, though your number one fan didn't look very happy. I'd think twice about accepting an invitation to the J. Edgar Hoover Building."

"I'll stick to videoconferences for now," Sanderson said.

"Sounds like a wise plan. Rotor failure on that helicopter, eh?"

".50 caliber rotor failure," Sanderson said.

"Works every time. I'll be in touch shortly with more details. You might consider acquiring some more satellite phones. You're going to be a busy man."

"Already in progress. I'll have a mobile communications suite here by midday tomorrow. Full satellite coverage, high speed bandwidth...the works. No need to keep this place a secret any more. Just keep me posted if anyone has a change of heart over there," Sanderson said.

"I will. Just make sure you take a lot of pictures of that helicopter. I'd like to see one with you in the pilot's seat. I'll pass it on to remind everyone."

"Take care, my friend. Thanks again for betting on an old horse," Sanderson said.

"I only bet on winners. See you shortly."

Sanderson hung up and walked into the kitchen to find a strong drink. He stopped halfway, with a better plan already forming. There was no sense in drinking alone, when it was clearly time for a celebration at the compound. He just wished everyone could be here for it.

Chapter Sixty-Two

10:18 PM
Falls Church, Virginia

Karl Berg started to fade away into a long overdue slumber. He'd finally been ordered by Audra to catch a few hours of uninterrupted sleep before Europe awoke. His alarm was set for 1:00 AM, which gave him a few hours to enter a deep restful sleep. Petrovich's team would still be on the road, which was the only reason he had been allowed to leave. A few of the offices adjacent to the Operations Center had been converted to sleeping quarters for duty personnel. He needed more than a few broken hours of institutional sleep on a thin mattress more suitable for a state penitentiary inmate.

His cell phone rang, lifting the heavy blanket of unconsciousness and jarring him back into the world of the living. The phone continued to ring, and he slowly moved his hand over to the night stand, homing in on the light from his BlackBerry screen. He lifted the phone above his face, still lying flat on his back, and read the caller ID. He didn't recognize the number, but knew who it might be based on the foreign prefix.

"Karl Berg," he whispered.

"You sound like shit, my friend," a deep voice said in Russian.

"I'm trying to catch a few hours of sleep, no thanks to you."

"I don't sleep very well anymore. Old age, they say."

"Are you sure it's not the nicotine coursing through your veins all day and night? What time is it there? Four in the morning? I thought old people slept in," Berg said.

"I decided to take an early morning walk. You know…to make sure I don't have a fan club. I'm at a pay phone halfway across the city. I haven't used one of these in years. Kind of reminds me of the old days."

"In the old days, all of the public phones were bugged," Berg said.

"They haven't monitored these phones like that in years. Cell phones ruined it for them. Still, they electronically troll the lines for certain phrases. I hear they even do that in your country now."

"I wouldn't be surprised. So, how did it all play out on your end? Will you be taking a trip down the lovely Moscow River?"

"I don't think so. Our insider removed any possible trace of her work. There will be a witch hunt soon enough, but we've been careful. Oddly enough, they think our Russian friend was responsible for his own abduction. They're convinced that he defected with the help of your Special Forces team. Your team left quite a mess on the streets, which was impressive given what they were up against. We have twelve bodies to recover."

"Two of them are ours," Berg said.

"Interesting. I don't think anyone here knows that. Twelve is the number I'm hearing. And how is the grand prize holding up? I assume he'll be given political asylum and a nice townhouse in the Midwest?"

"He didn't survive the interrogation, but we managed to make a few connections with the information he provided. We're working on them right now."

This wasn't true, but the less Kaparov knew about the fate of Anatoly Reznikov the better. Less than a dozen people knew that Reznikov had survived the brutal interrogation outside of Stockholm. Petrovich and Farrington understood the implications of an active Russian bioweapons program and did their best to keep him alive while producing immediately actionable intelligence. Technically, they had killed him four times in thirteen minutes during the course of their interrogation, but the high tech equipment and medical staff somehow kept him alive. In this case, the ends justified the means.

"I assume that my office will be the first to hear of any impending biological threats to the Russian Federation?"

"Of course, though I didn't realize your career needed a boost."

"It didn't, but I can't be outdone by one of my old adversaries. Congratulations, Deputy Assistant Director."

"I'm not even going to speculate on how you garnered that information. Thank you, Alexei, for everything. We're on the right path to stopping this threat. Give me a call if you need to make a quick getaway."

"I appreciate the offer, but I have a hefty pension coming my way and I plan on collecting it in rubles. Plus, I hear that smokers are discriminated against in your country."

"They most certainly are, though I'm sure we can find you a nice spot down south, where you can smoke all you want."

"I'll keep it in mind. Well, I don't want to steal away any more of your beauty sleep. I have a feeling the upcoming days are going to take a toll on your good looks."

"You aren't kidding. Stay safe, my friend. I'll be in touch," he said and hung up on Kaparov.

Berg was the only person who knew that Kaparov had provided the CIA with Reznikov's address and he had no intention of ever exposing the Russian's name or position. Berg had made this clear to Bauer and Manning from the start. He had made some questionable calls in the past, but he could never intentionally give up a fellow field agent. There were still a few rules he held inviolate. He placed the phone back on the nightstand and started to consider what Kaparov had said about the days ahead. Mercifully, he drifted off before any concrete thoughts formed, or he would have found himself staring at the barely visible ceiling for the next three hours.

EPILOGUE

Later that evening

South 20th Street
Newark, New Jersey

Three figures hid toward the back of a crumbling driveway tucked between two duplex houses, keeping close watch on the driveway entrance and the adjacent backyards. They wore dark street clothes and black ski masks to blend into deep shadows. A few feet away on the decaying back porch of the battered two-story structure, a woman concentrated on picking the locks to a door that led directly into the first level apartment.

Her mask was pulled to the top of her head, exposing a portion of her shoulder-length blonde hair. She tested the doorknob, which turned slightly, and whispered into the shadows next to the two-story deck. The three men guarding the area walked carefully up the deck's rickety stairs and produced suppressed pistols. They silently entered the darkened apartment and split evenly into two groups. One group headed for the hallway leading to the bedrooms, and the other proceeded through the kitchen into the front room.

If the two FBI agents assigned to watch the apartment had been awake, they would have witnessed several flashes rotating quickly through the windows of the ground floor apartment. Ever diligent, their surveillance equipment recorded the light show, along with close-up images of the four masked intruders behind the duplex.

Deep in the backyard of the apartment, one of the men removed his ski mask within sight of the powerful night vision enhanced camera lens. The smart lens whirred as it made a few minor adjustments, allowing it to take focused pictures of each figure, while continuing to capture a wider framed video of the apartment. The surveillance camera clicked several times, causing the agent sleeping on the nearby couch to shift. Across the street, a tall black man tightened the straps on his backpack and disappeared with his group through the backyards.

The two agents would rise early and review the digital playback from the camera, eventually catching the only unusual thing they had ever seen at this location. So far, the stakeout had proven to be as boring and mind-numbing as every other. They had been told that more agents would arrive at some point tomorrow morning to bolster each watch section. This news had been the only interesting development in the five months they had been assigned to the stakeout rotation. They weren't told why more agents had been assigned, but everyone had heard rumors about a coordinated effort between the Newark and New York Police Departments to map out Muslim neighborhoods in the Tri-State area. With three mosques within walking distance, the West Side neighborhood definitely qualified for extra attention.

The End

To sign up for Steven's New Release Updates, send an email to: stevekonkoly@gmail.com

Please visit Steven's blog for more on *Black Flagged* and future projects: www.stevenkonkoly.com

Made in the USA
Charleston, SC
04 August 2014